CHASING SECRETS

© S.J. See 2026
This book may not be duplicated, republished, shared or distributed without the express permission of the publisher, except for brief quotations in reviews or a similar context. To obtain permissions, review copies, or schedule an author appearance, contact the publisher: editors@emerald-books.com
ISBN: 978-1-967628-10-0 | $18.95 US $26.95 CAD |
PUB Date: March 10, 2026 | 306 pages
Library of Congress publication data has been applied for.

THE ORDER
CHASING SECRETS

BY S.J. SEE

Author's Note

As with all the best told stories, *The Order: Chasing Secrets* carries a thread of truth. This novel is inspired by real historical events that captured Ireland's attention in the early 1900s and left its mark on the country. While much of the backdrop is rooted in fact, this story is ultimately a work of fiction—shaped, stretched, and reimagined for the sake of storytelling and enjoyment.

For those of you who found yourselves intrigued by this history, I encourage you to seek out the facts we know about the disappearance of the Irish Crown Jewels and the heroes of the revolution that shook Ireland in 1916. The true history is every bit as fascinating as the tales we weave from it.

Dedication

To Ric, for pushing me to be the very best I could be and daring me to finally chase my dreams. May our life together always be an adventure!

Prologue

THE YEAR WAS 1907, DUBLIN CASTLE, DUBLIN, IRELAND.

The path out past the castle was dark and surrounded by trees, which blocked his view of the night sky, stealing what little light the moon provided, creating an eerie ambience before him. The master had said he would know when to prepare for their departure. A single siren would sound to let the carriage boy know he was coming. They would have to leave quickly and as quietly as possible. That would be difficult, considering Dublin Castle was constantly encompassed by aristocrats and socialites, even at this time of night.

The carriage boy fiddled with the cool leather of the horse's reins. He knew there was a good chance he was assisting in a criminal act. Still, the master had promised he would be compensated for his loyalty, so at the night's end, he stood tall and stuck it out regardless of nerves and waited for the signal.

Suddenly, a high, piercing sound shrieked from Bedford Tower, making the boy's stomach lurch. But the awful sound ended as soon as it had begun. The carriage boy stood off the coach's step and looked at the tower in shock.

No, he couldn't have, the boy thought.

Was he crazy?

Off in the distance, a tall, suited figure covered in a heavy black cloak and fitted with a top hat walked swiftly out of the castle grounds. The carriage boy shook his head, and with a sudden new fear guiding his moves, he gathered the reins, opened the door to the coach, and hopped up into the coach box to await the master's presence. Crazy or not, he was now entirely committed to whatever scheme his master had cooked up.

The man approached and tipped his hat kindly to the carriage boy.

"Master Lynch," said the boy.

The man nodded. "Terrance, all ready to go?"

The boy sat up straight and returned one curt nod. "Right as rain, sir."

"Perfect. Get us to Glendalough and fast, Terrance. We have business to attend to." And with that, the man folded into the back of the black coach and drew the curtains shut before closing the door behind him.

Taking one last look to his left at Dublin Castle, Terrance took a deep breath and cracked the whip. He was now confident that if caught, he would be charged as an accomplice to a crime—and a serious crime at that. For as Master Lynch had approached, Terrance noticed a dark brown stable satchel tucked under his left arm hidden perfectly beneath his heavy cloak. Knowing he had just come from Bedford Tower, Terrance already knew what the papers would read tomorrow:

Crown Jewels of Ireland Stolen. Suspects Still at Large!

# Chapter One

Modern-day, Villanova, Pennsylvania

Ava

"Moving on. Can anyone tell me the importance of the Tuatha Dé Danann?" Professor Burke asked.

A few hands unenthusiastically lifted into the air around me. I bided my time, looking around to see if anyone could actually answer the question correctly.

Doubtful, I decided. At least until I noticed Connor Cook and Makenzie Rain sitting over in the corner. The three of us shared many classes in the past, so I knew just how smart the two were. It was possible they could answer the question correctly without a second thought. If they had raised their hands, that is. But like me, they both sat quietly watching the scenario play out before them.

It was the beginning of my last semester. My Celtic Mythology class was small that year, with only about twelve students. Which was still a decent amount considering the class was not a popular one. Still, sitting in this small room, looking over the class and seeing half the desks filled made me irritable. By this point in my studies, I had hoped to find this class so small that I would be able to get one-on-one time with the professor, but unfortunately, that was not the case.

I sat in the back corner off to the opposite side of Connor and Makenzie, surrounded by strangers. Let me rephrase, surrounded by mere acquaintances. It was true, I knew most of the students here, but while I knew their names, I didn't actually know them. Connor and Makenzie were the only two I had ever interacted with outside of class, and it hadn't been often. So technically yes, the rest of the class were strangers to me. Though they seemed to all know each other well enough to feel comfortable. Must be nice.

It wasn't that I didn't make friends easily, but more like I didn't have the time. Between my studies and my part-time job, I always seemed to be in a rush. I didn't have time for friends or dating, for that matter.

Professor Burke stood in front at the head of the class near his desk. A single whiteboard hung on the wall behind him. His desk sat a little off to the right, holding a heavy leather bag of books. "Yes, Marley."

My eyes flitted over to the blond girl with pink lowlights and tons of piercings, layered in shades of black. Marley Lewis.

She was your typical artsy rich girl who dressed specifically to piss off her parents. Her persona screamed rebellion. I'd like to say she passed her classes using her looks and daddy's money, but she surprisingly knew much more about historical subjects than I had first gathered from her. This fact did little to impress me, though. It wasn't the harsh outward demeanor that forced me to keep my distance.

No, it was her attitude.

Despite truly knowing her trade, which I could respect, she still had an entitled frame of mind that drove me insane. She had a habit of assuming that she was the best at anything and everything she set her mind to. And she always expected to receive instant praise, she thought she deserved for those achievements. My best guess was it was a byproduct of being hand-fed everything her whole life.

Here we go, I thought.

"Tuatha Dé Danann," she stated, "are fairies, little people. Part of the folklore in Ireland. Many people still believe in them today."

I stifled a laugh because in this small class, they would surely hear that and get the wrong idea.

Wrong.

"They are where we get our American versions of leprechauns. They are known to create chaos and trouble wherever they go. Which is why many people in Ireland still fear them to this day."

Wrong again.

Genuinely surprised at her uneducated answer, I could not fight the urge to roll my eyes.

"Close," said Professor Burke. "But not quite. Can anyone else enlighten Marley? How about Ava? Would you like to add to the conversation?"

I raised my eyebrows in the professor's direction.

3

Professor Burke was kind. In his mid-sixties, graying with glasses. He looked like a typical history professor. He was a brilliant man, though. One who I believed was squandering away his knowledge here at the university. It was a great school, don't get me wrong, but he could have been so much more.

The first one of Professor Burke's classes I ever sat in was during my second semester of my undergraduate program. While my studies already surrounded the rich history of Ireland and its people, Professor Burke was the one to introduce me to the legends and conspiracy side of Ireland, which, at the time, I had not yet investigated. The way he spoke about different events with such a suspicious view changed my perspective on things and taught me to search deeper to find the truth behind every story we uncovered.

For me, a lot of that intrigue focused on the Irish Independence War of 1919. Professor Burke had been kind enough to lend me a few of his books on the topic, and I have been enjoying taking his classes ever since.

By then, Professor Burke knew me well enough to know I had no interest in correcting Marley. Participation wasn't my thing. "Remember, twenty-five percent of your grade rests on your contributions in this class," he reminded me smugly.

I tried not to scowl, that was rude, and instead, I sighed and conceded. "The Tuatha Dé Danann—it means the people of Danu. They were an ancient race believed to have been made up of supernatural beings—one might refer to them as gods. The leader of these beings was a god known as the Dagda, which means the good god. The Irish believed they inhabited the island long before humans."

Marley glared at me.

"So, as I said, the fae."

I bit my lip, frustrated. I was raised to be polite, but in the most recent years, that had become more problematic as I just didn't have the energy or care to put up with stupid people anymore. But I knew what my mother would say, 'You never know what someone else is going through.' And I found that to be true most days. But good Lord, have mercy, did this chick get under my skin. The internal struggle to keep my mouth shut was already coming loose at the seams when I pulled my eyes from her and scanned the room in an effort to drop the issue at hand.

The rest of the class was silent, but then my eyes caught Connor's from across the room. He sat back in his chair, watching us. His head tilted, arms crossed over his chest. He perked a single brow at me as if to entice me to continue.

I was never one to make a scene, but I let my intrusive thoughts get the better of me. I pinched the bridge of my nose as if pained. Realistically, though, the only thing about this conversation that depressed me was the American educational system.

I closed my eyes, shaking my head. "No—see, first, the Irish do not refer to them as fae. They use the term *aos sí*. And while the folklore might trace back to the Tuatha Dé Danann, it is only one of many theories that make up the *aos sí*. Therefore, you cannot simply consider the Tuatha Dé Danann a cover term for the *aos sí*. Secondly, they are definitely not where our American leprechauns come from—the Tuatha Dé Danann were believed to have been strong and inspiring magical creatures, not chaos-creating elves. Which would mean that the current Irish do not fear them, as Marley said."

"That is correct, Ava. Thank you." Professor Burke clapped his hands together and turned away to grab his pointer.

I glanced sideways to find a seething Marley Lewis glaring at me. This time, I smirked back at her and whispered, "Better luck next time," before returning my attention to my laptop, eager to relieve myself of the situation.

I had only managed to type a couple more sentences before the class erupted in whispers. I looked up to find a newcomer standing in the doorway, greeting Professor Burke enthusiastically with a handshake as if they had gone way back. However, the guy had a regal appearance that did not suit a college campus.

He wore a tailored charcoal gray suit with black stripes and a dark forest-green tie. His shoes clearly cost a pretty penny, as did his cufflinks. He had black hair salted with gray, much like Professor Burke's. Although on this man, it said *distinguished* and not just *soon-to-be retired*.

"Class, may I introduce the recruitment officer and, most importantly, director of the National Museum of Ireland, Dr. Thaddeus Balor. He is an old colleague of mine who is here on business in the US."

I sat up straighter in my seat. We all knew why he was here. This was kind of a surprise as they didn't normally hand-deliver invitations. But we all knew what it meant. Someone at Villanova had been accepted into the NMI's internship program in Ireland. This was a big deal.

Dr. Balor smiled politely and raised his hand to the class in greeting, then looked back at the professor with a smile. "And, of course, to visit old friends," he said with a nod toward Professor

Burke. There was a hint of an accent in his voice that sounded like it could be Irish, which added to his appeal.

"Sally will be delighted to have you for dinner tonight, I'm sure. The floor is yours, Thaddeus."

Professor Burke sat at his desk as Dr. Balor approached the center of the dimly lit room. "Thank you. As your professor mentioned, I am a recruitment officer representing the National Museum of Ireland. I don't usually deliver these in person, but in this case, I had business nearby and decided to drop by and visit your professor here. I expect most of you are surprised to see me," he said with a smirk. "For those of you who are, let me explain. Every five years or so, we offer a special internship program to the most promising students in this field worldwide. Only a select few students from schools in the US are chosen each round to come and work with us."

"As I am sure most of you are aware, these internships range in multiple historical departments, from record-keeping to exhibitions. The selected students will come to work with us for the next year under a paid internship program. They will be offered a chance to continue their selected studies abroad in Ireland. This year, many of you from your university applied for this program. And after a thorough screening of every applicant, we have made our final decisions."

Dr. Balor turned to look back at the Professor over his shoulder before continuing on.

"Before we continue, those of you who have been accepted should be sure to thank your professors here for their enlightening letters of recommendation they wrote on your behalf."

Professor Burke simply nodded his thanks to Dr. Balor and awaited the answer. Who got in?

This internship was so selective, it was rare that students from Villanova got accepted. The vibe in the room shifted, and my classmates were silent. A paid internship in Ireland was a dream come true for most students, including myself. Or it would have been if I didn't have other responsibilities to attend to. I knew that even if I was chosen, I doubted I would be able to accept.

When this was originally presented as an opportunity to me, I was over the moon. I had studied hard for this. Put everything I had into it. My thesis surrounded a major Irish conspiracy that few knew about. I had wanted nothing more. Just thinking about it sent a shiver down my spine.

A whole year, I would get to study historical artifacts, research original documents, and learn from the best in my field. There, I would have the chance to track down the secret community that protected Ireland and trace their footsteps back to ancient times. I could finally experience real history that impacted many lives. Who wouldn't want that?

My family, however, had been less than thrilled with the idea. They didn't want me too far away from home. They had even discouraged me from the idea before they had even had the chance to look into it. And it all frustrated me so much that I kept my distance after that. But at least I understood why.

My thoughts slid toward my sister, and I bit my lip. I knew they were right; I needed to be here at home. And while I understood their push back, I couldn't deny that part of my soul sank at the thought of missing out on this opportunity. Why couldn't I just, for once, have something of my own? Something that wasn't laced with trauma or grief.

I shook off my thoughts and looked back at the front of the class. There was no use dwelling on the impossible. Who said I had even been accepted anyway? There were twelve very capable, very promising students in this class. It could be any one of us.

Dr. Balor held up a single manila envelope. You could feel the anticipation in the air like static electricity. "In this envelope," he continued, "I have the names of two promising students from this university who have successfully made it past the application process."

In front of me, Marley smiled widely as if she expected her name to be on that list. I scoffed. Please don't be her. Please not her. Anyone but her.

Yeah, I realize it was petty, but I never claimed to be mature.

We waited.

It felt like Dr. Balor was moving in slow motion as he reached into the folder, drew out a piece of paper, and held it before him. "Connor David Cook and Ava Tyler Metheny."

I blinked. He said my name. I couldn't process the information fast enough, because I just sat there staring at him with surprise, while everyone else seemed to have glued their eyes to either myself or Connor.

I looked over at him; he seemed just as surprised as I was.

Connor was a tall guy with kind blue eyes that he hid behind black rectangular wire-framed glasses. He had fluffy, dirty-blond hair that curled to one side and resembled the fur of a golden retriever. His sharp square jawline drew the girls' attention, as did his honest smile.

You could tell he was toned and worked out, but for the most part, I knew he tended to hide in the library.

I didn't know much about him other than he was a decent guy. He was an archaeology major, and I was finishing my graduate program in Irish Studies. We rarely talked outside of class. But on the occasions we had, I found his company enjoyable.

Until now, though, we had never had much in common.

"Will those two students stay after class, please? If you have a class to follow, I have been assured you will be pardoned. Thank you." And with that, Dr. Balor stepped back and passed the command of the class back to Professor Burke.

I sat back in my chair, thinking over the possibilities that awaited me. If only life had not tied me so strictly to home.

A paid internship at the National Museum of Ireland . . . a full year paid internship, nonetheless, was insane. I couldn't believe I would have to turn it down.

Chapter Two

I watched the rest of the students file out of the classroom. I waited until it looked like Connor was ready to greet the men in the front of the room before I came to my feet. I met Connor halfway, and we silently walked to the pair together.

Dr. Balor reclined against the edge of the professor's desk. He and Professor Burke seemed to be catching up on life. Professor Burke cleared his throat, trying to hide his laughter at something the other had said when we approached.

"Ava, Connor, congratulations!" the professor said, standing up and holding out his hand to shake ours. We both smiled and accepted. "This is a fine honor indeed! Not many students from the US are chosen."

Dr. Balor, behind him, nodded with a smile and crossed his arms at the desk. "He's quite right, you know. You two are like needles in a haystack." Connor bashfully nodded back. He looked as if he was unsure how to respond to such a compliment. I glanced at him, trying not to laugh at his embarrassment, but he caught my eye and blushed, his smile growing genuinely wider. "Thank you, sir," he said.

"Let us get down to business, shall we?" Dr. Balor stood and turned, and his sports jacket swung behind him. He retrieved two black leather binders from his briefcase. He handed one to each of us.

"Both of you have the grades, the selective studies interests, and the letters of recommendation we have been looking for. And I've personally read your thesis on the Order of St. Patrick, Ava. I must say it was quite impressive," he said with a wink.

"Tell me what brought on your interest in a group like that? Was it something you found? Family lineage perhaps?"

His question surprised me.

"Actually, I came across them while researching the Independence War of 1919."

His face fell a fraction, but Dr. Balor shifted and moved on quickly.

"All well, anyway. We at the National Museum in Ireland would love to have a part in helping you develop those skills. The first packet will tell you about the program and how someone with your talents can be useful to us, even at your young age. Inside, you will find information on the different departments in the museum you could choose to work for, and, of course, the paid internship itself," Dr. Balor explained.

"The second packet in there will give you information regarding our rules and regulations while on museum grounds, as well as your campus housing. We have high expectations for our interns at the museum, so I encourage you to read it carefully. If you find you cannot live up to our conditions, this internship may not be for you. Lastly, you will find a packet consisting of all the forms required to accept this position and a list of contacts who can start you on the process of transferring you to the Emerald Isle. Hopefully, if everything goes smoothly, we should have two new members joining our team within the next two to three weeks!"

Dr. Balor finished with a confident but calm smile.

"Unfortunately, though, that means you'll have to miss graduation," Professor Burke chimed in from the side.

Of course it did. That would never fly with the McKennas

I flipped through the packets. There were lots of rules, expectations, and requirements I would have to meet to make this happen. If I were able to, that is . . .

The biggest issue would be bringing my guardians on board with this program.

My heart was racing. Of course, this was one of the most exciting things to possibly happen, and yet, as much as I wanted it, as much as I yearned to take the position, I knew I couldn't leave home. My insides were a box of mixed feelings, all bubbling up at once into a volcano of anxiety.

"What about payment? Is there information in here about that?" Connor asked. That snapped me back to reality. I looked away from my papers to Dr. Balor, waiting to see exactly how big of a payment we were talking about. If I was lucky, it would be enough to offer me something to send home, which might make going to Ireland plausible.

"Of course! The first packet will have all the payment information. There will be a list of different departments you could potentially work for, each with its own allowance if you will. Now, understand that because the two of you are studying two vastly different things, the departments offered to you and their salaries will be very different. It might be best not to disclose the wage information to anyone other than family." I flipped through the first packet until I landed on the list of departments I had been approved for on page seven.

> *Records Keeping . . . $25,000 US Dollars*
> *Artefact preservation . . . $35,000 US Dollars*
> *Ancient Expeditions . . . $30,000 US Dollars . . . $75,000 Dollars additional*
> *Artefact Trades Market . . . $18,000 US Dollars*

My eyes stopped at the third line. "Is this like annual, or how does this work?" Dr. Balor smiled at my sudden interest.

"I assume you are referring to your third department offer. Yes, the first number is your yearly salary. You will be compensated biweekly; however, if you manage to complete certain tasks, you will be paid accordingly. That second number is the average amount for those tasks. I should warn you, though, those tasks will be challenging. They don't come easy. Some of my colleagues have been working on the same case for years, hoping to resolve it, and they never do. I believe you also have a similar offer, Mr. Cook."

"Will we get to choose which department we would like to work for?" I asked without taking my eyes off that ridiculous number.

"Yes," answered Dr. Balor. "Any of the departments you are approved for will take you. We just need to know your decisions by next Thursday. From there, should you choose to work with us, a representative from the department will contact you and begin preparing you for your transfer to Ireland."

This was a game-changer. That kind of money could change everything, but I would need time to consider this. Shifting my thoughts back to home, I bit my lip. A call to Eamon was surely in my future. He would be able to help me sort through this information and make the best decision for both my sister and me. If there was any chance of me being able to go, he would be the one to hear me out.

Chapter Three

Connor

Connor couldn't believe his luck as he stared down at the folder. This was a big deal. Though he obviously had applied for the internship, he never thought he would fit the bill. He also knew how rare it was that they recruited students from Villanova, so to be one of two who were considered made him even prouder.

He smiled to himself. He knew instantly that his mom would be thrilled. She had Irish roots and had always been proud of her heritage. If he was being honest, it was one of the reasons he was taking the Celtic Mythology class to begin with. Yes, he needed the class to round out his studies, and an additional class with Ava was a bonus, but he had known his mother would be ecstatic when she found out he had registered for it.

Taking the actual class was a small price to pay for putting a smile on her face. Especially since she had worked so hard to get him into this program in the first place.

Connor's home life had been a little tainted. He had only been three days old when his dad walked out, leaving both him and his mom behind. And while men had come and gone, none had stuck around. They had said that her shifts at the hospital were too long, or the time she spent with her son was too much—and so it had always just been the two of them. And Connor made sure nothing got between them.

By the time he had started his sophomore year in high school, he had become painfully aware of just how much his mother had given up to make ends meet and get him to where he was. And because of that, he felt like he owed it to her to put in the effort to be the best he could be.

Now it was his turn to give a little something back. With the money from this internship, he could do that. It may not be a lot, but it could help pay off some of their bills, so maybe she wouldn't have to work so hard.

Connor took a deep breath of affirmation and looked over to where Ava had been standing just seconds ago. His smile faded as he watched the slender girl with dark brown hair and jade green eyes disappear into the bustle of the hallway.

Part of him was disappointed that she hadn't lingered to discuss the internship with him, but he knew her well enough—she was always on the move. It was rare that she ever stayed in one place for too long. He had never been quite sure why this was.

Originally he had thought she had a boyfriend. But a couple months ago, after spending a whole afternoon to gather his courage, he decided to stop by her work to grab a drink. He had made small talk with her and she actually volunteered to pick out a drink for him. It was during that one short conversation that he found out she was single.

He remembered it clearly: she smiled at him from behind the counter and made him a caramel chia tea.

"Doesn't your boyfriend get bored on his own? I mean since you're either working or studying all the time?" he had asked her with sweat pouring down his back.

She had glanced at him with a sheepish smile and shook her head. "Oh, no boyfriend. Good Lord, between this job, family life, and school, I have, like, no time!" She handed him his cup and he nodded.

"I can understand that. But you gotta get out and experience campus life sometime, right? Won't ever get this opportunity again, ya know?" he said with a partial shrug.

Ava had just sighed. When the bell on the door behind him rang and alerted them to a bunch of students entering the café, Ava glanced back behind him at the crowd forming and blew out her hair from her eyes.

"Sometime, I wish. I gotta get back to work, but it was nice talking to you." She dismissed him.

Connor raised his hand in a wave as he started to make his way toward the door. "Yeah, I'll see you around, I guess!"

Her face looked doubtful, but she smiled back at him anyway. "Maybe," she had said, then moved on to the next customer.

Connor shook his head at the memory and glanced back down at the folder again. He found himself excited for both the internship and the idea of getting the chance to know Ava Metheny a little better.

While the two hadn't had many classes together, they tended to frequent the same places—mostly the library and the coffee shop. He had only had the guts to speak to her a handful of times after that conversation, and neither of those times had been personal.

Connor tapped the folder in his hands and closed it. Smiling to himself, he made his way to the exit. He sensed that he would soon get to know her much better.

1903

Dear Mr. Lynch,

It has come to our attention that you have been involved in illegal activities, including distributing handouts to certain families and trading goods without the knowledge of the English government. Such actions require a level of courage that is rare, and we would be grateful for the opportunity to support you further by offering our resources and connections.

If you are interested in discussing this further, we would like to meet with you in person to explore this mutual opportunity. Please join us at O'Donnell's Pub in Cork on the evening of Saturday, 4th August.

We look forward to collaborating with you in the future.

Anonymous

Chapter four

AVA

Outside, the brisk air whipped my hair into a mess as I made my way off campus. Though spring had arrived, the air was still chilly, which forced me to cling tightly to my jacket as I walked. I had barely left the main pathway when I pulled out my cellphone and dialed Eamon. The phone rang twice before a female voice answered.

"Ava! We weren't expecting to hear from you today. I thought your Thursday schedule was pretty packed with classes?" Millie had answered the phone, to my surprise.

I sighed. "My third class got out early, due to an unexpected interruption. Is Eamon around?" I asked anxiously. It wasn't that I didn't want to talk to Millie, I just knew Eamon would handle the news better. Admitting I had applied behind their backs was going to be hard enough without Millie derailing me. She tended to get stuck on the wrong details, and I didn't want her intervening before I had the chance to discuss this with Eamon properly.

"He's getting Ryker ready for soccer practice but should be down in the next few minutes. What kind of interruption are we talking about? Something interesting happen today?" she asked sincerely. I groaned inwardly. Why did she have to ask that? I tried not to lie to Millie. She had done so much for my family. The least I could do was be honest with her. I took a second to brace myself then answered.

"Very. I got accepted for that *paid* internship at the NMI in Ireland." I could hear her drop the pot into the sink.

"I thought you decided not to apply for that?"

I hesitated. How was I going to explain myself out of this one?

"Well—"

"Ava, we talked about this." I could hear the disappointment in her voice loud and clear. I hated that I had upset her. I knew Millie always had the best intentions at heart, but I was struggling to live like this. Constantly in the shadow of the past. Pushing against the current of the dimming future. Despite everything going on, a part of me still craved escape, to do what I wanted without fallout.

In a better world, that would have come naturally, like it did for everyone else. In my world though? I was trapped by decisions that both allured me and damned me.

"I know we did, but to be fair, I never actually thought I'd get in! And then, I did so—" Millie's sigh over the phone was enough for me to know she wasn't pleased with this.

"And you say it's a *paid* internship? Are you sure?" Typical Millie, always a sceptic.

"A hundred percent. I have the packet in my bag; I already memorized the numbers."

"Who's it for?" she asked, and the scrubbing of the dishes in the background resumed.

"The National Museum of Ireland."

Millie took a long breath in. I couldn't tell if she was impressed or nervous. "You know I am not happy you went behind our backs with this after we told you this was not a good idea," she said blatantly.

"Yeah, I know, but other than the situation with Jules, you never told me why. You just looked over the information and dismissed it without cause. Millie, this is everything I have been working toward. I couldn't have dreamed of a better internship. If I play my cards right, I could make connections here, maybe line up a job for the future. I could also send back money to help pay for Juliana's treatments. These are all positive things. Something good is finally happening in my life, and yet you're still skeptical. Why can't you just be happy for me?"

The sounds of suds and dishes paused again, and I knew I had pushed her too far. Playing on Millie's heartstrings was a dangerous game. Sometimes it worked and other times it didn't, but to my surprise, today was my lucky day, and she caved in.

"Sweet girl, I am happy for you. I know how hard you've worked for this. I just—"

"What?" I challenged, forcing her hand, even though I was out of cards to play.

"I just want you to be careful. That is all. Ireland is so far away. Eamon and I won't be able to help you if you get into any trouble there."

"Millie, I'm an adult. I'm not the little girl you used to read bedtime stories to."

"No, you are definitely not. Alright, fine, but you'd better talk to Eamon about this one. This is your big news, so you get to be the one to tell him. He'll be down in a second."

I breathed a sigh of relief. Thanking God, Millie hadn't decided to disown me for going against her wishes. "That's exactly why I called." I stopped and bit my lip before asking my next question. The one I was dreading the answer to. "How's Jules?"

Millie's silence told me everything. Neither of us really liked to talk about it, but we couldn't avoid what was happening any more than we could stop the rain. "Not well. She's been needing to rest a lot, more than normal. It's like her energy only lasts so long before she has to give in and sleep it off for the rest of the day."

That didn't sound too bad. That I could handle. "Good," I said, "she needs her rest."

"You don't understand what I'm saying, Ava." Millie stopped what she was doing and held the phone closer to her ear. "Juliana is slowing down. In a way no six-year-old should be. The doctor wants us to try a new treatment, but it is a lot of money, and our insurance won't cover it because it's experimental. On the flip side, if we don't figure something out soon . . ." Millie trailed off. "I honestly don't know how much time we will have left with her."

I stopped on the gravel path and tried to take in what she was telling me. From what I could grasp, it was either we tried this new treatment, or we gave up, and that wasn't an option. Juliana was everything to me—and the McKennas. I knew Eamon and Millie were doing everything for her, but clearly, it wasn't enough. A part of me feared that nothing would ever be enough.

Maybe it was my turn to step up.

"You should come home to visit her, Ava. She needs to see you."

"How much?" I suddenly asked.

"What?"

"How much does the treatment cost?"

Millie sounded exasperated. "No, you're not listening, Ava—"

"Millie, *how* much?"

Millie sighed again. "She would need surgery first, around a hundred fifty thousand, and then monthly injections for the next year—at least ten thousand a pop. The insurance would be able to help with the surgery, but not the injections."

A hundred and twenty thousand, then. Hell, the injections would be nearly as expensive as the surgery itself. I couldn't promise that much, but if I took this internship, I could probably put a decent-sized dent into that price tag. If only I could complete one of their "specialized tasks." I bit my lip. My mind was partly made up, but I definitely needed to talk to Eamon. If I truly intended to see this through, I would need his help.

"Okay, just have Eamon call me."

"Ava!"

I didn't wait to hear it, so I hit the red button to end the call. I grimaced because I knew I was being disrespectful, but I also knew Millie wouldn't be as open-minded as Eamon, and it would be much easier to convince her once he was onboard.

At about nine thirty that night, Eamon rang my phone, primarily to discuss my rude behavior. While he was a mild-tempered man, he did not take well to disrespect, especially toward Millie, who had done so much for me. The more mature part of me understood where he was coming from. So, I bit my tongue, trying to hold in my anxiety as I waited for him to finish scolding me. The minute he allowed me to explain, though, I took the opportunity and ran with it.

Eamon listened carefully as I told him about the internship and all its benefits. He kept silent while I apologized profusely for going behind his back and even though he had initially objected. It sounded like he contemplated each detail, but I knew a storm was coming.

"So what I'm hearing is that despite my concerns, you went ahead and applied for the internship anyway and now that you've been accepted, you've come back to apologize, plead your case and all, because you think you can get the money to help pay for Juliana's treatment?"

Well, when you put it that way.

"It's not just about Jules; it's about living my life and securing my future."

"Securing a future that takes you even farther away from your sister, who's nearly six feet in the ground!" he roared back. "How do you not see the problem there, Ava?"

I did. Of course, I knew he was right. But I also knew that if we didn't come up with that money soon, she would be dead anyway. If this was the only way to make some extra cash fast, then

I was going to risk it. I knew the McKennas would call me home if it was too late.

I took a deep breath in.

"I don't need your permission, you know. If this is the only way to get her the treatment she needs, then I'll be content to go with or without your approval."

Eamon was silent over the phone for a good minute. At one point, I almost thought I'd lost his call. But a rustling over the phone caught my attention just before I was about to hang up.

"I'm not going to lie and say I'm happy about this. You know how Millie and I feel about your priorities here. But you are right, I can't stop you. And if you insist on going, then I will help you. I promised your mother years ago, we'd always watch out for you, and while I think you are making a mistake, I know how much this means to you, and I understand your intentions behind it."

My heart about jumped in my chest at Eamon's agreement to help me pursue this.

This was real! I was going!

"I know you think this is a mistake, but I promise you, I'll work hard to make this worthwhile. I will fly home as often as I can to see her, and I'll get that money! Please, all I ask for is a little faith in me, Eamon."

Eamon was tentative in responding, but he too caved in the end.

After getting all the information, he was quick to step in and pick apart the internship and its flaws. I knew he had agreed only because I had threatened to go at this alone, but after a while, it seemed like he was truly looking to help make this plausible for me.

A part of me wondered what had deterred him from the idea in the first place, after all, this was exactly how Eamon had met my mom, through a program just like this one.

My mom's name was Triona Metheny. She was a first-generation Irish American woman whose parents had come from Tipperary. She had chocolate-brown hair and crystal green eyes. She was adventurous, daring, and mischievous in the best way. And she loved nothing more than her family. Over the past couple of years, I had been told that I mirrored her in nearly every way. It was something that I tended to hold onto to keep her close.

My father had been a fun and adventurous type. Born in the United States, with no siblings, he learned at a very young age how to entertain himself, which gave birth to his many different hobbies. He was always taking us camping, teaching me how to fish or shoot. He encouraged me to practice karate when I was little because he had said ballet was too delicate and I was no flower. And like both my mother and I, he loved history. Growing up, he always put us first—before work meetings, before extended family conflicts. We were everything to him, and he made sure we knew that. I admired him for that. As a child, I thought the three of us were inseparable. But things never stay the same for long, and at some point, something has to give.

I would never have guessed that he would leave us the way he did. My dad had left when I was eighteen, and shortly after, Mom decided to adopt Jules and welcome this little spunky two-year-old into our home. That was four years ago.

Like me, my mom was a history major. She had met Eamon McKenna when she had studied abroad in Scotland. They both went to the same college and entered the same program in their junior year. The two had gotten close, but nothing ever blossomed between them.

Once they arrived back in the States two years later, my mom introduced Eamon to Millie, her childhood best friend, and they hit it off immediately. At their wedding, a short year later, Eamon had returned the favor and set up my mom with a man named Aiden O'Donnell—my dad. The four friends had stayed in touch for years until one day, my dad just up and left. He left no note—no reason why. One day, he was just gone.

And then Mom died. And that was it. Everything changed after that.

"The specialized tasks sound intriguing, I admit, but I'm not sure we should hold our breath on that money. Based on the documents you sent me, it sounds like completing these sorts of tasks is rare. But I'm willing to support you if that's truly what you want to do. I think it would be good for you to get out and do something new," Eamon said.

I peeled my eyes away from the family photo of my mom, Jules, and me at the corner of my desk and scrolled down to reread the information about the specialized tasks. "What about Millie?" I asked, continuing to page through the documents I had scanned into my computer.

"Millie will support you and whatever you decide to do as long as you apologize for being a major pain in her ass this afternoon!" Millie yelled from somewhere behind Eamon. I guess I had been on speaker the whole time and hadn't known. Eamon laughed, and I apologized with a smirk; none of us could ever stay mad for very long. We all learned the hard way that life was just too short for that.

"Ava, you have to promise me you'll go into this with the understanding that... this may not... save your sister," Millie added gently. I stopped for a minute to look back at the photo.

"I know. But if it could help, I have to try at least."

"Then we will support you every step of the way. Your mother would be proud to see you going overseas!" said Eamon.

"Alright, alright then, now that we're all on the same page. What do you need from us?" asked Millie, and I knew she was all in.

"Well..." I spent the next couple days filling out forms, expediting my passport, and contacting the people listed in the binder to let them know I had accepted the position. Eamon played a big part in helping me organize the forms and passport information to help make things easier. By the following Friday, with my passport in hand, I was packed, standing at the international gate at Pittsburgh International Airport heading to my layover in Boston.

Chapter Five

Connor had also accepted an offer at the museum, and they had booked our flights simultaneously. From Pittsburgh International Airport, we had one connecting flight through Boston. At that time, we boarded Aer Lingus to Ireland. In total, it was about eight hours of flight time. Looking around, I noticed a lot of younger people on the flight out of Boston, along with a few older couples. I wondered how many were interning at the museum like we were.

As the flight took off from Boston, Connor settled his headphones on the back of his neck and he opened his hand to offer me a pair of thick blue earplugs. "The plane's earplugs are pretty cheap. I figured you'd want to be well-rested for tomorrow."

I smiled back at him and took them. As I was finding out, Connor was a hidden gem of a person. Kind, respectful, and apparently prepared. Though he wasn't my type, I enjoyed the camaraderie. It was strange to think we'd never spoken outside class before. "Thanks, I never even thought of that. I appreciate it."

He returned my smile and shook out his hair with his hand. "No need to thank me. If I'm being honest, they hadn't been very expensive at the airport either, but I figured they would be better than these." He held up a smaller pair of white earplugs with his other hand that the airline handed out for free and shrugged.

I practically snorted at his honesty. His smile widened as I laughed. Seriously, how had I missed the chance to get to know this guy before?

"Well, thanks anyway." I twirled the earplugs he had given me in my hands. I wanted to ask him about the internship, but I wasn't sure Dr. Balor would consider it appropriate. Still, I was dying to know. After tossing the question back and forth in my head, I finally turned to him and scrunched up my face apologetically.

"Do you mind if I ask what department you signed up for? I know we're not supposed to share that information, but—"

"But you can't figure out what kind of job I could possibly have working for an Irish museum as an archeology major?" he finished for me. I blushed and looked down at my hands, feeling guilty. I hadn't meant it as an insult.

"Am I that transparent?" I asked. He smiled and shook his head.

"No," Connor simply replied. Being an archeology major, I couldn't deny that I had been surprised to see him in my Celtics Mythology class this semester. I couldn't picture him involved in anything I was studying.

I looked at him and waited for him to explain. He suddenly looked bashful yet again and started to set up his laptop on the food tray. "Believe it or not, I decided to get into Expeditions Operations."

I sat back, a bit stunned, and deepened my smile. This I never would have guessed.

"It may surprise you, but believe it or not, while I am majoring in archeology, I am minoring in computer communications."

I popped an eyebrow, still trying to follow how that helped pave his way onto this internship. "A tech guy, cool. But how does that help with anything?"

He laughed nervously. "Well, it means I can help communicate with those who are actively on expeditions. I can assist them while on the job, in almost anything they need, and all from the comfort of my desk."

I sat back. "Oh." That made more sense to me now.

"The museum had offered me Archeology Expeditions and Artifact Preservation, which are both things I would like to pursue, but I felt it might be better to get behind the computer and see how these expeditions go before I sign up for them. I spoke about it with Dr. Balor, and he said I could always switch departments halfway through the year if I preferred to try something different."

I smacked him playfully on the arm. "That's so cool, though. You know, I signed up for expeditions."

"I figured you'd be in something like that."

"Will you be overseeing my expeditions?"

Connor shook his head and shrugged. "I honestly don't know. I looked into it a little deeper, and it turns out they have multiple expeditions departments. Did you happen to see which department you signed up for?"

"Uh, yeah. Missing Artifact Expeditions."

Connor's face lit up. "That's amazing. That's supposed to be some of the most exciting work the museum has to offer. They can be incredibly dangerous, though. Did the department rep say how long your training would be before they assign you to one?"

"Two weeks. But I will meet my advisor tomorrow. He's supposed to be a major part of my training."

Connor nodded as the drink cart rolled by. "Very cool. Maybe we will get to work together." I turned back to the TV screen in front of me. I had been mindlessly fiddling with it the whole time we had been talking, and now the third Harry Potter movie was about to start.

"Yeah, that would be awesome. It's nice to know I'm starting this new adventure with at least one familiar face. It's not so scary when you have friends looking out for you." Connor's smile was genuine when he agreed and returned to his screen.

We landed in Dublin at two a.m. Eastern Standard Time. I hadn't slept very well on the plane, aside from the hour or two I had gotten when I'd fallen asleep on Connor's shoulder.

A small black bus was waiting at the airport after we got our bags and went through customs. At least thirteen other students had joined us on their way to the campus grounds where our dorms and classrooms awaited us.

Much to our dismay, though, the instructors had informed us that we wouldn't be shown to our rooms until nearly seven p.m. Dublin time. They explained that we would adjust better if we stayed up for the day. I groaned aloud when I realized it would be two p.m. in Pittsburgh.

Connor looked just as exhausted as I felt. He leaned his head back on the bus seat, his eyes closed, wire glasses slowly sliding toward the tip of his nose. Come to think of it, I couldn't tell if he was awake. I turned and looked out the window.

The bus was approaching a massive concrete building with four white stone pillars, holding an awning over the front entrance. The architecture gave the essence of a historic castle. The building was surrounded by five other buildings, breaking off in different directions in the distance. Each building in the background held two letters over the front in more stone. Statues of famous figures were placed at the arch of each building's entryway. The buildings read *S.H.*, *G.R.*, *M.L.*, and *D.Q.* I pondered what those different initials could possibly stand for.

As the bus came to a stop at the end of the clean gravel path, Connor's eyes groggily opened. The driver hit a few buttons, then pulled the lever in front of him, and students began to file out one by one.

I followed behind Connor off the bus, and then shuffled off to the left of the group of students gathering beside the opened door. There were several other young people, all dressed in relatively the same uniforms. Most wore nice jeans, a skirt, or slacks accompanied by a museum shirt. The shirts were forest green with dark navy blue trim, and the initials *I.N.M.S.* were embroidered above the right breast in the same navy blue.

Off to the left of the group stood a girl in a dark navy pencil skirt. She wore her museum polo underneath a navy blue blazer. She stood out to me because of her jet-black hair and dark brown eyes. Her skin was pale, and her frame was petite, but she was taller at second glance. She looked like she could defend herself just fine despite her size. She wore small black heels, which gave her a little height and made her look more professional than the others. But what struck me most about her was how her eyes danced over the students before her as if they were fresh meat.

"Irish National Museum Studies," Connor whispered to me. I pulled my eyes away from the girl to look up at Connor towering beside me.

"What?" I asked, confused.

"The initials on their shirts. That's what you were trying to figure out?"

"Oh! Uh, yeah."

A tall, pale, blond woman who was no doubt older than the others stepped up to address the group, and the students quieted down. "Welcome to the Ireland National Museum's, Celtic Studies Internship Program. We are so excited to have you here. As you have been informed, we will not have you settling into your housing accommodations just yet. It is in your best interests to stay with us until the early evening hours to help you adjust appropriately to Ireland time. In the meantime, your bags will be taken to your assigned dormitories."

Connor and I exchanged a look.

"Behind me are your department representatives. They will show you around the campus today to help you become more familiar with your departments and our college grounds. They are here to assist you with anything you may need. Please do not hesitate to reach out to them. Are there any questions before we continue?"

When no one raised their hand, the woman clapped her hands and welcomed the others behind her. "Wonderful! Each department representative will call out the names of those students in their department. You are welcome to follow them from there. Good luck, and welcome aboard!"

The woman stepped away as clapping ensued, and a tall, dark-haired male came up to call out the first few names on the list. Those students grabbed their purses and backpacks and followed him toward the building that read *D.Q.* Three more walked up and called out names before the girl I had been studying stepped up to the front.

"Ancient Expeditions: Ava Metheny."

Oh, goody, I thought. She looked like she could eat me alive.

I took a deep breath to clear my nerves. I had decided to come into this with a positive attitude, and that wouldn't stop now.

I turned and gave Connor a fist bump. "Catch you later?" I asked.

Connor nodded back, smiling as I walked away. "Definitely."

As I approached, the girl stuck out her hand and shook mine. She smiled at me with a genuinely sweet smile, and my nerves melted away.

"Calista Scott. A pleasure to meet you," she said. I could just pick out an accent, but I wasn't sure where from. I didn't think she was from the US, though. Maybe I could ask her later. It would be nice to have another friend here on campus. I was sure Connor would eventually grow bored of me.

"Ava, pleasure is all mine." Calista turned and started guiding me down a separate gravel path toward the first building that read *S.H.* She turned around and proceeded to walk backward so she could see me as I soaked in everything. I was slightly impressed she could do that in heels. Large and luminous trees stood between the buildings—their limbs gaining leaves by the minute. Mixed with the cool Irish breeze, it made for the perfect spring feel. Getting a closer look at the buildings, I could see they were more recent, unlike the first building. Their architecture, while beautiful, proved to be cleaner and more modern than the building we had walked away from.

"Beautiful, isn't it?"

"Incredible," I whispered as I looked up at the building.

"The building we left is known as the Main Hall. Most of your studies will happen in that building. It also houses the main library and a small assortment of computer labs and communication centers. That is where all the record-keeping students work for the most part. You, on the other hand, will be out on the field most of the time, but when you are on campus, your training will take place here, at Stoker Hall." She finished waving her hand at the marvelous building before us.

"Stoker Hall?" I asked. The name sounded familiar, but I couldn't place it entirely. Calista nodded.

"Named after famous author Bram Stoker. Each of the remaining buildings is named after a famous Irish figure." She pointed to the next building behind Stoker Hall as we came to a stop under its gorgeous archway. "Green Residence is named after the famous historian Alice Stopford Green. McCarthy Lodge was named after famous Irish explorers Timothy and Mortimer McCarthy, and Dowling Quarters in honor of Jonathan Dowling, a famous Irish Scientist."

"Stoker, Green, McCarthy, Dowling," I recited, pointing to each building.

"Precisely. Aside from Stoker Hall, they are housing units for us here. Each equipped with its own café."

"And what's different about Stoker Hall?" I asked.

"This is where you will dive headfirst into preparing for your expeditions," she said proudly. Then she smiled at me and turned on her heel toward the great big wooden doors of Stoker Hall. "Follow me."

Chapter Six

Stoker Hall's main lobby was laid out in luxurious, mahogany wood flooring. Off to either side was an arrangement of dark wine and gold-accented love seats and loungers. A giant coffee bar separated the lounging areas in the middle of the room. Beyond the lobby doorways, at the back of the space were two elaborate staircases that created a half-moon when they met on level two.

Calista walked me through the different halls, pointing out classrooms, the library, and the main computer room. We ascended the left staircase and came to a stop at a huge open window that looked down onto a ginormous gym. A navy and green track encircled the gym.

Protective mats filled the area in the middle, aside from one spot off to the side that held another space of wood flooring about the size of a tennis court. An assortment of weights, punching bags, and equipment was scattered throughout the rest of the room. There was even a rock climbing wall off to the left.

A man in his late twenties was in the middle of the room using the weights. From this angle, and from what I could see, he was quite the view. He was lean in the torso but broad in the shoulders. He wore black basketball shorts, a dark gray t-shirt, and black tennis shoes as he lifted. I couldn't see much from this angle but I could definitely appreciate his body type as his muscles bulged under the lines of his t-shirt.

Calista clasped her hands behind her back and smiled admiringly at the man a floor below us. "And that is your expedition advisor, Elias. He will accompany you and oversee every expedition you go on for the next couple of months," she said, then turned slightly my way and added for my benefit, "But don't worry, I will always be around too."

I knitted my eyebrows together, unsure if she meant it as a possessive response to my working with him, or if she just wanted me to know she was always available. I looked back down and watched him closely as he sat up from the bench press. He was clearly fit, with muscles packed on each arm and nicely toned shoulders. I wouldn't blame her if she was staking her claim. He was definitely the type girls could get possessive over.

Calista shifted suddenly, and I pulled my eyes away from him and followed her. The length of the window looking into the gym matched the length of the hallway. There was an elevator at the end, but right before we came up to it, Calista opened a door on the right and flicked a switch, illuminating a large, relatively dark room even with the lights on. It was filled with computers, radars, and a few big screens on two different walls. I had only ever seen something like this on TV. At the back of the room was a large table fit for at least eight people, and behind that, against the wall, was a decent-sized bookcase lined with hundreds of what appeared to be historical and geographical books.

"This is the Expeditions Communications Lab. While on your expeditions, the team supporting you will meet here. They will have access to your location at all times and be informed of every detail of your expedition. Any help you need, you will find from the team here. Downstairs, we have two separate suites for your team to stay in while your expeditions are taking place; that way, they have easy access to the lab, should you need them in the middle of the night."

"Wow," was all I had to say. This place was huge.

I imagined people sitting around with radio sets and headphones contacting us from afar. I turned back to Calista, who had been watching me. Her smile had returned to her face. "Will you be on my team?" I asked. She nodded.

"Yes, I am what they call the Team Manager of Operations. I oversee the Expeditions Operations Teams in all departments. Still, the main team I work with is Missing Artifacts."

"That's so cool. So, we will be working together then?"

She nodded. "Yes, I will almost always be in your ear," she said, using air quotes, and laughed. I turned back to get a better look at that library, but Calista cleared her throat. "The hall of records is down the opposite way. It has more books and documents. It should have everything you need to prepare for any future expeditions. Elias will be able to brief you better on how that works over the next two weeks of training." Calista stepped out of the room, and I reluctantly followed her.

The elevator required a key code. Apparently, access to the gym was granted only to those training for expeditions.

Connor had said there were multiple expeditions you would go on, but to my understanding, not all of them would require the same type of training. I assumed archeology expeditions didn't require such physical training.

I was not looking forward to this part of the training. It wasn't that I was unfit or lazy, but I also rarely hit up the YMCA. Not knowing how intense this training might be made me a little apprehensive.

The man we had been watching from upstairs dusted off his hands on his shorts and began to make his way toward us. Calista's smile deepened the closer we got.

Getting a better look at him, I understood why, and I felt a blush creep up my cheeks as Elias approached. Lord, have mercy, he was more gorgeous than I had thought.

He had rich brown hair with hints of caramel between the layers that were longer on the top of his head. He was clean-shaven, allowing his nicely cut square jaw to steal all the attention from his soft brown eyes that resembled honey. Freckles peppered his high cheekbones making him appear younger than he was. His lips were full and inviting, and I could just barely see a dimple in the middle of his chin. His ears peeked out from underneath his hair showing off a rather pointed ear on one side and a rounded ear on the other.

Huh, must have been kissed by the fae.

He stopped about five feet away from us. Calista turned to me. "Ava, this is Elias Andrew Cassedy."

Elias held out his hand, and I took it in mine.

"Ava Metheny. Nice to meet you."

He nodded and looked at Calista.

"As I said before," she said, "he will be your expedition's advisor. From here on out, you will report to him."

"Don't worry, I don't bite," he said and flashed me an unforgettable smile. I was surprised that he had no accent and, in fact, seemed to speak with a sort of Midwestern vibe.

"Sounds promising," I retorted.

Calista looked between the two of us, then shifted from foot to foot as if suddenly anxious. "Well, then, I guess I should let you get acquainted. I'm sure Elias has many things he'd like to introduce you to before the clock strikes seven tonight. Ava, Elias will have my number for you if you have any further questions.

You'll be stationed down at McCarthy Lodge for the remainder of your time with us."

She handed me a folder that had been on a bench nearby. It was filled with my lodge information. "If you have any concerns or questions, I will be more than happy to assist."

I thanked her for showing me around and started to page through yet another folder of information when she abruptly turned back to us before exiting the gym.

"Oh, and Elias? She just got in—try not to be too hard on her tonight, will you? She's exhausted as is."

Elias gave her a genuine smile that told me there was history there. Calista returned it with a wicked grin, shaking her head, and began to exit. "I make no promises," said Elias, and the elevator doors closed.

He looked over at me, and his smile faded. I tried not to take that personally. He shifted his eyes back to the weights, sitting uncomfortably in the corner. I again found myself fighting the urge to groan.

I was not prepared to lift weights at this ungodly hour. It was honestly kind of a miracle that I was still standing, but I figured at this point my body was merely operating on adrenaline from exploring the campus. I hated to be this person, but now that my thoughts had returned to my lack of sleep, my body began to feel heavy.

"We're not *really* going to work out tonight, right?"

Elias scoffed and shook his head. "No. Come on, I'll show you where we'll start." I mindlessly rubbed my eyes and followed him to the elevator. We rode back up to the second floor in silence.

Usually, in that situation, I would have felt awkward, but by that point in the evening, I didn't have the energy to notice. We passed the communications room and headed toward the only room Calista had not shown me—the hall of records.

Like the communications room and the gym, this room was locked with a keypad. Elias typed in a four-digit passcode and yanked on the golden handle. He held it open for me, and I entered a room that looked like something out of *Beauty and the Beast*.

Rows of books lined every wall. Rolling ladders leaned against the shelving to help people reach the top. This room was even more significant than the actual library they had in the Main Hall. But it smelled like dust and mothballs. I curled my lip at the odor.

Elias walked over to the large table in the center, where he had a chaotic stack of old documents, multiple history books, and various maps in the middle. I let out a slow whistle, suddenly awake. Clearly, he had already started his research.

"What on earth is this mess?" I asked and glanced up at him. He scowled at my comment, and I muttered an apology. I stepped closer to the chaos to inspect it. As I lightly paged through some of the papers before me, I began to grasp just how old some of these things were. I expected that a few dated back to the late 1800s, if not older, but I wouldn't know for sure until I could read through each of them one by one.

Elias scoffed. "This mess—" he waved his arm at the papers before us—"is your playground. This is where your specialty comes into play. I've gathered as much information as possible. Still, I suspect we will need a few more days here in the hall of records before we begin planning our journey."

I looked sideways at him as if he had two heads. Then it clicked. "I have an assignment already?"

"*We*," he corrected. Right. We. Whatever. I held back my automatic response to roll my eyes—it wasn't polite. As handsome as he was, I had expected him to be more . . . charming. I was wrong. "Yes, we waste no time here."

He seemed to bite the inside of his lip like he had been working on this for months, a puzzle he just couldn't crack. Then, after a second of pondering to himself, he blinked back at me. "What?"

I could tell he was trying to deflect his awkwardness back at me. I shrugged and shook my head, raising my eyebrows innocently. "Nothing. So, what exactly is the assignment?"

Elias smiled mischievously. It was the first time I got a glimpse of real excitement in him. He stepped forward, pulled out one of the chairs at the table, and gestured for me to sit down.

"I don't know if you know this, but they give us your enrollment information so we know a little about our team before they arrive. Based on what I've read about you, you're going to love this."

I cocked an eyebrow back at him. "Intriguing, go on."

He reached over me from behind my chair and pulled a very old clipping forward. At the top of the article was a black-and-white photograph of Dublin Castle. "Our first assignment. The Missing Crown Jewels of Ireland."

My smile faded.

1904

Dear Brother,

I received your letter the other day. I am so pleased to hear that things are going well for you in Cork. I am happy to inform you that I will be returning home in the next couple of months. Work is calling me back for a short time. Though Tipperary is a wonderful place, it is not home. It will be nice to see you all.

I must admit, it feels as if St. Patrick himself has blessed me with an opportunity I never could have imagined. The work I will be doing is exactly the sort of opportunity I have always dreamed of. This will not be like any previous job I've had; this role will change the course of my life, I just know it.

Oh, brother, if you only knew.

I wish I could give you more details, but alas, I find my hands tied at this moment. I do dislike keeping things from you, but perhaps this one is for the best. Of course, I will be sure to inform you of anything serious.

In the meantime, please pass on this information to our mother, and give Nathanial my love. I look forward to seeing you all very soon.

Until we meet again,

Lynch

Chapter Seven

I was no stranger to the history of the heist that had taken place at Dublin Castle over a century ago. At the time, it had been the crime of the decade. Strategically planned and carried out without complications. Whoever did it must have prepared for weeks.

My eyes wandered over the papers spread out on the table, and I reached over to start looking through exactly what Elias had compiled so far. "May I?" I asked before touching the historical documents.

Elias nodded, watching me from underneath his lashes. "That is kind of your job," he replied sarcastically. Then he shifted his tone and spoke a little more seriously. "This is what I could find on the subject, but it wasn't as well documented as I'd hoped. Honestly, I wasn't entirely sure where to start. Other than what I have gathered here, I'm not quite sure where else to look."

So, he wasn't meant to be the brains behind the operation. I was. Shocker.

I sighed, trying to get the negative and short-tempered thoughts out of my head. They weren't helping. Despite Elias's attitude, I needed to try to get along with him. We were set to be working together for the unforeseeable future after all. I had to try to be kind, even if he wouldn't.

Flipping through documents and history books with marked pages, I came across an ancient and crumbling map of Glendalough and gently—very gently—handed it to Elias. He took it into his hands as gingerly as I had passed it. With the vibe in the room suddenly serious, he laid it on the table, away from the remaining papers and books. He grabbed his chair and sat down beside me. "We start here, at Glendalough," I said confidently.

Elias looked up at me curiously, waiting for me to elaborate. Still, the look in his eye told me he was testing me and was not being truthful about the amount of information he knew. I narrowed my eyes on him.

What reason would he have to withhold knowledge?

I was in no mood to play his games. "What do you actually *know* about the Crown Jewels?" I asked.

If he wanted to test me, fine, then I would test him in return.

His eyes moved away from mine, as if disappointed. He ran his tongue over his teeth before answering.

Clearly, he didn't trust me with this information for whatever reason. That was okay—I had to remind myself just how high the stakes were, and decide how much I truly wanted to trust him in return. So, it seemed we stood on mutual ground in that respect. But we were never going to get anywhere without sharing information first.

I sat back in my seat and spun the pen on the desk around as Elias finally answered. "Based on the information I was able to find, I know that the jewels were made of Queen Charlotte's jewelry collection. In total, about 394 precious stones were used to design these specific pieces."

I nodded. "Correct."

Elias seemed to ease up. "The prime suspect at the time was a man known by the name of Andrew Phineas Lynch," he continued, "but he was pardoned as a suspect because he was found to have been in Scotland at the time of the theft." I looked up at him smugly.

"And why did they suspect Andrew Lynch then?"

Elias blinked twice at me, then looked down at his papers. "They were stolen from Dublin Castle during a party that was being held by the vicar that night, and he claimed to have seen Andrew at the party but . . ."

"But . . . ?"

Elias scowled. "He was drunk, and when witnesses said they saw Lynch in Scotland, the account was thrown out."

Smug smile still holding on, I nodded at him, and he rolled his eyes.

"Very good."

"Alright, enough, clearly you're poking fun at me."

I raised a lazy shoulder. "You wanna test me? Two can play that game. And trust me when I say I know my stuff."

Elias held up his hands in surrender. "Fine. Point taken. I'm sorry I just needed reassurance you are in this for the right reasons."

I scowled at him, offended that it would even be a question he would consider. "I have a job to do here, Elias. That's all; I'm not here because of the treasure. I'm not here for fame. I'm here because of my love—" I broke off my sentence, unable to stifle my yawn "—for history."

Elias studied me momentarily then nodded and looked away, a bit ashamed. "To be fair, you wouldn't believe the amount of people I've had to report because they hoped to gain riches from whatever we were looking for."

I tilted my head to the side and looked away. I didn't doubt he was telling the truth. People these days were sleazy and consistently fake. And I didn't necessarily blame him for questioning my motives either. I, after all, was here with that same motive in mind. But he could never know that.

"Can we get back to the topic?" I yawned again. "At hand."

Elias nodded. "The only other thing I could find was that historians believed it initially ended up somewhere south of Dublin."

I nodded and tapped the map in front of him.

"That is correct. Glendalough to be exact. But there's so much more to this story. The Crown Jewels were stolen in 1907. Later in 1916, an unexpected rebellion of the Irish, known as The Easter Rising, happened. This revolution proved to be a disaster for them, yet they continued to demand their independence, which eventually led them to the Irish Independence War in 1919.

"At the time of the theft, the British ruled over Ireland. They used Dublin Castle for many political meetings. However, the British decided to house the Crown Jewels of Ireland there in the Bedford Tower, along with a few other priceless items—all of which were taken back by the British after the Irish Independence War ended in 1921. All except the Crown Jewels of Ireland."

I fished through the history book until I came across the chapter dedicated to the Easter Rising in 1916 and shoved it toward Elias.

"The jewels didn't belong to the Brits, though," Elias interrupted.

"No, they didn't, but they didn't really care. The jewels actually belonged to a secret society called the Order of St. Patrick. They were known as the protectors of Ireland."

Elias processed this information before looking back at me. "So . . . you're saying . . . ?"

I mindlessly rubbed my forehead and passed him yet another new article with a black-and-white sketch of an empty Bedford tower.

"Historians argue that the Republic of Ireland planned the heist—or more specifically, the Order of St. Patrick. The conspiracy theory is that they stole the jewels to protect them from falling into British hands permanently. The jewels were special, you see. Unlike most of Queen Charlotte's collection, they were not used in coronations for the royal family but were actually used in knighting ceremonies for the Order itself. They had been gifted to them specifically for this purpose. So, for the Order, this was personal."

I slid yet another paper with a single symbol across the table. A knot with three swirls going off in three different directions. A triskele.

Elias picked up the document and intensely studied the symbol, running his fingers over the grooves in each swirl. He seemed to be lost in thought, and for the second time that night, I got the feeling he was hiding information from me or at least playing dumb. But I didn't know why.

Without thinking, I snatched his forearm and held it up, pointing to a bare patch of skin there, but Elias quickly withdrew his hand from me.

"Relax," I joked, giving him a glance. "The knights of the Order were branded right there by that mark. All of them. If he stole the jewels, Andrew would have had to cover it up somehow."

Elias cleared his throat. "That wouldn't be too hard, considering he was probably wearing a dress suit at the time," Elias responded mindlessly, rubbing his wrist. I shook my head and rubbed my temples; exhaustion was really setting in. Elias glanced over at me with a slightly worried look. "Are you still with me?"

I closed my eyes and nodded, then rested my head in my hand. "Just exhausted."

He looked at his watch and raised his eyebrows. "Shit, it's way past seven and past time for dinner. I'm sorry I wasn't keeping better track of the time. If you're up for it, they probably still have stuff out in the main hall. Otherwise, I can walk you back to McCarthy Lodge if you prefer."

As if the weight of the world suddenly sat on my eyelids, I slowly opened my eyes and looked over at Elias. "I think I'll pass on dinner." Elias looked back at the documents sprawled out on the table with a disappointed expression, then stood and grabbed my backpack off the floor.

"I can carry it," I insisted as I came to my feet.

"It's fine. I got it, really." His tone was a bit short but I shrugged and let him take it. Whatever tension we had at the beginning of the evening seemed to be subdued. How long would that last? Who knew? But for now, I was thankful. As we exited the elevator and entered the main floor of Stoker Hall, Elias glanced over at me.

"While we're walking, do you mind filling me in on how we end up at Glendalough?"

I raised an eyebrow at him, giving him a sideways glance, and nodded. I yawned once more before I began, though.

"The conspiracy theorists say that once the Republic of Ireland had their hands on the jewels, they took them back to Glendalough for safekeeping. From there, though, it is unclear where they went."

As we walked, Elias kept one hand wrapped around the strap of my backpack on his right shoulder and his other hand in his pocket. He kept his eyes on the ground as we walked. I kept my eyes straight ahead, as I was afraid I would fall over if I didn't.

"I thought you said they thought the Order had stolen the jewels? And why Glendalough?"

"The Order was part of the Republic of Ireland. And they agreed the jewels should remain with them since the Order of St. Patrick was an Irish Order and not tainted by the Brits. They chose Glendalough for its significance. Glendalough is a place of spirituality. They believed St. Patrick and God alike would bless their endeavors there."

"But Glendalough hadn't been in use for many years. What was left that they could use?"

"Incorrect. It had been refurbished at the end of the nineteenth century and was housing a new monastery. They partnered up with the Republic of Ireland to save the jewels. The monks were a big part of the knighthood in the Order, so it made sense they would side with them."

Elias looked up as we approached McCarthy Lodge's big wooden doors. He reached out and held open the door. "Do you have a theory as to who actually stole the jewels?"

"Yep, Andrew Lynch."

Elias frowned. He seemed surprised. "Boy, you really worked hard to find that hidden gem, didn't you?" he asked. I gave him a look of irritation that said *are we really going to go through this again?* Elias rolled his eyes but lifted a hand in truce once more. "Okay, fine, sorry but—"

"Ava!" I looked up as we walked into the open light of the lobby and saw Connor waiting up—barely—with a cup of coffee in his hand.

"I was wondering where you were. I didn't see you at the dining hall," he said as he approached us. He held out the mug and looked at Elias. I accepted it gladly with both hands, smelling the comforting scent before taking a sip. Connor was about the same height as Elias, if not a few inches taller. But where Connor was tall and toned, Elias was lean with muscle. I looked between the two of them before wiping my mouth and introducing them.

"Sorry, I'm losing it. Connor, this is Elias Cassedy. He's my expedition advisor. Elias, this is my friend Connor from school. He's an archeology major."

Elias's smile was tight. "Archeology? Nice." He said it as if it was a nerd thing but held out his hand to shake Connor's regardless. Connor gave him a fake smile in return.

"Yeah . . . but I'm overseeing Expeditions here for the time being. I'm working with Calista Scott." Connor turned back to me. "I believe she showed you around earlier this afternoon, Av."

I nodded.

When did Connor start calling me *Av*? Did I like that? My eyes thoughtlessly danced between the guys' feet until I decided I didn't really care and hugged my mug closer to my lips.

"Oh, Calista is something special; you'll have a good internship with her for sure," Elias said. I opened my eyes and gave him a quizzical look. Had they been a thing before? They certainly acted weird enough around each other, I had noticed.

"Sure, I bet." Connor looked at me as I closed my eyes yet again and took my last sip of coffee. "Come on, Av, let's get you to your dorm."

Elias took a step toward us and offered his hand out. "Do you need me to show you? I'm not bunking in McCarthy this year, but I have before; I could carry your bag and show you around if you want, Ava?"

I looked over at him, but before I could respond, Connor interjected. "Nah, man, thanks, but we got it. I can carry that for her."

I made a face. I was beginning to dislike this show of testosterone that was going on here. It was too late for that shit, and there was no reason for it. What did Elias care for anyway? It wasn't like we had hit it off. "No, both of you can go. I'll be fine from here on out, really. Thanks, but I'm a big girl. I can handle getting to my dorm room by myself." I reached out to take my bag from Elias. He didn't argue.

"Elias, thank you for the coffee, and Connor, thank you for walking me back. I appreciate it." They both gave me a weird look, and it took me a minute to realize my mistake.

I smacked my hand against my head and handed the empty coffee mug to Connor, who put it on a nearby coffee table. "You know what I mean!"

Elias chuckled and shook his head. "Fine," he said.

"You're sure you don't want help finding the dorm?" Connor asked, but I held up my hand.

"I'm sure."

"Alright then, I'll let you get to bed."

Elias turned to walk back out the double doors we had come from but stopped abruptly and called out, "Oh, I almost forgot, Ava! Due to your jet lag today, we will both have tomorrow off, but I will expect you to be at Stoker Hall's gym for training at six thirty a.m. sharp the following day. And be dressed to train. The key code is in the folder Calista gave you earlier today. I also wrote down my number and slid that in, should you need me. Calista's number is on the back."

I pulled out the folder from my backpack, knowing I'd need it to find my room anyway. "Six a.m. sharp, got it."

"Six thirty." He corrected his tone a bit more seriously this time. "I'm not a monster. Get some sleep, Ava. I'll see you around."

# Chapter Eight

1904, County Cork, Ireland

Andrew walked down the cobblestone street toward where he had left his brother to wait for him in the open cart. The brothers had gone into town in search of a few things from the local market. Andrew had split off just after they'd arrived, claiming he would pick up the last few items on their list and meet his brother back at the cart. That had been a lie. Instead, he had just come from a meeting with one of the members of the Order at the blacksmith's and was hoping Elijah wouldn't have too many questions as to why he had been gone for so long.

Much to his surprise, though, as Andrew made his way up to the cart, he realized his twin was nowhere to be found. Andrew set his bag of items into the cart and stepped away, looking down the main street for Elijah. Andrew gave the horse in front of him a look and patted its nose, then pursed his lips and left the cart behind to go search for his brother. It didn't take long to find him.

Two blocks down, Andrew heard a commotion from a back alley to the right. Looking down the narrow side street, shadowed by the day's activities, Andrew saw three men standing around another blond male crumpled on up the ground. His bag of possessions was sprawled around him, some damaged. The man was using one hand to prop himself up on his knees while the other was wrapped around his stomach in pain. The men around him laughed in his humiliation as he groaned.

"Hit him again, Seamus, for good measure," the smallest one of the bunch said with a curt nod as if he was serving justice and not acting like a tyrant.

"Better be careful; we wouldn't want him to like it and start to fancy you, now, would we?" the second, bigger bloke joked and playfully punched the third man standing between them. He let out a howl of a laugh as the man Andrew knew as Seamus McDowell smugly cocked the side of his mouth upward in a sinister smirk.

Seamus McDowell had been a schoolmate of both Andrew and Elijah's. They were roughly the same age. His parents were on the richer side and didn't know what it meant to want for anything. That upbringing had pretty much cost Seamus his humanity.

Andrew had known they had suspected Elijah's little secret, but he had never had proof that they were the reason behind his brother coming home beaten up and bruised on multiple occasions.

The smallest of the three companions looked around the alleyway nervously. "If you're not going to finish him off, we better be getting back to the market, Seamus, before someone spots us or worse, he finds someone nearby and reports us."

"Now, now, Connell, don't be ridiculous." Seamus bent down to look at Elijah. His smile was grotesque. "Elijah wouldn't dare be stupid enough to risk his life like that, would you, Elijah?"

"He might not, but I wouldn't mind placing that bet," Andrew said and stepped out of the shadows of the alleyway. He rolled up the ends of his sleeves as he came into the light. He figured it was about time he flaunted his newfound authority.

So much for doing well in Cork, Andrew thought to himself with a frown.

Seamus frowned and stood up straight, eyes narrowing on the other brother. Elijah barely turned his head in Andrew's direction.

"Ah, well, if it isn't the better brother, here to save the day."

Seamus folded his arms over his chest and smiled as if accepting the challenge. But his confidence was short-lived. Andrew lowered his arms, sleeves rolled up to the elbow, and revealed the new branding he had just received at the blacksmith's.

The Order of St. Patrick was a local legend. Stories that were told between school kids. Gossip passed through word of mouth in pubs.

The rumor was they were part of a rebellious group that was out to challenge the British for dominance of Ireland. But only the bravest and most determined warriors were chosen to be knighted into the Order.

They held places in the highest parts of society and had members everywhere. No one in their right mind would mess with them, and Andrew knew it. They were marked by the symbol of a single triskele branded onto their skin—the very same one Andrew now sported on his left forearm.

Seamus seethed after seeing the mark. Connell behind him shrank back, eyes wide. Even the big bloke looked frightened.

Andrew came over to stand beside his twin and held out his other arm for Elijah to grab onto. Elijah took it and came to a standing position. Connell and the other man began to retreat further into the alleyway. Seamus stepped backward as well, preparing to head out.

"You'd be wise not to share my identity with anyone now, ya hear? I'd hate to think what would become of men who ruined the reputation of a member of the Order."

As the other two men fled, Seamus stuck around one last second to look Andrew straight in the eye.

"This isn't the last we will speak, Andrew Lynch, mark my words." Then he disappeared back into the shadows.

# Chapter Nine

Modern-day Dublin, Ireland

Elias

Stepping out into Dublin's brisk, cool air, Elias hunched up his shoulders and pulled his coat collar closer to him to try and protect his neck from the chill. He was walking fast toward Dowling Quarters when the phone in his jacket pocket buzzed. He glanced around the dark and pulled the phone to his ear. "Yeah?"

"Hey, you got any news for me yet?" the girl on the other end asked in a sweet voice.

Elias shrugged. "Not much. I definitely think the board of directors chose wisely this time, thank God. This girl seems to know what she's talking about."

"That's great! Sabane will be pleased to hear!"

"Yeah. I'm thinking this time we might actually have a shot."

"All good reports. You'll have to keep me posted and let me know if you need anything."

Elias nodded to himself as the light from Dowling Quarters got brighter. "Will do. Hey, have you spoken to my aunt recently? I think I'll have to stop by and see her soon." He could hear clicking as the girl on the other end started typing something while they spoke.

"No, but I could give her a call. I haven't had the pleasure of catching up with her in a while. It will be nice to chat with her again."

Elias smiled. His aunt had a way of making everyone feel like they were family. "Yeah, if you wouldn't mind just letting her know. I'll probably reach out myself once I have a better idea of when, but I suspect it will be within the next few weeks." Elias ran up the stone steps of Dowling Quarters, wanting to escape the chilling Irish wind. He opened the door to the dorms and entered, walking right past the lobby up the stairs, heading for floor two.

"So . . . how are things with you and Calista? Have you two gotten back together yet?" she asked, and Elias rolled his eyes. He realized that Kayleigh had to be bored, stuck behind a computer screen all day, but sometimes he worried that she knew too much about him.

He pulled out his key from his pocket, holding the phone to his ear with his shoulder, and opened the door. He had expected the room to be dark, but instead all the lights were on but dimmed. Elias dropped his shoulders, already knowing what he had just walked into. He grabbed the phone with his hand.

"Speak of the devil," he whispered to Kayleigh.

"Ohhh! What's happening?" she asked, intrigued, but Elias shook her off.

"Nothing. I gotta go."

"I'm sure you do! Give her a kiss for me! Team Lottie all the way!" Kayleigh hollered as he ended the call.

Elias turned off his phone and shoved it back into his pocket before sighing and entering the room. The room was reasonably small, with just a closet, desk, bed, single chair, and bathroom. It resembled a tiny hotel room. Elias had to walk down a small hallway that allowed an entryway to the bathroom off to his left before he saw Calista lying casually on the bed in nothing but her matching black bra, thong, and stockings from earlier that day. She grinned at him and licked her lips as he shut the door behind him.

"Surprise," she said in a raspy voice. Elias raised his eyebrows and shook his head at her as he came to a stop right in front of the bed. He didn't move from his spot, but he also couldn't stop his smile. *Shit.*

He thought they were done with this. They had broken up almost a year ago and were still hooking up. Usually, that kind of thing wouldn't have mattered to him. All this meant nothing to Elias, but he suspected that it meant everything to Calista. They were friends—good friends. He truly cared about her and wasn't willing to lose the friendship over hurt feelings.

"We said we weren't going to do this anymore," he reminded her.

Calista pouted and sat up on her knees. She crawled over to kneel before him on the bed. She moved her hands up to cup the back of his neck, and she began to play in his hair. "But it's so much fun," she whined.

Elias, trying to stand firm, slowly pulled her hands away from him, and then he pinned her wrists to her chest. He looked down at her and shook his head. "We both know it's a bad idea, Lottie."

Calista shrugged and tilted her head mischievously. "Who cares?"

"*I* care. How was your first day with your new intern?" he asked, trying to distract her. In the past, they had made a habit of trash-talking the newbies. He had hoped he could use this and the promise of a drink out at the pub to convince her to put her clothes back on.

Calista rolled her eyes. "Boring as usual." The way her *r*'s curled sent a shiver down his spine and made him wince. He was not going to give into that accent of hers. No way. He would stay strong, he told himself.

"He's almost as dull as your new intern. I swear the board of directors has got to do better. These two are downright unintelligent. I don't know how I'll get through a year of this. Especially with her. She seems like a total fraud."

Elias cocked his head in surprise. That had not been the vibe he had gotten from Ava at all. Tired, yes. Sarcastic and witty, yeah, a little, but not dull or unintelligent. "I don't know; Ava really surprised me tonight with how much she already seemed to know about the assignment. She might just be smart enough to help me crack the case," Elias countered.

Calista scowled. "That dimwit? Oh, please." Calista looked down at his hands, still holding hers together against her nearly bare chest, and seductively smiled back at him. "Besides, I don't want to talk about her anymore. I have . . . *things* . . . to attend to," she purred, and Elias knew he was in trouble.

"We agreed to keep our friendship strictly professional this year, remember?"

Calista sat back up on her knees and yanked her hands away from him. Elias let his hands fall to his sides and tilted his head idly at her. Calista gave him another pouty face, batted her eyelashes at him, then popped her shoulder so that her right bra strap fell to the side, leaving a visible gap between it and her A-cup breasts. Elias took in a slightly unsteady breath. The new view of her was hard to walk away from, and she knew it.

Knowing she'd won, Calista shuffled forward on the bed and grabbed the hem of his t-shirt. She pushed her hands underneath the fabric and started to creep up his abdomen. Elias was helpless to stop her. He looked over at his desk as Calista slowly pulled up his shirt.

"We can't keep doing this, Lot, we're not—" But Calista abruptly snagged his face between her hands and growled at him seductively.

"Oh, God, just *shut up*!" she said, and she brought his mouth to hers. Elias gave in.

Chapter Ten

AVA

Two days later, I was up bright and early, heading into the gym, coffee in hand. I still wasn't quite sure what kind of work we'd be doing, but I was prepared no matter what it was. Or so I thought. Sporting navy blue leggings and a sports bra under my black cutoff shirt, I was ready for action. But I had also brought along my reading glasses, just in case we decided to hit the books again.

Elias was waiting for me over by a wooden bench off to the side of the track. I walked up to him as he closed a small brown leather book and tucked it away in his gym bag. He rubbed his hands together. "Ready to get to work?" he asked.

I took one last swig of my coffee and nodded. "I just need to refill my water bottle, but I'm prepared for whatever you have to throw at me."

Elias raised his eyebrows at me but was otherwise unfazed. "Oh, I'm sure you'll regret that statement before we're through today," he said.

I shook my head and turned away from him, making faces at his expense toward the wall. I tied my hair into a high pony, then checked to ensure my shoelaces were tightened before standing up and putting my hands on my hips. I was determined to prove that I wasn't weak. Elias ignored it.

"For most of the expeditions, you will need to rely on your sense of smarts, but there will come a time when you will be required to do things that are out of the physical norm. And that is the reason we train here." Elias turned to look at me with a serious expression on his face. "I take this training very seriously and need you to do the same. Not knowing how to respond to certain situations could get you killed. It will be daunting and hard, but I need you to push through. You can hate me if you want, but trust me when I say it's worth it to be prepared when you're out in the field."

I took a deep breath and stood up a little straighter. These were not exactly the words I wanted to hear, but I understood where he was coming from. It seemed like Elias had been doing this a long time, and if he said it was important for my safety, then I would trust him on this and take it seriously. I nodded back at him, biting my lip. "Okay, great, where do we start?"

I wasn't sure if he had noticed his demeanor suddenly change from the sarcastic ass I was getting to know to a man who seemed to be haunted by the actions of his past. I softened my features to seem less combative and stopped to listen to what he had to say.

Convinced that I would take the training seriously, Elias smiled smugly and crossed his arms over his chest. I didn't like the look he was giving me. "I hope you enjoy running."

For the next two hours, Elias and I ran the track around and around and around until I threw up. Ever the gentleman, he waited patiently for me to finish before giving me an apologetic smile and ushering me onto our next task. Despite my stomach, I never gave up. Four hours after we had arrived, he finally called it quits.

I walked over to the bench we had initially started from and fell onto the wood. I grabbed my water bottle, leaned forward, and doused the back of my neck. Elias walked up to join me.

"How are you feeling?"

I stopped and slowly turned to look at him with a scowl. He snickered at me, so I took the opportunity to shake out my soaked hair, no doubt getting him wet in the process.

"I tried to warn you." He shrugged innocently. I sat up, still trying to catch my breath. Once I could think straight without seeing double, I looked over his way. He had fished out that little book from his bag and had shoved his nose back into its discolored pages.

"So how exactly does all this work? You've stated that I'm pretty much the brains of the operation, but where do you come into play?" Elias snapped the book shut and glanced at me, eyelids half-mast.

"I am your advisor. I oversee all expeditions."

"Yeah, I know that already, but what does that mean? How did you get—" I waved my arm drastically in front of me. It felt like moving Jello in slow motion. "Here?"

Elias raised an eyebrow but sat down beside me. He handed me the book. It automatically opened to the page marked with a single satin bookmark. I looked at it quizzically, flipping through. I couldn't read a single word. "It's in Gaelic," I said.

"That's how I got here. I was a bilingual communications major. I am fluent in English and Gaelic, but my minor was Celtic Studies. Since I started here, I have expanded my knowledge of Greek and Latin. I'm not fluent, but I can read them well enough. I'd like to learn a few others, but I'm finding myself short on time. I started doing expeditions at the end of my internship year for different departments that they thought would need a lot of translation. Eventually, I switched to studying Celtic history full-time and then accepted a position here assisting with interns."

I sat back and processed that. Gaelic, Greek, and Latin? "Damn. That's impressive," I admitted out loud.

He crossed his arms, slightly uncomfortable, and nodded. "Yes, but I'm nowhere near your qualifications regarding Irish history." I looked over with an apologetic grimace. Yes, indeed, I had noticed that when he had first said it.

"Yeah, there's a big difference between Celtic Studies and Irish Studies, but I tried to let it slide."

He chuckled under his breath. "Basically," he continued, "I'm here to lead the expedition, and you're here to provide the map. But I can help along the way. I have certain interests, which might pique your interest later on down the road. But realistically, so you know, *everything* regarding the assignment, *every* decision, *every* task, has to go through me for both of our safety." He sounded stern, and I got the feeling that something unexpected had happened on a previous expedition. This was the second time it felt like his whole persona had changed. I wondered if I should be worried. Maybe I could ask Calista about it.

"Okay, you're in charge. Got it. Anything else?"

"Yes. We work as a team. None of this *one the brains, one the brawn* shit. I don't play that game. I can help with the history stuff; I'm just not as well-versed. Just like I will be training you at the gym, you should look at the room of records as your place to train me." I weighed my head back and forth. I could roll with that.

"Okay, deal."

"Good," said Elias, standing. He threw his little leather book into his bag, zipped it shut, and motioned for me to join him. "Then let's get started. Take a half hour to shower, then meet me upstairs. Two weeks is all we got to plan and prepare, and I don't intend to waste it."

And that's precisely what we did—we hit the books and weights for two straight weeks. I was proud when Elias pulled out his notebook one day and showed me notes he had taken from our discussions. And then he congratulated me the first day we worked out without me spilling my guts.

After a couple days digging into the books, we had maps laid out everywhere and notes all over the place. We had gotten so far that I was content with the information we had on the Order but not so keen on our lack of knowledge surrounding Andrew. It wasn't until one night while flipping through a book I had paged through at least a dozen times by now, that I came across a picture of a man and a woman dressed in their finest clothes from an upper-class party in 1907. I nearly jumped out of my seat when I recognized the face of the man in the top hat.

"Elias! Come here and look at this!"

From the opposite side of the long table, Elias lifted his eyes from the book in his hands with curiosity. He set it down and stepped behind me at my chair as I pointed to the picture of Andrew Lynch and a woman named Bridget Hayes. Elias used his finger to follow the words on the page beside the photo to gain a better understanding.

Bridget Hayes was a famous pianist at the time whose growing career was taking Ireland by storm. According to the book, she was known to have many suitors but only one who ever stuck around, and that man was Andrew Lynch.

"This picture was taken in Dublin in 1907," Elias mused.

"You think it could have been taken on the night of the heist?" I asked. While my gut told me yes, we really had no way of knowing for sure.

"Couldn't have," he replied, but the look on his face told me he was also second-guessing himself. He moved back over to grab a book we had sitting out and open on the desk between us, flipping through its ginger pages. "Bridget Hayes is not listed on the guest list that night."

"But neither is Andrew, and we know for sure he was there," I insisted.

"We *think* he was there," he corrected. "There were still witnesses there who placed him in Scotland that night, remember?"

This was true—which posed a problem. How could both stories be accurate? There was far more evidence placing Andrew in Dublin that night than in Scotland.

Elias seemed lost for a minute. He turned the book's pages again. "Although—"

"Although what?"

I stood up and scurried over to look at the book myself. Elias lowered it for me so we could both inspect it further. "There is a Celene Hayes listed."

"Her sister?"

Elias turned to look at me. "Could it be possible that this Bridget Hayes got him his ticket into the party that night and they used the sister's name to keep the police from being able to track them down?"

"That would definitely answer a few questions!" I bounced up on my heels, excited at the prospect of a new clue. Could Bridget be a new lead to this mystery? I intended to find out everything I could about her and more. Maybe she would lead us to the next clue in Glendalough. I still wasn't sure this new lead would explain how Andrew could be in two places at once—but I hoped it would be fruitful. It was worth a try.

"I'll pull her up on the computer, you see if you can find out anything about Celene!" I instructed with newfound glee in my voice. Elias chuckled under his breath and shook his head as he walked away.

I wouldn't have called us best friends, but we were working our way toward a friendship. At the very least, we could tolerate each other for the most part, and that was something.

Chapter Eleven

Connor

Connor relaxed outside a local coffeeshop that he and Ava frequented regularly. He was nursing his fresh hot coffee when a fit of giggles burst through the regular bustle of the morning traffic that filled Dublin's streets.

He saw a mother and her young son spinning around as they headed toward another shop across the street. There, they stopped and waited. The boy was just out of his toddler years, probably three or four at most. Connor smiled as he watched the boy lift his hand to show his mum a flower he had picked for her, and she responded by scooping him up and planting kisses all along his cheek.

The boy let out another laugh when she picked him up and flipped him upside down, tickling his tummy, just as a man came toward them from the other direction. The man smiled and gave a quick kiss on the woman's cheek before picking up their son and taking him from his mother's arms so he could lift him into the air.

Connor returned his line of sight back to the mug in his hands. He let out a sigh and decided not to go down the emotional path that such a scene normally evoked in him.

He already knew his dad wasn't coming back. He had accepted that long ago, but now that he was in his twenties, he was interested in finding someone to build a life with. The desire to become a better man than his father weighed more heavily on his heart than it had in his youth. However, his new life all started with finding the right woman, and he understood that.

Connor had been so lost in his thoughts about the future and the mixture of his past that he hadn't noticed Ava approaching.

He lifted his eyes and his smile widened. She looked back at the cute little family as they rounded the corner, but returned his soft smile and pulled out the chair next to him. She accepted the coffee he had snagged for her and brought it to her lips with a hum of appreciation.

"Got something you want to share with the class?" she asked him, leaning her head in the direction the little family had departed from. Connor followed her gaze but shook his head and lowered his eyes back to his own cup.

"No, just considering the future while keeping the past in mind," he replied. Ava narrowed her eyes at him suspiciously.

She put her cup down and rubbed her hands together to create friction and looked around. "Considering the future?" she asked, surprised.

Connor lifted a single shoulder.

"Aren't you a little young to be worrying about that type of thing?" she asked. Connor chuckled but shook his head and sat up a bit straighter. Lord help him, she was quite something to look at.

Ava was an all-natural beauty with her tanned skin and her popping jade green eyes. Her lips were thin and yet somehow full at the top. Her hair was wild and free. And the way she often set her gaze on him gave her eyes a mischievous and seductive look that he couldn't get out of his head.

Connor shook out his head and brought himself back to the present.

"Probably, but at least I know what I want. Isn't that something everyone wants?" Connor asked. Ava seemed uncomfortable as she hunched her shoulders a bit and stared down her coffee cup. Connor's smile faltered. He hadn't meant to make her uncomfortable.

"I suppose."

"You suppose, but?"

Ava threw her eyes up at him making sure he knew she didn't like being cornered into this conversation. However, she clearly respected him enough to tell him the truth because she answered nonetheless.

"But . . . it's not something I foresee in my immediate future."

Connor furrowed his brows at this answer.

"How come?"

"Because if I'm being honest, I didn't have the best father figure in my life to demonstrate what a good husband and father should look like," she said as if it didn't bother her. Connor averted his eyes and took a sip of coffee.

He hadn't thought of it from that point of view. He had always had a woman in his life to look up to. He knew exactly what kind of person he wanted his future wife to be because his mother had been a great example to him growing up. He frowned. Perhaps the only way of truly saying sorry for pushing her to be open with him was explaining that he understood.

"I get it. My father left too. Right after I was born. But my mom was always a positive presence in my life. So, I was lucky." Connor glanced up at Ava and was relieved to see a smile back on her face. It softened her features as she nodded and sipped her own coffee.

"Mine was too."

"I guess I just keep getting caught up in this idea of finding something extraordinary while we're here," Connor explained. Ava weighed the thought in her head then nodded.

"I think that's pretty common for people who take a step out of their homeland bubble. There's so much of this world to explore leaving us with so many possibilities. It makes sense that we would find ourselves with a deeper longing for happiness while here." She turned to glance out at the street.

Connor watched her for a second admiring her ability to be open with people and still guard herself. He knew she was tough—that much had been obvious to him after her first week of training with Elias, when she came to their coffee date covered in bruises and barely able to walk. But this inner strength was a whole new level—one he understood and respected.

He normally didn't share this kind of stuff so early in the morning, so he figured it was time he changed the subject.

"How's training coming along? Elias learning anything in your midnight study sessions?"

Ava whipped her head back to him with wide eyes and set down her coffee. "Yes! I'm actually surprised. The way he had tested me the first night made it seem like he had no idea what he was talking about, but the more we research, the more he retains. I must say I'm impressed."

Connor frowned. It was not the response he had been hoping for. "Quick learner," he said.

Ava nodded enthusiastically. "Very. Ya know, honestly he's kind of a dick, but I'm learning a lot from him. I think between my expertise in history and his knowledge of the mission field and how it all works, we might actually be able to find something constructive on this journey next week. With your help, too, of course."

She almost seemed in awe of her new partner. He tried not to scowl but instead flashed her a smile and wiggled his eyebrows at her.

"Of course, Elias is great and all but let's be real for a sec. You know you'd be lost, completely in the dark without me," he joked and Ava laughed at his confidence.

"Oh, of course I would! How could I possibly go on without you? You are my rock, Connor!"

He smiled, something genuine, and he leaned forward to tap his cup against hers. "Damn right I am, and don't you forget it!"

Ava made a sarcastic face at him, mocking him behind giggles, but she couldn't hide her smile any more than he could hide his. Once their fits of laughter had died down again, they both looked out into the streets of Dublin once more and simultaneously sighed.

"Promise me something?" Connor asked her, breaking the silence. Ava turned back to look at him.

"Promise me that sometime during the next twelve months here, we will eventually get out and go explore Ireland together the way we hoped to." He turned toward her now to return her gaze. "Promise we will find something extraordinary here."

Ava's smile lit up like fireworks on the Fourth, and nodded. "Of course we will. That's not a promise. That's a fact."

# Chapter Twelve

1905, County Cork, Ireland

It was dark and Andrew walked at a slow pace so as not to draw attention. Beside him, Elijah had a decent shiner. He kept his head down, allowing his hair, which was a little longer in the front, to hang over his face, and followed quietly behind him.

Andrew had prayed to St. Patrick that they would take him. They had to; he didn't know what other choice they had. Elijah would surely have to leave Ireland if it didn't work. He was not safe here in Cork anymore. Of that, Andrew was sure.

They came up to the door of the local pub, O'Donnell's. Inside was a dimly lit bar at the back, with scattered tables. A musician sat in the corner, spinning the fiddle in his hands and working the crowd. The small group around him had their glasses raised as they sang along to "The Rocky Road to Dublin." It was a good night for a meeting; Andrew was sure no one from outside would hear them over the festivities.

He approached the bartender, who was drying pint glasses, and tipped his hat to him and Elijah. Elijah watched curiously as the man leaned over the bar to call out to them. "What'll ya boys be havin' tonight?"

Elijah's eyes flicked to Andrew, who leaned closer. "We're here to see the barkeep," he explained.

The bartender leaned back and sized up the two. "So ya think yer blessed then?" he asked.

"Ey, the road rises to meet me, brother." The bartender stood back and inhaled deeply as he scanned the room for anyone watching them and curtly nodded without making eye contact. "She be wait'n for ya through the backdoor to the left down the stairs."

"*Go raibh maith agat,*" Andrew responded in Gaelic. "Have them send down two glasses of Jameson."

"On it, sir." The bartender turned around to start getting their drinks ready as Andrew walked past the bar to a door off to the left. He pushed the handle, and they entered a darker hallway that led down a set of stairs into a cellar.

The cellar was made of substantial concrete slabs; torchlights illuminated a long rectangular table at the back of the room. Five men sat behind it in dark cloaks with hoods that covered their facial features, but Elijah could tell that most of them seemed to be a bit older. A few others loitered around the miscellaneous chairs that were placed in the room.

The group quieted down as they entered. Andrew stepped into the middle of the room. Elijah stayed put at the front of the entryway, a little caught off guard. The man in the center addressed Andrew.

"Ah, young Andrew Lynch. You have requested a meeting of the council. Please tell us exactly what all this is about."

Andrew, unlike Elijah, seemed to show no fear as he looked straight on and explained the reason for their meeting. "Lord—"

The man held up his hand. "Thou shall not speak thy name whilst we have an audience with a civilian!"

The men scattered throughout the room, who were younger and closer to Elijah's age, glanced at him and waited for Andrew to continue.

"My apologies, sir. I am here out of desperation, to seek the help of the council," he explained. The man in the middle seemed to accept his apology and gestured for him to continue.

"My brother is in danger. He has been the victim of multiple muggings within the last four months. Some of the attacks left him close to death. Even now, he shows proof of a recent encounter. I cannot intervene much more without drawing attention to our cause, and yet if I should leave him to go about his daily way, I fear one day he may not return home." Elijah watched wide-eyed as the men in the room looked between Andrew and him, no doubt inspecting that proof.

"And what exactly is it you would like the council to do for him?" a hooded figure off to the far left side of the table asked with a huff. Andrew turned to him, standing his ground. He didn't show any indication of backing down despite how bitter the man in the hood sounded.

"To induct him."

The group of men, both behind the hoods and scattered throughout the room, gasped as if Andrew had just told their secret—the secret Elijah had already put together for himself. Whispers from one to another led to shouting.

"That's enough!"

"Who does this lad think he is?"

"He shall be punished for this!"

"I told you Lynch was not ready!"

Elijah, held in place by fear, gulped as the bartender approached him from the stairs with a tray of assorted drinks. The men all hushed as he passed out glass by glass and then finally reached Elijah, handing him a glass filled halfway with whiskey before retreating upstairs. Elijah watched Andrew in front of him, staring at the ground as he swirled his drink. He was not as patient and took a swig at once without thought, hoping it would calm his nerves. Andrew continued while it was briefly silent.

"I realize I'm asking a lot of the council. But I have a plan that would make great use of Elijah to us." More whispers littered the air.

"What use could this boy be? He can't even fight his own battles, Andrew. Clearly, he's useless to us. Do you make us out to be fools?"

Andrew swirled his whiskey once more, then took a swig. "If you don't hear me out," he threatened, "you might be."

"Why, you son of—"

"That's enough, Marcus!"

One of the men to the right slapped the table in front of him hard. He was reining in the room. He stood up and leaned over the table to face the man on the opposite end of the table. "I've had enough of this back and forth. We get nowhere hearing you squander his every attempt to speak. You will sit, and you will hear what he has to say, and then and *only* then will we decide what we want to do as a group. But you do not speak for all of us. Mind yourself."

The other man grumbled from under his hood but otherwise didn't respond. The one who had just stood up for Andrew turned to face the two boys and removed his hood.

The man was much older than Elijah had expected him to be. He was bald with a string of white hair encircling the outer edge of his head. He had kind, sunken eyes and was wearing a thick wooden cross around his neck. A monk, Elijah realized.

"Please go on, Andrew," he said and seated himself.

Andrew, who had been leaning his hand on a nearby chair and held his glass in the other, looked between the monk and the other hooded figure off to the left with a smirk.

"Thank you, Abram. Elijah and I are twins. Identical twins at that, we can easily make it seem like we are one person who is in two places at once."

At this, the man in the middle sat up straighter, giving Andrew his full attention.

"Elijah is clever, much more clever than me. He can be of use to the Order in other ways that I cannot. If you induct him, you get the best of both of us. I can train him in other things he may need help in. He could be a great political asset to us if you let him."

The man in the middle suddenly flipped his hood back and revealed himself to be a local lord of justice: Lord Michaels. He was a little younger than the monk but held much more power.

"So, what do you suggest we do? Fake his death?"

"Exactly. Put to rest the life of Elijah Lynch and bring to life the double agent of Andrew Lynch." More whispers erupted from the group. The monk studied Elijah with precision. Two more hoods fell, one belonging to a blacksmith and the other to a sailor.

"This actually could work well for us, Everett. We could use a spy amongst us."

"This could change the way we think of future operations."

"Can you imagine what door this could open to us?"

"And what if they're caught? What then?"

Elijah tried to keep track of the conversations but got lost somewhere in the middle. The monk held out his hand and silenced the group.

The last hood fell, finally shedding light on the face that had scorned Andrew before: Marcus O'Neil. As Elijah had expected, he glowered at Andrew with his arms crossed. Clearly, he wasn't in favor of the idea, but if all had dropped their hoods, this must have been a good thing. Because if they didn't decide to take Andrew up on his offer, that meant that they were now exposed to a non-member of the Order. Elijah could only assume that would bring about his swift death and soon after, Andrew's. It was a fifty-fifty shot if they would make it out of here alive.

"I do have a few questions. What sparked these attacks?"

For the first time since entering the room, Andrew actually looked nervous. He looked down at the floor for a moment then back at his brother. Elijah understood his concern and knew it shouldn't be his brother's cross to bear, so he sucked in all his inner strength and stepped to the center of the room to stand beside his brother. Andrew kept his eyes on the ground, and Elijah spoke up.

"I am not like other young men. Sir, I'm . . . different." He looked over at Andrew for support despite knowing he needed to do this on his own. Andrew looked back at him, fear showing in his eyes but he gave his brother a small smile of encouragement anyway.

"I don't particularly fancy women . . ." He spoke cautiously, but Marcus grew impatient.

"Spit it out, man!" he shouted, and Elijah nearly jumped.

"I'm a homosexual, sir. But I have never acted upon my desires!"

The monk Abram let a look of disappointment cross his face. He turned away, shaking his head. Whispers started up again, and Elijah found himself desperate for both his own sake and his brother's to make them listen.

"I don't know how the men found out—I have never told another soul this, but they did, and they took every opportunity to make me pay for my sins."

The monk looked back up at Elijah and, with narrowed eyes, inspected his bruises.

"And how then does Andrew know if ye never told a soul?" Marcus asked in spite.

Andrew stood up straight and faced Marcus with an irritated look. "I'm his twin; he didn't have to tell me. I just knew."

"Well, if you figured it out, then, and these men sussed it out also, then how do ye expect to go on missions disguised as Andrew and intend for others not to just suss it out?" he asked.

This was a good question, one that made Andrew turn to Elijah.

"I'll train. I'll study my brother's every move. It will be like acting. I'll take notes on how he responds to things; I already know him better than most; I will just perfect his finer mannerisms and work on acting them out."

Andrew almost smiled but turned his head to the council, who sat silent before them and waited.

Marcus O'Neil responded with a distaste for the idea. "I don't know, Everett, I don't like it. If it doesn't work, it's going to be an awful big mess for us to clean up. Look what happened to Oscar Wilde! We can't have that association amongst our ranks." Elijah openly frowned.

"Hm, he makes a hefty point." Lord Michaels tossed his head from side to side, weighing in on the offer at hand. The man on the other side of Abram said something about the concerns of how they would pull off such a giant lie. Michaels nodded, understanding the complications with that as well.

The sailor beside Marcus showed interest in the idea, giving them easy options to help Elijah escape the radar safely out at sea with him while they "killed him off." Lord Michaels shrugged, then finally looked to Abram, who was still thinking.

"Abram? What say you?" He folded his hands, and the whole room focused on the monk.

Abram held everyone's attention for a moment longer before he spoke to Elijah directly. "Though I don't condone your life choices, young man, I can see that you are not without a brave heart. At the end of the day, that is what makes a man of honor. Someone willing to put his life on the line for what is right. Do you know what it is that the Order does?"

Elijah's heart skipped a beat; he didn't want to look to his brother for help, but he also didn't know much about the Order; all he knew were rumors.

"Rumor has it, you are collecting members to fight the Brits."

Lord Michaels shook his head and smiled as if that was what he wanted people to think. "Not exactly," he said. "The Order is intended to protect Irish heritage and Celtic culture at all costs for the good of our people. We work to return what is ours back to its rightful owners and to bring peace to the island. We are grand in numbers and even grander in heart. We cherish all people under the Celtic family tree and offer hope to those choosing to seek refuge within our ranks."

Andrew smiled at the last part. He felt confident they had won over the council.

Abram nodded.

"Though you think I wouldn't side with your cause, I see great potential in you, Elijah Lynch, the same fire your twin beside you has in spirit. I believe you could be of great use to our cause." He then turned to speak directly to Lord Michaels.

"Though the logistics of the mission at hand may be like squeezing water from a stone, once we have convinced the world of Elijah's death, I believe we can use the brothers to our advantage," said Abram. Lord Michaels nodded with a smile.

"And who knows, there's a lot of politics going on in Dublin Castle these days. That might be a great place for the two to start." Abram stared Andrew down as he spoke, drawing concern from his twin. But a mischievous twinkle danced in the old monk's eyes to ensure he meant no harm.

Different council members whipped to look at the monk as if they had just been slapped with a realization. Even Marcus seemed to have changed his tune. One after the other, each one nodded with Abram. And a decision was reached. Elijah Lynch would soon be put to death.

Chapter Thirteen

Modern-day Dublin, Ireland

Ava

I breathed heavily in the gym. My sports bra was soaked at the back, my body exhausted and sore. I was hot, tired, and ready to give in, but I didn't give up. Elias was pushing my limits today by adding a second hour of training. Our preparation time was running out, and I knew he was trying to make the most of the little time we had left, but good God, my body longed for rest.

Stray strands of my hair stuck to my forehead as I squared up to Elias with my fists raised in front of my face. I clenched my teeth against my mouthguard to release the tension building from the anticipation of his next swing.

I watched him closely, as he gradually stepped to the side, teasing me. The movement caused his torso to twist slightly, sending beads of sweat trickling down the ripples of his bare abs, drawing my gaze. My eyes tracked the droplets down his body as if in a trance, and Elias capitalized on the distraction.

His left arm lashed out toward my face, and I barely had time to duck his attack. I cursed myself silently, knowing it was my damn fault for keeping my eyes on his perfectly chiseled torso rather than up where his deadly fists lay waiting to strike. I pulled my head back quickly, preparing for another blow, but Elias surprised me by using his right foot to hook my ankle and pull it out from underneath me. I landed on my backside with a thud.

"Lord, have mercy!" I squeaked from my position on the floor. I lowered my hand to rub away the soreness now entering the one part of my body that wasn't yet aching. Elias wanted a full house out of me, and he managed to achieve one tonight. My entire body was now in pain from what I knew was our last session together. I looked up at him from my spot on the mat and frowned. Elias paid no attention to me as he adjusted his wraps on his wrists.

"Take five and grab a water," he said, nodding toward where our bags rested on the bench to the side. I rose to my feet and made my way over, muttering under my breath the entire way. I raised my hands to my head, removed the padded cover from it, then leaned forward to shake out my hair and pour the spare bottle of water I had brought over my ponytail.

"You know I can hear you, right?" he asked, eyeing me from the far end of the bench, a towel draped in his hands. He casually leaned against an exposed support beam.

I shot a glare at him as I redid my ponytail, grabbed my Yeti, and took a long swig. After wiping my mouth with the back of my hand I turned to face him.

"Sorry, I didn't realize I had hurt your feelings," I taunted.

Elias smirked.

"Oh, I wouldn't worry about that. If anything, you inflated my ego. So, thanks," Elias turned his eyes back to his hands as he refastened his bands, then patted his shoulder with the towel.

"Inflated?"

He looked back at me with his smile, which blossomed quickly into that grin I rarely got to see but thoroughly enjoyed viewing.

"Of course! What kind of man would be upset that the biggest distraction of their female opposition was their own body?" he teased. Then he made a show of glancing down at the goods before returning his gaze to mischievously meet mine.

"I'm a little biased, obviously, but I'd say all the time in the gym has paid off if that's all the distraction I need to get in a good hit on you."

For the love of all things green, he had noticed. I needed to think quickly to hide this humiliation growing inside me. The last thing I wanted was for Elias to think I was crushing on him. He would either pity me or hold it against me, and then I'd never hear the end of it. Either way, neither of those options was good for me.

I faked a laugh and shook my head.

"Wow, you must think highly of yourself. Trust me, hon. I was not distracted by the sight of you."

"Could have fooled me," he sang and made a show of slowly dragging the towel down his chest.

"Oh my God, stop that, you're being ridiculous," I chastised, but I couldn't contain my smile. Elias ran the towel slower over his right peck and then moved onto his left and lifted his eyes so he could watch me squirm.

My eyes tracked his movement, much to my dismay, but I quickly shook my head, trying to dismiss it. I needed to prevent him from continuing this game of his. It was becoming far too embarrassing on my part. So, I did the only thing I could think of and used the only weapon I had. I lifted my water bottle and jostled it toward him, splashing its contents in his direction.

"Hey!"

"You seemed to need a reason to use the towel properly, so I offered you one," I told him, then sent another spout of water flying. He stepped back, trying to miss the wave heading for him, but I still managed to hit my target, and I laughed.

Elias stepped forward and flicked his wrist out, snapping the towel in my direction. I jumped back as the fabric whipped at my knee. "Ow! Why did you do that?"

"Me? You soaked me with water!" he accused. I suppressed a giggle as I rubbed the back of my knee gingerly. I shrugged and stood up straight, preparing to go again.

"To teach you a lesson! You are not as special as you think you are!"

"Oh really?" Elias stepped forward and snapped his wrist again, sending the towel hurrying towards me, but I managed to move quickly enough to avoid it. He advanced once more, and I stepped back out of his reach, dancing on my tiptoes around the movement of the towel.

"I'll have to remember this technique when it's time to practice on your footwork later," he said with a laugh. "See, you just need the right motivation."

I threw the contents of my Yeti at him again, soaking his head this time. He stepped back to shake out his hair. Water splashed in different directions, causing a shriek from me and making me throw my hands up to shield myself just as I heard the familiar click of heels enter the gymnasium.

Elias stopped playing around and turned his now serious face toward Calista. Her eyes carefully scanned the floor between us to keep her shoes out of the puddles we had made, then moved up to shift nervously between the two of us.

"Am I interrupting something?" she asked, her voice cold and clipped.

Her eyes stayed put on me, and I shifted my stance uncomfortably before shaking my head.

"No. Just releasing some tension in the room," I told her. Unwilling to remain under her intimidating gaze for long, I turned abruptly and fished out a dark gray t-shirt from my bag and threw it over my head to cover myself in her presence.

"I see," she turned her scolding gaze onto Elias now, who ran his hand through his hair, slicking it back so he could focus. Calista walked up to him and snagged a new t-shirt from his bag, handing it to him, making sure to place her palm over his bare stomach possessively. Elias took the material from her but did not move otherwise.

"The arrangements have been made for tomorrow evening. Everything will be prepared and waiting for your arrival in Glendalough," she told him. Elias nodded.

"Hattie rearranged a few things to ensure there will be two available rooms so that you don't have to share. Make sure to thank her for that when you arrive," Calista purred beside him. Elias's jaw clenched, but he remained still, only nodding in response.

I wasn't sure if I was meant to join in this conversation or not. The way she spoke to him sounded territorial and intimate, so I looked away and pretended to search through my bag for something.

"I'll have the proper paperwork delivered to your room and on your desk by eight tonight, love. I'll speak with you soon."

I lifted my eyes just in time to see Calista drag her nails down Elias's back before stepping away from him and heading toward the exit. She nodded politely to me as she left, and I returned the favor.

Once we were alone, I turned to Elias, whose shoulders had dropped and who seemed to be shaking his head in irritation. I still didn't know the full story between them, and up until now, I hadn't cared. But looking at Elias now told me that whatever was going on between them was strained at the moment and causing him some stress.

I moved to make my way back toward him, hoping I could ease whatever was bothering him. For the most part, Elias had been stoic, grumpy, and professional. This playful side of him hadn't been shown yet, and I found I preferred it over the usual one he shared with me. I was desperate to bring that side back.

"She didn't seem happy with us," I said, returning to my place in front of him. Elias shook his head.

"No, she rarely is with me these days," his statement was an afterthought of whatever his inner monologue was playing inside his head. I shrugged.

"Well, you did make quite a mess." Elias's eyes shot to mine.

"Me?"

"Maybe if you hadn't gotten water all over the floor and created a slipping hazard, she would have been in a better mood."

"Sure, go on, blame the guy. Everything is always our fault!" Elias threw up his hands, mockingly defeated, and spun slowly around for dramatic effect. But before I could register his movements, he flicked his wrist again, causing the towel to snap back toward my ankles, making me jump. Water sloshed onto the floor as I wrestled with my own feet to stay upright.

"See, you prove my point! Everything is your fault." I raised my nearly empty water bottle at him again, preparing to toss the rest of its contents at him, but Elias moved first.

"That's it!" with impressive speed, he dropped the t-shirt Calista had handed him and fisted both ends of the towel in his hands. As I stepped forward to toss the water, he mirrored my movements, wrapping the towel swiftly around my wrist before throwing his weight to the left. I gasped in surprise as my wrists connected with the beam with enough force to send my bottle flying out of my hands and tumbling onto the floor.

Elias then released one end of the towel and flicked his wrist again, snapping the towel at my ankles. "You're done," he said confidently. His smile lit up his face once again, though it was not as wide as before.

I stepped back, rubbing my ankle with a smirk, and eyed him briefly before looking over at the bottle lying on the floor.

"Alright, that was cool," I said, pointing to the towel. Elias shrugged and pretended to dust off his shoulders.

"That's what you get when you don't take your training seriously," he stated matter-of-factly.

"What form of boxing was that?" I asked.

"It wasn't. It was jujitsu."

The wheels were turning in my mind now, pondering what kinds of things I had been missing out on. Of course, Elias had taught me a few moves, but mostly, they were offensive. However, that was fun; that was defense. I was keen to learn more. Being small and thin didn't give me much support, but simple moves like that could really improve my game. Not that I should ever need to use them, but still.

I knew what Elias had planned for the rest of our afternoon session, but I suddenly decided on other plans. I shifted onto the balls of my feet as he bent down to grab his shirt and throw it over his head.

"Teach me that!"

Chapter Fourteen

Finally, after two long weeks of morning and afternoon workout sessions and nightly studying, the day came for us to leave for Glendalough. My excitement had been hard to contain.

This would be the first time I managed to escape the city walls of Dublin and see the island in all its beauty. I was eager to delve into the history that graced Glendalough and also to admire the lush splendor of its surrounding hills.

Elias hoped the trip to Glendalough would only take a couple of days, but I wasn't so sure. We had a good starting point; however, that didn't guarantee success. The Crown Jewels had been missing for so long for a reason. The clues were few and far between, and most of them related to conspiracy theories, that we couldn't always rely on.

I suspected we would find something at the graves in Glendalough. The Lynch brothers were buried there along with several other known members of the Order, including Father Abram Malachy, the infamous monk who spoke at the trials after the Easter Rising. So, I knew there had to be something there to give us a hint and lead us to our next steps.

Elias, on the other hand, was interested in scanning the grounds to see if anything from the Order's first meeting house had been left behind. While some structures in Glendalough were newer, built for tourists the historical landmark attracted, most were remnants of the monks who inhabited the area in the tenth, eleventh, and twelfth centuries.

Because of this, Elias was keen to take the time to examine the magnificent structures for any signs of the Order's presence. It was rumored that the Order of St. Patrick used to meet there before they vanished sometime in the nineteen forties, and he suspected they had used one of the original structures for their gatherings.

With all of that in mind, we couldn't be certain how long we would be there, and my best guess was closer to a week at the least.

After a long session with Elias, Connor and I had met up for dinner at a local pub to celebrate our first assignment. Though it had been hard to find the time, he and I had made daily coffee a habit—we would meet before training to catch up and chill. I began to enjoy those meetings thoroughly. I was going to miss him on our trip.

The following day, Elias and I packed his car outside Stoker Hall. Calista and Connor came down to see us off. When they approached, Elias was just finishing tying our bags onto the car's roof. Calista walked up to the car dressed in a stylish red sweater with faux fur around the collar. She looked up at Elias sweetly and waited for him to climb down.

Connor hung back with a slight smile carrying two cups of coffee. He had brought me coffee for our last coffee date. I smiled at him and walked over, leaving Calista and Elias alone. He handed me my coffee.

"So, this is it . . . our last coffee date. What a shame."

I smiled and brought the paper cup to my lips. "I know. I thought about continuing the tradition with Elias, but it wouldn't be the same." Connor made a face and glanced at Elias, who had just climbed off the car and was speaking in hushed tones to Calista.

"I hope not. He's great and all, really, but—"

"But he's kind of an ass?" I asked, and we both giggled.

"You said it, not me."

The moment I had shared with Elias the afternoon before was imprinted in the back of my mind. I had enjoyed seeing him a little more relaxed. But that part of Elias had come and gone. And the grumpy, irritable, stoic person I was used to had returned bright and early this morning when he snapped at me for being five minutes late.

I shrugged and looked back at the two huddled closely together. Calista wrapped her arms around his neck and fiddled with his hair. I knew I had no reason to be this way, but something in me didn't like the way she touched him, and I scowled. "I didn't know they were together," I said aloud before I could stop myself.

Connor followed my line of vision to where Elias and Calista stood. He narrowed his eyes in suspicion but shrugged. "Calista talks about him an awful lot, but she has never mentioned they were dating." That was good. No wait, why did I think that? I was pretending I didn't care.

"Anyways," Connor said, bringing the conversation back to us. I turned around to give him the full attention he deserved. "You think you will be okay out there on your own?"

I nodded and shrugged. "Of course. Besides, Elias will be with me the whole time, and I suspect we will have to check in here regularly with updates."

"Yeah, Calista says we should hear an update from you weekly. I'm just hoping you won't be gone that long; there will be way too much for us to catch up on."

I laughed. "And not enough coffee in the world!"

Connor chuckled. Then, he pulled me in for a hug, and I let him. Hugging Connor felt weird to me. I wasn't usually the hugging type, but he was nice and warm against the cold air. Plus, it felt good to know someone here cared enough to hug me this way. I wrapped my arms around his waist and squeezed. "Be careful, please."

I pulled back to look up at him with a goofy smile. "I will," I promised.

"I'm only a phone call away." And I knew he meant what he said.

My friendship with Connor had become one of my favorite parts of being in Ireland. He was a genuinely kind soul, and I knew I could trust him fully. I pulled away from his grasp and looked at Elias, who was waving me over.

"Time to go," I said and looked up at Connor sheepishly. He smirked and held his fist to me just as he had our first day in Dublin.

"Catch you around?" he asked. I bumped his fist with mine, then began walking backward toward Elias's car and winked at him. "Definitely," I replied.

Elias and Calista were still talking in hushed tones when I reached the two. Not wanting to intervene, I nodded at Elias and jumped into the passenger seat up front. I buckled my seat belt and waited. I didn't mean to spy on them. Still, I couldn't help but notice Calista lean toward Elias up onto her tippy toes and kiss his cheek. Then he said something to her that I couldn't hear and joined me in the car. I sat back with a gross look on my face. But by the time Elias had turned to ask if I was ready to go, I hid my irritation and gave him a small smile instead.

Chapter Fifteen

The trip to Glendalough was not long. It was relatively short, in fact. Elias drove the whole way, since I was not accustomed to driving on the opposite side of the road—something I would have to learn in the future.

I spent the time listening to my murder mysteries podcast through my headphones while Elias listened to his music through the car stereo. We barely talked. We had spent so much time together over the last couple of weeks, and yet the only thing we had discussed was the expedition. We never spoke about family, traveling, or dreams. It was about work with this guy. We had very little in common.

While driving, I kept looking at my phone. I knew Millie would expect me to check in sometime soon since I hadn't talked to her in a few days, but with no service, I wondered if I would get that chance.

"Is there a place that I will have cell service? Either on the way, or once we arrive?"

"The Inn that Lottie booked for us should have service so you can call your mom," he replied.

I turned my head out the window so he didn't see me wince. For some reason, that felt like a punch to the gut. I wasn't sure I wanted to flaunt my family scandal to him just yet. So, I chose to hide my reaction.

"Thanks."

"No problem," said Elias. We sat in an awkward moment of silence before I couldn't take it any longer. It had been nearly thirty minutes of silence already, driving me crazy.

"Who is Lottie?" I asked. I hadn't remembered meeting her, but there had been a lot of people I had met over the last few weeks, and it was hard to remember everyone's names.

Elias looked over to me with a weird expression on his face. Almost as if I was sporting two heads. "You met her."

"Uh . . . I did?"

"Yeah, Calista? She's the one who showed you around the campus until she passed you over to me." Calista . . . right. How had I not put those pieces together?

Two things about that statement didn't sit right with me. One, he implied that he had some sort of dominance over me—"passed you over"—and I wasn't sure how I felt about that. And two, the cute but weird nickname he had for her. That made me uncomfortable for some reason, but I couldn't quite pinpoint why.

"Why do you call her Lottie? That sounds nothing like her name." I tried to ignore it, but the way the sentence came out sounded a little bitter. Elias looked at me with an eyebrow raised as if to ask why I cared. I blinked and tried to clear my face of any emotion.

"Calista and I go quite a way back," he explained. "We started the same year and became close quickly. We weren't in the same department at first, but our schedules aligned at the time, so we spent a lot of time together that first year. Later, we both took on full-time training roles as interns' advisors, which kept us close. I call her Lottie because I used to joke that her full name, Calista Scott, sounded like Camelot. Eventually, I shortened it to Lottie."

I was not fond of that at all, I decided. "So, you guys *are* a thing?" I asked, trying not to sound conceited. Elias made a face as if he was suddenly offended that I would think that.

"No! Not anymore, anyway." So, they had been together. That explained the weird interactions I had noticed between them.

I glanced in his direction. He wore a smug smile that let me know I wasn't hiding whatever emotion this was as well as I had hoped.

"Neat," was all I could muster. I couldn't figure out why this bothered me so much. It wasn't like I had claims to the guy. Hell, I barely just met him. Elias looked over to me, briefly taking his eyes off the road to call me out on my hypocrisy.

"What about you and that guy Connor?" The way he said his name came out childish. I was stunned that he would ever think there was something between us. I don't know what planet he was living on but that was definitely not the case.

"Connor is just a friend."

Elias scoffed as if he wasn't buying the story I was selling. "Oh please, he was all over you that first night. I simply asked if you wanted help getting to your room, and he got all pissy with me."

I threw my hands up and laughed. "Right, and Calista or Lottie," I said in air quotes, "wasn't acting the same that night?" I shook my head again.

Elias frowned.

"Connor and I barely spoke before this trip. Honestly, I didn't have many friends on campus—too busy."

Elias snorted and made a sharp turn on the steering wheel. "I find that hard to believe. I don't understand why you are so upset right now."

I leaned my head back, thought about it, then regained my composure and turned to right myself to sit facing front. I folded my hands on my lap for a split second, then decided that wasn't normal enough. I propped my head on my arm and looked out the window. "I'm not."

Again, Elias gave me a sideways glance that said I wasn't fooling anyone. "Right, well, Lottie and I haven't been a thing for a long time, and whatever you and Connor have is really none of my business."

"And besides," I interjected, "you and I are just colleagues," I said matter-of-factly.

Elias refused to show any emotion. "Yup."

"Fine. Friends then."

"Eh," he said, pretending to weigh that back and forth in his head. I smacked his arm playfully and cracked a genuine smile for the first time.

I sat back, feeling like I had hit the Lotto, being able to make him smile. I noticed it was getting darker the more we drove. I hadn't realized just how late it had gotten. When we arrived in the area, it was almost ten at night. It was far too late for us to check anything out before morning, I suspected.

Elias pulled up to a big, white house with brown trim. It was in the middle of nowhere, hidden deep within the trees up on a hill. Two lanterns illuminated the only light onto a gravel path. "Hattie must be in the barn," Elias said, leaning forward to look out my window at the bed and breakfast. He opened the door and stepped out of the car.

"Come on. Maybe we can take a look at the graveyard briefly before she comes out to greet us." That sounded like a bad idea to me. Alone, just the two of us, in the dark, in an ancient graveyard? I couldn't say this was something I was thrilled about, but I opened my door and stretched my legs while Elias dug in the trunk of the car for a pair of flashlights.

He handed me one and pointed his flashlight down a smaller dirt path to the right that was overgrown with weeds and thorn bushes. This was not a good idea.

"That's where we gotta go."

I looked up at him, and I have to admit, I felt terrified. "That looks like the place people go to die," I said to him, hoping he would change his mind. What was his rush? Elias tried to hold in a laugh but it escaped regardless of his efforts.

"In a way, it is." Ha, ha . . . very funny. I wrinkled my nose and zipped up my jacket. I hadn't dressed appropriately for this. Clearly, he wasn't going to back down, and I refused to show any weakness.

"Great. Lead the way."

Chapter Sixteen

I followed Elias down the dark path. He pushed aside tall weeds and low-hanging branches as we moved. At one point, my hair had gotten caught in a thornbush, and Elias had to stop to come back and work it out of my hair. Note to self: ponytails from now on.

Finally, after about ten minutes of walking, we came across a bridge to an opening that held a few tall structures of stone, a massive graveyard in the middle, and a smaller patch of graves off to the right. He led us to the lone graveyard, clouded by thick trees and next to the trail. This was separate from the main graveyard the tourists visited and didn't hold nearly as many gravestones. It wasn't that well-kept either. Elias sucked in a breath and stopped at the front.

I wasn't quite sure what had caught him up, but as for myself, the simple beauty of raw history before us was amazing. It brought a chill to my bones and shifted the vibe between us. I stepped toward the first stone, shining my light on different graves. Elias stayed back for a second.

I knew what I was looking for, though. It took me a couple minutes due to the degradation of the stones, but finally, I found it. I stopped and crouched down to inspect it. The stone read:

Andrew Phineas Lynch
Beloved Brother
Brave Hero
1883-1916

I traced the words on the stone with my fingers, letter by letter. After two weeks of studying this, we were digging up natural history. My heart was racing when I felt Elias's presence behind me. His flashlight cast a dim glow over the worn-down grave of Andrew Lynch. I looked at him over my shoulder. His eyes seemed to be searching the stone for some hidden clues, but I hadn't expected to find anything here, tonight, in the dark. I returned my gaze to the stone as Elias walked away.

I had to admit, I had been surprised not to find the triskele anywhere on his grave. Especially given all he had sacrificed in the end. A sudden chill came over me, and I tugged my jacket tighter.

"I doubt we are going to find anything tonight. We should come back in the morning, Elias."

He shook his head; he had the little leather book out again and was paging through it. "There's got to be something here," he said. But I couldn't tell if he was talking to me or the book. It wasn't the first time I had wondered exactly what that book was. But he seemed to always have it.

"It's getting colder," I said, "and I don't like being out here in the dark. We—"

Elias snapped the book shut and strolled over to the opposite side of the graveyard. He ignored my pleas. "Not many people know this," he interrupted, "but Andrew was actually one of *three* brothers."

I shook my head and followed him, confused.

"What?"

"He had two brothers."

"Yeah, so what?" I asked.

Elias continued. "Nathaniel was his younger brother by seven years, and Elijah."

I still wasn't connecting the dots. His flashlight lit up stone after stone until he stopped at one and smiled. I came up behind him and looked around his shoulder. I kept myself close to him to hide from the wind. He didn't seem to mind.

This stone read:

Elijah Mattheas Lynch
Beloved Brother
Loyal Friend
1883-1905-1955

I had to reread the stone aloud for it to sink in. I shook my head. It didn't make sense. What little information I could find on Elijah had simply said he was Andrew's younger brother. Nowhere did it say younger by two minutes?

"They were twins?" I asked in disbelief. Elias nodded and looked back at me with a toothy grin. "But wait—"

I pointed to the three years labeled on the stone. "Why are there three years listed?"

Elias kept his head turned toward me so I could hear him, but his eyes were fixed on the stone. He used his flashlight to point from one year to the next.

"The first year is the year they were born. The second year—"

"Is the year the history books listed his death," I finished.

"Right, and the third year is the year he actually died."

"He was seventy-two when he died? But wait, why fake his death?"

Elias bit his lip and shrugged. His eyes flitted back to the little book in his other hand. "I don't know. But there had to be a reason."

At that moment, the wind blew a considerable gust toward us, causing my hair to fly in all directions. I buried my head into Elias's shoulder, and his hand came up protectively to block us from the wind as best he could. He looked up into the dark sky. Thick gray clouds were rolling into Glendalough fast; now was the time to leave.

"There's a storm coming. We better head back. We will have to check this out tomorrow, first thing."

I nodded, not looking up, and let Elias guide me by my hand back toward the bed and breakfast.

The Inn was very homey on the inside. Two separate rooms had been prepared for us on the upper level, each with its own bathroom. They were across the hall from one another, on beautiful hardwood flooring. Once we had returned from the car and unpacked our bags, I settled into the old-fashioned claw-foot tub off to the side of my room. It took me twenty minutes of soaking in the hot water to feel my toes.

When I finally felt like the Irish chill had left my soul, I reluctantly climbed out and dressed in my plaid PJ pants and hoodie. I opened my door and tiptoed up to Elias's open door. I had planned just to walk in, but when I realized he was on the phone, I stopped and waited behind the door frame.

"No, the drive wasn't bad . . . Yeah, no, I agree . . . I think she will be fine . . . Be nice, Lot. Everything's cool . . . Yeah, tomorrow we will phone you in for sure. I've got some things I'll need you and Connor to look into anyway for us, so I'll be sure to shoot you an email tonight . . . Of course . . . Yes, I do too . . . Sure. Night, Lottie. We'll talk soon."

I stayed where I was for a second, thinking over my next move. There were a couple things to unpack here. The first exciting thing was that it sounded like I would get the chance to talk to Connor over Zoom sooner rather than later. I was thankful for that. However, I wondered why we would need to have a phone conference with the team this early on. It wasn't like we had come across anything worth announcing. And secondly, it was pretty obvious they had been discussing me at one point, and I wanted to know what was said.

I just decided to face the situation head-on and confront Elias, but when I turned to go into the room, I ran face-first into Elias's broad chest. He held his arms out to grasp my shoulders to stabilize me. "Whoa, I thought you were in bed already."

I shook my head. "No, I just was in the bath," I replied.

"Oh, well, it's good that you're here anyway. I want to show you something I think may interest you." I took a steadying breath as he let go before following him back into his room. I had to shake off the chill that went down my spine when he touched my arms.

I followed him to where he had a stack of papers organized into different piles on his desk. Okay, now *this* is what I should be focusing my attention on. This made sense to me.

Some papers were his notes, while others he had taken from the room of records. I didn't think that was allowed, but I wouldn't say anything. Elias tended to be grouchy when you argued with him, and I wasn't about to poke the bear.

He sat down at the chair and fished out his notebook with different dates and his own version of the Lynches' family tree. "While you were settling in, I couldn't get what you had asked about the dates on Elijah's grave out of my head. Unfortunately, I wasn't able to figure out the answer to your question—why did they fake his death? But I think I figured something else out."

Standing behind him and looking down over his shoulder, I accepted a paper he had in his hands with an article about the heist, and when they had ruled Andrew out as a suspect.

"Andrew Lynch was found to be innocent because why?" he asked.

I shrugged and looked down at him, only slightly irritated. We had already been over this. I didn't need the article to tell me the answer; I already knew.

"Because there were several witnesses placing him at an event in Scotland. But what does that have to do with anything?"

Elias looked around at me. "But there *were* witnesses who say they saw him at the vicar's party in Dublin too."

"Right, but due to a lack of evidence, they concluded he was innocent."

"What if the witnesses were right? All of them?" he asked. I squinted.

"That's not possible. You can't be in two places at once."

Elias looked at me waiting. "Unless . . ."

I looked away from him, thinking this through, and suddenly, an old memory of the Olsen twins on *Full House* came to mind. The light inside my head suddenly flicked on in surprise.

"You have an identical twin," I whispered, "who everyone believed had died two years prior! Oh my God, Elias, you're a genius!" I said, shaking his shoulders in excitement.

Elias turned back to the papers in front of his desk, and a smile crept up on his lips. I had noticed I was beginning to see more of those lately, and I decided I didn't mind them. He had a nice smile, and it was a relief when he wasn't so grumpy.

"And here I thought that was supposed to be you," he said.

I put one hand on the back of his chair and fanned the papers mindlessly as I discussed our theory.

"So, Andrew and Elijah split up. Elijah makes a public appearance in Scotland, posing as his brother. At the same time, Andrew heads to Dublin Castle to carry out the plan."

"Right, Andrew gets there, gets the vicar drunk so he doesn't notice, and then *bam*! Pulls off the greatest heist of all time."

I scratched my chin. Something was still missing. "But how did Andrew get into the vault?"

Elias frowned and picked up his leather book, opening it midway. His eyes read through a few lines before he responded quietly. "He used the keys."

I already knew that. It wasn't exactly what I meant. "Thank you, Sherlock. How did he get them?" Elias shook his head, closed the book, and looked back at me.

"I don't know, but that sounds like a good question to start our day tomorrow. Are you up for an early morning? Calista called just before I ran into you. She wants us to video conference with our team back in Dublin."

I yawned and nodded. I placed my hand on his desk and leaned my weight into it. "Yeah, that's fine, nine a.m., okay? Or were you thinking a little earlier?"

"Nine is fine. That will give me time to shower and meet you downstairs for breakfast," said Elias.

"Great. See you in the morning then." I turned to make my way out of his room.

"Oh hey, Ava?"

I turned around as I reached the doorway and rested my hand on the wall.

"Yeah?"

"I almost forgot. Calista asked that I let you know she's going to be in contact sometime tonight or tomorrow. She said she had something to discuss with you about your paperwork." My paperwork? What paperwork? I didn't have anything that had gone through her.

"Uh, sure. Thanks," I said and began to make my way back across the hall to my room.

"No problem. Sleep well!"

I entered my room and grabbed the knob on my door. "Yeah, you too," I said. And closed the door behind me.

1906

Dear Nathanial,

I've been meaning to write to you and check in, but putting the right words on paper has proven to be difficult. I know it was quite a shock to lose Elijah so suddenly. None of us saw it coming. I'm sure it must be hard for you now that you're the only one of us still at home. I know how our mother can get, so please, if you ever have any trouble or need me, just send a letter, and I will come as soon as I can.

I truly don't understand how you manage to get through all of this so well. You have shown such bravery despite the circumstances. I must say I was impressed by your ability to stay strong during the funeral. Elijah would be proud too. I, for one, can't believe he's gone. It feels as if the world has shifted, and, at least for me, it will never be the same.

They say a rainbow only appears after the storm. So I will cling to the promise that this grief cannot last forever, as should you. Stay strong, little brother, and never forget who you are.

Wishing you the best,

Andrew Lynch

Chapter Seventeen

I had no sooner closed the door to my room when I received an email from Calista-Lottie? Whatever.

I slid off my slippers, tiptoed across the hardwood flooring to avoid my feet getting cold, and jumped into my singleton bed. It was a classic wood-framed bed with four posts. It was covered in clean white linens and a beautiful hand-knitted red quilt on the top. The bed moved an inch when I landed, and I froze instantly, making a face, afraid I had broken something. But when nothing else followed, I relaxed and snuggled quickly under my covers.

Ireland was so much colder than I was used to. I had been here for almost a month and had yet to adapt. In Pittsburgh, it was still around seventy-five degrees. I pulled the covers up to my nose and laid my head on the pillow. I stuck my hand out of the edge of the covers so I could look at my phone.

Congratulations on making it to your first destination, Ava!

We look forward to regrouping with you and Elias tomorrow for an update. Until then, the museum's board of directors would like to offer you an additional assignment while you work on your current one. This assignment is optional—the one you are currently on should always take priority. However, should you choose to accept, you will be compensated $500 US per accomplishment.

Again, we cannot stress how important it is that this new assignment does not interfere with your current one, so please, if you feel they will overlap in a way that you find distracting from your current mission, we encourage you to refrain from proceeding. If you are interested, however, please respond with a yes, and the instructions for the second assignment will be sent to you. If you still believe you can do both simultaneously after getting more information, then we will move forward accordingly.

We look forward to hearing from you soon.
Sincerely, the team manager of operations,

Calista Scott

I sat up with a jolt and blinked at my phone. This wasn't a question. Of course I wanted to know what opportunities awaited me here. If I could possibly make a little bit more money to push back toward Juliana's treatments, then you can bet I was going to do it. The question was, what was it? And could I skate by doing both? They had made it sound like there was a possibility that it would be more complicated than it sounded. How would I know if I never inquired about more information?

I looked back at my phone and typed one word back.

YES.

It didn't take long for the following email to come through, almost as if it were an automatic message.

We are so glad you are considering taking on a second assignment! The following information is strictly confidential. It is not to be shared with anyone, including your current Expeditions Coordinator. From here on out, in this mission, you work alone. You will have four separate tasks to accomplish. Each one will be sent directly to your phone after completing the previous one.

A couple of items have been taken off museum property for previous expedition use but have yet to be properly returned. All we ask is for you to locate those items and help us return them to where they belong. For every item you are assigned, you will be given a general location as to where you may find them, as well as a drop-off location. We will have someone from the operations team retrieve them from there.

So, what do you say, Ava? Are you prepared to take on your next mission? Please think about it and respond by 8 p.m. tomorrow. Again, we look forward to hearing from you and hopefully working with you even more in the future.

Sincerely, the team manager of operations,

Calista Scott

I rolled myself over so that I was no longer on my side and instead leaned back against the bed frame. This was intriguing. I wasn't sure what artifacts I would be granted the luxury to inspect with my own hands, plus again, that money was so tempting. But could I manage to snag those and focus my full attention on my current assignment at hand? And all without telling Elias?

I threw my head back and looked up at the wood ceiling. Elias . . . While we weren't close, I still felt uneasy about lying to him. It was something I struggled to do normally anyway. But this was important. And for some reason, the museum didn't want him to know what I was up to. Morally, I felt I couldn't accept it. But greedily, I knew I had to.

Turning my head to the right, my eyes landed on my old photo in a white wooden frame beside the lamp on my nightstand. It was the only personal item I carried with me while traveling. It was the first thing I unpacked when getting to a new place and the last thing to pack when leaving.

The picture was from a carnival we had gone to with Millie, Eamon, and Ryker. It was of us four girls hugging each other and laughing at something Eamon had said when he snapped the camera. It was before Mom had died, before Juliana had gotten sick. It was one of my favorite memories.

I turned back to my phone and dialed Millie. The phone on the other end rang five times before going to voicemail. *That's right* . . . I thought and sighed. It was way too late there for her to answer. She would be sleeping by now. I snuggled back under my covers and switched off my light. I had until tomorrow morning to decide, and maybe, if I was lucky, I could get ahold of Millie before then.

I spent the next ten minutes perusing social media before putting my phone on silent, setting my alarm, and turning in to go to sleep. I would have to figure out the right thing with Millie tomorrow. And if I didn't, I would simply have to just accept the position without her opinion.

The next morning, my alarm went off bright and early at 6:15. I got up, bathed, and got ready for the day before trying Millie for the second time. However, when it went straight to voicemail, I started to pace the room silently. I was due to meet Elias downstairs for breakfast soon, and I wanted to figure this out before I came face-to-face with him. Plus, I knew there was a chance we would not have cell service for a good part of the day, and I didn't want to lose the opportunity should I be interested in taking it.

I dialed Millie for a third time and got her voicemail again.

Ugh, you have got to be kidding me! I thought. I gently tapped the end of my phone on my forehead in some weird hope that it would bring clarity to the situation while I paced the room.

Okay, think, think, think.

Though Elias and I didn't really know each other well, I knew him enough to know he wasn't a bad person. And while I hated lying to people, I wasn't really lying to him that much anyway; I just wasn't going to tell him about it, that's all. That was fine, right? I didn't owe him anything and wasn't doing anything wrong. So why was I making such a big deal about this? Why did it feel so off?

I shook my head and looked down at my feet, which were still sockless and unprepared to get breakfast. I stepped over to the bed and bent over, pulling on my socks and boots right after. I sat there, letting my phone go to Millie's voicemail once more before I shook my head and headed out the door.

That was it. I had made my decision. Jules was far more important than any weird feeling I had about this. I would just simply have to overcome it for her sake. I stepped out of my room, looked back at my phone, and typed two more words into the conversation with Calista.

I'm in.

Then I walked down the edge of the hall and tromped down the stairs into the kitchen. As I entered the room, I looked around for the first time, seeing it in the light, and took everything in.

There was a small coffee table with a bowl for keys to the side of the entryway. The left side of the wall was lined shelving units that held an array of cute farmhouse-type things like porcelain plates with paintings on them, cow figurines, and an Irish cross. A barn in the back was visible through a large window at the rear. On the opposite end of the room was the sink, oven, and refrigerator. Toward the back wall, another much larger window shed morning light onto a large wooden table fit for eight people which was directly in the middle of the room.

Elias sat in the middle of the table, looking at his open laptop. He had done the same thing I had decided to do and dressed a little warmer today. He had a black thermal on under a light brown jacket, and he wore jeans and thermal socks with boots. His eyes were focused on the screen and he scratched his chin. I noticed he hadn't shaved today and was letting his beard grow in, giving him a scruffy and rugged sort of look. I did not mind that at all.

A woman in her mid-sixties was standing off to the side of the kitchen. She had just pulled out a pan full of homemade cinnamon rolls from the oven and was wiping her hands on her red floral apron when she noticed me. She turned and gave me the biggest smile I'd seen in a while and threw her arms out to hug me as she approached.

Elias glanced in my direction without a word. His eyes were cold. Someone had woken up on the wrong side of the bed.

"Oh, my goodness! You must be Ava! I'm so thrilled to have you with us! Elias has told me so much about you!" she said in her thick Irish accent.

I patted her on the back and gave Elias a surprised look from behind her. Elias rolled his eyes and returned his attention to his computer.

"Really?" I asked as she pulled away. Hattie waved her hands in the air and shrugged.

"Well, no, Elias doesn't really talk about anything now, does he? But he did give me the basics, and I got a more personal profile from Calista last night. So . . ." She leaned back and smiled at me.

She was slightly plump, with short strawberry hair matching her rosy cheeks and blue eyes. She was a genuine sweetheart; I could tell immediately. I returned her smile just as a whistle went off. Hattie's eyebrows shot up, and she rushed back to a kettle in the kitchen.

"Everything smells . . ."

"American?" she finished over her shoulder.

I smirked at her response. She wasn't wrong. Compared to most of the breakfasts I had here in Ireland, this was much more . . . normal for me. Most of the time, I just had eggs.

"Delicious is what I was thinking," I said and sat down.

"As it should," said Elias. "Hattie is an amazing chef, and you should thank her for allowing us to stay here last night. She had to cancel another reservation in order to get us each our own individual rooms." I heard his slightly irritable tone.

I chose to sit away from him at the end of the table so I didn't catch his lousy mood in case it was contagious. It frustrated me a bit to see him once again acting this way. After yesterday, I kind of thought we had broken through that ice, and things had changed, but I guess not. I tried not to pout as I pulled out my chair.

Hattie once again waved him off. And she turned to pour the kettle into two mugs. "Oh now, don't listen to him. He's always grumpy in the morning before he gets his coffee."

"There's coffee?" I hadn't anticipated being able to have coffee again. At least not until we had arrived back at campus, so this was a pleasant surprise.

Hattie brought over the three cups, two with black coffee and another with a tea bag sticking out the side. She set them on the table before us and returned to grab the freshly iced cinnamon rolls and some cream and sugar. She sat beside me, across from Elias, and brought the tea to her lips, carefully testing it before taking a sip.

"Of course, and cinnamon rolls! I have been working to house the museum's students while on expeditions for many years now, and I am lucky I get to see Elias at least three times throughout the year for those. I know what he likes, so I keep these things around so he keeps coming back." She flashed Elias a grandmother-type smile, which seemed to soften his demeanor a bit. He lifted his cup to her in thanks and took a sip.

"And it is greatly appreciated, Hattie. Thank you."

I sat back, stirring the cream into my coffee, and glanced between the two. They seemed to have a solid, family-like connection, which was nice. It wasn't a side I had seen of Elias yet. Up until now, he was a very stern, focused, determined, and utterly sarcastic individual. It was nice to see him in a different setting for once.

I sipped my coffee for a second while Hattie dished out the cinnamon rolls. Coffee was glorious, I decided.

Elias's laptop suddenly started ringing, and his screen opened up a video. Calista, Connor, and Dr. Balor were crowded on his screen, waiting for us. Elias sat up straighter and set down his coffee, now in full work mode.

I stood up to come around and stand behind him so I could join the meeting. Hattie made a face, then gave me a sheepish wave and left the room.

"Good morning, explorers!" Dr. Balor greeted.

"Good morning, Dr. Balor. To what do we owe the pleasure?"

Chapter Eighteen

Elias

Dr. Balor sat at the desk in front of him, dressed in a classic gray suit and tie. Lottie, Elias had noticed, was wearing a similar gray dress suit with her blue blouse. He assumed she had dressed a little more professionally to appease Dr. Balor. She seemed a bit stiff next to the man, but then again, Elias was a bit stiff when he had answered too. He shook out his shoulders in an attempt at appearing more relaxed and folded his hands in front of him.

Elias was uncomfortable, to say the least. He didn't trust Balor at all and hated the fact that he was sitting in on this particular expedition. It was unusual for a member of the board to get involved in expeditions, so what was he so interested in this one for? Elias had also heard rumors about Balor, which didn't do his reputation any favors.

There were stories involving black market sales and difficulties working with other groups involved in hunting down artefacts. However, to his knowledge, nothing had ever been proven, and he had a history with the museum itself, which is why they never looked further into those rumors. Elias had tried to uncover the truth about him some time ago but hadn't found anything worth reporting.

Connor, who sat on the opposite side of Dr. Balor, had a computer sitting in front of him with a set of headphones on. He wore his wire-framed glasses today and was staring into the middle of the screen in front of him, focusing on moving his wireless mouse around. When he saw Ava on the screen, however, he smiled up at her and waved. She returned the friendly greeting and made a texting motion with her thumbs to him. Elias bit his tongue.

"How is everyone doing this morning? Ava, I hope you are getting along well?" Dr. Balor started.

Ava, who was standing behind Elias, leaned over him and put her coffee down to the side of his laptop. She smiled and nodded. "Yes, sir, Hattie had us starting the day off on the right foot with some perfect American coffee!" she said enthusiastically.

Elias played with his cuticles, mindlessly fidgeting as she spoke. He always got a little nervous when his companions on these missions mentioned Hattie's name to anyone on the board of directors. Though he knew she did her job well, and overall, they had been pleased with how she had taken care of their explorers in the past, he didn't want her caught up in the politics of it all.

"Wonderful. That's always good to hear! She is one of the best, and Elias here can vouch for her, I'm sure!"

Elias faked a smile and nodded. "Definitely."

"Good, good. Now, you are probably wondering why I'm sitting in on this conference today."

Ava, behind him, tilted her head to the right and waited.

"I will be overseeing this operation personally and assisting your team here—" he motioned to Connor and Lottie beside him—"along the way. This is a critical mission for the museum. And the directors would like to be kept in the loop, as much as possible, on this one."

Perfect. Just what Elias needed. Balor watching his every move. Elias tried not to roll his eyes or show any emotion. Ava, the ever-oblivious puppy dog behind him, nodded politely as if this was terrific news.

"We can manage that for sure, sir. Just have Calista inform us when you would like to conference us in, and we will be in touch at our earliest convenience," Elias said.

Elias's mind started turning, coming up with all kinds of ways that he could get out of these video conferences. He was hoping the following location would be someplace without Wi-Fi.

"So, what have we found out so far?" Balor asked.

Elias took too long to think about a carefully worded lie, so Ava answered the doctor first. He took a breath in irritation and sat back, looking over his shoulder at her as she did. He was having a hard time keeping his anger in check.

"It turns out Andrew Lynch had a twin brother, who may not have died as early as everyone thought he did." Ava went on to explain what they had discussed last night after taking a quick look at the graveyard. She filled them in on every single word.

Connor took notes on his laptop as she did. Elias was confident that they would have every bit of information that Elias currently had. He crossed his arms and waited till she was finished, then leaned forward and took a swig of his coffee to keep up the happy charade.

"It sounds like you are off to a great start!" Lottie said, looking relieved that her team had something for her to show to the doctor. Balor also looked happy with this information and clapped his hands.

"Yes! You two are doing very well. She makes a great addition to your team, Elias; I think I see a partnership in your future!" he teased.

Elias tried to hide his distaste for the matter but failed. Lottie smirked, catching his reaction. Thankfully, Ava had not noticed. "We shall see, I suppose," he simply said.

It wasn't that he didn't like Ava; he just wasn't sure he could trust her, and he was only really using her as the missing brains of the operations. He had a job to do, and that was that. He didn't tend to make friends on these missions. That was a huge mistake.

The museum preferred that he worked with a partner, so it was much better if he just recycled the new blood every time they did recruiting. That way, he didn't have the chance to get to know anyone and no one had the time to dig too far into his past.

Lottie was the exception. She had managed to worm her way into his life long before he had started doing missions, and he wasn't about to filter her out now because of them. No, he trusted her. They had history.

"You will have to excuse him, sir. Hattie says he's not much of a talker before he has finished his morning coffee, and it shows," Ava said apologetically, but her tone said she was also teasing him.

Elias narrowed his eyes at her, and the doctor chuckled.

"That is quite alright. It sounds like the two of you have much to get done today, so we won't keep you any longer. Calista will be in touch once we are ready to conference you in again."

Elias gave a curt nod, and Dr. Balor stood up and exited the communications lab on the screen.

Lottie stood center screen, ready to sign off. "Text me when you can, Elias. Otherwise, I'll try to call later tonight." Then she turned her attention to Ava and smiled radiantly.

Elias sometimes forgot how beautiful she was. They had been friends for a long time and lovers a couple of times, even recently. But it had been a long time since he had thought of her in any romantic sort of way, and that was probably for the best. She, like

Hattie, was another person Elias didn't want getting caught up in his mess. However, she was much more challenging to keep out of it than Hattie was.

"Good luck out there, Ava; remember, if you need anything, I'm always around." Then she winked at her, and the screen went dark.

Ava smiled thoughtfully, and Elias wondered what that was between the two girls there at the end. But it only took him two minutes to decide that he didn't care. He crossed his arms and leaned back in his chair. "We need to talk," he said.

Ava looked over at him, her mouth full of cinnamon roll like a deer in the headlights.

"Take a seat."

Ava, wide-eyed and slightly irritated, walked back to her chair from the other end of the table and took a seat. She swallowed her bite and set the remaining half of the cinnamon roll on the plate in front of her. *At least she listens,* he thought.

"Let's get one thing straight. During this temporary partnership, I am in charge. You don't act, you don't think, and you certainly don't speak unless I say so. Especially in a meeting with one of the board members. Do I make myself clear?"

Ava curled her lip slightly and sat back in her chair, eyeing him with disdain. It was such a different vibe between the two than the night before. And he knew he was probably giving her a little bit of whiplash, but he had to make this point very clear to her. He couldn't allow her to go running her mouth again like that to the wrong people and risk everything. No, he had to keep her in check, whatever the cost.

Ava also crossed her arms, looked down at her feet, and shook her head, mumbling something to herself that sounded like "*Well, that made that decision a whole lot easier.*" But Elias couldn't be sure.

She scoffed and looked back at him indifferently. "Of course, my apologies. See, I had gotten the wrong idea in my head that we were actually working on this as a team. But I will learn my place. Be the good girl that I am. Sorry I embarrassed you." And with that, she slid her chair back, causing it to slam into the edge of the door frame behind it, and stomped back upstairs.

Elias rolled his eyes and sunk his face into his hands just as Hattie walked in, looking after Ava. She looked over at Elias at the table, shook her head at him, and poured him a second cup of coffee.

"Elias, I know ya were raised better than that," she scolded.

Elias lifted his head slightly to simply lean on his hands for support and accepted the mug.

"That's no way to treat a lass, especially one as sweet as she. Ya know, ya won't find any better," Hattie said and sat down across the table from him.

Elias rolled his eyes, full force this time, and shook his head. It was like this with Hattie; she was always trying to set him up with some girl on these missions. But she knew better. "I'm not interested in my partner, Hattie. And it has to be this way. You know that as well as I do." He shook his finger right back at her.

Hattie stared at him for a second, waiting to see if he'd budge. However, she grew frustrated when he didn't and waved her hands in the air, rustling her apron on her lap. "Oh, fiddlesticks. They run your life more than you run your own. That's not the way they want you to live, and you know it. Take a chance, Elias, live awhile, why don't ya? Ava's a nice girl. At the very least, she deserves your respect."

Elias had already figured he was being too hard on her, but it was for Ava's own good. It had to be this way. It was always better for people to think of him as a total jerk than to get too close. "I was respectful," he said, knowing it was an absolute lie.

"Don't you lie to me now, Elias Andrew! You and I both know you weren't." Hattie stood up and started putting breakfast away. Elias sighed. There wasn't much he could do now.

"Respect has to be earned," he finally said, and Hattie turned to look at him as she scrubbed the mug Ava had been drinking from earlier.

"She's here, isn't she? Partnered up with you? And on her first mission, no doubt! Clearly, there is something special about her."

Elias scoffed and folded his hands in front of his mouth. He leaned his elbows on the table and looked to the right of him, down the green-painted hallway Ava had left from. "Doubtful. Word on the street is she's here because she's the daughter of someone powerful. Someone Balor can use to his advantage."

"Balor," Hattie cut in, "is only her ticket in. The board must have seen something promising in her to grant her the internship. She is intelligent, thoughtful, and kind. Don't ya dare make a fool of me by treating her any worse than she treats you."

Elias glanced up at Hattie, who had her back turned to him. She was right. The board must have found something special about Ava. Otherwise, she would have never made it in. Elias thought back to the day they met. She had also managed to prove herself and her intelligence on the first day. Maybe Hattie was onto something.

Elias frowned. He hated admitting he was wrong. Especially to Hattie, who would no doubt hold this over his head if he said it out loud. Elias looked sideways at the woman and sighed. "Yes, ma'am."

He came to his feet and walked around the table to stand next to Hattie. He leaned over and kissed her on the cheek. Hattie stopped to look up at him with pride in her eyes. He looked down at the woman he had known all his life and smiled sheepishly. Hattie dried her wet hands on her apron and brought them to Elias's cheeks.

"Ah, yer a good man, Elias. Your mother would be proud. Just try to keep yourself in check, shall we?" His smile turned genuine, and he kissed her one last time on the forehead, then passed her and headed back to his room to get ready to head back out on the road.

As he walked down the hallway, he passed a faded family photo of a mother and her four young children around the tree at Christmastime. A young girl and three young boys, all under the age of seven, the last being just a baby. Elias had seen it many times before, and every single time he did, he used it as a reminder to call his sister. She still had those same blond curls to this day.

Chapter Nineteen

Outside, the air was still chilling as they made their way back to the graveyard through the woods. Ava walked silently, making sure to always be two steps behind him. She hadn't said a single word to him since they had raised voices in Hattie's kitchen.

Elias couldn't help but think she was acting a little childish. But then again, as Hattie had pointed out, he had let his temper get the best of him. Though he appreciated the peacefulness, he wasn't going to be able to allow this much longer; otherwise, continuing to work with her was going to be a bear of a task. And Elias needed her to trust him. He just knew better than to trust her.

"Are you going to give me the cold shoulder for the remainder of the trip?" Elias asked as he stopped to push away a rather large tree limb from the path.

"Depends, are you going to continue to be a huge dick?" Ava questioned.

Elias stopped abruptly and spun around on his heel just as the branch he had brushed aside whacked itself back into place, hiding Ava from his view. Ava gasped, acting as if he had done it on purpose, and he rolled his eyes before pulling the branch back to see her. Her scowl was the same one she had given him before.

"That was rude."

Elias motioned for her to go through. "So was calling me a dick. And I didn't do that on purpose." He began to follow behind her petite figure.

"Yeah, right."

"You're acting childish," he rebutted.

This time, it was Ava's turn to spin around on him. Her eyes were blazing green and spitting daggers his way. He had clearly hit a nerve.

"I'm being childish? I was doing my job! I did what I was asked! Dr. Balor wanted a verbal report on our progress, and I gave it to him. Yet you act like I tied a scarf around your mouth and purposefully prevented you from speaking. I've earned my right to be here whether you like it or not, and I will act accordingly!"

Elias just stared down at her feisty demeanor with his eyebrows raised. His lips held a firm, straight line in hopes of hiding his smirk. But the moment he spoke, he lost control of the situation and chuckled under his breath. "Is that so?"

Ava stepped toward him and whacked him on his arm. Elias playfully jumped back as if hurt and rubbed his elbow, his smile growing wider. "Yes! You ass!"

Elias laughed for real this time. Still rubbing his arm, he looked around before turning his attention back to her. The two had entered the open field of green that led them across an old bridge into the open field that held three large stone structures, which the monks in the tenth century had built. They had arrived, and he hadn't even noticed. "I believe you! I believe you."

Ava shook her head. The frown on her face was starting to bleed into genuine hurt. Elias reached out to snag her upper arm.

"Ava, wait." He pulled an unwilling Ava back his way, and she came to stop in front of him but avoided eye contact. "I know you belong here. The board would not have invited you to join us without doing their research on you first. No matter who recommended you."

Ava returned her attention to Elias. "Recommended me? Who recommended me?"

Elias thought it over for a brief moment before he decided not to tell her the truth—that Dr. Balor had been the one to request she receive an invitation to join them. Especially considering he really didn't want her snuggling up to him and becoming a kiss-ass. No, he needed her on his side. So, he shook his head instead and shrugged.

"I don't know, but that's not the point. The point is you're smart. You truly know what you're talking about. According to Lottie, you're supposed to be one of the very best in this field. For your age, that's pretty impressive. They would not have put a newcomer on this case unless that was the case, and here you are, so . . ."

Ava looked away, pondering his words. Elias realized he was still holding onto her, so he pulled his hands back, and her arms fell to her side. Though a gray sleeve covered it, the contact had sent chills up his arms for some reason, and he found himself wondering why he had reacted that way.

"I'm sorry I was rude before. Hattie is right. I'm not a kind person before ten."

Ava bit her lip and crossed her arms over her chest. Her thick army-green vest made a noise as it rustled. Elias hadn't stopped to notice her appearance earlier this morning. Her ponytail, which was held up by a charcoal ball cap, whipped back and forth. She wore jeans and hiking boots, just like him.

Ava was somewhat of a surprise to him. She was so much different than what he was used to. Lottie was a lipstick-and-heels type of girl, but Elias could see that Ava was a little more down-to-earth.

She waited impatiently to hear what he had to say.

"But I must be clear: those meetings need to be held in a particular manner. I need to be the one who decides what information to share and what not to. I only want you to speak when spoken to. It's not a seen-and-not-heard type thing but more of a political type thing. Please? Just trust me on this?"

Ava gave him an odd look, then shook her head and looked off toward the hills that surrounded them. "Fine," she huffed. "But eventually, you'll owe me answers. I don't like being kept in the dark." She turned to continue toward the graves.

Elias took a big breath and shook out his hair to clear his head once Ava had finally turned around. It was doubtful she would get what she was looking for in that department. Elias would lead her on for years before that happened. But for now, that promise was directing Ava forward, so he let the words hang in the air between them.

Looking out over the land before him, Elias had forgotten how much he had loved it here in Glendalough, especially on a beautiful day like today. Most days, it rained in Ireland, but today, they were blessed with a sign of St. Patrick himself, and so the sun was shining down.

The grass was as green as it gets. It was easy to see how Ireland had earned the nickname the Emerald Isle. The hills just grew and grew in every direction. A rather large stream flowed off to the left of where the graveyard and rundown monastery sat between two huge mountains of rock and green grass. The stones, as they came up to them, gave the area the perfect final touch of historic culture.

"Hold on a sec," Elias called to Ava as she ventured further past him. She stopped and turned to meet his gaze as he inclined his head at the giant tower before him. He palmed the stone of the old building and tilted his head to get a better look. "I want to inspect the buildings first, see if we can find anything there before we move onto the graves," he told her. Ava nodded and made her way back to his side. He knew it was unlikely the tower would hold any clues for them, but it was worth checking out.

If he had to guess, the old stone church that now sat in ruins was their best option, but he would save that one for last and give it the most amount of time to inspect. Ava circled the tower briefly and came back to incline her head to see the top. She seemed to have noticed the door wasn't on the ground, and therefore, they had no way in.

"This structure is a dead end. I'm gonna move onto the church and check it out real quick before I make my way over to the headstones," she announced. And Elias watched her go. She had no idea what she had just walked away from, but he was sure that if she knew, she wouldn't have left so quickly. Maybe one day he'd tell her that Father Abram Malachy, the monk who led the Order through the trials leading up to the great revolution, at one time inhabited this very tower. He tapped the stone twice before stepping back and walking away.

Up ahead, the old monastery was gated in the front, the only entryway inside. It was the only building still standing fully intact, and it would take time for Elias to get into. He frowned, cursing himself for forgetting about the gate, and pulled out his cell phone from his pocket to reveal his lack of cell service. Elias was impatient. Calista would be no help unless he chose to wait another day to come back here to get inside, but what choice did he have?

Frustrated with himself, he pulled his eyes away from his phone and glanced up to find Ava walking through the rundown structure on the left known as the Ruined Church. Her fingers traced the stone walls as she moved through the rubble's entryways, humming to herself. Elias was sure this building had not been used by the Order, but he kept following her anyway, enjoying the view until she finally led him out the exit and headed towards the small set of graves on the right.

Ava reached Andrew's stone first and kneeled beside it. She rested her hand on the top and studied the words etched on the front. Elias stepped past her to Elijah's grave on the opposite end of the graveyard. The place wasn't very big—it only held about twenty-five or so stones, but who actually knew how many unmarked graves were here? Elias tried not to think about that. It was definitely something he intended to look into later, though, if he ever got the time.

The front of the stone was the same as it had been the night before, with three dates lining the bottom. Elias stepped around to see if there was anything on the back. They had not gotten the chance to look at the stone up close with the storm rushing in the night before. To his surprise, there was a lot more wording than he had anticipated, including the triskele sign, which both he and Ava had been looking for the night before.

"The mark of the Order is on the back," Elias called over to Ava. She hurried around to the back of Andrew's grave to check it out. Elias started to read through the words on the back of the stone, but it didn't make much sense to him.

> *That I should rise, and you should not*
> *Good night and joy be to you all*
> *They are sorry for my going away*
> *They wish me one more day to stay*
> *And drink a health whate'er befalls*
> *Good night and joy be to you, lass.*

Elias read the back over again in his head. He recognized it from somewhere, but he couldn't pinpoint where it was from. He dug into his pocket and pulled out the leather journal. He hoped the Gaelic from within its old pages, would shed some light.

On the other end of the graveyard, Ava was still inspecting the back of Andrew's stone, whispering to herself. "But since it fell onto my lot . . . Elias? Does Elijah's grave have wording written on the back?"

Elias looked up from his book, which didn't seem to have any connection to their topic at hand currently, and nodded. "Yeah, but I can't make sense of it, though it sounds so familiar." He drifted off, lost in thought, and flipped the pages. He hoped if he skipped ahead, maybe he would find answers—no such luck.

Ava made her way to him, and he shut the book. Frustrated, he returned it to his jacket pocket. Ava stepped in front of him, reading the words on the back of the tombstone, then gasped as if she had caught onto something. She quickly ran back to Andrew's grave to reread what she already knew was there. Elias followed her curiosity and read Andrew's stone from over her shoulder.

"It's the lyrics for 'The Parting Glass'!" she exclaimed.

Yes! Of course, it was! That's why he had recognized it, but Elias had only ever known the song in its Gaelic version, and it seemed to be out of order, which is why he had had trouble placing it.

"The Parting Glass" was a song known to be sung at funerals and Irish wakes. It was meant to be a tribute of sorts. The way it's done is by passing around a pint or a shot and raising a toast to the deceased's honor. It is supposed to be the last drink you have with the departed. When done right, it can be a beautiful sentiment.

Elias had seen it done at many wakes he had attended throughout the years. It was very traditional. A part of him was impressed that Ava even recognized it, let alone before he did. But he also was learning not to underestimate her.

"But the lyrics are all out of order." Elias stepped back and walked over to Elijah's grave once more. Something about this wasn't right. Elijah had to have a reason behind the mixed-up lyrics. Walking back and forth many times, Elias began to notice a particular discoloration in the stones that only seemed to mark certain letters, which was odd. If there were going to be watermarks, for example, or any type of discoloration, it wouldn't just randomly single out specific words.

Elias threw open the book again and came across a page that talked about tools used back in the day. That was it! Elijah was sending them a message! It was here in literal black and gray right before his very own eyes!

"He discolored their stones!" Elias came back to stand beside Ava and pointed to a blackened *m* on the back of Andrew's grave. Ava pondered this, then, suddenly, she began to dig into the bag she had resting on her shoulder and pulled out a piece of paper and a pen.

"I bet if you're right and we put the lyrics together, that will give us the proper order of the colored letters." Ava walked back and forth between the graves, careful to write them in precisely the same order as noted on the two graves. Once she was done, the lyrics read:

But since it fell onto My lot
That I should risE, and you should not
I'll Gently rise and softly cAlL
GoOd night and joy be to you all

Of all the <u>C</u>omrades that <u>E</u>'e<u>R</u> I had
They are s<u>O</u>rry for my going away
And all the <u>S</u>weethearts that e're I had
They'd wish me one more day to stay
So fill to me the parting <u>G</u>lass
And dr<u>I</u>nk a health whate'er befalls
Then <u>G</u>ently rise <u>AN</u>d sof<u>T</u>ly call
Goodnight and joy b<u>E</u> to yo<u>U</u> las<u>S</u>.

"*Lass* is not in the original," Elias stated, looking over her shoulder.

Ava shrugged, focused on picking out each individual letter from the mix. "Doesn't matter. I'm guessing he needed that last *s* to send his message properly." Elias didn't like it but figured she was probably correct.

"M-E-G-A-L-O-C-E-R-O-S G-I-G-A-N-T-E-U-S." They read the letters back, stood up, and started to pace around Elijah's grave. She stated and restated the letters before turning to him and asking if it meant anything to him in Gaelic. Elias shook his head slowly, still thinking.

"No, it sounds Greek. But it's not a word I am familiar with. Or at least all put together it doesn't sound right, but the first half sounds like the word *Irish* in Greek." Elias pointed to her paper.

"Greek?" Ava pulled out her phone and typed in the letters.

"There's no serv—"

"I'm channeling your hot spot." She looked over her shoulder playfully. "Thanks."

Women.

Elias stepped closer to read over her shoulder.

No results showed on the first search, but on the second, Ava split the word down the middle, and they got a hit. It left them with the Greek words *Megaloceros giganteus*. "Irish elk."

"Irish elk. The next clue is Irish elk?"

"Irish elk have been extinct since the Ice Age," Elias stated, which didn't make any sense.

"Could it stand for something more?" Ava asked, confused.

"No, Elijah wouldn't have a riddle within a riddle. The only Irish elk around now are in . . ."

"The museums!" Ava jumped up so abruptly that Elias had to take a step back. "There is a painting of one in the Carnegie

Museum! It's pretty old and a part of the Celtic exhibit. You think that could be it?"

Elias wasn't familiar with this museum and, therefore, had no idea, but it was as good a guess as any. "I suppose so. Do you know the name of the artist? Maybe if we do some research on him, that would give us a better indication of its involvement," he said.

Ava shrugged and pulled out her phone. "The artist was a man named Beckett Lowery," she stated, studying the screen. Elias nodded.

"Born in 1867, County Clare, died in 1929 at the age of sixty-two from tuberculosis in Glendalough." Ava's eyes shot up to him, and he gave her a look in return.

"Do you think this Lowery guy may have been a member of the Order?" he asked her. She shook her head and looked down at her phone. Her shoulders sank in defeat.

"I really don't have any way of knowing," she said, and Elias could hear the disappointment in her voice. He frowned, too. So, it was up to him then to figure this part out. Elias made a mental note to give Kayleigh a call once he got back to Hattie's place.

"The Carnegie Museum might have more answers for us regardless," Ava said, looking back up at him, still hopeful.

"Which is where?"

Then Ava's face fell, and her excitement faded as something unbeknownst to him dawned on her. "Pittsburgh! We're going to Pittsburgh . . ."

Chapter Twenty

1907, DUBLIN, IRELAND

St. Patrick's Hall was lively tonight as Andrew kneaded the palm of his hand. Dressed in his finest suit and sequestered off to the side of the luxurious ballroom, his eyes scanned the crowd, looking for the familiar face he had lost since re-entering the party.

He had just stepped out for a moment to do some verifying of the grounds. He couldn't imagine where on earth his beauty of a companion had disappeared to in that time.

He was just about to head toward the bar when a flash of bright red curls caught his eye. Bridget Hayes slithered through the crowd of heavy drinkers, with her eyes on him and her lips pulled into a seductive grin. Two glasses of champagne graced her thin fingers, one for herself and one for him, no doubt.

Thanks be to God. He needed it.

Though everything had gone according to plan thus far, Andrew had yet to pull off the most crucial task of them all and was becoming anxious to move forward and get the hell out of here. Something to take the edge off would do him some good.

Bridget approached him now and handed him a glass as she turned and curled herself around his arm. She lay her head on his shoulder lovingly.

This was all a ruse, he told himself.

This was the story they had been presenting to people for over a year now. The happy couple who ran with only the most elite and prestigious crowds in Dublin. Who partied most nights and worked hard amongst the suits by day. The perfect pair that was madly in love with one another and could only be separated by Bridget's many tours as a sought-after musician.

That's what made this story perfect. That was the key factor that sold the lie they were living and would undoubtedly save his ass tonight, as long as she could pull it off.

With Bridget out touring the country, Andrew would never be questioned about his whereabouts, which gave him time to sneak off to Glendalough frequently without being noticed. Andrew would have to remember to thank the redheaded devil when this was all over and their breakup became public. She was risking a lot for him.

Andrew shifted in his suit, his collar tight from Bridget's grip on his sleeve. As more people began to enter the room, Andrew gently pulled them both back and out of the spotlight, into the shadows.

Bridget nestled his shoulder fondly and spoke only loud enough so he could hear.

"Have faith, my pet, it will all work as according to plan."

Andrew nearly snorted but shook his head instead and took a sip of his drink for courage. Ever the queen of positivity, this one.

"As long as you are as good a liar as you say you are and your sister Celene is as grand a pianist as I've heard, then this should go off without issue," he responded. Bridget stood up straighter to look at him, her blue eyes already scolding his negative comments before she spoke.

"Celene is a wonderful pianist. Don't you dare question her ability. And shouldn't you be more concerned about *your* sibling, as he has the more infectious skeletons in his closet, should we be caught?"

"I am more concerned about *our* next steps rather than theirs to be honest. They have the easy job after all," Andrew once again shifted his weight, but this time so he could peer down at the blue eyes looking up at him under her barely tamed curls. He smiled sincerely at her and was blessed with a dazzling smile in return.

"Oh, come now." She purred once again, resting her head on his shoulder.

"That's easy. Once you've acquired the Jewels, you head out to the east wing where Terrance is waiting while I distract them. When they ask later where you've gone, I'll simply say you left early with a cough. And they'll be so drunk and I in right mind, they won't be able to argue. Then I'll leave shortly after to avoid arousing suspicion—it's a perfect plan," she recited confidently.

Her red lips quirked even higher as she continued.

"Besides, it can't be all that hard; in fact, I think you'll even enjoy it." Her words were laced with an electricity that had always run between the two of them. Andrew's smile blossomed into a grin against his will. They always did have fun together.

Bridget and Andrew had met a few years ago at a social event held by one of the council members of the Order. Her father was a member as well and had brought both her and her sister along in hopes of finding them husbands.

Truth be told, Andrew and Bridget's connection was instantaneous, and he had made sure to inform her father of his interest in his oldest daughter. But Bridget had other plans. Despite what her father wanted for her in life, Bridget had always been sort of a wild one. Andrew had since cursed himself for not noticing this sooner, after he managed to sneak her home that very night and uncover the real woman that lay beneath the formal skirts and petticoats.

It was now obvious to him that he would never marry this woman, no matter how hard he tried or how much she liked him. She had other dreams set in sight, and he was just another ride in her fast-paced adventure.

Celene, Bridget's younger sister, however, was not as brave and had fallen in line with her father's wishes, choosing to step away from the piano to pursue a normal family life. While Celene thrived at home, Bridget set out to make a name for herself.

Despite her father's best efforts to settle her down, she had much higher aspirations in life and was determined to accomplish them. One by one, she began to make her way through Dublin's elites and managed to impress them all with just a stroke of her fingers over the ivory keys.

Nearly three years later, everything had changed for her, and yet nothing between the two of them had changed. She was still the apple of his eye that would never ripen. Andrew looked over his shoulder at the sound of a burly laugh booming from off in the entryway, his face set in a permanent mask of calm collection at this point.

The vicar was making his way into the ballroom, which meant the time for action was fast approaching. He leaned down and jostled Bridget on his arm to grab her attention.

"Did you sign Celene and Ryan's names on the guest book?"

Her head bounced swiftly in a nod.

"It's all set."

She lifted her head again to follow the vicar as he made his way through a crowd of drunks sloshing about toward the back of the room. His eyes were ghostly, but the smile on his face and his slow movements told Andrew it was time.

"You think he's intoxicated enough?"

Andrew gently pulled away from her and readjusted his suit, setting his glass on the table behind him and retrieving his hat, bag, and cloak from the chair next to it.

"Yes, I think now is our best chance." He turned to look at Bridget now as they prepared to part ways. With her eyes full of sternness, she nodded in return. Andrew smiled at the woman he truly did love and leaned down to leave a quick kiss of encouragement on her lips. She blinked and gave him another genuine smile before squeezing his hand in hers.

"In another life, my love," she whispered to him, and he believed it. Andrew squeezed back once more, then stepped back further into the shadows as he watched this beautiful woman get to work.

She tossed back the rest of her drink, then made a scene of throwing her hands up and announcing that the entertainment had arrived. Andrew watched with pride as she made her way to the piano in the back corner and began to tickle the keys with such talent the fae would be envious. Then, as the rest of the party was distracted, Andrew disappeared from the room.

Chapter Twenty-One

Modern Day Glendalough, Ireland

Ava

Surrounded by beauty, I sat there thinking through my options as Elias dialed Calista. The moment she picked up, he walked away to discuss our next destination. I wasn't sure I wanted to invite the oh-so-arrogant Elias Cassedy into my family home, but logic told me that it would be nearly impossible to go home and not actually *go home*. If I did go back to Pittsburgh and not visit Jules and she found out, she would be super-disappointed with me. However, sneaking away without Elias noticing would be even more difficult; nothing seemed to slip past him. That didn't leave me much of a choice.

"Yes, and we'll need both a meeting set up with their museum director there and hotel rooms for the time being," Elias said into the phone.

I could hear Calista ask him for how long. He shrugged his big, broad shoulders, looking off into the hills; I wasn't quite sure who that gesture was for—me or him.

"I can't possibly know that, unfortunately. But I doubt it will be that long. Get us the meeting first and then book the rooms. I—"

"No need," I cut in with gritted teeth. I brought my fingers to the bridge of my nose and pinched the spot in hopes of preventing a headache from coming.

Elias looked down at me, confused, and told Lottie to hold on, then covered the phone to ask what I had meant.

I sighed and climbed to my feet, and looked at him with a forced smile. "My family is from Pittsburgh. If it's okay with you, I'm sure they won't mind you staying with us for a few days."

Elias looked from me to the phone and then back again as if he was suddenly uncomfortable with the situation but didn't know how to handle it. Calista, on the other end, spoke up through his fingers, and he removed his hand, put her on speakerphone, and then held it out in front of us.

"You are on speaker phone, Lot."

"Okay, hello, Ava!" I stepped closer to Elias and tried not to look at him.

"Hey, Calista! I was just telling Elias that my family lives in Pittsburgh. If it's okay with him, we could stay there for the time being."

Elias took a breath in and let it out, taking his eyes off the phone and looking over my head. I couldn't get a good read on what he was thinking. He was definitely unsure about this plan, but I didn't really see a way around it. Of course, if he wasn't comfortable, he could always stay at a hotel, and I could stay with Eamon and Millie; that would be by far the best outcome. But somehow, I doubted that would happen.

"That actually would save the museum a lot of money. Elias? Do you have any opposition to this? Would that be okay with you?"

I stepped back and looked up at Elias with a polite smile, trying to let him know it was okay if he chose to stay at the hotel. Still, I wasn't sure I got the right message across.

He didn't move, just glared in my direction, but agreed nonetheless. "Yeah, that would be fine."

I looked at the ground and took a step back. Damn. It didn't work.

"How early could you get us a flight out, Lot?"

"Considering you two will have to travel back to the campus to pack before you go, probably not until tomorrow evening. I will send you both an email with your ticket information once the flights are booked."

"Perfect, thank you, Lottie."

"Yes, thanks, Calista!" I said and reentered Elias's personal space. It seemed to take everything in him not to step away from me.

"Not a problem at all—that is what I am here for! Happy to help! We will reconnect once you guys are set up in Pittsburgh.

Until then, I'll see you both once you get back on campus grounds! Toodles!"

Elias and I said goodbye, and he hung up, then casually stepped back and pretended to readjust his shirt. I looked off into the woods, where we would be hiking through momentarily, then back at the graveyard surrounding us with slight disappointment of my own. I let out a sigh and took it all in.

There is so much history, so much beauty, and so many wonderful things to explore, and yet such a short time to do so. Elias caught me staring off at the hills.

"It's hard to pull away from, isn't it?"

I shook my head, knowing exactly what he meant. "This is an absolute dream job, and yet, somehow . . ." I let my words fade into the wind around us.

"And yet, somehow, you still miss the magic that grows freely here." He sighed and dug his hands into his pockets. We sat there and watched the long grass on the hills sway back and forth, each of us lost in our own thoughts.

"If you had the opportunity, what would you prefer to do with your time here in Ireland? Other than expeditions?"

I paused. What a loaded question. There was so much I'd do, so much I wanted to explore and see. And while I assumed I would eventually get there, it was clear to me that I wouldn't get the opportunities I thought I would have right away. "There are a few places I'd love nothing more than to explore, but honestly? Out of everything? You want to know what I'd do?"

Elias looked over at me, his eyes shaded by his hat, waiting to hear what I had to say.

"Do you remember the Order I told you about when we first met? The Order of St. Patrick?" He nodded, and I let my eyes wander to the stream between the mountains. "I'd track its roots. I'd find the Order."

Elias didn't have any reaction. He just looked away to admire the view in front of us and bounced on his heels. I supposed the wind was getting to him, but I wasn't sure I cared. Just one more moment to take it all in was worth being cold for another second. I couldn't blame him for his disinterest in the Order. I had never really explained its significance in a way that showed its true heroism.

"I didn't think that was still a thing. I figured, by the way you talked about it, that it had died off long ago."

"I'm not so sure. Recent events suggest it could still be around. But even if it is dead, to know exactly where it died, to know where the last meeting was held, who the last knight inducted was, would be amazing."

Elias stayed put but watched me as I stepped over dirt by Andrew's grave. I walked to the opposite side, where Elijah's tombstone sat and bent down to trace my fingers over the triple spiral symbol etched in the stone one last time.

I would be back without a doubt to follow a path these brothers had set out for me in hopes it would lead me to the Order one day.

"These brothers, if what I think is true, may be two of Ireland's biggest revolutionary heroes. And yet the world will never know." I shook my head and closed my eyes to briefly bless the stones before standing up.

"No, but we do. And maybe that is good enough for now."

I looked at Elias thoughtfully and smiled at him genuinely. He got it. The beauty of this place, the pure history and love for this culture here. He understood how I felt about this place. It was nice to know I was not alone in this love.

We made it back to Hattie's a little later than expected. Elias disappeared into his room for a couple minutes to phone Calista again and let her know we wouldn't be getting back to campus until, at best, later in the day tomorrow. I stayed in the kitchen with Hattie and chatted about the expedition and her family history while we ate lunch.

She took the time to tell me all about her sister, the one with the four children in the picture frame I had seen down the hall earlier that morning. She had been beautiful and kind, and she loved her kids; she was Hattie's youngest sibling and only sister. Hattie had been devastated when she passed from complications of cancer. I gave her my condolences and told her about my sister. We tried not to cry as we held each other's hands in mutual hatred for the disease.

Hattie also talked a bit about her relationship with Elias. She explained that he didn't used to be as stoic as he is now. According to her, he even learned to play hurling before he started taking his missions so seriously. It was only after one of his partners on an expedition a couple of years ago fell from a rock high on a mountain and was seriously injured that he changed.

Somehow that didn't surprise me. Despite his closed-off and composed demeanor, Elias seemed like the type of person who had become hardened with experience. It made me feel remorse for the way I had treated him that morning. But I also felt grief. The part of him that had enjoyed life seemed to have died from that point on, according to Hattie. Between the loss of his mom and the accident of his previous partner, which he blamed himself for, he felt a lot of pressure to do things right. I decided to make sure I asked about that in a little more depth from Elias himself later.

After Hattie had finished her lunch, she had to leave me to my thoughts while she went outside to water the garden. I took the opportunity, though, to text Millie and let her know I'd be home within the next couple of days. I had just taken another bite of the delicious stew Hattie had, of course, handmade from scratch, when I got an email with our flight information for late tomorrow evening. But before I could even open the email, a second one came through with my first official solo assignment.

The item was an old watch from the early 1900s or maybe even before. It looked like an old military trench watch. I had seen one before, just like it, but I couldn't remember where. It had a reddish-brown leather band and was circled in gold. The gears were left to turn under clear glass. The top case closed over it to hide the edges of the gears and show the hands of time.

Apparently, the watch had been left in one of the inn's rooms by another explorer on a recent expedition. I studied the watch and noted that Calista wanted it personally delivered to her by the time we returned to campus for proper cleaning. Easy enough. I figured I'd peruse the rooms after I finished packing and continue my conversation with Hattie.

The rest of the afternoon, Elias and I spent time further inspecting the old rundown church. He swore we would find answers to and when we didn't, he resorted to calling nearly every person on his magical list of contacts to try and get us access into the stone monastery that was still intact and locked up by iron gates. But the earliest we would be able to gain access wasn't until next week, and we simply couldn't wait that long. Deciding to put that search on pause, knowing we had gathered what we had come for at least, we decided to make a plan to come back out and check out the monastery when this was all over.

This seemed to please Elias finally, and we made our way back to Hattie's Inn.

Later that night, after Elias and I had both rested and packed and met Hattie downstairs for dinner, I set off to look for the missing item. My first thought was to ask Hattie. If I wasn't supposed to talk to Elias about it, I assumed it was to prevent other explorers from getting in trouble for leaving behind such a precious item. But then I thought better of it: I figured it was best not to ask for her advice after all.

I took a walk through two other unused rooms on the upper floor and even moved things around on my own before I decided to look in Elias's room. The door, though, was locked from the inside, so I took a stroll down the stairs.

Upon walking back into the kitchen, I noticed that there, on the little end table by the entryway right in the middle of the bowl for keys, was the watch!

Thrilled that this assignment had been easier than I expected, I gingerly picked it up and placed it in a small cloth bag I had brought for my reading glasses and set it in my suitcase before jumping in the shower. As much as I loved being in Glendalough, this wet, cold, Irish air was still something I was getting used to, and I couldn't pass up soaking in the steam from a hot shower.

I had just gotten out, wrung out my hair, and wrapped my towel around my torso when the door swung open, and Elias barged into my room. I jumped back briefly, startled, and clung to the towel around me.

"Excuse you! Don't you knock!?"

"Oh, my God!" He held up his hands. His cheeks began to flush as his eyes took in the sight of me. A warmth spread across my own cheeks in response. I watched as his eyes grew dark with a desire he was trying desperately to hide. Still, with great effort, he eventually returned his clouded gaze to meet mine.

"I'm so sorry. I was just, uh, looking for something," he explained casually as if he had nowhere else to be.

I narrowed my eyes at him. "And you thought you would find it in my room?" I shot back. He shook his head and shrugged. He didn't make a move for the door, and he didn't apologize further; he just stood there and continued to try to explain his reasoning.

"Well, no, I—"

"Then get out!" I picked up my slipper and threw it at him. He shifted his hands to try to block it, but my fuzzy cow slipper hit him on the shoulder.

A playful smile escaped from his lips. "Ow! What did you do that for?"

I picked up the other slipper and threw it at him, nearly missing his head. He was lucky he had ducked just at the right moment. "The fact that you have to ask is an answer enough," I said.

Having run out of slippers to throw, I marched forward and used my only free arm to whack him on the shoulder. Elias was careful not to touch me, this time striking him straight in the chest and pushing him back through the doorway.

"Why are you still here? Get out! Lord almighty."

He couldn't help but chuckle as I shoved him out the door using all my strength. I went to smack him one last time, but he caught my wrist in his hand before it made an impact. He held it firmly, unwilling to let go, and looked down at me with a spark in his eyes. "Wait, Ava—"

My irritation simmered as I looked up at him from under my eyelashes. He towered over me with strength and a control over the situation that I hadn't realized I'd lost.

So, I stopped fighting him and huffed. I gave him a face to let him know I was listening and that he could continue. But this was only because the look he was giving me had pushed me into submission and I couldn't find the will to pull myself out of his grasp. And a wicked smile crept over his face.

"Does this mean I have to take you to dinner now that, you know?" And he motioned to my partially covered body.

I let out a screech of annoyance, my resolve returning to me once more. He laughed, letting me go, then stepped away. I spun on my heels, then slammed the door in his face, and this time, I set the lock.

Chapter Twenty-Two

Elias

The following morning started out on the wrong foot for Elias. First, he burnt his tongue on his coffee. Then he accidentally knocked over a picture frame hanging in Hattie's hallway, which broke into two pieces upon hitting the ground. That was going to cost him.

His shower that morning had been freezing for some reason, and above all else, he still couldn't find his watch.

He searched everywhere for it—his car, his suitcase, he had even walked in on Ava getting out of the shower. He never actually got the chance to ask her. He had been too distracted by her tiny figure in nothing but a towel and had completely forgotten why he had barged in on her in the first place. The whole situation had surprised him.

His heartbeat picked up.

He quickly squashed whatever arousal she had sparked within him and tossed the image of Ava out of his mind. He didn't have time for distractions, and he certainly could not fall down that rabbit hole with her, of all people.

He shook his head to himself, regretting that he had ever gone in there to begin with. In truth, he hadn't really thought the watch had been in her room anyway, but he was at least hoping she had seen it.

Looking at the clock on the wall had told him he was running out of time. So, he decided to table the search for now and get his things packed.

He would have to ask Hattie about it later. At the very least, once the mission was through, he could come back and look again. If it was lost at the inn, he knew it would be in good hands once it was found.

Once he had gathered his belongings into his bags, he took a seat at his desk and started to put together the Lynch brothers' files he had brought with him from the museum. As he was collecting the pages one by one, he came across an old picture of the twins, with Elijah holding a small leather-bound book and Andrew carrying a decent-sized satchel.

That reminded him of something, and he snagged the page and walked straight over to Ava's room.

Though there were definitely some things he needed to keep secret from her, this was one she would indeed find out sooner or later. If she realized he was keeping information from her, that could spell disaster for him. He figured it was best if he told her now.

Ava wasn't in her room any longer, though; in fact, none of her stuff was, which struck him as odd. Maybe she had already taken her things down to the kitchen, he thought, and so he rushed down the stairs two by two.

His eyes grazed the kitchen and landed at the bottom of the stairs when suddenly a tiny figure ran into him from the side. Ava, he had noted some time ago, could be pretty clumsy when she was not paying attention.

He put his hand out on the wall to his left to catch himself. Ava's hands flew up to his chest in an effort to steady herself, but then, out of embarrassment, she snatched them away as if he had bitten her. She blushed under her ball cap, her hair still damp from her morning shower, and avoided his eye contact.

"Whoa, where's the fire?" he asked her.

She dropped her head, shielding herself from his gaze, and shoved her hands into the pockets of her black jeans. "Sorry, I didn't see you there," she said.

"Clearly. Where were you going so fast?"

Ava finally looked up to him and shrugged sheepishly, almost as if she was trying to hide something. Elias narrowed his eyes in suspicion but decided to hear her out. "Just running upstairs to grab my last bag to put in the trunk is all."

"Uh-huh." Elias didn't buy it but figured it didn't really matter, and he didn't really care. He shook his head, pulled out the paper with the picture of the brothers, and shoved it into her hands.

Confused, Ava evaluated the document. "What's this?" she asked.

"This is what I was coming to find you for. It was in the files we brought from the room of records."

Ava's lips perked up at the corners like she knew he was in trouble for something. "You mean the files that *you* brought from the room of records," she corrected him.

"Po-ta-to, po-tah-to," he replied.

"You know she's going to kill you once she finds out you took those without permission, right?"

Elias just blinked at her innocently. But really, he was wondering how she had known that. "Yeah, I think I can handle her. Anyway, I wanted to show you this." He pointed to the satchel Andrew had around his shoulder.

"This is in every photo I have found of Andrew. It's an old satchel that was used at the time, much like a briefcase. I looked it up to see if I could find one online, and I found a version from 1899. I believe it's the same version as the one Andrew carried with him everywhere," he said, and the two started to walk. Ava continued to inspect the photo as they talked.

"What's the significance?" she asked, looking up at him thoughtfully.

"If I am right, this may be the same satchel the brothers used to keep the jewels in." The pair entered the kitchen and stopped. Ava leaned against the sink and continued to study the paper in her hand. Elias leaned on the table, his back facing the wall that held the window out to the back of the inn.

"I've seen other pictures of the brothers, previous to 1904, before the heist. There's not a single one where he is wearing this satchel. It's only after 1904 that it starts showing up."

Ava shrugged. "Okay, so what's your point? He bought a new satchel in 1901?"

Elias gave her an exasperated look. "Nooo," he said, drawing it out and pointing to the photo. "This satchel, this model satchel, had a metal box inside, like a lock box. One that needed a special key in order to open it, and each key was personally made, so there were no copies."

Ava sat back and contemplated this. She let her hand with the paper fall to her lap as she crossed her other arm around her waist, holding onto her elbow, and looked past him out the window.

"Look, I know it's a stretch, but I think it's a lead worth following."

Ava was zoning in on something past him. Her eyes had grown wide, and her mouth fell open just barely. Elias figured she was still trying to process this theory and was just too tired to do so quickly. He stepped in front of her and waved a hand at her, trying to rein in her attention back into him.

"Ava?"

"Fire," she whispered. Her breath had quickened, but Elias hadn't noticed.

He frowned. He had never picked her for the easily offended type. "It was just a joke, Ava," he replied with a thread of annoyance in his tone.

Ava suddenly snapped out of her trance and sprang into action, throwing the paper down on the table behind him. "No, Elias! FIRE!" she yelled and ran out toward the door that led to the back of the inn.

"What?" A look of confusion crossed his face as he followed her stare. When he saw the barn out back smothered in flames, his eyes grew wide and his stomach dropped.

"Hattie!" Elias threw a chair aside to get to the door. Ava sprinted ahead of him toward the barn, and Elias realized what she had planned to do before he could stop her.

"Ava! Wait!" But it was too late. She ran straight into the entrance of the barn without hesitation and disappeared into the smoke between the flames. Elias followed.

In the barn, Ava found Hattie crouched down as low as she could get in a horse stall, her face covered in soot and one arm over her head while the other tried to forcefully pull her horse, Nigel, out from his spot in the back of the stall. Ava got to Hattie first and wrapped her arms around the woman as she coughed.

"We have to leave, Hattie! The fire's almost blocked the exit," she yelled. Hattie looked from the horse to Ava and then back again, clearly in distress about leaving him behind. Nigel, in response, threw himself back onto his hind legs. It forced Hattie to drop the reins, and the pair stepped back. She nodded sadly at Ava but let her lead the way just as Elias reached the two. Hattie's eyes grew wide.

"No, Elias, go back! I will follow you!" she yelled. But Elias shook his head and turned to grab the reins Hattie had dropped as Nigel let out a fearful neigh.

"I'll get him, you go!"

Hattie pulled away from Ava's grasp, stepped toward him, grabbed his arm, and pleaded with him to leave the horse. "Not without you! Please, Elias!"

Ava looked back toward the exit as a beam from the ceiling fell close to the door, sending a few ducks who were already on their way out running with their wings spread in panic. She bit her lip and turned back to Hattie and Elias, trying not to panic herself.

She had only been in the barn a minute, and yet she felt like she was melting and her lungs were on fire.

"Ava, get her outta here!" Elias roared over the smoke. It was an order, not a request.

Ava grabbed Hattie's arm more forcefully this time and began to drag her away from him, and Elias tried to cajole the scared horse. Hattie had tears streaking down her face as Ava led her to the exit. She couldn't see anything but bright yellow and white flames licking the walls around them; the air in the middle was dark gray and filled with smoke.

Ava clasped Hattie's hand and pulled her down into a crouch, hoping she might be able to see a bit better if they were underneath the smoke. It wasn't much, but it was something.

Hattie let her weave them through the flames and wood beams that were falling and creating a zigzag path toward the exit. When they got to the front, it was blocked by the overly large beam that Ava had seen fall earlier. It was lying on the ground at an angle, with the top against the side of the barn. It was so big the bottom was resting against what had been large bales of hay beside the other wall and were now engulfed in flames.

Ava tried to find a way around but couldn't. She looked back at Hattie, unsure of her next move. "I think we're going to have to try and jump over it!" she yelled.

Hattie looked past her and took a second to evaluate the situation before nodding. Behind Hattie, Ava noticed a barrel that had just barely caught fire. She ran over to it and thanked the Lord that it was empty and, therefore, relatively light. She pushed the barrel over onto its side and then gave it another good push so it rolled, putting out the small flames that had only been sitting on the bottom.

Hattie caught on and helped Ava quickly roll the barrel over to sit in front of the fallen beam. Together they used an old saddle to support the barrel so that when they jumped, it wouldn't move. Ava gave Hattie a push. "You go first."

"But—"

"Go!"

Hattie stopped arguing, pulled up her now dirty skirt with her hands, and stepped up onto the side of the barrel. When her boots seemed stable, Ava said, "On the count of three, one, two . . . three!"

Hattie jumped and disappeared through the flames. Now, it was Ava's turn. Terrified, she knew she didn't have any time to waste. Mustering up her courage, she followed suit and jumped up onto the barrel. She took a glance back, hoping to see Elias, but when she saw nothing but smoke, she turned around and jumped with all her might in between the flames.

Elias had been able to calm the terrified horse long enough for it to allow him to mount it. Thankfully, he had been riding Nigel his entire life, and the horse trusted him. He kicked Nigel in the ribs, and the horse took off through the blaze, smoke, and fire, nipping at their heels as they flew through the crumbling barn.

Once they had reached the entryway, the great beast jumped over a barrel and a beam that had been blocking the path out. They suddenly entered clear air, where Elias was able to let out a tight yet difficult breath. He spotted Ava and Hattie out of the corner of his eye holding onto each other and waiting for him.

Nigel had no plans to slow down or stick around, so Elias took his chances and jumped off the horse, then tucked himself into a ball so he hit the ground rolling. Ava and Hattie rushed to him to verify that he was okay.

Once they had all checked each other, Hattie ran back into the kitchen to call for help, and Elias sat on the wet grass, watching the barn he had known fall into splinters. The two said nothing as Ava walked over and sat down beside Elias. She reached out and laid her hand on his arm, and this time Elias didn't flinch. They sat together in silence watching the flames continue to burn as the smoke coated the night sky.

Chapter Twenty-Three

Elias struggled to leave Hattie after the fire. He couldn't fathom how it had started in the first place, but had made a call to Kayleigh to ensure someone came to check things out. He was assured that there would be a report on the damage done and that he would receive a copy. For now, he had work to do, and thankfully, Hattie understood that.

With the fire disrupting their plans, Lottie kindly went ahead and changed their flights to depart in two days, giving them an extra day in Dublin to regroup. This worked out nicely, as Elias and Ava had decided to drive back and visit the place where it all began—Dublin Castle.

As the bus transporting them to the large tourist attraction came to a stop in front of the towering gates leading down the gravel path toward the monument, Elias felt an unshakable sense of foreboding. This was where it had all begun in his mind. Yes, Glendalough had been a major part of it, but Bedford Tower held the evidence within its stone walls. Well, what little evidence there was, anyway.

Elias kept to himself as he followed Ava off the bus and started down the gravel path. He had been here many times before, but it had been a while. Still, everything around him felt familiar, leaving him relatively unfazed. Ava, to his left, however, stared silently for the first time in ages, stunned by the magnificent architecture before them. Her eyes flicked from the steeples reaching toward the sky, down to the decorated windows below, and then to the reason for their visit here in the first place, Bedford Tower.

Elias smirked and looked away, not wanting to spoil this for her. He suspected she hadn't had the same opportunity to travel as he had. It was invigorating to recall how remarkable certain places like this, which seemed ordinary to him, could be. Seeing them through fresh eyes once again was a blessing.

They stepped out of the light of the day and into the castle, stopping briefly at the ticket desk where they snagged maps of the building and made their way toward St. Patrick's Hall. That's where the party hosted by the vicar would have been held that night all those years ago. Ironic now when you think about the fact that the group that presumably stole the Jewels was titled after the very same saint.

"Just a bit farther here, down the corridor," Elias said, guiding Ava through the labyrinth of hallways. Ava trailed behind, gradually absorbing everything. When they reached the Hall, Elias exhaled and moved to open the door. Ava looked up at him questioningly.

"St. Patrick's Hall is often used for big diplomatic events. Sometimes, if it's big enough, they close off the whole castle, but for most events, they just rope off this room. The biggest event held here are the presidential inaugurations," he explained. Ava's eyes grew wide, realizing what they could have missed had something been going on that day. Elias stepped into the great hall, and again Ava's eyes scanned around the giant room.

The Hall was a large rectangular room with beautiful wooden floors and deep blue walls. A golden pillar, which started halfway up the wall and stopped just before reaching the ceiling, sat between sets of large open windows on one side and large mirrors on the opposite wall. Banners were placed above each pillar in the small space between them, drawing your attention skyward toward the magnificent ceiling.

Elias inclined his head, then turned around and walked backwards so Ava could see and follow in his footsteps.

Above them, three large canvas paintings captivated the eye the moment you looked upwards. The middle one was the most famous and, by far, the most stunning. It depicted King George III on his throne, flanked by two noblewomen, surrounded by figures from ancient times. An angel and cherubs flew overhead, symbolizing the church's watchful eye over his reign. Gigantic glass chandeliers hung between each artwork, floating above them and unifying the room.

"The middle painting is King George III flanked by Britannia and Hibernia by Vincenzo Waldré, 1788–1802," Elias told her, his smile blooming as he noticed her mouth was now agape. He continued to walk backwards toward the front of the room, where the exit nearest to Bedford Tower was. "I'd close your mouth if I were you," he teased. "Wouldn't want to catch a fly that way."

Elias chuckled as Ava shot him a look and shook her head, then quickened her pace to join him at the corner of the room where he had paused to observe people inspecting their surroundings. As she stood beside him, she gazed across the floor and began to recall what they knew of the conspiracy theory involving the Lynch Brothers on the night the Jewels were stolen.

Elias felt the shift in her demeanor and adjusted his mindset as well. Though she was a good distraction from his concerns of Hattie, he needed to remain focused on their task now.

"So what do we know about this night?" he asked, reviewing the information they had collected during those nights studying together before Glendalough.

Ava took over.

"We start in St. Patrick's Hall, with a dazzling girl on his arm. That's how he managed to get into the party in the first place. Andrew came as the date of Bridget Hayes, the famous pianist who had been a personal invite of the vicar at the time, hoping she would grace them with her gifts," she stated aloud.

Elias nodded and started to imagine the couple standing arm in arm in the back corner, dressed in their finest and talking quietly while sipping champagne. As if before his very eyes, Elias watched as the pair noticed the vicar entering the ballroom, intoxicated and slurring his words as he laughed loudly and staggered his way through the room.

In his mind, he could see Bridget kissing Andrew on the cheek before stepping away from him, heading toward the grand piano at the far end of the room, her flowing white and black skirts trailing behind her as she moved. Bridget expertly captures the attention of the entire crowd, drawing them to the back of the room while Andrew slips backwards and disappears into the darkness of the outer hallway.

Ava turned her head toward the entrance beside them and gestured to leave the room and walk down the corridor. Elias followed suit. They strolled on, recounting the tale they had crafted based on their imaginations and the few facts they possessed. Elias watched as the imaginary figure of Andrew walked carefully ahead of them, leading the way toward Bedford Tower.

"While Andrew and Bridget are in Dublin, they send Elijah and Bridget's sister, Celene, to Scotland to perform in Bridget's place, and they sign Celene's and her husband, Ryan's, names in the guestbook here."

Elias stepped in, filling in the next piece of the puzzle.

"Right, ensuring that Andrew could not be tracked. It would be the vicar's word against theirs, and he was a known drunk. So then, Bridget distracts the partygoers with her music, and Andrew quietly slips out of the room and makes his way toward the Office of Arms located in Bedford Tower, where the Jewels were now stored in a safe."

Andrew's figure in front of Elias veered sharply right into the next unlit corridor and then turned left. Just as he was about to ascend the stairs of Bedford Tower, he halted at a large door set to the left. He cast a knowing glance at the door before continuing onward.

Together they walked until they reached the same door that had almost diverted Andrew on his way to the jewels and stopped in front of it. The door was now large and made of sturdy material, with a modern keypad positioned to the side. This was the strong room, known for being highly secure and nearly impossible to breach.

Had the Jewels been hidden there at the time of the heist, Andrew's mission would have undoubtedly failed, and the British would still possess the Jewels today, just as they do now, along with all the other artifacts stored in Dublin Castle at the time apart from the Jewels themselves.

Ava carried on with their theory. Her eyes scanned the length of the door.

"The Jewels were meant to be stored in the brand-new, state-of-the-art, strong room that had been built by the vicar to keep them safe. But due to some intervention by the Order, they had measured incorrectly and the safe didn't fit, so they were placed into the Office of Arms instead."

Elias crossed his arms over his chest and thoughtfully gazed down the length of the door that led to a room beneath the castle. "Thanks to Lord Michaels' recommendation, the Order was able to assign one of their own to the project of constructing the strong room under the guise of a carpenter. A carpenter who misjudged the amount of space needed to store the safe containing the Jewels and ended up providing the construction crew with incorrect measurements, which forced the vicar to place them in the only mildly secure room in the castle: his personal library, the Office of Arms in Bedford Tower.

"Thinking out loud here, Andrew was lucky the vicar was not clever enough to keep a guard stationed at the door to the tower during his parties. That could have caused a serious issue," Elias remarked. Ava agreed.

"I'd push that further and argue the Order was very fortunate that a man like the vicar was even appointed as the custodian of the crown jewels in the first place. He was neither wise nor responsible. Essentially, all of his dirty laundry was aired after the jewels went missing, and he was promptly sacked following the investigation."

They turned to ascend the stairs of the tower, passing a few tourists. There were fewer steps than most people expected at this point in their tours. Bedford Tower was only two stories high, but as Elias noted, that had worked in Andrew's favor.

Pausing their conversation halfway up, they waited until they were nearly alone on the steps before continuing. Andrew's ghostly figure, however, trotted up the stairs swiftly, unable to wait for them to catch up.

"The key was the next step in the heist," Ava went on. "The vicar's office was not secured, but the safe was and had only one key, which he kept on his person at all times. That is where I always struggled. How did he get the key?" Ava asked, glancing over at Elias thoughtfully.

He had an answer, thanks to his little book.

"The first key was notably in his inner pocket once the police arrived that night, but the second key wasn't found till the following week by a groundskeeper outside by the eastern wing. I'm assuming Andrew mastered the art of pickpocketing in his time preparing for this and managed to snag the second key upon his arrival when he greeted the vicar."

Elias wiggled his fingers in the air. Ava bit her lip, thinking this theory through.

"That or Bridget could have also. After all, she would have received a warmer greeting, making it perhaps easier for her."

The imaginary figure of Andrew appeared at the top of the stairs, hesitating before the set of double doors, as if lost in thought. Sweat trickled visibly down the side of his face as he placed his hat on his head, tied his cloak to ensure a swift escape, and briefly glanced over his shoulder at them before grasping the golden knobs on the forest green doors labeled with the letters O. A.

"Possibly. Anyway, Andrew reaches the Office of Arms and opens the door—"

"And all hell breaks loose."

Chapter Twenty-four

1907, DUBLIN, IRELAND

Sweat gathered on Andrew's brow as he approached the double doors he had only inspected a few times before.

Downstairs, Bridget's piano music floated up to him, shifting from a haunting, eerie ballad to a lively, upbeat tune that he was sure had most of the crowd on their feet. Finding reassurance in her music, Andrew glanced over his shoulder one last time, placed his hands on the doorknobs, and pushed open the doors to the Office of Arms.

Sirens came alive, emitting a wailing noise that would normally have made Andrew cover his ears to shield himself from the terrible sound. But Andrew didn't have the luxury of time. He expected the sirens to be triggered by the safe doors, not the doors to the Office. Now he was running out of time.

Quickly, Andrew stepped into the room and made his way around the giant glass-encased safe that held the Jewels. The safe was over half the size of the room created in the shape of a hexagon and sealed with gold trimmings at both the top and the bottom. He ran to where the door to the safe sat, pausing only briefly to dig his gloved hand into his suit pocket and pull out the long silver key.

Andrew thrust the key forward into the lock and turned the handle until he heard a significant click. The glass before him popped forward, releasing itself from the confinement of the tight seal.

Without delay, he entered the safe and flung open his satchel, unlocking the box within, then very carefully turned to pick up the Jewels and gently place them into the padded compartments of his own portable safe hidden in his leather bag.

One by one, he packed each piece into his bag, locked it, and threw the leather-bound cover over the artifacts he now carried.

A commotion started downstairs, and Bridget's music had noticeably stopped. Now was the moment to make a run for it. Andrew sprang out of the safe and nearly flew down the stairs in a rush, making sure he wouldn't be caught with nowhere to hide.

He had just reached the bottom of the stairs when the sound of footsteps echoing down the hall reached his ears. Trying to stay calm, Andrew sharply turned left out of the open door of the castle into the garden, where an old woman sat on a bench, looking around bewildered—Mrs. Rugford, a woman of high class who usually attended these events with her grandson and was known to be out of her wits.

She was the perfect disguise.

Whipping off his hat and satchel in a hurry, he threw them high up onto a branch in the tree above, out of sight for now. Andrew then sat beside the woman and took her hand in his, ready to play his part.

The old lady turned to him now and smiled as if they had been lifelong friends.

Andrew barely knew her.

"Hello, deary," she cooed sweetly. Andrew smiled openly at her, just as three men approached the garden's entrance. Two large dogs on leashes accompanied the first man, baring their teeth and growling fiercely. Drool dripped from their mouths and flung onto the ground as the dogs fixed their gaze on Andrew and his new-found partner in crime.

Andrew stared at the vicious beasts and found his façade now cracking just slightly.

He had not been informed about the dogs.

The two men with the dogs were breathing heavily as they came to a stop outside the garden and turned their attention to the pair. The third man, however, didn't stay and frantically ran upward from where Andrew had just come from.

The dogs sniffed the air briefly and began barking, standing on their hind legs, but their owner restrained them.

"Quiet, Rosche!" he scolded, then turned to Andrew.

"Aye, either of you see anybody run out of the tower there?" he asked gruffly.

"Why yes, sir, a very good-looking young man fled the tower just moments ago, in fact!" Mrs. Rugford said, cutting off Andrew's response.

Andrew froze in his seat.

"Where'd he go?"

The little old lady pointed back in the direction of the castle that led them back into the state rooms. "Lovely lad, wasn't he hon? He went back into the ballroom to join the party. I think he liked the music," she said sweetly.

The men glanced at each other briefly, and Andrew didn't blame them.

The lady was mad.

The dogs began barking again, and it took everything in Andrew not to look upward at his satchel hanging in the tree.

"Back into the ballroom, ya say?"

This time, Andrew answered. "Yes, sir, I think he meant to slip past you through the crowd," he explained.

The first man yanked again on the leashes of the dogs, who were getting more worked up by the minute and gave a curt whistle to quiet them down. "Enough. Both a ya!" he hollered, frustrated now. "And whater you two doin all the way out here, then, huh?"

"Just getting Granny here some fresh air," he told them. Mrs. Rugford leaned over and pinched the side of his cheek adoringly.

"Can't you hear the alarms going off? The party's over, take your granny and get out a here!" the second man snapped.

"Aye. Come, Frances, the police are on their way, maybe we can head him off at the front," and with that, the two men retreated into the castle, dragging the two vicious beasts away with them.

Andrew watched the men leave, relieved that neither of them was someone he recognized. The vicar, however, who was now upstairs at the top of the tower, shouting shrieks that competed with the wailing of the sirens, certainly would be. If Andrew didn't get out of there quickly, he would be responsible for ruining the entire operation.

Andrew turned and patted Mrs. Rugford's hand gently and stood, grabbing his belongings from the tree as quickly as he could. He tipped his hat to the woman and began to make his way hastily toward the single black coach that awaited him in the darkness, far from the other drivers.

"Mrs. Rugford, thank you for your services," he said jokingly.

But the old bat chuckled and replied, "Anytime you want to cause trouble, you know where to find me, deary."

Chapter Twenty-five

Modern-day Pittsburgh, Pennsylvania

Elias

Ava stared out the window of the plane as they touched down in Pittsburgh the following afternoon. They had both tried to sleep on the flights but to little avail. He looked over at her, now oblivious to his staring.

Elias had used the time he spent awake on the plane to go over the events of the last twenty-four hours in his head. There was a lot to process.

Both he and Ava had been a little shaken up by the time they arrived back in Dublin that night. But it was the image of Ava running straight into the fire, without a second thought, to rescue someone she barely knew, that had imprinted on Elias's mind.

The kind of courage that took, the sort of kindness and bravery she had shown in that moment was something to admire. Not many people were like that. Not many people put others first in the way she had. He found himself quite stunned by her now as he continued to watch her.

Ava had been quiet, he had noticed, since they had boarded their connecting flight in Boston. And that had surprised him. For an ordinarily chatty girl, she had kept to herself most of the trip. He suspected he could chock it up to her simply being tired.

Still, there was something telling him that she was acting differently for a reason. He followed her gaze out the window to the bright city, decked out in black and gold, and considered what could be bothering her.

Once they made it off the plane, the pair hightailed it to baggage and then got an Uber toward Ava's family home. The drive was about forty-five minutes outside the city, farther from the bright lights and the one-way chaos of Pittsburgh. The neighborhood they pulled up to was in the suburbs northwest of the city. The houses around them were sprawled out evenly and separated by large luminous trees.

Elias wouldn't admit it, but he was thrilled that it was much warmer in Pittsburgh than it had been in Ireland. Though he loved the cold little island, every once in a while, it was nice to let his blood thaw out.

The car pulled up to a quaint little two-story house with blue shutters and matching trim. Ava took a breath and smiled slightly before stepping out of the car.

Elias grabbed their luggage from the trunk, and then followed her inside. At first glance, it looked like no one was home, which was a relief to Elias. But it only took a few seconds for all that to change.

"Knock, knock," Ava said, shutting the front door behind him. She had just barely enough time to set down her purse when a child came running out of the other room, full speed ahead, and crashed into Ava. She had apparently expected it, though, and had opened her arms in just enough time to catch the brown-skinned boy. She stood up and pulled him into a tight hug as he giggled into her hair.

Elias took a step back and watched everything unfold.

"Ava!"

"Ooh, Ryker! Look how big you've gotten! Holy cow, you must be seven feet by now!" Ava set the boy down, who shook his head at her playfully and shrugged.

"I said that too, but the school nurse said I'm only four foot seven this year. Of course, I don't believe her, though, because I finally passed up Mary Keepler in my class, and she's close to six foot two!"

"Sorry, kiddo, but Nurse Tara doesn't usually lie about these things," Ava said, bending down to plant her hands on her knees so she could talk to him properly. The boy, Ryker, made a face and scrunched up his nose at her as if he didn't like her answer.

"Hey, at least you're tall enough now to ride the Jack Rabbit at Kennywood, right?" The little boy started to jump up and down in excitement.

"Right!"

A tall man in his mid-forties with the same brown skin and short black hair walked into the room with a large smile. His eyes were a light brown similar to Elias's own. Scruff decorated his jawline, graying in parts. His deep laugh echoed in the room as he approached.

Ava stood and beamed up at the man who walked right past Elias and wrapped her up in a giant bear hug. He held her there for a moment before taking a step back to look her over as if he hadn't seen her in years.

"Ava. It's been too long. We have missed you around here."

"You have no idea how much I've missed being here. I have so much to tell you!" she said, and her face lit up in the same way Elias had noticed it had when they were in the graveyard, and she had put the letters together to form the next clue. It was a contagious look of pride and excitement, and Elias couldn't help but smile a bit to himself, knowing full well she intended to tell this man all about her time in the Emerald Isle.

"You're not the only one."

A female voice entered the conversation. A little girl walked into the kitchen, followed by a woman who chose to stay back for a moment, leaning against the door frame of the entryway and watching.

The man who had been hugging Ava looked over his shoulder, smile still in place, and stepped back to join the woman, who Elias assumed was his wife, at the entryway.

The little girl slowly ran up to her as Ava fell to the floor and wrapped her up in her arms. Her hand brought the little girl's cream, bald head to her shoulder, and she closed her eyes as they embraced. Elias's smile faded as he watched the interaction. A single tear fell from Ava's eye as she held onto the little girl for dear life.

The little girl was different than the three people he had already seen; she was very clearly not related as she was of Asian descent, and these people were clearly not.

But then again, Ava wasn't either of those nationalities, which left Elias a bit confused, but he ultimately decided it didn't matter; Ava clearly loved these people, and they loved her, and that was all he needed to know.

Ava took a deep breath to steady herself and pulled back to look the little girl in the eyes. She was smiling widely at Ava while Ava was watching her intently as if to memorize every single detail of her face. "Hey, baby girl, how ya doin'?" she asked. The little girl shrugged and kept her eyes glued on Ava.

"Okay. I have trouble breathing sometimes, but Millie says it's just because I'm using my powers too much."

Ava's eyes widened in mock surprise. She looked up at the woman who stepped forward and then back at the little girl still in her arms. "Magic powers! Since when do you have magic powers?" The little girl giggled and held up her hands.

"The nurse told me when I was getting my blood drawn at the hospital last week."

The woman with long dark braids held back in a bright pink headband stepped forward and put her hands on the girl's shoulders. "Juliana was coloring pictures for other kids in the ward, and they told her she has special powers that make people happy wherever she goes," the woman explained.

"And they sure were right, huh, Jules? Did you tell her what you and Ryker have been working on since?"

Juliana shook her head, which held a yellow and blue bow around it and giggled. "We've been making get-well cards for the people in the hospital."

"And thank-you cards for the nurses!" Ryker said, and he stepped up to be a part of the action, but his dad pulled him back to him gently. Ava looked back and forth between the two kids and clapped.

"Wow, that's awesome, guys! I'm sure they absolutely love that! That is so kind of you!"

"My cards have flowers on them," Juliana told her.

"And my cards have superheroes!" Ryker said. He pulled away from his father's grasp to make a swift karate chop in the air before him. Ava laughed, shook her head, and stood up.

"So cool. You guys are so creative."

The woman nodded, still smiling, and looked down at the two children. "Hey, why don't you guys go finish the cards you were working on so we can talk to Ava and her friend for a second?"

For the first time, the little girl turned around and tilted her head all the way up to look at Elias with a smile. Ava watched the two interact. She wrung her hands out as if nervous about his presence suddenly, so Elias smiled back at her in an effort to soothe her. Then he turned his smile to the child before him. "Is he your new boyfriend, Ava?"

Ava's smile dropped, and she looked back at Juliana in shock. "Good Lord, no! When have you ever known me to bring a boyfriend home? Jules, go get your cards. I'll come find you in a little bit. I promise!"

Elias let a snicker escape, but when Ava shot him a look, he straightened and covered it with a cough.

"Okay!" Jules said and turned to grab Ryker's hand and pull him out the door.

Ryker rolled his eyes at her and jokingly said, "She drags me everywhere!" And then they were gone, leaving the four adults in the kitchen.

Ava shook her head and let a smile return to her face as the woman stepped forward to embrace her. She gently rocked her from side to side before dropping a quick kiss on her forehead and stepping back. The man in the background had shifted his gaze to Elias with narrow eyes.

Elias shifted and straightened his stance to seem presentable. He didn't have a reason to try and impress the man, but he knew things would be easier on the two of them if he did.

"My darling Ava. Look at you! Ah, sweet girl, you are just what this house needed. A little bit of sunshine."

Ava beamed and kept her hand held tightly with the woman's, then stepped back.

"Yeah, I'm always sunshine and daisies. Especially at seven thirty in the morning," Ava said, then shifted her gaze to Elias. He lifted his jaw and gave her a small smile, acknowledging her. She moved to stand beside him. "Guys, this is Elias Cassedy."

Elias stepped forward and shook the woman's hand first before getting a firm squeeze from the woman's husband. Elias could feel a slight bit of tension emanating from the man but wasn't quite sure why. He eventually settled on the idea that he was just protective of Ava, which Elias could understand.

Despite the fact that he couldn't pursue any type of feelings or relationship with Ava, even if he wanted to, it didn't mean he was blind. Hattie was right on the money when she had said the girl was stunning, and Elias knew it especially after he caught her in her towel.

"He's my Expeditions Advisor. Elias, this is Millie and Eamon McKenna. They are my family."

The two looked over at him expectedly. Millie with a smile, Eamon with a perked eyebrow.

Millie was beautiful with the same dark skin as her husband and son if not a shade lighter. Her smile was warm and welcoming, her chocolate eyes gave off a calming presence Elias couldn't ignore. She was someone who immediately made people feel cared for just like Hattie always did for her travelers at the inn.

Elias instantly liked her based on that similarity alone. He turned and nodded casually in their direction.

"It's a pleasure to meet you both," Elias replied, giving them genuine smiles. Millie, oblivious to her husband's apparent uncertainty about Elias, seemed thrilled to have him.

"It's so nice to meet you, too! Ava has told me so much about you! She was so excited to get to work with you guys; I hope she is behaving herself."

Elias chuckled, and Ava scowled.

"I'm always on my best behavior, thank you. I am an adult, you know."

"Are you?" Eamon asked, taking his eyes off Elias, who finally let out the breath he had been holding in since the two had made eye contact.

"I couldn't remember. It's been so long since you graced us with your presence."

Elias noticed Millie trying to hide it as her smile faded, and she tapped her husband's arm lightly as if to say *not now*. He looked at her with a raised eyebrow but listened to whatever his wife was trying to tell him. Elias realized there was something clearly going on here that they didn't want to get into with him there and figured maybe it would be a good time for him to excuse himself.

"Millie, do you have a restroom I could use?"

Millie snapped out of whatever fog hovered between her husband, Ava, and herself and turned on her smile again. "Oh, of course!" Millie turned to Ava and motioned to the back door. Eamon's face suddenly dropped in quiet concern as if he had anticipated what was going to happen before Millie even said anything.

"I'm so sorry. I'm sure you both are jet-lagged. Ava, why don't you take him back to the apartment and get him settled in? You two can get your rest, and I'll cook up something special for dinner at five. How does that sound?" Ava nodded, and Eamon just watched everything unfold with wide eyes and pursed his lips.

"Yeah, that would be amazing. Then I was thinking I'd take Elias into the city tonight. Mark Fitzpatrick is playing at the Emerald Ale, so I figured I'd show him around town."

"Oh, I'm sure you'll enjoy him, Elias; he's quite the show, I hear. Yes, get some rest, you two, and we'll see you for supper. Oh, and Ava?"

Ava picked up her backpack, and Elias picked up the luggage, following suit. "You and I will have a discussion about you-know-what sometime before you leave this week, ya hear?"

Millie's tone said it wasn't a question. Whatever it was they needed to talk about was something serious enough that she was demanding it in a motherly tone, and yet something Ava seemed to know needed to happen. She nodded in understanding before shuffling out the back door, and leading Elias into the back yard toward a quaint little shed.

Chapter Twenty-Six

1907, Glendalough, Ireland

The carriage ride had been long and stressful for Terrance. He kept weighing the pros and cons of helping Master Lynch escape Dublin Castle. He knew what awaited him if they were eventually caught. Jail time, an unfair trial, no doubt, and most likely death. He also knew that helping Master Lynch meant a consistent job, which he needed to support his family and earn good money for his loyalty. He had accepted the position as the Lynches' coach driver despite the rumors that they were part of the rebellion. So, to some extent, he had expected this.

The horses drove the coach up alongside a long, old stone wall. Eventually, it brought them to an archway of stone, sealed with an iron gate. A single lantern was lit on the left side. Terrance sat and waited.

His anxiety grew in the dead of night, with nothing but silence and the horses purring to accompany his thoughts. Finally, a hooded figure stepped out from behind the gate. He never lifted his hood or showed a light on his face for safety purposes. Instead, he simply held his staff still and said in a deep voice, "Are you blessed, me friend?"

Master Lynch had indeed provided him with the proper response. So, Terrance tipped his hat at the man and replied, "The road rises to meet me, sir."

The man didn't nod or remove his hood. He didn't say anything, either. He simply and slowly walked back to his seat, hiding behind the wall among the bushes, and let the gate swing open.

Terrance gently whipped the reins, and the horses guided them again through the old monastery's path back into the dark. Surrounded by the old graves and more large trees, Terrance's heart raced as a new fear crept in.

They followed the winding path through the creepy graveyard until they came to an old cottage lit by multiple lanterns and torch fires. A few men in monk attire and a few in regular clothing awaited them.

Terrance brought the horses to a stop. Without a second thought, he jumped down and intended to open the door to the coach for Master Lynch, but he got out before Terrance could get to him. Terrance sucked in a breath.

"Master Lynch! I am so terribly sorry, I was slow."

The man waved him off again, kind as before, and shook his head, his satchel tucked carefully beneath his arm still. "Not at all, boy. You were fine. I just have urgent business to attend to. Come."

Terrance checked on the horses, then followed the master toward the men. The man in the middle of the solemn group was an elderly monk, twice the age of the others. He donned burlap robes and wool shoes. He was balding in the middle, and the only hair left on the top of his head was white. He stepped forward.

"Andrew."

He looked as anxious as Terrance felt. Andrew stuck out his hand, and the man took it in both of his with a concerned look. "You made it back safely. We worried you had come into some trouble."

He shook his head triumphantly. "Not a chance, Abram. Everything went swimmingly. I was able to get in and out relatively undetected, and my good man Terrance played his part well." Lynch reached back and clapped Terrance on the back. He was so surprised he actually jolted forward from the force. Terrance straightened his hat while Lynch smiled back at him.

"Thank you, sir."

"In fact, I would back the decision to induct him, should the question arise if he be worthy!" said Andrew Lynch.

The old monk nodded and sighed as if tired. Terrance seemed to notice that even though their plan had been a success, Abram was still unable to wash the concern from his face. "We may discuss that later. For now, Terrance, please follow Ashton to the stables to attend to the horses."

Terrance, knowing his primary loyalty was to Master Lynch and not the old monk, glanced in his direction.

"Do as he says, Terrance. Abram is of mighty importance around here. Before you go, though—" Andrew reached out and grasped Terrance's hand firmly.

Terrance's eyes widened as he felt the coolness of sterling sitting in his palm. Terrance released his hand and held it out to inspect the currency with a bit of shock. He had expected to be compensated well, but hadn't expected this much.

"Sir?"

"Thank you, my friend. I look forward to working with you in the future," he said. Ashton stepped forward and ushered him away.

Andrew turned toward Abram.

"I assume you were successful then?"

Andrew smiled mischievously and pulled out the satchel from under his cloak. Abram's face showed only the slightest sign of relief. He held out his hands and took the satchel from Andrew.

"And the boy? Does he know of the crime you have committed?"

Andrew looked back toward where Terrance had disappeared into the dark. He squinted, pondering this for a second, before simply shrugging his shoulders. "I'm sure he has an idea, but he has nothing to confirm or deny his own theories."

The old monk nodded; the sagging skin on his chin bounced as he did, and he turned to walk in the other direction. "Very well, then. It's probably for the better until he is cleared. No life lost that way."

Andrew agreed. He liked Terrance. He saw real potential in him. Seeing Abram beginning to disappear from his place into the dark, Andrew, still dressed in his finest suit and hat, ran up to catch him. "Abram, wait a moment!"

Abram didn't stop for him, though, and instead kept walking. "Has he returned yet?" Andrew asked, concern showing on his face. Abram barely glanced his way as he kept up his stride.

"No, but my sources tell me he should be back soon, if not tonight. You should go get your sleep, Andrew. We have much to do in the morn—"

But before he could finish his sentence, a quiet birdlike sound pierced through the night. To anyone out this early in the morning, they would assume it was just the sound of night, animals rustling about. But Andrew knew it was a message to the Order. Someone was arriving at the gate. Andrew stopped dead in his tracks and looked back down the path he had come from. He was here.

Abram had stopped, too, to look back in that direction. He didn't waste much time on the siren, though, and waved his hands off to Andrew before continuing on.

"Don't stay up too late, Andrew. Our work is just beginning!"

Andrew let him fade into the night without a second thought this time. A second black coach led by two beautiful, deep brown horses pulled up to a stop in front of the old cottage. Andrew didn't waste any time walking back to meet the coach.

He had just stepped into the light when a man his height stepped out of the carriage. He was dressed in a fine black suit and cloak with a top hat. He had sandy blond hair and dark brown eyes. His face and frame were a little thinner than Andrews, but that aside, they were identical. The man turned to him finally, and Andrew relaxed for the first time since the man had left. "Elijah." He smiled.

Elijah smiled back and leaned forward to clap him on the back. "Brother." The two exchanged a quick hug and each stepped back to look at his twin at arm's length. Andrew subconsciously looked Elijah over for cuts or bruises, while Elijah's eyes searched for something else.

"Did you get it?" Elijah asked. Andrew nodded with a smile.

"Abram is putting them somewhere safe. Did you have any trouble?" he asked his brother anxiously.

"Not a bit. No one suspected a thing. I did run into an old fling of yours, though. *That* was unbearable. Thank God Celene was there to usher her away." He laughed, and Andrew laughed with him.

"Marjorie, ah, yes. I honestly don't know what I was thinking when I entertained her all those years ago."

Elijah shook his head with a smile. "In the future, brother, allow me to set you up with a woman. I have much better taste in these things than you, after all."

Elijah was silent as they walked for a moment, then he slid his brother another mischievous smile and said, "Ya know, Bridget's not a bad catch."

Andrew shook his head, his face mimicking that of his brother, and put his hand on Elijah's shoulders to direct him toward their bunkers, hidden back into the woods. "In another life, perhaps. For the future, though, make sure it is indeed a woman and not a man, will you? We may be identical, but our tastes are not entirely the same."

Elijah chuckled to himself as they walked, finally feeling safe now that he and his brother were reunited. As they walked through the yard, they passed a newer grave set off to the side of the path amid several other gravestones.

The stone read:

Elijah Mattheus Lynch
Beloved Brother
1883–1905

Chapter Twenty–Seven

Modern-day Pittsburgh, Pennsylvania

Elias

The inside of the shed was designed to look like a tiny home. The entrance was across from a countertop with a sink, oven, and microwave all along the wall. Off to the left was a small olive-green couch facing a small TV that was mounted toward the top of the wall. On the right side was an upstairs loft with a queen bed and a ladder leading down the side. The loft opened into a full bath with a small shower, toilet, and sink. The smallest barn-style sliding door Elias had ever seen had been left open so he could see into the bathroom.

Everything was either cream, brown, or olive green, which made the place feel more spacious than it was. He was impressed. For Ava, it seemed perfect.

"You live here?" he asked. He looked around at the space, trying to figure out where to put the bags.

Ava sheepishly smiled at him as she took her bags from him. She walked over to the wall that held the ladder to the loft, opened a door on the side, and gently placed her bags in there. "Yeah, Eamon built it for me a couple years ago so I could have my own space when I was home from school and to make more room for Jules's stuff."

Elias nodded. That made sense. He was sure she had some medical equipment in her room, and it would be hard to fit Ava and her stuff in there with all that equipment as well. Her condition seemed to be the elephant in the room, which Ava was not quite willing to acknowledge.

She walked past him and pulled the couch out into a full bed. She opened a drawer underneath the mattress, pulled out some sheets, a blanket, and a pillow, and laid them on the couch before him.

"The bathroom's right over there; feel free to wash up if needed. There are towels and shampoo in the cabinet beside the mirror, you'll see. Otherwise, I'm going to rest for a bit before dinner if that's okay. You're more than welcome to watch TV—the remote's on the desk beside the bed—or sleep as well, but we will probably want to be ready to go about four thirty if you're up for going out to the pub tonight?"

Elias nodded. "Sure." His eyes felt heavy, too, and he stifled a yawn. At this point, it was pretty clear, at least to him, that he was captive to whatever Ava wanted to do, at least until their meeting with the Carnegie museum director. The fact was, he was in her territory, and therefore, she had the advantage. However, some rest would be good, he agreed, but only after a shower, for sure.

After Ava climbed up into the loft and snuggled so deep into the blankets that Elias could no longer see her, he jumped into the tiny shower. He cleaned up a bit and then stretched out on the pullout couch.

When the alarm on his phone went off at four, Elias got up only to find Ava already awake and reading in her loft. She had already changed, cleaned up, and gotten ready for the night ahead, so Elias grabbed his clothes and took his bag into the bathroom to change. He threw on a plain black t-shirt and jeans and cleaned up his hair from sleep, but by the time he stepped out, Ava was already gone.

He met her on the porch of the small unit, which had a white fence and a little porch swing. Ava closed her book when he exited and looked up at him. She looked a little different to him here in Pittsburgh, almost as if she had a natural glow that she didn't seem to have back in Ireland. She was wearing a casual white sweater with black stripes and jeans. Her chocolate-brown locks hung loosely around her shoulders under a black ballcap that had a golden *P* on the front.

"Ready to go? Millie made a roast and potatoes for us! I haven't had her cooking in ages, but it's amazing!" she exclaimed. She stood up and picked up her worn black jacket from the swing.

Elias was excited, too, at the thought of a home-cooked meal. Other than when he went to visit Hattie, he never really got anything home-cooked. "Whenever you are," he said and followed her inside.

Dinner was different than what he was used to, and for that, he was grateful. Though his sister was able to cook pretty well, she wasn't nearly as talented as Hattie or Millie. And most of his dinners these days were either spent with Lottie or by himself. It had been a long time since he had had a sit-down meal with anyone younger than the age of ten, and here he was with two children who were eager to officially meet him and ask him any and every question they could think of. It definitely wasn't his norm, but he didn't really mind. They were both great kids, and he found them to be rather entertaining with their questions.

After dinner, Elias thanked Millie for her hospitality. He followed Ava out to a bright blue Honda Civic she had hidden under an old tarp. About a half hour later, they entered the city, where Ava led him to a little Irish pub on the corner with the words *The Emerald Ale* hanging above the doorway.

The place was decently packed; every seat at the bar was taken, and there were high tables scattered across the room—all occupied. Elias scanned the space for a place to sit when Ava suddenly snagged his hand and dragged him into the pub. She slithered through the crowd like a pro and managed to grab a small high table in the back just as an older couple was leaving.

It was a perfect spot, really, close enough to the musicians in the corner that they could hear the pub songs but far enough in the back that they could also engage in conversation if they wanted to. That was precisely what Elias had planned to do. She had brought him into her world willingly, and now he had some questions. This quiet version of Ava was a little unsettling to him, and he needed to change that.

Ava waved over a waitress who wiped down the table for them and asked for drink orders. Elias cut Ava off before she could order and asked for two shots of Jameson to start. Ava sat back and looked at him, surprised, but a smile played at the corner of her lips.

"Why'd you do that?" she asked. Elias shrugged, smiled, and leaned back in his chair as the waitress returned with their shot glasses.

The way the room was set up had the musicians playing directly in front of them, so their chairs were side by side, closer than Elias was expecting, rather than across the table from one another. In this proximity, he could practically feel her excitement buzzing from her.

"New town, why not?"

"Can I get yinz anything else?"

Elias picked up the menu with the beers on draft. He pointed to a few he had never had that were local, but Ava shook her head and readdressed the waitress for them.

"He'll take a Yingling, and I'll take a Jameson and ginger ale."

"A Yingling and one dirty ginger. Got it!"

Elias watched the girl leave, and his eyes narrowed in suspicion. He had never let anyone order his drinks before, let alone this woman. He slid his gaze back to her with accusing eyes.

"That better be good, or you're paying."

Ava snickered in a way that made him feel uneasy and looked down at her full shot glass before shaking her head at him. "You'll like it, I'm sure of it. Besides, new town . . . as you said, why not? So, what are we toasting to?"

Elias raised an eyebrow at her. "You don't need to give a toast for every shot, ya know."

She reached over and elbowed him playfully. "Of course you do. That's why each language has its own version of it."

The waitress returned with a bottle for Elias and a short glass for Ava. Elias took a sip of the beer; it had a malty, sort of amber taste to it, and Elias decided she was right. He would be sure to trust her regarding his drinks in the future. "Oh, really?"

"Yes, the Italians say *salute!* The Greeks say *stin ygeia sas!* The English say *cheers!*"

He rolled the neck of the bottle in his hands around between his thumb and forefinger. "And the Irish?"

Ava got a mischievous twinkle in her eye. "*Sláinte!*" She held up her shot glass, and Elias clinked it with his.

"To our next adventure. *Sláinte!*" he said, and they each threw back a shot. Ava made a face as she set her empty glass down on the table. Elias shook his head at her, grinning.

"You literally ordered a drink with Jameson in it, but you can't take the shot?"

Ava rolled her eyes at him, then tossed back a gulp of her drink as a chaser. "It's masked by the ginger ale," she explained.

"Tsk! Tsk!" Then Elias took a breath, leaned his forearms on the table, and began to swirl the neck of his bottle around again. "Alright, so are we going to talk about the elephant in the room?"

"Which one? Your God complex or your ability to leave every room you are in looking like a tornado swept through it?" she asked, blinking up at him innocently.

He dropped his jaw. "What? I don't have a God complex." Ava raised her eyebrows, teasing him, and looked away dramatically. "And I keep my things tidy, thank you!"

She looked back at him like he had two heads. "Did you make your bed before we left?" she asked.

Elias looked away as he thought about it, then he snapped his mouth shut. They both knew he hadn't. Ava laughed and turned to check out the musicians who had just stepped up onto the stage. "No, I meant the McKennas," said Elias.

Ava, who had been watching the band set up, turned back to him, a questioning look on her face. She leaned her elbow on the table, rested her chin on her hand, and used the other to take another sip of whiskey.

"Don't get me wrong, your family is . . . wonderful, but . . ."

Ava refocused on her lap, a little nervous. Elias's playful smile had faded as well as he waited patiently for her. He had decided, though, after seeing this simple response from her, that he wouldn't push her for details if she didn't want to share, but after a second, she sat up straight and answered him.

"Ah, I was wondering when you were going to ask," she said as she mindlessly played with a napkin on the table. She refused eye contact with him after that. He watched her intently. She took another big breath and seemed to sag into her chair. She looked away from him and spoke.

"My dad left when I was eighteen, so right before my freshman year. Before that, it was only him, my mom, and me. We were happy, or at least I thought we were, but then, one day, he was gone. I had been at school, and my mom was at work when he just spontaneously packed up all his stuff and disappeared in the middle of the day. He never came back."

Ava returned to the napkin and took another drink.

Elias was curious to know more. "Did he say anything?"

She shook her head. "No, just left a note saying he couldn't stay any longer. And that was that. We never saw him again. After that, my mom decided to foster a child. That's how Juliana came into our lives. She was only two or so when we met her, and we fell head over heels from the get-go. My mom adopted her shortly after. And life was good . . . for a bit."

Ava took another sip, and Elias noticed her glass getting low, so he motioned for the waitress to grab another round in hopes it would relieve her stress. Ava thanked the girl who brought her a second drink, and Elias shook his head when she asked if he was ready for another.

"Then, three years ago, my mom was in a car accident."

Elias took a breath and pulled his eyes away from her. She deserved to tell this with some privacy, so he took a swig of his beer.

Ava stared blankly at the space before them, her voice monotone as she recounted the last couple years of her life.

"She was hit by a drunk driver going seventy-five miles an hour. She never saw it coming." Her voice trailed off, lost in her tortured memories. Elias didn't know what to say.

"I'm sorry, Ava," he whispered. Instead of watching her, he watched her hands play with the curled-up napkin still on the table.

"Millie and Eamon took in Juliana and they swore to watch over me, but I was already a legal adult by then. They had been lifelong friends of my parents so I had known them growing up," she explained. "After that, I dove head-first into my studies. Then, a couple years ago, Juliana was diagnosed with cancer."

This time, Elias stared at the beer in his hand. He had known the diagnosis was coming, but hearing it attached to a string of losses somehow made it worse. This girl had been through the ringer in the last several years. Even one of these events was terrible enough, but it was like a never-ending domino effect for her. One trauma right after the next, each one stealing away someone she loved. Elias shook his head mindlessly, trying not to let the pity he felt show on his face.

Elias considered himself lucky. He had only suffered through the loss of his mom, and that was bad enough, but his entire family being picked off one by one? He had no idea how she did it, how she forced herself to tackle each day with a positive attitude and a smile on her face.

"Millie told me a couple months ago, right before I took this internship, that they are running out of funds—and treatment methods. Nothing is really working right now, and she's slowing down. That's part of the reason I was so eager to get started. Was for . . ."

"The money," Elias finished, and his eyes widened slightly, though Ava never looked up at him to notice.

His heart dropped, leaving a sour taste in his mouth and a pain in the pit of his stomach. Of course she needed the money. Of course she was counting on that to save her sister. Elias wanted to smack his palm against his forehead in this awful bit of luck, but he didn't want to draw her attention to him. Ava turned to him anyway, clasped her hands together in a praying motion, and began to explain.

"I know that's not the answer you were hoping for . . . you were right to question my intentions in the beginning, but I swear, the money is only a bonus. I really do care about my work here."

There was absolutely no reason she needed to explain herself to him, especially for that. There was a big difference between the people he had worked with in the past who were less than worthy of this internship and Ava.

She finally locked eyes with him; her green eyes hid tears along their rims that she refused to unleash. Elias sat up straighter and shook his head animatedly.

"You do not have to apologize for wanting to save your sister, Ava. Any decent human could understand your reasoning, and it's very apparent you love what you do for the museum. That's all I really need to know for this to go smoothly for us. I could care less what made you sign up."

Ava gave him another sheepish smile, took a sip of her drink, and then looked back down at her hands. "Hattie said you would understand, considering your mom and all."

He stopped and jerked his head. His startled chocolate-brown eyes collided with hers. She looked back at him innocently and waited patiently for him to respond.

Ava had caught him off guard. He didn't know how, but somehow, she had figured out who Hattie was. Elias suddenly felt very exposed, and he didn't like it, nor did he know how to handle it. Especially since she had just shared her deepest, darkest scars with him, part of him felt as if he owed it to her to admit his truth, or part of it anyway.

"I—Hattie told you?" he asked, a little flabbergasted.

Ava slowly shook her head and looked toward the bar before returning to look at him. "She told me of her sister who passed from cancer, and I put two and two together."

Elias's eyes skated around the table for a bit, uneasy before landing back on her.

"I hope you don't think of me as dense," she laughed, and Elias faked a smile. But Ava seemed to be able to tell that he was a little bit on edge, so she continued. "You're the spitting image of the boy in the photo with her. Plus, I figured Hattie had to be related to you somehow, considering the way she talks about you."

He decided the best reaction to this news was to refrain from reacting. So he looked at his beer and sat back instead, taking in all the information he had just gotten and what she had confessed. It was a lot.

"I'm sorry about your mom."

He appreciated her sympathy but didn't want to dwell on the past. Elias looked back at her without showing any emotion. He waved the bartender over for another round. Screw it. How could he possibly lie himself out of this one anyway?

"Thank you. It was a long time ago. I was thirteen." He paused for a second, then looked back at her sternly. "So, you know, no one at the museum knows that Hattie and I are related, and I would like to keep it that way if you don't mind."

Ava tilted her head, not understanding. He could appreciate her uncertainty. Hattie was such a gem and so loved by everyone that it wouldn't make sense to an average person outside the situation why he would want to keep their relationship hidden.

"I don't really want her caught up in all the museum's . . . politics," he explained, still questioning the wording in his head. Ava seemed to accept this answer, though, and shrugged.

"Your secret is safe with me."

She shifted her frame so her shoulder bumped into his and lifted her glass to her lips. "Though I don't know why you would want to hide the fact that you're related to such a sweet woman. More people might actually like you if they knew," she teased. Elias rolled his eyes.

The waitress appeared a few seconds later and dropped off a new drink for each of them and cleared the old glasses they had finished. This, despite the fact that Ava had still been working on her second drink.

"You have three siblings?"

Elias glanced her way and nodded. God, she was observant. He had never been this open with anyone before. Not even Lottie knew much about his family, let alone about Hattie. He didn't necessarily like the fact that she was learning more about him but suspected that this was information she would figure out anyway if she really wanted to.

"I'm the middle child. My sister Alana is the oldest, then there is my brother Nate, and my younger brother's name is Tanner."

"And your dad? I didn't see him in the picture. Is he still around?"

Elias took a swig to get the bitterness this question brought on out of his mouth. "Yeah, he's a professor in my hometown."

"Which is?"

Elias smiled at her playfully and wiggled his eyebrows. "Somewhere near Boston." He wasn't stupid. There were still lines he wouldn't cross. While Elias couldn't deny he had a soft spot for Ava, he wouldn't be so careless as to let those feelings get him in trouble. He would never jeopardize his family's safety for anyone.

Ava practically jumped back as the band started up in the background, and she slapped her hand down on the table as if she was offended, even though it was clear she wasn't. "Don't tell me you're a Red Sox fan!"

Elias grinned.

"Lord help me! Don't say another word, or they will carry us out of this city in body bags!"

Elias cocked his head back and chuckled. "Oh, and what? Are you going to try to convince me the Pirates are a shoo-in to win this next season?"

She tried to make a face of extreme offense but couldn't do it without a smile and laugh slipping through, and he knew he had her. "Well, no, but they've had . . . some great players . . . in the past. You never know!" She laughed as soft guitar music played in the background. Elias was glad to have changed the topic.

The band hushed the crowd and introduced themselves. They started playing an old Irish song called "Tell Me Ma." It was a fast and catchy tune that had Ava, along with most of the crowd, raising their glasses and singing along. Elias smiled and watched, and she continued to down her drinks and sing along with the band, clearly enjoying herself.

The night had turned out to be much more revealing to him than he had expected. He did not typically get entangled in other people's personal lives. Much in the way he protected Hattie, he protected the people he worked with, too. He even had secrets from Lottie. But mostly, he kept his distance for his own safety.

He looked down at his third beer of the night and realized that now was probably a good time to stop drinking. He was allowing himself to get a little too loose-lipped with Ava, and he needed to be careful.

He set down his drink and looked over at her. She was on her fifth, swaying back and forth to the music. Elias realized it was probably better he stopped drinking for another reason as well. Someone was going to need to drive them back, and it clearly wasn't going to be her.

Chapter Twenty—Eight

Elias sat and watched the woman in front of him in wonder. Just a couple days ago, she had been a real thorn in his side, a hindrance with only one appeal to him. But as he watched her smile and laugh and completely let her spirit run free, he was left in a sort of awe.

There was a natural pull to her that he couldn't seem to shake. It wasn't necessarily romantic (though he wasn't about to deny the fact that he was attracted to her in a way he knew he really shouldn't be) but more protective and . . . impressed, maybe? He wasn't sure if it was the alcohol in his system or the complete vulnerability she had shown him earlier. Still, he did know that she wasn't anything like he had expected when this started. This chick was tough. She was intelligent, a hard worker, and a fighter. And given everything she had gone through, she didn't let her past control her life the way Elias had allowed his to.

For the longest time, he had shielded himself, set up walls, and refrained from getting to really know people, all under the guise of safety for the mission. He had been doing it so long that he hadn't realized that part of himself, the part that actually enjoyed life, began to slip away.

The moonlight came in through the window and people began to filter out of the pub, so Elias decided it was probably time to get this chick home. He had already cut her off earlier without her noticing and paid the bill; all that was left was to find the car and get her keys. Elias leaned in close to speak directly into her ear as she hummed along to the slow song the musician was playing on his guitar.

"Hey, ready to get out of here?"

Ava flipped her head toward him with a goofy grin and her hat fell onto the floor. Elias bent down to pick it up and set it on his own head. "You lost your hat privileges for the night," he told her, then flashed a teasing grin. Ava narrowed her eyes playfully but sighed and leaned against the table with her chin resting on her hand.

Her hair bounced from the sudden movement. "You have other plans?" she asked.

Elias smirked but grabbed her hand from under the table and directed her toward the door. "Come to think of it, I do."

Sleep, he thought.

Ava jumped down off her barstool without letting his hand go and shook out her shoulders as she followed him through the dwindling crowd. Once out on the dimly lit street, she leaned into him and looked up to see his face from under the hat. Elias tried to hold back a laugh when she swayed into him a couple times. He tightened his grasp on her hand though to make sure she was steady; the last thing he wanted was for her to fall.

"Better be something fun," she said with a laugh and held her hand to her nose as if it was the funniest thing she had heard all day. Elias shook his head at her. Good Lord, she was tanked.

"Only if you enjoy counting sheep," he replied.

Ava scrunched up her nose, making a childish face as they continued walking. "That sounds incredibly boring," she said.

He laughed. "It's not supposed to be fun. It's supposed to be restful. I need your keys, by the way." He stuck out his hand for her.

Ava, who was watching the ground beneath her feet, suddenly turned to look back up at him, hugging his arm as she did so. This made Elias lose his footing and sway them both a little to the right, but he was able to catch himself and steady them before they went plowing face-first into the asphalt.

"Ya know, there's always a way to make counting sheep more . . . interesting."

He looked back down at her, shocked she even suggested anything along those lines. Whether she was drunk or not, part of him wanted to laugh, but an even deeper part of him wanted to explore that thought and see where the option would lead the two of them. Eventually, he shook his head at her with a gentle smile, doing his best not to upset her, all while putting his own dirty thoughts to bed.

"By counting them in Spanish?" Ava made a face and rolled her eyes. And Elias prodded her again. "I need your keys, Ava."

"I don't speak Spanish," she said with a frown and kept walking.

She seemed to be pouting as they turned into the lot where she'd parked her car. Elias looked up at the starry night. He said a silent prayer that he would be able to get her home and in bed without giving in to her sudden advances. He only returned his eyes to hers when she tripped over her own feet, and he had to put his other hand out to keep her from falling forward.

"Stop trying to trip me!"

Elias gave her a pleading laugh and held out the hand that wasn't still holding onto hers. "I'm not, Av. Will you please give me your keys? I need them to drive home."

She abruptly pulled away from him. Elias had to fight to hold onto her hand but eventually let her go since they had reached her car anyway. Ava turned to face him and pointed an accusing finger at him, placing her other hand on her hip.

"Ya know, for all the talk Hattie did about you being the wild child and adventurous, you really don't know how to have fun."

He rolled his eyes at her playfully and took a step forward to retrieve her keys. Ava mistook his actions and took a step back until she had her back against the car. He sighed. He wasn't sure if she was disappointed that he wouldn't "count sheep" with her or if she was implying that she wanted to go do something else, but either way, neither of those things were happening tonight, and for her own good.

"What kind of fun are you referring to? I have plenty of fun in my own time, I assure you."

Ava scoffed and placed her hands behind her back, leaning on the car door, and looked out to the right. "Oh, I bet you do."

Elias frowned. That was not what he meant, and he had had enough. He leaned forward, blocking any path she had to escape and he reached behind her back. Startled, Ava snapped her head to him, wide eyes, and they came face to face, close enough that he could smell the Jameson on her breath.

His eyes might have hazed over for the briefest second as he fished her keys from her back pocket. He pulled them from around her and dangled them in front of her face. Ava blinked for a second. "Not that kind of fun," he replied and clicked the unlock button, then opened the passenger door for Ava.

Her eyes danced wildly around his face so close to hers. He knew he should move away, step back, and usher her into the car, but he stayed where he was, against his better judgment and said, "I think that's your cue."

She stared up at him with foggy eyes. "I think you missed yours," she whispered. Elias pulled his eyes from hers but didn't move. Instead, he looked past her into the night, knowing that allowing this was a mistake. However, he couldn't find it within himself to pull away from her as she stood up on her tippy toes and closed the distance between them.

He closed his eyes when her lips softly brushed against his, leaving the gentlest of butterfly kisses there. She must have only meant that to test the waters, though, because, in the next second, she had reached her hand up and wrapped it gently around his neck, using it to pull him down to her.

Her kiss was so hot and slow, it sparked a fire within him, heating him from the inside out. Her tongue danced across his own and he lost his will to pull away. He braced his hands on the rim of the car above her head. He had been lying to himself ever since Glendalough. He had wanted this more than he realized. But it had to stop. This wasn't right. She was intoxicated and even though he was tempted to give in, he didn't want to take advantage of her in this state.

Ava's movements became more urgent, and Elias knew he had to pull away. He couldn't do this with her here. She deserved better—better than a guy who couldn't commit. Better than the back of a car in a dark parking lot. With great effort, he pulled his head away from hers. Ava looked up at him, waiting. But he just shook his head at her, his gentle smile back in place, hiding his frustration.

"Not like this," he whispered. Ava nodded and seemed to understand what he was saying. "Come on, let's go home."

It didn't take long for her to fall asleep on the drive home using the navigation system. So, Elias had the whole forty-five-minute trip to replay tonight's events and process all these thoughts. He was so confused he didn't know what he felt. He knew what he was supposed to feel, what was safest for the two of them, but something in him had been triggered by her story and then again as she "let her hair down."

This wasn't a thing, he decided. No, it couldn't be. Hell, he had just hooked up with Lottie again a couple weeks ago! Yet here he was, still entertaining Ava's earlier offer in his head as if it was something he could genuinely pursue. Why was he acting like she was suddenly the sun, moon, and stars? Nothing between them had really changed. She was still his partner, and he was her superior. They weren't meant to be, and even if they were, Elias didn't believe in that crap—end of story.

By the time they got back, the McKenna house was dark and quiet. Ava was snoring lightly in the front seat as they pulled into the drive. Elias figured this was probably for the best. As quietly as he could, he got out of the car, unlocked her apartment door, and came back around to the passenger's side to open her door. She never moved. He unbuckled her seat belt, gently picked her up, and carried her back into the tiny home.

Once inside, Elias looked between his bed on the main floor and her bed up in the tiny loft. He would wake her if he tried to get her up into the loft or, worse, whack her head on something, so instead, he laid her down on his bed and tucked her into the covers before retiring to the loft for the night.

As he lay there in the dark, thinking over everything, he looked to his left. He noticed a little picture frame with a photo of Ava, Juliana, Millie, and a woman who Elias assumed was Ava's mom.

Seeing that picture reminded him of his own family photo currently decorating Hattie's inn, and that's when he decided whether he would further any type of friendship or relationship with Ava; he would always be around to look after her.

She had lost so many people in her life that she could use someone in her corner. For as long as she walked around the Emerald Isle, he would always be there to make sure no one hurt her again.

—19-10—

My darling B,

I cant believe the new year is nearly upon us. And yet I have heard little from you, since you've arrived back in Dublin at the beginning of the fall. I dare say, it has been far too long since your letters have graced my desk. But perhaps I am more to blame for this than you are.

I acknowledge that I have not been very proactive in our conversations, but I hope to change that soon. I am eager to hear about your adventures travelling around the country. Our homeland is truly a beautiful sight. What I wouldnt give to be in your shoes. And oh, the parties you must attend! I cant imagine they are as exciting as the one we attended together a few years back, though, eh? Now that was a party. Perhaps it is a good thing you are settling down now in a permanent theatre. Maybe now, I can sneak away for a visit more often.

Regrettably, my reason for writing to you this time isn't solely social. I am certain your father has informed you, but we have been receiving numerous concerns about increased violence in other areas daily. The council has requested that I contact you to inquire about the situation there in Dublin. How serious it is and what you have observed.

I hope you can write back soon as I am yearning to hear from you again.

Wishing you the best,

A. Lynch

Chapter Twenty-Nine

Ava

The morning started with a major headache that was only comforted by a strong, woodsy smell. I squinted into the morning light and looked around, trying to collect my bearings. My head was peeking out from under the blankets, looking across the room toward a bathroom door.

Steam curled up from underneath it, letting me know that Elias was using the shower. I blinked, suddenly realizing I was in his bed rather than my own. I jolted myself around and glanced under the blankets, then breathed a sigh of relief when I realized I was still fully dressed in my attire from the night before.

But how did I get here? Why was I not in my bed? What happened last night? I was in the middle of racking my brain to try to bring back my missing memories when Elias exited the bathroom in a t-shirt and jeans. I slid deeper under the covers and drew the sheets up to my nose in embarrassment. Elias snickered as he stepped fully into the room, and I groaned, covering my head with his blankets.

"What's wrong, Little Sheep? Got a headache?" he asked.

I curled my lip. *Little Sheep?* What did that mean? "Yes," I said, my voice muffled by the covers. "Why am I in your bed?" I squeaked.

Elias laughed and stepped forward, setting something on the end table beside the bed and tapping my shoulder. I slowly pulled the covers down to my nose and peeked out to look at him. He was standing there, holding out three pills. A glass of water was on the table.

"You were completely out by the time I pulled into the drive. I didn't want to wake you by trying to get you into the loft, so I gave you my bed and hopped into yours."

I stared and blinked for a second, then decided that didn't sound too bad. So I sat up and took the pills, then chased them down with the glass of water.

"Thank you," I said and swung my feet out to sit on the edge of the bed.

Elias turned away to grab something off the counter. When he turned back to me, he had a sticky note in his hands. I took the small pink paper from his hands and recognized the handwriting immediately.

Coffee pot is on inside. Meet me when you're ready. —M

"Millie left this on the door for you."

I sighed. I dropped my hand to my lap, knowing what I was in store for. Which led me to another thought: I hadn't heard from Calista in a while. I had been hoping she would have had a new assignment for me by now, but I suppose there wasn't much for me to collect for the museum here in Pittsburgh. I doubt many explorers come here on assignments usually involving exotic locations around the world—not the steel city of black and gold. Disappointed there wouldn't be a chance for me to earn another $500, I glanced up at Elias, who was leaning against the countertop sipping his coffee. That brought another question to the forefront of my brain: "Why do you keep calling me 'little sheep'?"

He looked up with a smug smile and let me simmer for a second. He swirled the coffee in his mug and wiggled his eyebrows at me. "What's wrong, Little Sheep? Don't you remember anything from last night?"

I chose to not return his gaze. I didn't want to admit that I was indeed missing a few spots from last night. I pursed my lips and finally rolled my eyes. "No."

"Don't worry, Little Sheep, nothing too exciting happened. Nothing to report, anyway . . ." Though his grin never wavered, the way he said it with a sigh left me wondering if that was really true.

Was there more to the story than what he was leading me to believe?

I chose to leave it be for the moment and return to it later. I didn't have the energy to try and figure anything out. But I would definitely revisit the subject later.

I stood up and brushed past him to grab my bath caddy from the closet under the ladder. I entered the bathroom, but before I closed the door, I turned around and pointed my finger at him. He gave me a silent playful look, daring me to say something.

"I hate you," I declared.

Elias let out a full barking laugh, one I'd never heard from him before. It was musical and full of warmth and so lovely to hear. I closed the door behind me before I got pulled back into a conversation with him.

I tried to keep my shower short, but the hot water felt good as it pelted my throbbing head, and I ended up spending a bit of time on the floor of the shower due to some leftover dizziness. Afterward, I combed my hair, got dressed, and met Elias out on the porch. He was on the porch swing, still sipping his coffee and flipping through his phone. He looked up at me and I took the seat beside him. He glanced at me curiously from behind his mug. I was wasting time, and we both knew it.

"Don't you want your coffee?" he asked.

I withdrew, unsure how to answer. "Of course I want coffee. I just don't want to talk to Millie . . ." I indeed had some memories return to me while in the shower, and one of those was of me spilling my guts to Elias at the pub. I could only imagine what he thought of me now: *She is a mess; her life is a disaster. That poor kid.* All things that accumulated into something I didn't want. Pity. But given the circumstances, he didn't appear to be fazed. I was sure he could guess what Millie wanted to talk to me about.

Elias thought about it for a minute. "So, make coffee in the apartment. You have a Keurig."

I shook my head. "I'm out of K-cups. You must have used the last one."

He scoffed. "Well, buckle up, then, because I'm pretty sure if you don't go in to talk to her, she will come to you." He was right. Of course he was right, and I hated that. But regardless, I stood up from the swing and walked past him.

"Yeah, I figured as much. Hey, if it's okay with you, Juliana has really been itching to go to the zoo. I was thinking while I was in town . . ."

Elias nodded, like he already knew what I was going to say. "You'd like to take her today before we meet with the director? Yes, that's fine with me. I don't mind checking out the city with you guys for a bit."

I nodded my thanks, then looked back at him and sighed, crossing my arms over my chest. "You gonna be okay here for a bit while I chat with her?"

He shrugged. "I'll be fine. I have to call Lottie anyway. I don't think she's all that thrilled that I didn't call last night."

Oh, right, "Lottie." They spoke on the phone almost every night, it seemed. I started to walk away, but I stopped and turned to scowl at him. "I thought you *weren't that close?*" I said, using air quotes to make my point.

He rolled his eyes, smug as a bug in a rug. "Don't worry, Little Sheep, we're just friends."

"Worry? Why would I care?" I asked but turned my face to hide any blush that was creeping into my cheeks, unconvinced but also uninterested in going down that rabbit hole today. I turned to head into the house.

Millie was in the kitchen, drinking her tea and reading a book. When she saw me come in, she raised her eyebrows as if she already knew I had drunk too much the night before. She stood up, shaking her head at me, and walked over to grab me a cup from the cupboard. I accepted it and filled it with the delicious chocolate hazelnut coffee she had brewing for me.

Since Mom died, Millie always seemed to know what I needed, even if I didn't know it yet myself. I sat down across the table from her, letting the aroma from the coffee open my senses. "Girl, you are so lucky Eamon drove the kids to school today. He would not be thrilled to see you hungover after your first night home."

She was right, of course, Eamon would kill me if he knew. I moaned overdramatically and slumped forward, sliding my hand under my chin. "Elias asked about the family last night," I explained. Millie paused.

The look she gave me expressed exactly what I was feeling at the moment. She leaned forward and tapped my arm from the other side of the table.

"You hadn't told him yet?" I shook my head and nursed my coffee. "Oh boy, you're gonna need another cup, then. No wonder you're hungover."

I looked down at my hands on the table and shrugged. "I honestly wasn't expecting it." She brought over the whole pot and set it down on top of a potholder next to the cream and sugar. She gave me a slight frown and sighed, understanding my pain.

In the midst of everything, sometimes it was hard to remind myself that I wasn't the only person who had lost people in the chaos of the past seven years. Millie and Eamon had lost just as much.

My mom and Millie had been close since grade school; they had known each other their entire lives. They told each other everything. They were together for every holiday, even when they had started families of their own. When Mom died, Millie's soul had never quite recovered, and you could see it in her features. Her kind eyes always looked exhausted.

Helping Mom recover from my dad leaving us had put quite the strain on her, and then when Mom died, her heart broke. And after Jules was diagnosed with cancer, Millie seemed to have trouble picking herself back up. But somehow, she did—every day, just like I had.

Each morning, we got up, got dressed, and put on a smile for the two kids in the family. The ones we loved the most. We took the brunt of the pain and hid it away deep in the darkest corners of our minds. Millie was better at discussing things because she had to deal with it on a daily basis; I, however, tried my best not to. I blinked away my thoughts and took another sip, bringing my hand up to pinch the bridge of my nose.

"You had to suspect he was going to ask when he met us, didn't you?"

"I mean, yeah, but I hadn't expected it at that moment."

Millie shrugged and leaned forward onto the table. "What did he say?"

I explained what I had found out about his family and his mother. We talked a bit about how she'd lost her battle to the disease when Elias was thirteen, and how I noticed it affected him much more than he realized. Millie listened and nodded every so often.

Our stories (Elias's and mine) were pretty similar. We had both known great loss and had both overcome it. We found a common love of history and sought to use it as our way to escape our troubles. Millie smiled as I told her about the things we had found so far and about the pieces I was slowly putting together about Elias one by one.

The more she listened, the more she seemed to lighten up, which, in turn, made me open up more.

It had been a long time since the two of us had had the chance just to sit back and have girl talk, and it was nice. Millie had always been more of an aunt to me than anything, but when Mom died, and she took on more of a front-and-center motherly role in my life. That was when she and I stopped talking so intimately. This was refreshing.

"You sound like you might like this guy," she finally said, trying to hide her genuine smile behind her mug. I narrowed my eyes, criticizing her judgment.

"No, not possible." Was it? I struggled to remember what had happened between Elias and me after we left the pub, but a blurry image of my body pressed up against his was stamped into my brain. I couldn't tell if it was real or not but every time the image popped up, chills ran down my spine.

Millie shrugged and set down her mug, looking out the window. "I don't know. You talk awful highly of him."

I shook my head, trying to hold my stance. I didn't like him. I couldn't. I didn't have time for guys, let alone one as problematic as Elias—the king of hot and cold, who couldn't even figure out his feelings, let alone care for mine. No. She was simply misreading everything I had told her. I laughed helplessly, trying to deny it all, but that picture in my head was so real.

"I don't have time for guys, *especially* one as stubborn and as . . . as . . . *arrogant* as he is! I have responsibilities of my own to worry about. You, Jules, the internship. I can't get mixed up in as a relationship."

Millie cocked an eyebrow and sat back, not believing me for a second. "A second ago, he was an intelligent and attractive young man, and now you're calling him stubborn and arrogant?"

I held up a hand. "I never said attractive."

"You didn't have to! You just went on and on for about ten minutes straight, telling me all about his love for history, his work ethic, and his sense of humor! What do you think attraction is, girl? Take a good look at yourself; there's something there between the two of you. You're just too scared to pursue it."

If my jaw could have dropped to the floor, it would have. I sat there mouth agape, looking at Millie with mock shock. She waved her hand at me, the mug moving around the air and threatening to spill onto the table. She smiled at me and pointed a finger.

"And secondly, just because you have responsibilities doesn't mean you can't have a relationship. You owe it to yourself, Ava, to find love and make mistakes, whatever they may be. Stop trying to live up to this perfect life. You'll never have fun that way. We only get one stroll around the block; take it from your mother and make it count. You've been through so much these past few years; it's time to give yourself a break and do something for you for once."

The mention of my mom brought a serious tone to the conversation. I closed my mouth and sat back, truly surprised that this conversation had taken such a sharp turn so fast.

I had spent most of the past couple of years either deep in my studies, or at the hospital with Jules. I didn't allow myself time for anything other than a part-time job to try and help Millie and Eamon with her expenses. I wasn't sure if it was all as easy as Millie was making it sound, but she was definitely right about one thing, and I knew it.

All this time, I had blamed my lack of social life on my circumstances, claiming I had other things to worry about or more significant things to focus on. But in reality, I had decided that it wasn't fair for me to try and allow myself to be happy and live a good life while others I loved could not.

How could I go on allowing myself to have fun and be excited about things when Jules was consistently fighting to take a deep breath? How could I go off and enjoy the bright summer days, wasting time at the beach or on vacation, when my mom was six feet under? How could I allow myself to fall in love when so many people I knew had lost the love of their lives? It wasn't fair. And knowing it wasn't fair had kept me from enjoying life.

Millie reached forward and took my hand in hers, drawing my eyes up to meet her own. "We both know I had a completely different conversation planned for this morning. But in light of all that you've told me, I want you to try, Ava. I want you to pursue this thing with Elias. He's a good guy, and he seems to treat you well. Even if you don't fall in love, at least make a friendship out of this. You deserve the world, my darling. Please try to find what makes you happy. We will take care of the other stuff from here. Don't you worry."

# Chapter Thirty

ELIAS

Ava appeared to be lost in some sort of trance. Whatever she and Millie had spoken about had caught her off-guard. Of course, she was also probably still nursing her hangover, so that could explain her quiet demeanor. Initially, Elias had thought perhaps it was something to do with her sister Juliana's health. But he scrapped that thought when he noticed Ava constantly glancing in his direction as if he been doing something she disapproved of.

Then, a thought hit him. Did she remember last night? Elias decided it was best if she didn't; that way, she wouldn't know how easily he had given in to her, how smooth their chemistry came to them. Elias chewed on the inside of his lip, hoping that wasn't the case. Regardless, without a doubt, she had something on her mind that was troubling her, and for some reason, it had something to do with him.

Once Ryker and Juliana had arrived home from school, Ava and Elias packed the two up in her car and headed off to the zoo for a few hours. Ryker was a typical ball of energy bouncing all over the place in excitement over all the animals they had to see. At the same time, Juliana, for the most part, watched in wonder.

Elias loved to see how the two kids were bonded. It reminded him of his siblings back in Boston. Ryker never seemed to wander far from Juliana and was looking back to check on her when he strayed ahead of the group. Even though they weren't blood-related, it was clear that Ryker loved his sister, and Juliana adored him in return.

Ava loved every moment they got to spend with them, and it showed. She sported an ear-to-ear grin all day, holding Juliana's hand as they walked. When Juliana got tired, Elias lifted her onto his shoulders and carried her. For this, Ava was grateful since she had brought Julianna's nebulizer and was carrying it around in her backpack.

Despite how much energy both kids had, Ava never got tired of their questions, their outbursts, or their zoomies. Instead, she seemed like she was exactly where she was meant to be. This sparked Elias's interest, considering every time he saw her in a library, she also seemed to be just as comfortable. He had always assumed that was her altar.

Still, as it turned out, family may actually be her true motivation. These were two sides of the same coin that made up the woman before him, and he was beginning to grow fonder and fonder of her with each moment he spent getting to know her.

Unfortunately, because of Juliana's condition, the trip wasn't a long one, only a couple hours at most before they had to return the kids to the house so Juliana could rest.

Elias took a call to Hattie during their downtime.

Once they returned to Ava's apartment, they had a bit of time to waste before their meeting in Carnegie. Elias had been pleased to relax on the couch and read further in the brown leather journal he carried, but when Ava started giggling from her bunk and looking down at her phone, he got distracted.

Who could she be texting that was so funny? Ava caught him staring and laughed, flashing him the screen of her phone. "You should hear Connor's updates from the museum. He's been comparing his time with Dr. Balor and Calista to that of an old Donald Duck cartoon."

Elias raised an eyebrow at her, not understanding the humor in this.

Ava shrugged. "Guess you have to be in the moment." Then she returned to her phone.

Elias was less than enthused. He had met Connor and had yet to be very impressed. He was a nerdy kid with an average body who was possessive and studying something no one cared about.

Elias shifted from his spot on the couch and suddenly climbed to his feet. Ava's reaction to Connor's texts had irritated him, so he figured he would distract himself with a conversation of his own. So he dialed Lottie's number. "Better call Lottie. Didn't get the chance this morning like I had planned and I'm sure she's missing me."

He knew this bothered Ava and was hoping to use it to his advantage. He stepped out onto the front porch just as Lottie picked up. He smiled to himself smugly, satisfied when he caught Ava's curious eyes following him out the door with a frown.

"Hello?"

"Hey, Lot, how are things?" He took a seat on the swing and put his phone on speaker so he could pull out the journal and practice his double-tasking. Calista sighed over the phone, and Elias could see her clearly rolling her eyes as if she were sitting right beside him. He smirked. "That bad, huh?"

"Some of these new recruits, I swear!"

Elias chuckled. They had always enjoyed trash-talking the *new meat* as they arrived and started their first tasks. But they hadn't had much time to do so this round.

Usually, this was a tradition they held every year in Lottie's dorm room. In past years, they had started with a movie, popcorn, and alcohol and eventually ended in a hookup. But after the accident involving his partner a few years ago, Elias didn't feel much like continuing the tradition. Instead, he had come up with a new fitness plan for the recruits that he insisted all of his new partners follow during their training and before their first expedition. This was to ensure nothing like that ever happened again.

What he had come to realize through the unfortunate experience was that as annoying as they were, the new blood was, for the most part, untrained and uneducated in survival techniques. And they were part of someone's family. It didn't matter that he was in this program for alternative reasons; he still wouldn't allow another human to get hurt on his watch again. Having to meet his previous partner's family in the hospital that night had scarred him, and he just didn't look at the new recruits the same.

Elias shook his head to himself. Lottie was ever the pessimist. "Connor giving you trouble?"

Lottie moaned in a way that let him know she was frustrated. "No, not yet, anyway. He may be a little boring, but he's nothing if not useful. Balor seems to really like him, so I'll keep him on my team for now. No, I was referring to the guy from Dowling Quarters who keeps sneaking in during the middle of the night to screw the girl down the hall. God, is she loud!"

Elias laughed and flipped the page of his journal. He had been a little disappointed that Lottie approved of Connor. She usually was the one who had dirt on everyone, and Elias had hoped she had dug something up on Connor that Ava would find unforgivable. However, he also knew that Lottie understood how the accident had affected him and he was sure she had been trying to change her mindset about the new recruits for his benefit.

"How about Ava? Is she as big of a prude as she acts?"

Or maybe not. Elias quickly grabbed the phone, which was still on speaker, and turned it back to personal mode so Ava couldn't overhear their conversation if she came outside. "Originally, I thought so, but it turns out, she has rather impressed me so far," he said.

Lottie scoffed from the other end. "What'd she do? Take her top off?"

Elias didn't respond directly to her jab at Ava. "No, I'm not that shallow. As it turns out, she is much more intelligent than I gave her credit for, and she even managed to pick out a good beer for me at the pub the other day."

"Uh-huh." Lottie did not sound enthused.

Elias shrugged. Though he did keep secrets from Lottie, they were few and far between. "She did hit on me, though," he admitted.

"The tramp."

"Says the girl who tried to seduce me in her dorm room a couple weeks ago."

She laughed seductively. "First, I didn't try; I succeeded, and second, I have no idea what on earth you are referring to, sir. I am a lady!"

Lady, my ass, he thought.

Lottie dropped her voice to a sexy purr over the phone and continued. "You know, I don't mind you being . . . shallow."

Elias shook his head, uninterested. It was always about sex with her. They barely had a normal conversation anymore that didn't involve work or sex. He wished he could just go back to the good old days when they were just friends. If Elias had his wish, he would have never tried to hook up with Lottie; they would have just stayed friends. They were good together that way. He truly appreciated her when she wasn't trying to rub him down.

"Oh, I know you do. Too bad you don't have a boyfriend to be shallow with," he pointed out. He could practically hear her pouting from his remark.

"Fine, push me away, Elias Cassedy. Just remember how great you had it. Let those memories of scorched lips haunt your dreams forever."

He highly doubted that. Though she had tried, she hadn't been able to get him into bed before they left for Pittsburgh, and she wouldn't be able to now. He didn't want to hurt her feelings, but he was over being Lottie's toy and preferred just being her friend.

"Maybe I will go find Connor after all. To be fair, he is very attractive in a nerdy sort of way, but you can't deny those lean muscles," she said.

This time, it was Elias who scoffed. "Yeah, however small they might be."

"Don't be jealous, Elias; green doesn't look good on you."

Elias made a face just as the door to the apartment slowly opened. Ava stuck her head out, and Elias turned and nodded to her. "Green always looks good on me. Nice try, though. Hey, I gotta get going; we're going to be leaving for Carnegie here in a minute."

Ava stepped out of the apartment and motioned for him to see if he needed anything from it before locking it behind her.

Lottie shifted her voice back into work mode, and Elias practically sighed in relief. It could get taxing having to fight off her advances that way. Most of the time, he gave in just enough for her to be happy with the attention but not satisfied. But as he looked over at Ava, who leaned against the railing behind her, waiting for him, he softened. Things were changing between the two of them, which meant soon enough, things would have to change between him and Lottie. She wasn't going to like that conversation.

"That's great! We still haven't had a Zoom meeting since Glendalough, and Balor is going to want that conference soon. I'll text you a time for tomorrow morning once you've met with Carnegie's director."

"Great," Elias said sarcastically, but only Ava noticed; she eyed him from behind her phone curiously.

"Okay, I'll let you go, love. Oh! And tell Ava to expect a text from me soon if you please."

Elias knitted his eyebrows together and looked between Ava and the space in front of him as if Lottie was there. "Why? What's going on between the two of you?" he asked suspiciously. He had noticed they were texting quite a bit, but it always seemed to be work-related and not necessarily friendly. He didn't like being left out of work discussions. This made him nervous.

Ava, in the corner, widened her eyes as if she was afraid she was somehow in trouble and redirected her attention to her phone.

"Nothing at all, my sweet! Just girl talk and paperwork. You know!" Lottie waved off his concerns nonchalantly. Elias decided it was definitely something, but he would choose to open that can of worms later.

"Whatever, I'll talk to you later tonight," he told her, and with that, he ended the call. He glanced over at Ava, who had this expression on her face that said, *I didn't do it.* "Lottie said she was going to text you later today. Something about more paperwork."

Ava sat up with a fake smile and shrugged. "Great, should we go?"

Elias shook it off. Whatever the two girls were up to would have to wait. It was time to get back to work.

"Let's."

Chapter Thirty-One

AVA

Knowing Juliana's condition was worsening was one thing, but actually having to witness it on a daily basis was another. I could see why Millie always looked as if the light in her life had been blown out. I was emotionally exhausted from just a couple of days here. I could only imagine how Millie felt.

The more money I was able to put toward Juliana's treatment and help the family, the better. Whatever I could do to take a little bit of stress off the McKennas, I would do it. I owed it to them, and I could not lose Juliana. So I was thrilled when I received an email from Calista shortly after Elias and I pulled the Honda out of the driveway.

Good evening, Ava!

Excellent job acquiring your first assignment! It has been returned to its proper place at the museum and is being cleaned as we speak. Your next assignment is a piece that has been dropped off at the Carnegie Museum office for you. It is a donation to the NMI by a lone donor. Your meeting will start in the museum director's office—and that is where you will find the item. It will be placed in an envelope marked with the letters N.J.L. You will find it awaiting you in the mailbox marked for the Historic Office. As usual, please handle with care. You may return it once you have arrived back in Dublin. We will deposit your reward once you have completed the task.
Best of luck!

Sincerely,
Calista Scott
Team Manager of Operations

I brought my phone to my chest, smiling to myself. Finally! Elias glanced at me with a quizzical look just as a second message came in. I pulled my phone back, ignoring him, to read the second email.

"What was that look for?" he asked.

Elias, Ava, Calista, Connor

Dear Explorers,
The National Museum of Ireland is hosting its Annual Fundraiser Ball on Saturday 28.05 at Trinity College. All interns, staff, and students are expected to attend.
Formal attire is required. These events are critical to the museum, as they bring us the donations and support from the community that allows us to continue our expeditions. So please put your best foot forward. The event will commence at 7 p.m. sharp. We look forward to seeing you there!

Dr. Thaddeus Balor

"Dr. Balor was informing us of a fundraiser we are required to attend next week," I said, reading over the email once more.

Elias looked like he knew I was lying but turned back to the road and nodded. "The Annual Fundraiser Ball at Trinity College."

I let out a frustrated huff and openly frowned, not caring much if Elias saw. I knew him well enough to be open with him by this point so I had no reason to hide my feelings anymore.

While the event sounded like fun, that would only slow down our hunt, and I had absolutely nothing to wear. I frowned and put my phone down.

"Yep," I said dryly.

Elias glanced over again. "I figured you'd be thrilled. Isn't that like a girl's favorite thing? To get all dressed up and fancy? Plus, you'll get to see everyone again. There will be drinking and dancing and good food—what's not to like?"

I looked over at him with my eyebrows raised. "I never pegged you for the dancing type."

He smirked, this time keeping his eyes on the road. "Wouldn't you like to know?"

I envisioned Elias tiptoeing around a wooden dancefloor under bright multicolored spotlights, and my smile reappeared. Actually, now that I thought about it, yeah, I would.

"And you and I both know I'm not that type of girl."

Getting back to reality, though, I feared it would be obvious that I was low on cash when everyone else showed up dressed in elegant and exotic gowns, and I arrived in something from Amazon. I could ask Millie, but she'd insist I use the money I just sent her to buy something nice, but that would miss the point of why I took this position in the first place.

"If I'm being honest, I don't have anything to wear. Do you have any idea what a gown for an event like that costs?" I asked. Elias looked at me like I had two heads.

"Why on earth would I know that?"

"Exactly my point. While you get to rent your tux for the evening at a reasonable price, I have to buy a gown. There's no such thing as a cheap dress."

Elias ran his hand through the growing scruff on his chin. It was what he did when he was thinking things through, and I looked out the window. "Meanwhile, you're trying to save your money for Juliana . . ."

"Right."

"Hmm."

He didn't say more on the subject, and I didn't bring it up again. Instead, I set my mind to my new task. Keeping an eye out for that mailbox and slipping the artifact into my bag without him noticing would be tricky. He was going to be by my side, practically glued to my hip most of the time. I wondered how much trouble I would really be in if Elias caught me. I couldn't imagine Calista would care all that much.

When we reached the city, Elias parked in a nearby parking garage between level two and level three.

Since we were meeting with the museum director and we were both representatives of the N.M.I., we had chosen to dress up a bit. For Elias, that simply meant a slightly wrinkled dark green button-down over a black t-shirt and nice jeans, and for me, that meant straightened hair, a nice gray sweater, slacks, and a pair of heels to add a bit of professionalism.

It wasn't Calista's brand of poise and power. Still, I suspected that for a place like Carnegie, my business casual attire would do. As we walked toward the museum, however, I was beginning to reconsider the heels. After weeks of nothing but hiking boots and sneakers, these heels were starting to feel like walking on pins and needles, and it had only been twenty minutes.

We went through the main entrance just as the museum was about to close. Elias walked up to the security guard. The guard nodded, then stepped away for a moment, picked up the landline attached to the desk, and discussed our appearance with someone on the other end. "The assistant director will be down shortly."

Elias nodded, and stood back from the desk to wait. I watched as the lights for the exhibits started to turn off for the night one by one. Janitors and security guards were cleaning up and doing the final rounds.

A younger man with wire-framed glasses and a needlepoint sweater that made it obvious he was trying too hard to impress someone, walked up with his hands folded behind his back. "If you'll please follow me, Dr. Fort is nearly ready to see you."

We followed him up the stairs and down a hall that was labeled for staff use only. As we walked, I noticed a room that was open off to the right, just in front of the bathrooms. The room was small, with just a few filing cabinets, a punch card machine, and five rows of staff mailboxes bound to the side wall.

Bingo.

I wanted to stick my head in there, but Elias grabbed my hand as I fell behind, and I was so surprised that I allowed him to guide me into the first office instead.

"Please take a seat. The director will be with you shortly."

Elias dropped my hand, and I instantly missed the feeling of his warm palm against mine. That was something I could get used to. Instead, he pulled out a chair for me as if it was totally normal for him, and took a seat in the other. I slowly took the seat offered beside him, very confused.

What just happened? Not that I was complaining, but since when did we start holding hands? I shook my head, trying to refocus. I had to think about finding Calista's artifact; I didn't have time to ponder his actions right now.

I looked around the room in a daze, mulling over my options. I could try to snag the envelope before we left the hallway on our way out, but considering Elias's efforts to keep me close, I doubted I'd have enough time to find the correct mailbox without getting spotted.

A woman in a white blouse and dress pants stepped into the room and smiled as she stuck out her hand to shake both mine and Elias's. "Ah, Elias and Ava, it is so nice to meet you. Calista assured me you would be punctual, but alas, I didn't believe it. My apologies, I got caught up speaking to a visitor."

She was in her mid-forties with platinum blond hair pulled into a bun. She took a seat opposite us. She introduced herself as Allison Fort and got right down to business.

"Well, this is quite the story I have heard. Calista tells me you two are looking into the disappearance of the Crown Jewels of Ireland?"

Elias nodded proudly. "Yes, ma'am."

"How exciting! You know I studied abroad in Ireland once. Gosh, I loved it there."

"It's absolutely magical, isn't it?" I replied.

She beamed in her memories of the grand island and folded her hands on her lap. "Yes, quite right. It sounds like you have found a lead that has brought you here, of all places!"

Elias leaned forward, looking a little uncomfortable. To be fair, the chairs were not the best quality and were a little low for his tall frame.

"Yes. I don't know how much Calista told you of our expedition, but we would love a chance to inspect one of your pieces today. The painting of the *Megaloceros giganteus* by Beckett Lowery."

"Yes, she mentioned that. I do need to have an artifact specialist with you as you inspect it, just to ensure nothing gets damaged in the process, you understand. But at this point, they are just finishing up their report on a different piece and will meet us shortly. Until then, I'd love to hear what you've found. This part of the job was always so interesting to me; I regret not taking an internship like this when I was your age," she said.

That was it—my chance to sneak away. While Elias blabbed on about the mission, I could sneak away to find the envelope. Keeping both of them at bay while I searched would give me time to find the correct mailbox, and besides, Elias preferred to do all the talking anyway.

"Of course I—"

"Excuse me, Dr. Fort. Do you mind if I use the restroom while we wait?" I asked, standing from my chair.

"Of course, it is down the hall to the left right before you exit back into the museum. You can't miss it."

"Thank you." I disappeared into the hall and their voices picked up again.

I kept my eyes out both in front of me and casually glanced behind me to make sure there was no one in the hall. I ducked into the small room. The mailboxes were lined up alphabetically. At the top were the specific office mailboxes and, beneath them, the individual staff.

I located the mailbox listed as *Historic Office* and reached in but found nothing. Damn. Maybe I was too late? Maybe someone else had picked it up. I sighed in frustration and pulled out my phone. I was just about to text Calista when something caught my eye. One of the filing cabinets in the back corner of the room was labeled the same way, *Historic Office*.

I narrowed my eyes suspiciously. I glanced back out the door frame then tiptoed up to the cabinet. I couldn't open it . . . could I? Was that okay? This wasn't listed in the message Calista had sent me, but maybe, just maybe, it had been misplaced.

I took a final glance over my shoulder then tugged the drawer open. Multiple file frames bounced as I did, exposing several different documents and reports.

Then I saw it.

In the middle, in the file called *new artifacts*, was the envelope with the initials *N.J.L.* in big black Sharpie writing.

I snagged the envelope and shoved it into my bag. The writing on the envelope looked familiar to me. I assumed it was Calista's and threw the thought out as I closed the door and turned to get out of there as fast as I could.

I thought I had gotten in and out unscathed until I ran smack into the little assistant director, William. He stepped back to press his hands down his suit as if that could magically rid it of any wrinkles. He adjusted his glasses, glancing up at me skeptically.

"Miss Metheny, I did not expect to find you here," he said and pulled the files in his arms close to his chest as he waited for my response.

I batted my eyelashes at him and flipped my hair back. "Oh, silly me, I thought this was the bathroom!" I said, stepping past him.

William rolled his eyes. "No, that would be next door." Then, under his breath, he said, "The kids they are hiring these days . . . such a disappointment."

I smiled sheepishly at him and apologized, then found my way back to Director Fort's office just as she and Elias were exiting the room.

Perfect.

-19-1-1

My dearest Andrew,

 I am pleased to say that my days of attending grand parties are over. I no longer feel the need to play games or serve the whims of noblemen just to establish my reputation. Playing at the palace last month was an exhilarating experience. The King was exceptionally kind when I met him, and despite our political differences, I quite enjoyed my time there, much to my father's dismay.
 Returning to Ireland, however, was not as pleasant, I'm afraid. Things have indeed started to reach boiling points here in the city. While I was away, two men were beaten to death just the other day by the British enforcers! They were merely protesting their right to be treated with respect as employees! And they beat them to death with a baton! It is frightening to think what could happen if we continue down this path.
 I pray the next generation lives on to experience a better future.

 Sending my love,
 B. Hayes

Chapter Thirty-Two

As I approached Elias and Director Fort, he gave me an odd look. Still, he didn't say anything when I fell in step beside him. That wasn't necessarily surprising. Finding the envelope had taken more time than I had anticipated. So I simply smiled at him and kept walking to let him know I was okay.

The director pushed the door back open and entered the second floor on top of a grand staircase that led into on marble flooring.

Much like the National Museum of Ireland, the Carnegie held nothing back, sparing no expense to make the place feel like a palace, worthy of collecting the best artifacts to display—it was quite a wonder.

It had a way of making you feel like you were going back in time to each different period the room at hand had on display. When I was a child, it had been one of my favorite places to visit. Not much had changed, apparently.

The museum was now dark, with only security lights shining the way. We followed the director down the staircase and through several rooms until we came to one filled with an array of magnificent paintings, done by a variety of artists.

In the middle of the room, on a large desk illuminated by lights from underneath, was the painting in question—the *Megaloceros giganteus*, which Beckett Lowery had created.

It was lying outside its protective framing and was set up for us to inspect. A ladder above held an extra bright light.

I suspected that they had brought in extra lighting for us in hopes of preventing us from fiddling with the piece. I could appreciate their dedication to the artifact and decided I would try my best not to handle it at all.

Though Elias and I had yet to recognize the name of the artist Beckett Lowery, Connor, on the other hand, had. Apparently,

Lowery was a well-known artist who worked from the late nineteenth century to the mid-twentieth. His works were brilliant, obtuse pieces of nature, which were considered very innovative for his time.

Connor had explained that while he could not find any indication that Beckett had been part of the Order of St. Patrick, he had found a picture of the man, which included a shot of his forearm.

In the old photograph, the man's sleeves were rolled up, just enough to show a slight curve of a scar peeking out from under them. This was the only evidence we had found to connect Lowery to the Order, so we followed it all the way to the Carnegie.

An older woman in dress pants and a cardigan with glasses connected to a chain that hung around her neck waited for us over by the right corner of the giant elk painting. She was wearing bright white gloves and had a few tools sitting beside her on a rolling cart. She smiled when we walked in.

"Morgan! Thank you for being willing to stay late to assist us today," the director said.

We came to a stop in the center of the room. I had to step a couple paces back to see the entire painting in all its glory. Elias chuckled under his breath. I threw a glare his way but refocused my attention when the director turned to introduce us.

"Morgan, these are the representatives from the National Museum of Ireland. This is Elias Cassedy and Ava Metheny. Ava, it turns out, is from our neck of the woods, believe it or not." She smiled, and Morgan nodded.

"That's wonderful. It's nice to see people of your generation getting involved in this line of work."

I smiled at her and thanked her for her kind words.

"Morgan will take it from here, though. If you don't mind, I would like to hang around to see if you come across anything. This is all very fascinating to me," she said with glee.

Elias nodded. "Of course, ma'am. We would appreciate any insight you or Morgan have on the piece. Please feel free to join us."

Morgan stepped forward. "I'd shake your hands, kids, but I have already put on my gloves for the inspection. You can find yours on the cart. We do require them to be worn. But I request that you ask before touching anything; as I'm sure you can imagine, it is very fragile."

I stepped around her, set down my bag, and slipped on a pair of gloves.

The backdrop of the painting was a line of thick Sitka spruce trees in front of a glistening snowy mountain. In front of them was an icy pond that had captured its main attraction, the great Irish elk.

In total, there were three of them among the ice and snow, but there was only one that you could see up close. He was a large creature with giant antlers. He held his head up and his mouth opened happily into the air as if he was calling out to us. His large hooves were buried under the icy waters that held his reflection.

I had seen the painting here many times when I was younger but had never really appreciated it. Now, up close, I could grasp precisely how much work and precious time had gone into it. I could clearly see each delicate brushstroke, every swirl of color. I could imagine that it often left its viewer entranced. I, too, found myself in awe.

Elias, however, was more focused and got straight to work walking around to the side of the painting, and I took his lead and walked around to the other. Morgan stepped back, giving us some space while she began to recite some information on the artwork.

"This piece, as I'm sure you know, comes to us all the way from Ireland. It is titled *The Megaloceros giganteus*, the name of an extinct species otherwise known as the Irish elk, or the giant deer. It was painted in 1923 by Beckett Lowery while he was in Dublin. On a trip for the funeral of his sister, a poem was read that inspired this beautiful masterpiece and helped to assuage Lowery's grief. His wife nicknamed this guy Moose." Morgan smiled and nodded to the elk on the canvas.

"It was found among his things in his apartment in County Clare after his death from tuberculosis in 1929. His wife, Aine, said that the painting of Moose had once been one of his favorites, so she decided to share it with the world and donated it to the Carnegie when she moved to the States in 1942 with her granddaughter. Since then, many of Lowery's paintings have been donated to museums around the world."

I met Elias around the opposite end of the desk. He was studying the antlers on the beast in the painting while I chose to look closer at the edges of the canvas itself, which I noticed were beginning to fray. I squatted to further inspect it as Elias walked around me.

"Was anything unusual said by Mrs. Lowery when she brought it in?" he asked, but Morgan shook her head firmly.

"Nothing of distinction that I've been told."

"What about any tests? What was done to help preserve the piece?" I asked, but Morgan shrugged.

"No testing per se, but measures were put in place to restore the painting. This piece is pretty straightforward. The museum knew what it was getting ahead of time. So the painting's original stretcher was replaced, of course, and it was thoroughly and cautiously cleaned and varnished," Morgan explained.

Frustrated I wasn't finding anything, I let my gaze wander beyond the artwork to Morgan's cart of tools.

There were a few magnifying glasses, a couple of cleansing materials, a few pairs of tongs and tweezers, a couple of blacklight flashlights, a regular flashlight, a fourth pair of gloves, and a few brushes.

Elias stepped in front of me, blocking my view. I glanced up at him and then came to my feet. "And nothing was discovered during its preservation?" I glanced over at Morgan, who had not responded and instead was looking at the director with a knowing look.

"Was the preservation done here at the Carnegie?" I asked again with a look that demanded an answer.

This time, the director gave Morgan a short nod. She stood straighter and turned back to me. "Yes, ma'am."

Given the way those two were acting, I could only assume something had indeed been found while Moose was in the process of preservation.

"What about the fraying of the canvas? Has there been anything done to prevent further damage?" I asked.

Morgan shook her head. "That has only just begun. Until now, there was no need. But we have an appointment to address it this coming week."

I looked back at the edge of the cream-colored canvas beside me. The painting had been taken off its stretcher for the inspection, which really shouldn't have mattered to me, but something was nipping at the back of my mind, telling me to look closer. Though I had no idea what for.

Instead, I glanced back to Morgan's cart.

I stood up and walked back around the canvas to the cart. I picked up a blacklight, then looked back at Morgan and waved it gently. "What are these for?"

Elias was still busy trying to detect things with the human eye and wasn't paying attention.

Morgan smiled. "We figured you might want to take a closer look with those."

I looked back at work on the table beside me with suspicion. So they had found something. But how would Elijah have been able to—

"Elias?"

I snagged his forearm, tugging on it so he stopped what he was doing. I trusted the museum officials, but I wasn't sure what information he had shared with them and figured this was a better conversation to have between the two of us. Especially considering the Carnegie was a competitor in some respects.

Elias looked at me with serious eyes, and I had to shake my head to clear it of sinful thoughts before I continued. "You never told me how you figured out that Elijah colored the letters back in Glendalough," I whispered.

He knitted his eyebrows, unsure of what I was accusing him of or where I was going. He shrugged. "If it had been done naturally, it didn't make sense for single letters to be colored and not whole words. Why?"

I tilted my head toward Morgan and then motioned to the flashlight in my hands. "I'm wondering if it's possible Elijah would have used the same method for this clue as he did the one prior. Why else would they have blacklight flashlights sitting out for our use? That's not a normal thing to have at a museum. Plus, Morgan and Allison have been acting suspiciously. It's like they already know what we're going to find but don't know what to do with it."

Elias glanced sideways at Director Fort and then toward Morgan, who were both watching us with keen eyes. They didn't miss a beat.

Elias noted their weird behavior and leaned in closer to keep the conversation between the two of us. He put a hand on my elbow, moving me just right so that my body shielded his mouth from the two. Even if they could read lips, they wouldn't have had a chance.

"But even if that's true, Elijah used bird feces to discolor the letters. I don't think that would show up under blacklight."

I found this new information rather disgusting. "How do you know that? You never mentioned that before."

He shrugged. "You never asked. It was the only thing that made any sense. What else would he have had available to him?"

I stepped back and thought for a moment, racking my brain, but I couldn't come up with anything useful. "I don't know . . . blood? Milk, maybe? Water." I contemplated this briefly before Elias snapped his head up, suddenly causing me to throw him a look of alarm. "What about ferrous sulfate?"

"Huh? Uh, I don't know. I guess you might have found it in the city, I suppose, but what does that—"

"It's invisible ink!"

I was unimpressed by this explanation. "Come again?" I asked, wondering if I had heard him correctly. He had to be joking.

"You're knowledgeable at history, Av, but how about a little science? What happens when you mix water and ferrous sulfate?" Elias asked, leaning his head closer to my face than I had prepared for. I blinked and eyed his lips as heat began to spread through my cheeks. It took a lot of effort to regain my composure. I cleared my throat and glanced over at the two women watching us in the corner.

"I honestly have no idea," I whispered.

"It makes it colorless," Dr. Fort answered, stepping into the conversation and walking toward us. Morgan flanked her. Confusion was written all over my face as they joined the conversation. *You have to be kidding me*, I thought. The two walked up, polite smiles still plastered on their faces.

"Though it wasn't easy to get your hands on it back in the early 1900s, this painting has indeed been tainted by invisible ink," Dr. Fort explained. She grabbed the fourth pair of gloves and picked up one of the black light flashlights. She gave Elias a mischievous grin, then nodded and turned it on, pointing it directly at Moose. Morgan's smile fell a bit, but she allowed it nonetheless.

My eyes widened as the beam landed on Moose's reflection. "Elias," I whispered. There it was, painted in the reflection on the water of the great Irish elk. The initials that had sealed Moose's story and entangled it with ours.

E.M.L.

Elias grinned and placed his hands on my shoulders, shaking them slightly in excitement. I giggled.

"I can only assume by your reactions that you recognize those initials?" the director asked. Beaming, I nodded, turned on the blacklight, and began to run it over the canvas. Morgan scrunched up her face in disapproval but didn't say anything.

"What else is there?" I asked, but the director frowned and shook her head.

"I'm not sure what you mean?"

Elias stepped around me to examine the painting more closely. At the same time, I continued to brush it with the blacklight. "The invisible ink, that can't be all there is," he insisted.

I grew disappointed when I realized there wasn't anything more written between the brush strokes.

"We thought that was what you had been looking for?" Director Fort said, confused. Elias shook his head, his shoulders slouching forward. I could tell he was disappointed. But once again, I was convinced. The initials were there in blue light. Elijah had marked his territory; there had to be something.

I sighed, letting my gaze drop back to the fraying edges of the canvas. That's when something caught my eye. I bent down to look at it more closely. At first thought, it looked like there a faint yellow thread woven into the fabric on the back of the canvas. No, wait, that's exactly what it was.

"Morgan, did they line the back of this canvas with a wax resin?"

Morgan stepped forward surprised by the question. "We didn't see a need. Why?"

Elias stood behind me, but he knew better than to intervene. I pointed to the yellow thread at the top right corner of the back of the canvas that was hanging over the side of the table.

Morgan glanced sideways at me, then stepped away to grab tweezers and a magnifying glass. "I doubt it's anything, but I will approve further inspection. However, it must be done by a professional."

I nodded. Respecting her rules, I stepped back to give her space to check out the discoloration. Morgan repositioned her glasses and held the magnifying glass up to her face. With her free hand, she carefully used the tweezers to grasp the thread.

At first, it just seemed to unwind part of the canvas. At one point, she looked up and made a nervous face, which had me convinced she wasn't going to continue, but she got back to it and continued working. When a puff of air released dust from behind the canvas, and Morgan looked up with wide eyes I knew we had something. Her hands stopped hovering over the loose thread and waved us over.

I held my breath and came closer to look over her shoulder and encouraged her. She did, and it continued to unravel until the yellow thread was out. A little pocket had been threaded so intricately into the canvas back that it had been unnoticeable and was now open to us. It was only an inch and a half, maybe two at most, but it was there.

Morgan smiled and put down the tweezers. She then stepped back and motioned for me to inspect it. The room was dead quiet as I sat on my knees, eye level with the canvas, and looked into the pocket. I stuck two fingers in and pulled out a small note folded up and covered in dust.

Director Fort, behind me, gasped. I stood up and opened the paper.

A long line of tally marks . . . they weren't all the same length, and they didn't all have the tallies in the same place; each line was different.

I recognized the language right away, as did Elias. He smiled and shook his head. Elijah had done it again, this time in Ogham. His eyes slowly slid up to meet mine, his grin outlined by the lighting from the ladder above us, and I couldn't help but return it.

"Son of a bitch," Elias said in excited surprise.

The director behind us lit up, and Morgan looked pleased.

I turned and directed my attention to Morgan. "I assume we can't take this?" I asked.

Morgan made a face. But it was Director Fort who stepped forward. "I would rather you not, but I do have a pen and a piece of paper here if you would like to copy the runes."

Morgan dug into her cart and pulled out a slip of paper and a pen. I frowned at Elias, who shrugged, but passed the note to him so I could jot down the text, tally by tally. Elias continued to run his fingers over the old, wrinkled parchment.

"They're not runes; they are tally marks."

"From the ancient Irish language Ogham," Elias clarified, and I flashed him a smile. I wondered if he could read Ogham. The thought was somehow very sexy.

The director came over and took a look at the text herself, her face as pleasantly surprised as ours. I hadn't expected that; all this time, I thought there was something the two of them were hiding from us, and I was still suspicious of what this meant for our mission. What if they took this information and went off in search of the Jewels themselves? I looked nervously at Elias, who wasn't paying attention.

The director clasped her hands together in excitement. "All this time, I had expected you to find the pair of initials labeled on the front. But this! This is a new and wonderful discovery of Moose! We surely look forward to adding this grand story to his exhibit once you have found the jewels!"

Chapter Thirty-Three

LATE APRIL 1912, GLENDALOUGH, IRELAND

A buzz of rumors about the *Titanic* tragedy reached the Order's grounds in Glendalough. Many members of the Order, including monks, priests, and public officials, left for County Cove in an effort to help those mourning their losses and volunteer their services to the town that had last seen the giant ship take off.

Abram stayed behind to pray for Ireland's people. At his age, traveling such a great distance, only to then be put to work volunteering, would have been too much. Andrew and Elijah had also stayed behind.

Life had certainly gotten away from the brothers once Elijah joined the ranks. Andrew had been pleased at exactly how well his plan had worked. The town seemed to believe that Elijah had passed away without many questions about the circumstances. However, Andrew struggled to keep such an enormous secret from their family—all of whom honestly thought Elijah was dead. As unfortunate as it was, it was too great of a risk for their family to know the truth. Their little brother, Nathanial, appeared to have taken it hardest.

At Elijah's wake, Andrew wanted nothing more than to let his younger brother in on their secret. However, he knew that doing so would put Nathanial's own life in danger, and he couldn't have that. Andrew's mother, on the other hand, had acted as if she almost anticipated this day would come.

Surely she was upset that her son was gone. But the way she had spoken to Andrew after the wake made him realize that she had also known about the abuse that happened outside of the house. It was bad enough she never defended him in his own home, but to allow it to continue outside of the house after their father had passed had driven him mad.

His mother was an enabler. It made Andrew angry to think that despite her knowledge, she had never chosen to intervene. Had Andrew not stepped in when he did, his mother would have allowed it to go on until it inevitably killed him. Apparently, her reputation was far more important to her than the love she had for her son.

Things had changed drastically for the brothers since Elijah had been sworn in and branded by the mark of the Order. He had begun to study Andrew's habits and mannerisms in a way that had almost driven Andrew mad in the very beginning. He followed him relentlessly, taking mental notes, and at night would have Andrew question him on his likes and dislikes. Andrew hated the fact that Elijah, the brother he knew, was no longer.

However, other opportunities presented themselves to the pair as well. Andrew, to start with, had been much broader and more muscular than his twin, who had previously had little interest in working on his body and keeping up physical fitness. In an effort to make himself look more like his brother, Elijah had cut most of his hair, grown out his beard, and began to work out routinely alongside Andrew. They now started every morning with a run and ended most nights with a boxing brawl.

Elijah was a quick learner, and his appearance improved drastically within the first few months. By the end of the first year, they were indistinguishable. Andrew wasn't entirely sure that Elijah enjoyed working out the way he had. But Andrew had begun to appreciate their morning runs together. By the end of the second year, Elijah had finally stopped working so hard to be Andrew and started allowing more of himself to shine through. During this process, Elijah's confidence had bloomed, and Andrew had been glad to see his brother feeling comfortable in his skin again. He had gotten to know his brother better than he could have anticipated, even if Elijah had been trying to replicate him most of the time.

Since the big heist, Andrew and Elijah's "gift," as Lord Michaels had referred to it, had become very useful to the Order. They had been sent out on multiple missions that involved a wide range of jobs, from politics to other smaller heists and even a kidnapping to save the son of a deceased Order member. They were well known among the Order now and had the bunkers to prove it. The more accomplishments they completed for the Order, the grander the bunker the two got. Climbing in ranks, though, wasn't always luxurious, especially at a time when most council members were away in Cove.

Andrew and Elijah were helping Abram to keep things moving smoothly here, which was a challenging task. As part of their mission, the Order of St. Patrick sought to do good within their communities. They strived to help those clans in need. People from different parts of Ireland would send them letters asking for help on a variety of different issues, and most of the time, the Order would choose to step in.

On average, the Order got nearly twenty letters a day. Their name was getting out there in the best way while still being relatively undetected by the British. Although they did have plans in the making to challenge the Brits, now was not the time. Their people needed them first. And when the Order got its bearings and decided it was time, that's when they would strike.

Now, though, with most of the members gone, the sorting of letters and decisions of who they would help rested on the brothers' shoulders. Andrew was feeling the pressure of the Order weighing down on him as he sat at the desk in the small cottage that they used as their meeting hall most nights and flipped through each letter they had received in just one day.

Elijah approached his brother. He had just come in from a different meeting with another member who had recently returned from a mission. Elijah snagged a chair from across the table and dragged it over to the other side.

Andrew sat next to him, now leaning back in his chair, squinting as he focused on the letter in his hand that was marked from Kilkenny. Elijah didn't take his seat, though; instead, he leaned over the table, placed a cup of hot tea down for his brother, and picked up a different letter.

"There is a plague spreadin' near the shores of Galway and a family in Tipperary are looking for help feeding their seven children," Andrew said in a monotone. Elijah sucked in a breath.

"This one here is from a group in Belfast who claim the British have begun forcing people from their homes to grant sanctuary to other members of the United Kingdom." Elijah flicked the paper in his hands to straighten it, and Andrew put his own down to look at his brother.

Andrew wasn't given much time to respond, though, for at that very second, the high-pitched alarm sounded, informing anyone still on the grounds that there were guests at the gates. Andrew and Elijah stood up and looked out the window toward the path. Terrance came walking up the path. He no doubt would be here to inform the brothers of the intruder, and Elijah, ever the impatient lad, decided not to wait till the man reached the cottage. Instead, he turned and walked out the door to meet him. Andrew followed silently.

Terrance came to a stop on the gravel path before the old cottage and looked from one brother to the other. "There are intruders at the gates, sir."

"I can hear, Terrence, thank you," Andrew snapped. Elijah slowly looked toward his brother with a frown and shook his head at him.

"Forgive him, Terrance; he is under a lot of pressure as of late. Did you say there's a group of people?" Elijah said, eyeing his brother with a scolding look. Andrew rolled his eyes and placed his hands on his hips.

Terrance nodded to the two but turned to direct his answer to Elijah.

"Yes sir, a group of about six, maybe more."

"A family?" Elijah asked. Terrance shook his head.

"No, all men, sir."

"And what exactly is it they want, Terrence?" Andrew asked, his patience wearing thin. Terrance looked over at Andrew and then back at Elijah.

"They are looking for a meeting with the council regarding a matter they claim is of dire importance." The two brothers exchanged a look before returning their attention to Terrance. Each seemed to understand what the other was thinking.

"The council is not here. Tell them to come back later," Andrew ordered. The brothers chose not to waste any more time on this matter, and both turned to leave, dismissing Terrance. But he didn't move.

"I can't, sir . . ."

Andrew and Elijah stopped and turned around.

Terrance continued. "They claim they won't leave until a meeting has been set for today. They say the urgency is too great."

Elijah looked over at Andrew, waiting to see what his brother had to say. While they both were highly ranked within the Order, Andrew was still considered Elijah's superior and had the final say. It didn't matter that Andrew never made a decision without Elijah's approval first.

"They knew our men would be out on business covering the accident in Cove. This was planned, brother," he told Andrew.

Andrew nodded, thinking everything through. "They want a meeting, then they will get one, as unprepared as we are. Terrance, have the guards send them through, but only after you send a signal to the group still on the grounds that we have newcomers among us with questionable interests. Elijah, find Abram and track down Gideon McCoy and Darren O'Donnell. We will want them to sit in on this meeting in place of their father's presence as well. I expect our finest to be standing guard for an attack."

Terrance straightened his stance and gave Andrew a curt nod, then turned on his heel to sound a separate alarm.

Elijah started to follow his brother back to the cottage, knowing he had a different task but still wanting to reassure Andrew that they could indeed handle this. "Clear the hall tables for the meeting and make it presentable. I'll be back shortly. Let no man in before Darren or me is present," he instructed.

Andrew nodded and then disappeared into the cottage. Ten minutes later, the twins sat on either side of Abram, waiting for the group to set foot in the cottage. Darren and Gideon flanked the twins on either side. They were the younger sons of Jasper McCoy, the sailor who had snuck Elijah away on his ship while they held his funeral, and Wyatt O'Donnell, the blacksmith who had branded the twins.

From the window, you could just barely make out men hiding in the green grass of the hills surrounding Glendalough, waiting for trouble. Now was not the time for an attack. Most of the men were gone from the grounds doing work for the Order; the other half was away in Cove. Andrew feared what would happen if they were threatened.

Suddenly, the old wooden door to the hall opened, and a man in thick brown furs and dark-blue sleeves walked through. Tassels from his boots clanked as he walked. He was a big man; more broad than heavy, with a thick, dark-red beard that was graying in the middle. He wore a kilt in an effort to announce his superiority and leather cuffs to show off his riches.

Five men followed him into the room, and the door was closed by Terrance, who then took up his place as guard in front of it. Andrew rolled up his sleeves to show off the branding on his inner arm and crossed them over his chest.

"So this is the ever mighty Order of St. Patrick?" the man stated, arms held out in front of him to show the members of the current council. The man leaned forward a bit and held his hand up around his mouth as if he were about to tell them a secret. "Got to admit, I thought for sure I'd be a bit more frightened," he said, and he let out a howl of a laugh that shook his belly and threw his head back. His men chuckled behind him.

Seeing he wasn't getting the response from the council he was hoping for, he tapped his hands together. He looked around at his men before turning to address Abram. "Ah, well, enough of this. We've come to seek the assistance of the Order in a great plague that is destroying many towns and villages in Ireland. It is a cause I'm sure you can sympathize with."

Andrew sat forward. One of the letters had mentioned a plague, but he hadn't expected it to have spread so far already. Elijah, on the other side of Abram, tilted his head as a question.

"That be the plague of the British."

And there it was, just as Elijah had expected. He crossed his arms and looked down, disappointed to have wasted his time on this nonsense. Andrew sighed, but Abram nodded, to Elijah's surprise.

"We are aware of the trouble the British bring to Ireland," he said simply.

The man nodded, suddenly with fire in his eyes. Then he looked around the room and opened his hands, gesturing to the whole council.

"We hail from all over the country. Our group comes from many counties, as does yours. They call us the Rising. "

"Who calls you that?" Elijah interjected.

The man turned to him. "Our people!"

"Your people? Forgive me, but I don't believe I have ever heard of this group," Elijah stated. Abram looked curiously from Elijah to the man speaking.

"That is exactly why we are here. My name is Collin Leary. I speak as head of the group known as the Rising. We are built out of necessity to fight a common enemy. We have assembled a great group, an army of sorts, who seek to take down the British Empire. We are not small in numbers but small, perhaps, in reputation. And so we are here to seek the Order's help in an attempt to take back what is rightfully ours and restore Ireland to its former glory!" He finished his speech with his fist raised high in the air. The men behind him cheered and egged him on.

Andrew narrowed his eyes; the situation before him seemed increasingly threatening.

They had chosen to come at a time they knew their men would be away, and fate rested on the shoulders of the lesser ranks. They brought in backup and instilled fuel to fight with violence that couldn't be denied. They came claiming to seek the help of the Order.

Still, based on the way they had presented themselves, Andrew doubted they would take no for an answer. These people were out to start a war with the Brits. And they weren't here to ask them to join their cause. They were here to demand it when the Order was at its most vulnerable.

Still, the Order had been aware of their cause for many moons. It could not be denied that, eventually, something had to be done. But now was hardly the time. Andrew looked over at Abram, who spoke up first. "The Order is a peaceful group that seeks to keep the peace at this time. Eventually, there may come a time when our presence is required to intervene, but I doubt now is that time, friend," Abram said.

The man's eyebrows knitted together to form one furry caterpillar on his forehead, and he stepped closer to Abram, as if to make his presence seem more threatening. Showing true loyalty to Abram, both Andrew and Elijah shot up from their seats, prepared to step in front of the man if need be. Darren and Gideon, on either side, sat back watching, unsure of what to do next.

The man known as Collin looked between the two men and then back to Abram. "See here, monk. We know well of the plans of the Order, and we demand to see them fulfilled this year."

Abram held his hand up politely. "The Order has no plans at this time to deal with the British, Mr. Leary."

Collin looked outraged as this was not the answer he was clearly seeking, and he smacked his walking stick on the ground in anger. "What good is a group as powerful and as ruthless as ye be if you don't stand up for yer own people? How can you call yourselves protectors of the Celts when you don't stand up to fight."

"Fighting is not yet necessary."

"Of course it's necessary! You have seen what they've done to the people in Belfast; you've seen the jobs they take from our own, yet ya sit here and do nothing?" Collin was shouting now and drawing attention from the men on guard outside. Darren and Gideon slowly came to their feet as Collin's men stepped forward. Abram sat planted in his seat, unfazed.

"You say you've seen people hurt by the Brits, yet we have not yet seen that for ourselves. Can you produce proof?" At Abram's request, Collin blinked suddenly, taken aback, and began to rack his brain.

"Ah! There is always proof," he said and nodded.

"Then have it be brought to our grounds by sundown. Our council will talk it over tonight and have an answer for you by the time you reach us in the morning."

Andrew looked over at Abram, who slowly came to his feet and folded his hands in front of his chest. Collin narrowed his eyes at him and shook out his beard. "Fine. But beware, if ya don't join the cause, then consider yourself an enemy."

Abram nodded understandingly as the men began to back out of the hall. "Go now and be well, friend. May the sign of Saint Patrick himself bless you."

Chapter Thirty-four

MODERN-DAY PITTSBURGH, PENNSYLVANIA

AVA

Over the next half hour, Elias and I, alongside Morgan and Director Fort, touched every surface again with gloved hands and scanned it with the ultraviolet lights, but nothing else came up. The first text we found seemed to be enough for another clue all by itself, so Elias and I gave the final call and stopped looking sometime after nine thirty p.m.

I voiced my concerns about Director Fort and Morgan helping us find information. Still, Elias had assured me they had both signed forms agreeing that any further discoveries on the Irish elk belonged to the NMI.

The agreements stipulated that as long as they were permitted to add our findings to the Irish elk exhibit, they couldn't do anything with the information. That made me feel much better about sharing such detailed information about our mission.

Morgan finished up, but we spoke with Director Fort for another thirty minutes or so. After that, we said goodbye and allowed the director to lead us out through the service entrance on the side of the building. By the time we hit the dimly lit streets of Pittsburgh, I could barely feel my toes.

"My feet are killing me," I mumbled. I hadn't intended for Elias to hear me chastising myself for my shoe choice. But when we reached the parking garage, he walked me up to level one and stopped.

"Why don't you wait here? I'll go pull the car around," he said, looking up to level two.

We were parked somewhere between levels two and three. Even though I hated to sound weak and whiny, I loathed the thought of continuing the climb in these shoes even more, so I caved. "Are you sure?"

Elias shrugged. "Yeah, as long as you don't mind waiting here by yourself for a bit."

I looked around. I was in a parking garage next to an elevator, so I had a brighter light shining overhead. I could see just fine from where I was, and my back was facing the wall, so there shouldn't be any problems. Plus, this was the city I had grown up in; this was home. I had nothing to be afraid of.

I lifted a shoulder to Elias. "I'll be fine."

"Alright, I'll only be five minutes. Stay here."

I watched him fade around the bend into level two of the parking garage. It was lit enough that I could see that there were a decent amount of cars still on level one.

There must be some type of event going on, I thought. I stood there tired and inattentive to my surroundings, which gave the man behind me the upper hand.

Out of thin air, it seemed, a strong male hand cupped over my mouth, preventing my scream from going very far. A second arm slammed around my waist, practically knocking the air from my lungs. I tried not to panic, and my body suddenly switched into survival mode.

I screamed as loud as I could against the hands that held me in place. I brought my own hands up to the one covering my face and thrashed with all my might against the arm around my waist.

The man started to shuffle me off to the left side, and I felt I was losing the battle. I used every bit of strength I had. I threw myself forward then backward, smashing the back of my head against my captor's.

He dropped me in seconds and started to howl in pain as I fell to my knees, slamming hard against the ground. Dizzy and terrified, I looked back to find a mid-sized, broad man with a ski mask. Blood was pouring out of it, and he ripped it off his head and catered to his broken nose in his hands.

Holy shit, where was Elias?

I stood up and took a few shaky steps away from the guy down the slope of level one, unsure what to do next, momentarily immobilized by fear. Then, out of the corner of my eye, I saw lights from one of the parked cars off to the side flicker on. They cast a brief, blinding glow over the situation.

For the next few seconds, I thought someone had actually come to my aid until the lights dimmed, and I saw a second masked man behind the wheel. He revved up the engine, and I realized I didn't have time to wait for Elias. It was a fight-or-flight situation, and I chose the latter. I didn't have time to think; I didn't have time to look for options; I kicked off my shoes and ran down the ramp into the street. I took a sharp turn just past the gate. The street entering the garage was a one-way street going left. I hoped it might slow them down, but it didn't stop the men from continuing the chase.

A wooden bar, which guarded the garage, exploded into tiny shards behind me minutes later, much to my dismay.

I ran as fast as I could, not bothering to look back. Cars coming down the road veered off into the alleyways and swerved to avoid the maniac behind the wheel of the car chasing me. My feet scraped against the concrete sidewalk, slicing open the skin, causing sharp stabs of pain to weave their way up my legs.

I stumbled, feeling blind as I ran; the city around me seemed to blur past in muted shades of gray and black. Tears streamed down my face, making it hard for me to recognize exactly where I was going. Still, I pushed against the wind, propelling myself forward.

The black sedan had gotten very close, following me with terrorizing determination. I pumped my arms harder, my chest heaving, pushing my lungs to their limits.

It had just caught up to me when a popping noise sounded from the far left. It was followed by two even louder bursts closer by.

I turned around to see the black sedan swerve wildly then crash into a dumpster. The man who had attacked me in the first place jumped from the passenger seat and took off after me on foot.

I focused on the street before me, looking for alleyways that might split off and not lead to a dead end. The bustling noise of more prominent traffic pulled my attention up ahead. A bright four-way intersection came into view, and my heart leapt, knowing it would hopefully shed some light on the situation to other people in the area. Someone had to help me.

As I entered the traffic lights' glow, the man behind me collided with my back, which sent me flying forward. I slammed down hard on the pavement and bashed the lower side of my head on the sidewalk—a gush of metallic liquid bled into my mouth, tasting of rust. The side of my face ached like I had been punched.

I tried to collect myself so I could fight back, but my vision was blurring, and my ears were ringing loudly. I pulled myself up to a sitting position and tried to focus on a crack in the concrete underneath me.

I saw two of everything. Running was not an option anymore, and even if I could, I didn't think I would be able to physically pull myself up to a standing position. My head was too fuzzy. All my senses seemed to be offline. I put a hand to the side of my head, dazed.

The man took the opportunity and grabbed me by the back of my shirt, then flipped me onto my back so I was lying on the ground. He straddled my waist, and I watched in slow motion as his hands came up and curled around my neck, then squeezed tightly.

A second round of popping sounds rang out into the night. This time, they were much closer to me. Shards of concrete flew in all directions. The dark-haired man, with blood still covering his face, loosened his grip on my neck enough that I was able to turn my head away from flying cement.

A third round went off, this time from the other side of me and my attacker. It caused the man to try and take cover by curling himself into a ball on top of me. He wrapped his hands around the top of his head and squeezed his eyes shut.

Two more rounds went off around us. Even though my hands were free, I was seeing black spots. I couldn't process what was happening.

It wasn't until the man on top of me abruptly disappeared and I let my head fall to the side, stunned, that I even realized what the popping sound had been. We had been shot at. Beside me, where the concrete had exploded moments ago, was a perfect bullet hole, inches from my face.

I turned my head, still on the sidewalk on my back, and saw that Elias had finally found me. He took a few swings at the man first, then dropped him crumpled on the ground and returned to my side.

Elias looked like he had a twin I had never met before, and they were both staring down at me with concern. I thought he called my name, but my ears were buzzing, so I just blinked at him mindlessly, unable to communicate with him.

He put a hand around my neck and tenderly sat me up on the ground. He moved his weight around so he leaned my body against his, and he probed the side of my face, inspecting my jaw. My eyes finally began to refocus, and I could see Elias move his fingers around, pulling back only when I winced or shrank away from his touch. His face was pale, his eyes wide.

Moving quickly, he thrust an arm under my legs, wrapped the other around my back, and picked me up and placed me in a blue car waiting by the intersection. Again, he tried to talk to me, but I couldn't understand what he was saying. Instead of trying to respond, I leaned back against the passenger's seat. Elias jumped into the driver's seat and we took off out of the city like a bat out of hell.

I was tired, my head was throbbing, and my knees and hands were scraped. My feet were cut, bruised, and bloody. I didn't know why I was fighting so hard to stay awake when all I wanted to do was sleep. But something was telling me to keep my eyes open.

Someone wanted me to stay with them, but I didn't know who. After fighting for so long, though, I couldn't keep it up any longer, so I closed my eyes and allowed the darkness to swallow me whole.

Chapter Thirty-five

Elias

Ava's head was bleeding from at least one spot on the side of her jaw line and possibly from a second spot closer to the back. Her cream-colored face was smeared with dirt. Her long dark hair was in disarray; her jeans were ripped at the knees, showing scrapes and cuts.

But of all things, her feet were by far the worst. They were scraped and bloody and already bruised. Even though they looked to be the worst part of everything, Elias knew the head wound should be his biggest concern. He had addressed her multiple times, and she had not been able to respond to him once. That was not a good sign.

Elias pulled out his phone as he urgently drove the Honda through the streets of Pittsburgh. He didn't know where he was going, but he knew a hospital was out of the question. These people were after the jewels; he was sure of it.

He couldn't risk the Order by involving the police, and hospitals were too complicated to navigate without causing trouble. They had cameras everywhere, kept records of everything, and would surely ask questions he wasn't sure he could answer. But looking at Ava, whose head had just sagged into a terrifying unconsciousness, he knew he had to get her help soon. If Kayleigh couldn't find someone nearby, he would have to seek medical attention at a hospital, whether he liked it or not.

He dialed Kayleigh.

"Hello?"

"I'm in Pittsburgh; Ava was attacked, and she's bleeding from a wound on the side of her face; there may be multiple wounds, I'm not sure; I need help now!"

Elias could hear typing from behind the phone. "Okay, okay," said Kayliegh. "It looks like there are two members in the area who may be able to help. One is in Beaver County; it looks like it is owned by a sleeper agent, Ea—"

Elias cut her off. "That's all the way out by her parents! That's forty-five minutes away! I don't have time for that, Kay, she's unconscious!" Elias was trying to rein it in, but he was starting to panic at the sight of her slumped over in the passenger seat.

All the memories from the accident with his previous partner were flooding back. He was losing control of his emotions and he knew it.

"Okay, okay! Calm down! There is one closer to the city in Bethel Park. Owned by Amanda Snyder. She worked as a doctor for the army. She's ten minutes from you."

Elias took in a deep breath to calm his nerves. "Perfect, send me her details."

"Will do; I'll give her a call and let her know you're on your way. Anything else she should know about Ava's condition?"

Elias glanced back at the tiny woman unmoving beside him. "She's got cuts and bruises all over her hands and knees, and her feet are shredded. I think she only has one major wound on her jawline, but there is blood there and she has some bruising on her neck as well."

"Got it. I'll give her a call and text you her address."

"Thank you, Kay!" Elias hung up but didn't breathe even one little sigh of relief until he pulled into the short drive of Amanda Snyder's house. She stood outside, arms crossed over her chest in the dark, waiting anxiously for them under the porch light.

Elias barely put the car in park before he wordlessly snatched Ava and carried her into the woman's house. She led him over to a kitchen table in the middle of the room. She already had it lined with white sheets and a small pillow for her head. Elias gently set Ava down on the table and stepped back to let the woman work.

She instantly pulled out a tiny light and shone it into Ava's eyes, pulling each of her eyelids open as she did so. "When did this happen?" she asked.

"Fifteen minutes ago."

"What happened?"

Elias shrugged and shook his head in frustration. "I don't exactly know. I left her to go pull the car around, and when I returned, she was gone. By the time I found her, a man was on top of her, and she was like this," he explained, waving his hands out at her motionless body.

Amanda looked annoyed. "Why don't you go grab a beer from the fridge and wait out on the deck while I work? You're just going to get in the way here and cause yourself more stress if you stay in here."

Elias looked between Amanda and Ava, unsure what he should do. But Amanda was right. He could feel himself losing his cool.

"Beer's in the fridge. I've only got Ellie's Brown Ale at the moment, but I think you'll like it. Grab a couple and take them outside. I'll come get you if I need you."

Elias waited outside for what felt like a millennium. He felt helpless; he hated sitting useless, unable to help Ava as she struggled on a stranger's kitchen table. But Elias reminded himself that Amanda was a member of the Order. She was sworn to help them no matter what. She had taken them in on such short notice that Elias didn't think she'd had more than ten minutes to prepare. But she had been prepared nonetheless, and for that, Elias was extremely grateful.

Elias was working on his second beer. Out in Amanda's small backyard, he looked up at the night sky and the stars that twinkled above. His heart nearly jumped out of his chest when he'd first seen Ava lying on the sidewalk, being strangled and shot at by those men. He had a flashback to the accident two years ago when his then partner, Mark Adams, fell while they were rock climbing on a mission. He remembered the kid's unresponsive outline, his body crumpled and broken at the bottom of the cliff. His friendly, usually goofy smile was gone.

He waited in the hospital for the kid's parents to arrive. He would never forget the fear and panic in his mother's eyes in the waiting room hours after the incident while Mark was still in surgery. He could hear her sobs as they were told Mark would live the rest of his life in a wheelchair.

Despite what he had been expecting, Elias had not been reprimanded by the museum. It was an accident from faulty equipment they were given, according to the police report. He had walked away essentially scot-free, while Mark's life had been changed forever.

Elias shuddered at the memory and refocused his thoughts on Ava. How had he let this happen again? He would forever blame himself for leaving her alone in the parking garage in the middle of the night. He knew better. He had promised himself days before that he wouldn't let anything hurt her, and yet here they were. He'd failed her, and he felt that guilt deep within his soul. This was his fault.

His phone buzzed in his pocket. He pulled it out and looked down to see Lottie's number. He put the phone back without reading her message. Five minutes later, his phone went off again, and this time, he shut it off. He would make sure to inform her once he knew about Ava's condition, but he couldn't talk to her right now. He was too distracted to listen to her go on about trivial stuff when he was so anxious.

When he heard a creak of the door behind him, Elias jumped to his feet and came face to face with an exhausted Amanda. She sighed at him and smiled. "You good?" she asked, and he nodded. "She's not awake yet, but I got her cleaned up and stitched. She's going to be okay. You can come see her if you'd like. She's awake. Don't worry I explained that we are old friends."

Elias followed Amanda back into the kitchen, where Ava was now sitting up on the table, holding an ice pack to her jaw. Although her hands, knees, feet, and head had been cleaned, her clothes still bore some blood splatters. It had caked parts of her hair. Her feet were bandaged and also wrapped. Elias grimaced at the line of stitching glue Amanda had applied just along the side of Ava's jaw to mend the long gash she had received.

She blinked at him sleepily as he walked over and stood at her side. His hand came down gently and rested on her hip.

Amanda explained to both of them that fortunately, no serious harm was done to her jaw, but the gash would take some time to heal and would cause a rather noticeable bruise. While she wouldn't have any food restrictions, she might want to exercise caution and stick to soft foods for now.

Her hands, knees, and feet would recover in the same way. However, her neck might cause some soreness. Amanda suggested that, temporarily, it might be best to save her voice. At the moment, only two tiny spots had managed to leave any impressions on her skin. Thanks to the gunshots, the man hadn't had enough time to cause serious damage there either. For now, she recommended rest, pain relief, and limiting her vocal use.

Ava nodded dismissively, either too tired to argue or because she was still in shock; Elias couldn't be sure. Even with all this information and two beers in his system, Elias was still holding his breath; however, this time, he didn't let it show. His face had become a steel curtain, hiding every sign of fear in his eyes, stoic as ever. "Is it safe for her to rest?"

Amanda rummaged deep in the kitchen cupboard behind her, then made her way back into the light of the room with a bottle of Ibuprofen in her hands. She held it out to Ava, who took the bottle with a sad smile. "Yes. There is no sign of a concussion or any serious head injury, so I feel safe letting her sleep. You might want to consider getting a change of clothes though," she teased.

Ava looked depleted at the thought. Elias nudged her elbow pulling her attention to his.

"What's up?"

Ava shot him a glance, trying to figure out how to respond when Amanda had just said not to talk. However, the woman understood the assignment and had already retrieved a notepad and pen from a different cabinet. Ava scribbled down her answer with trembling hands.

I can't go back to Eamon and Millies like this. I'll scare the kids; Millie will freak out and Eamon will kill you!!

Elias didn't know what to say. She was right of course. It would not look good for them to return to her home tonight, that was for sure. He crossed his arms, thinking the situation through. "How long until the bruising goes down?" He knew this was a long shot, as it had barely started but he figured he would ask anyway.

Amanda shook her head and Elias instantly understood. No, they wouldn't be able to hide this forever. They would have to come up with a different plan.

"A week at least, maybe even more for her jaw there."

"Okay, well, it's too late to go back now. Let's find a hotel for the night, and we'll come up with something in the morning." Ava seemed to agree and jumped off the table with Elias's arm to steady her.

Ava stepped away from Elias to try and write out her thank you to Amanda, but the woman smiled politely and leaned forward to gently rub her shoulders, saying, "Anytime."

Ava tried to hand Amanda her notepad and pen, but she told her to keep it and wrote down her number on the front just in case they needed it.

Elias, in the meantime, sent a message to Kayleigh to get them a room at a nearby hotel and to send the directions to his phone.

Then the pair slowly made their way to the door, arm in arm.

Chapter Thirty-Six

To Elias's surprise, Kayleigh managed to get them into a rather nice hotel just ten minutes from Amanda's house. The only issue he saw was that it was only one room, whereas Ava probably would have preferred two. Elias didn't mind this at all, though. By this point, they'd spent enough time in close quarters that it really wasn't a big deal anymore, and besides, he didn't want to let her out of his sight. Not just yet.

After checking in with the front desk and collecting their room key, they made their way up to the third floor, where they planned to stay for the night. Elias appreciated that Amanda had thought to offer Ava a pair of Crocs and an old jean jacket to hide the blood on her shirt. He could only imagine the looks they would have received checking in with Ava in that state. He would need to send her a thank you note later for all her help.

Once in the room, Ava looked around blandly and frowned, catching a glimpse of the bathroom. Elias laid his backpack on the only bed in the middle of the room and tried not to take her expression personally.

"What?" he asked, taking a seat at the edge of the mattress.

Ava made a big show of writing out *"I have to shower."*

He wasn't quite sure what to say. He pursed his lips.

He understood why she might be timid about this. Her body was aching. She was both physically and mentally worn out. Her pain was manageable for now, thanks to the pills Amanda had made her take before she left, but that didn't mean her feet would be comfortable in a standing position for too long.

But it wasn't as if she had much of a choice; she had to scrub the blood off her shoulder and upper arms, and the warm water would help ease the ache in her muscles. Elias knew he couldn't do much, but he could at least help her get it ready.

"Sit, I'll get it going."

While she was in the shower, Elias had taken the time to text Kayliegh to thank her for her quick action tonight and to update her on Ava's condition. Then he began to outline the situation that had completely unraveled, hoping to clear his head a little.

These were the facts: They were staying in a hotel. Ava's parents currently didn't know what had happened or her whereabouts, but would have to find out eventually unless they came up with a cover story. They had no food or extra clothing except—

Suddenly, a thought dawned on him.

Ava was about to finish her shower and had nothing to wear but her dirty sweater, which still bore blood from her attacker's broken nose. Elias removed his green button-up from his shoulders and cracked open the bathroom door to toss it onto the towel rack inside.

He felt like he was quickly losing control. If the most he could do was ensure that Ava slept peacefully and comfortably tonight, then that's what he would focus on first.

One step at a time.

Elias took a seat at the desk opposite the bed and leaned back in the chair, returning to his texting conversation with Kayleigh. Ava didn't take long in the bathroom, and twenty minutes later she emerged slowly, wearing nothing but his green button-up. Elias did a double-take. The night in Glendalough sprang to the front of his mind.

Most of the buttons were secured, thank God.

The shirt reached just above her knee, leaving her lower legs exposed. Her brown hair was damp, and her eyes heavy as she padded over to sit at the edge of the mattress. "Looks better on you than it does me," he chuckled. Ava gave him half a smile in thanks, then rubbed her eyes. She pulled out her notepad, jotted down something, and then turned to present the page.

"Thanks for the shirt. What are we going to tell the McKennas?"

Elias turned fully to her now and shrugged. "I was just pondering that, actually; I think you should text Millie tonight so she doesn't worry and just let her know that we stayed out at the Carnegie longer than anticipated and are going back tomorrow morning. We booked hotel rooms in the city for the night, and then we can come up with an explanation for all this—" he motioned to her "—tomorrow over breakfast."

Ava quirked an eyebrow at him and turned her page over again to him.

Obviously, Elias knew they didn't have to tell the McKennas anything. She was a grown woman. But Ava preferred maintaining open communication with them, and they had become used to it. Elias could respect that. Coming in late was one thing, but not coming home on a night when she was in town only briefly for work with a stranger? It was understandable why they would worry.

"hotel rooms?"

She wanted to laugh, he could tell, but she suppressed her smile. Elias shrugged confidently and leaned back in his chair. "This was the only one they had! I don't know what you're talking about."

At this, she did smile. *"Sure."*

It was a relief to see her smiling again. The flow of conversation and banter was so easy for the two of them. Around Ava, Elias had begun to feel relaxed, which was a totally new experience for him. He was almost always on edge. It was a small price to pay for the job he did. However, another glance at her blossoming bruise reminded him of why he was always on edge.

When Ava reached for her phone to message Millie, Elias stood up and placed his phone on the desk. "Do you want me to take the floor?" he asked, gesturing to a spot on the floor beside the bed. Ava looked up at him, almost frowning, and shook her head.

"Okay."

He walked around to the other side of the bed and sat down with his back to her as she crawled over to her side and burrowed under the heavy quilt. Elias, opposite her, removed his socks and t-shirt, keeping the rest of his clothes on, settled under the covers, and switched off the lamp. He clung to the edge of the bed and stared up at the ceiling, now in darkness. Given his larger frame, it was a little difficult to give her the space she deserved, but he wanted to make sure she felt safe enough to sleep. However, sleeping for him tonight was likely to be challenging.

Ava stirred beside him a second before he felt her slender figure curl into his side. Her wet hair chilled the skin of his bare chest as she rested her head on his shoulder. Elias breathed a sigh of relief and wrapped his arm around her torso, pulling her close.

He couldn't believe how stressed he had been until that moment when he felt it all begin to wash away. Having her close now didn't feel like he thought it would; it wasn't sexy or romantic but rather refreshing. It wasn't like the kiss they had shared the other night. This was different. It felt like smelling the rain after a drought. It felt like finding the missing puzzle piece he'd lost.

"Thank you for saving me," she whispered. Elias turned and rested his lips on her head. His hand rested on her hip.

"You're not supposed to be talking," he whispered back. Ava wiggled beside him.

"Am I making you uncomfortable?" she asked.

"No."

"Good." She was quiet for a minute, then she whispered, "I wouldn't have slept in the second bed anyway," she admitted. Elias opened his eyes in the dark room now, afraid of what she would admit to next. But she didn't speak again, so Elias filled the silence with an admission of his own.

"I've got to be honest with you. When I finally reached that intersection, and I saw you . . . I went into full panic mode. It's been a very long time since I have felt that kind of fear." He let his words fade away.

Ava slightly drew back and propped herself up on her forearm to look up at him. Elias opened his eyes and shifted his position to rest his forehead against the top of hers. His admission had surprised not only her but himself as well. It was like he had crossed some line into uncharted territory. These were the things they didn't dare say out loud, but clearly, both of them wanted to.

They took a moment, allowing everything to wash over them slowly. All the pain, the fear, the anger was communicated between them without the need for any more words. She was so close, and they were both so vulnerable that it was almost intoxicating.

Elias didn't hesitate this time. He gave in to his desires. He leaned forward and closed the space between them. When his lips brushed against hers, she gently kissed him back. It wasn't a passionate kiss; it wasn't even that long. But it meant something. The gesture spoke volumes at a time when they couldn't find the right words. Elias pulled back slightly, not wanting to put too much pressure on her, and she nestled back into her spot against his side. He rested his cheek on the top of her hair, then pulled her in tighter.

Elias inhaled the scent of fresh lavender, and his heart finally surrendered its last resistance to her. He was done fighting this. They didn't need to have everything sorted out. He didn't have to work out what this meant for him and his place within the Order. They didn't need to figure out how to handle things moving forward. No, at that moment, they just needed to cling to one another as the rest of last night slipped into the past.

The next morning, Elias woke up to find Ava's arm wrapped around his waist. It felt right, but he knew they had some things to sort out, and Ava couldn't walk around in his shirt all day. Carefully, Elias eased her arm from his middle and swung his legs out of bed. After checking she was still asleep, he pulled on his t-shirt, socks, and shoes, grabbed her keys, and left a note on Ava's notepad before heading back into the city.

Chapter Thirty—Seven

Late April 1912, Glendalough, Ireland

Andrew paced the floor inside the hall. Abram paid him no mind as he looked through some of the letters the twins had gathered from today. Darren and Gideon held a short conversation as the two watched him. Elijah was sure his brother's anxiety was making the boys equally nervous.

They were only a little younger than the brothers. Darren and Gideon had both been inducted shortly after Elijah due to their fathers' reputations but had only been on one or two missions since they were branded. Neither was very active in the Order. However, with the current council on a mission of their own and due to the boys' family history with the Order, they were technically next in line to help make decisions.

Elijah didn't really know either of them all that well. Still, his brother was relatively close to Darren, who sparred with him on occasion during training. Darren's family hailed from the county of Donegal. Their ancestors had been some of the founding fathers of the Order of St. Patrick. And for that reason, there always seemed to be an O'Donnell on the council. Rumor had it that Darren's family was from the line of O'Donnells who had ruled Ireland for centuries until the British forced them out; descendants of the great Red Hugh O'Donnell. It's been said that St. Patrick himself blessed this clan, saying, "In hoc signo vinces!" *In this sign, you will conquer.* Their coat of arms held a cross to honor this.

As Elijah watched Andrew pace, he also noticed Darren's finger constantly twitching and Gideon's inconsistent, anxious breaths. No one but Abram appeared to be calm.

This would not bode well. Elijah had to figure out a way to put everyone at ease; otherwise, Collin would surely eat them alive once he returned. Elijah stepped away from the spot where he had been leaning against the window and walked over to whisper something to Terrance, who gave him a curt nod before disappearing into the darkness that had covered Glendalough.

Andrew stopped to watch the interaction and waited for Elijah to return to his side. Holding his chin in his hand as if still deep in thought, he waited for Elijah to explain. Elijah, however, gave him a look that told his brother to relax and walked by him toward the center of the floor where Collin had stood only a couple of hours prior. He addressed the group. Even Abram stopped what he was doing to look up.

"Gather your courage, friends. Our friends will return soon, and we need to be at ease if we want a fighting chance of not being corrupted or influenced."

Darren and Gideon exchanged a look, then Darren sighed and sat up straighter, trying to make himself appear more confident. Gideon looked from Darren to Elijah and bit the inside of his lip, still holding onto his concern.

"I know this is not the council we were expecting to lead us. You may not have been prepared to deal with such a dire situation so soon, but we cannot ignore this, and we cannot show them fear. We must stand strong. We all hail from great lineage. We are strong and wise warriors. We would not have been branded otherwise. Our call to serve our clan has arrived, and we must put our best foot forward and show our strength, not our weakness."

Just as Elijah said those words, Terrance returned from the dark carrying a tray with five drinks on it. Following Elijah's instructions, he handed them to everyone but Abram—who didn't partake—and held on to the last one for himself. Andrew understood his brother's motives and came to step up next to his brother, his glass raised, waiting.

"Take a sip, my brothers, and feel at ease. Tonight, they will return, and when they do, we will be ready for them!"

They raised their glasses and cheered before throwing their drinks back. Andrew relaxed a bit as he felt the warm liquid slide down his throat. He could do this, he thought. With Elijah by his side, he was invincible.

Abram smiled from his seat, watching the young men. After his push for the Order to induct Elijah, he had some concerns regarding his stature, his reputation, and, more importantly, Elijah's way of life. But Elijah had proven himself to be a wise choice, and Abram had grown just as fond of him as he was of Andrew. He was proud to be a mentor to such fine men. It was clear that one day, these two would lead the Order after he was long gone.

Just then, the siren went off, and Andrew snapped his head around to look out the door. Terrance shifted his stance, setting down his drink, and exited the building. Gideon stood up and relit lanterns around the room that were slowly fading as the twins returned to their seats. Together, filled with newfound confidence, the men awaited the return of Collin and the group known as the Rising.

A couple minutes later, Collin and his men walked back through the door. Though this time, he only brought along three with him to drop off the file he held in his hands. His eyes scanned the room, landing on the twins with suspicion. It was clear from the way they had handled his advance last time that these two would be a threat to his plan if anything actually went awry. Collin, at the time, had made a mental note to watch them a little more closely from then on. Andrew narrowed his eyes once Collins's gaze stopped on him.

"Here is the proof ye asked for. Straight and to the point. Things have gotten out of hand, and the time to act is now. If we wait any longer, as you have chosen to do so far, bad things will happen to our people. That is something the Rising will not tolerate. We will be back in the morning at dawn to discuss your intentions moving forward. At this point, ye either with us or yer against us," he declared, and he gave Abram one last look before exiting the building. That had been, without a doubt, a threat to the Order, and Andrew wondered how Abram would choose to respond.

Terrance waited for all the men in the room to exit, then swiftly made his way to Abram with the folder containing Collin's proof in hand. Abram collected it and opened the file. His eyes scanned the several papers he had before him. It wasn't much, merely some pictures or articles of different altercations involving the Brits and the Irish people in a variety of places across the country. Abram sighed, knowing this would not have been enough to encourage the regular council to act. However, he agreed with Collin that the time to intervene was indeed coming sooner than they had anticipated. Alas, Abram concluded that, given these circumstances, he was not quite sure what to do. He pursed his lips deep in thought and handed the file over to Elijah.

One by one, the members of the current council took a look at the evidence the leader of the Rising had brought to them. One could have easily mistaken this for the homework of a schoolboy if they hadn't known any better. Even Gideon McCoy had shaken his head, knowing this information meant very little to them. Still, the Order's job was to protect their people, and this, without a doubt, was going to be hard for them to continue to ignore.

Had the Order been aware of these things happening around the country? Yes. But up to now, they were few and far between. At this point, simply offering aid to the affected families was a better use of their resources than creating a scandalous scene and causing a war with the British that they were unprepared for. It all came down to one thing: They simply didn't have the numbers within their ranks. Andrew shook his head at a loss of what to do or how to respond.

"Any thoughts on what you want us to do, Abram?" Darren asked.

Abram looked at him with old eyes. "What would yer father say?" he simply asked the young man.

Darren crossed his hands over his chest, looking down at the table. Abram already knew the answer, but he wanted Darren to say it. Abram hoped he was helping him to step into his role as a leader if he simply guided him to think for himself.

Years later, Elijah would recall this teaching moment and note that it had indeed sparked a flame within Darren. Because of this conversation, he would grow to become one of the best leaders of the Order they had ever seen. And all because an old monk gave him the courage to think for himself.

"I know what my father would think. He would deny them the opportunity to work with us. There is simply not enough reason for us to intervene."

"And do you agree?" Abram tilted his head and waited.

"No. Not at this time. With most of our members away and not enough time to call them home, I think we should give them what they want. They are too much of a threat to us, and we are far too vulnerable. Plus, it is undeniable that things are beginning to escalate, and we are called to service for a reason," Darren stated.

Andrew turned his head violently toward the young man opposing him. "I disagree. Abram, to join league with these people now would be suicide, surely. Even at our best, we are simply not strong enough, not prepared enough to take on such a large enemy as the Brits. This would lead to the deaths of many clans. Surely, you see reason!"

Elijah scratched his chin thoughtfully, eyeing Abram and Darren before glancing at his brother sideways.

Gideon fidgeted in his chair. "He's right. To align with such a group is not our way. We cannot tarnish our reputation either. We must think this through, every aspect, in great detail."

Abram nodded, then looked back at the papers on the table, his old mind wandering many different paths, all leading him to dead ends.

Elijah cleared his throat. "What if we were able to do both?"

Andrew looked at Elijah with confusion. "And how do ye propose we do that? He has already seen you, Elijah; he knows there are twins amongst us."

Elijah shook his head at his brother with a chuckle.

"I'm not talking about us—or at least not in that way. But I do agree with Darren. We owe it to our people to keep a closer eye on the situation. So, I propose volunteering a spy. Someone from within the Order who we will send into the ranks of the Rising. They will infiltrate their grounds and keep us informed of their activities as well as the information they collect on the British. That way, once the full council returns, they can choose to act as they see fit based on the circumstances. This all while the members of the Rising are appeased. We can tell them that until our full group returns from Cove, we can only afford to send them one man but will surely send them our best to join their cause and work with them once the Order's council is restored."

Andrew inclined his head, thinking this through. This was brilliant. It held off the potential threat the Rising presented to the Order, all while giving them a chance to have eyes from the inside. Andrew looked up at Abram and awaited his response, but he had already come to his own conclusions.

Abram didn't need much time to ponder the idea; it was the only plan the Order could implement to move forward without harming its own. He nodded, approving of Elijah's brilliance; a smile of pride danced on his lips. He folded his hands on his lap and then looked around at the men.

"I think that is a wise choice. Who then shall we send into the camp of our possible enemy?"

The men discussed a few options, including Richard O'Connor, Killian Schrause, and Deacon Fitzgerald. All of the above were great options for this mission, having great reputations in their mission fields. Still, Abram kept a peculiar eye on Andrew. And it was then he knew what he wanted from him.

"I'll go," Andrew said, cutting off Darren and Gideon's conversation.

Elijah looked to his brother in surprise. "Don't be a fool, brother; you are needed here," he simply said, but Abram turned to him with a look only an elder could give, and Elijah stopped talking.

Abram then turned to the eldest twin and nodded. "It is decided. Andrew will join the ranks of the Rising and report to us on their strategies. This meeting is now adjourned."

It was decided by the highest member of their current council. Andrew would go, placing himself in the midst of danger. Elijah could not deny the terrible feeling he had growing in the pit of his stomach. But he could not overrule Abram. They both knew that.

Abram stood and began to exit the hall. He turned back to the men still staring at him and gave them one last look. "I'll see you at dawn to meet with Collin Leary."

And with that, the lights blew out.

Chapter Thirty—Eight

Modern-day Pittsburgh, Pennsylvania

Ava

I woke to find my jaw feeling tight, and the muscles along my face on the left throbbing. I let out a moan and twisted in the covers, reaching for the comfort of Elias, only to discover he wasn't there. I threw my eyes open and turned my head back to where his form should have filled half the bed, but my first instinct had been correct. I quickly scanned the room and listened carefully to see if the shower was running, realizing he was gone.

My heart shouldn't have felt the sting of betrayal so intensely, but in that moment, it nearly caved in on itself. That is, until I caught sight of his terrible handwriting, laid out on my notepad.

"Gone to grab us some clothes and breakfast. Got your size from your sweater tags. -E"

I breathed in a sigh of relief, pausing to steady my pulse. Somehow, in the last twenty-four hours, everything that had been going so well had completely fallen apart for them. Not only had I been mugged, but I'd lied to Millie again, and ended up in the same bed kissing the man I'd been denying myself for weeks. It was overwhelming.

But that was quite normal for me by now. Slow and relaxed wasn't something I was ever going to be; that had been made clear. Still, the memory of the night before—the terror I felt in those moments before Elias found me—was raw. I'd managed to navigate many of life's challenges, but this was something that genuinely frightened me. I'd never been physically assaulted like that.

Grief I was used to, but fear was a different emotion I didn't quite know how to deal with.

I never really considered the need to protect myself before. Sure, my dad had shown me how to use firearms when I was younger, and Elias had trained with me and demonstrated some moves, but in that moment, everything I had learned vanished from my mind, and I froze, only able to rely on my ability to run. I am now more aware of everything around me, more cautious, more anxious. The world is full of terrible people, and you never know where they might be hiding.

I had just started to spiral down the dark tunnel of anxiety when the door to our room clicked, and Elias's figure appeared in the doorway. My shoulders dropped, and my body relaxed at the sight of him. I took in a big breath to calm myself down from the panic attack I had triggered. He knitted his eyebrows briefly upon seeing me, and closed the door to the room behind him.

"You okay?" he asked. His eyes scanned my face as he made his way to the bed, and tossed a bag of items from Walmart and another from a local bakery onto the quilt. He set aside the drink carrier from his other hand on the desk in front of the bed and reached out to inspect me.

I didn't pull back from his touch but I could help the wince that escaped when his finger even gently brushed my face. "I thought you left me," I whispered.

Realizing I was in no real danger, he let out a breath and shook his head dropping his hands to his sides.

"No, I needed to go pick up a few things. It may not be the most stylish, but at least it will fit and be clean. I leaned more on the side of comfortable, but figured the turtleneck would help to hide the bruising on your neck."

I brushed my fingers over the fabric of the beige turtleneck he had chosen and gave him a small smile in thanks. His eyes found mine again and he took the seat beside me.

"How do you feel?"

"Sore," I whispered with a chuckle, then winced again. The movement hurt more than I had anticipated. Elias reached over to the desk across from him and grabbed the bottle of pills. He tossed a few in his hands and held them out to me, along with a bottle of water he'd grabbed at the store.

"Tylenol, to help until you eat. I'm not sure what you'll be able to tolerate so I snagged a few things," he explained and pointed to the brown bag between us. "There are eggs in there and a croissant for you, and if you're really struggling, I also grabbed you a smoothie."

I threw back the pills without a thought and thanked him.

"I wanna jump in the shower. Why don't you take your time getting dressed and check in with your mom?"

I watched Elias stride away from me toward the bathroom with his phone in hand, feeling a little disappointed. I wasn't sure what I had expected to come of last night, but I definitely knew I wanted more than what he was currently offering.

Feeling a little down, I slipped out from under the covers and stood up, taking a moment to stretch my feet and make sure they could support me before I started getting dressed. From inside the bathroom, I heard Elias's quiet voice fill the room a second before the shower turned on.

Calista was the only one I knew he would check in with this early, and I was curious to hear exactly what he had to say. So, I slowly crept over to the side of the wall and extended my ear towards the closed door.

Elias sighed into the phone from the other side. "I know, I know. I'm sorry I didn't answer last night. I was dealing with a problem with Ava and had to shut off my phone for a bit."

Calista's voice rang through the buzz of the shower, but I couldn't make out exactly what she was saying.

"No! Actually, we found what we were looking for. But we will most likely be extending our stay here for another day or two. Last night, something happened when we were leaving Carnegie, Ava . . . got in an accident."

An accident? I was surprised to hear him lie about what happened last night—and to Calista, of all people.

Elias was silent for a moment, but I couldn't hear Calista speaking on the other end, so I wasn't quite sure what was happening. When he finally spoke again, he sounded annoyed. "She's okay, thanks for asking. I got her checked out late last night but she's a little roughed up."

The muffled voice picked up again on the other end.

"A gash on the side of her jawline, some decent bruises and cuts," he responded. Calista carried on.

"Uh, yes, sorry. We found a note stitched into the underside of the painting. It's written in an old Irish language we haven't deciphered yet. Ava and I will work on translating it once we return to Dublin."

A hand slapped something, and Elias let out a frustrated breath on the other side of the door. "He wants a meeting today? I mean, I guess I can make that work, I just—No, I understand. Yes, it's fine. Sure. Okay, I'll send you a text when we're available today, but it probably won't be until early this afternoon. Okay great, I'll talk to you soon. Yeah, I love you too. Bye."

I stepped away from the door. Steam that seeped out from underneath the door frame swirled around my ankles. Elias swore they weren't together, but it had always been quite obvious they were close. And Calista was determined to make a spectacle of it every time she was around.

Picking up the clothes Elias had bought for me and ripping off the tags, I wondered where that left me. Even if Elias and I moved forward, would I always be the third wheel in their friendship? Calista was important to him, and I liked her enough, so I wanted to make it work, but I wasn't sure she'd be very pleased with me. I couldn't blame her—breaking the girl code was a serious offense. I was getting ahead of myself; so far, nothing had come of last night. Everything had changed inside me while the truth of our relationship remained bare in the room around me. We weren't together. We were just two people working on a project who had bonded through trauma. That was it.

I eased into the pair of loose jeans and pulled the turtleneck over my head, carefully avoiding the side of my face. I walked over to the mirror attached to the desk and gave myself the first look since the attack last night.

I blinked at my reflection. It looked worse than it was. My eyes were hooded and lacked luster today, lips pale, but the paint-like splotches of bruising on the side of my face, surrounding the vertical gash and glue strips, were more than enough for me. Feeling insecure, I suddenly turned my eyes to my dark hair and ran my fingers through it, brushing out all the knots.

Elias cleared his throat from the entryway of the bathroom and drew my attention away from the mirror. "You look fine," he said with a small smile, and I felt a flicker of hope in my chest. "Not everyone can pull off that shade of purple," he teased, holding out his hand. I took it and let him guide me past the bed to the small love seat by the window.

"How are your feet?"

I looked down at my feet and lifted my shoulders. They hurt a little today, but the pain meds helped, and they definitely weren't as bad as I thought. As long as I wasn't on them for too long, I figured I'd be okay.

Elias squeezed my hand. "I booked the room for two nights, so I figured we could hang in here today and just relax and let you rest before we head back."

Thank God. I had no intention of walking around town today. We had mostly been on the go since Glendalough, too, so having a day just to rest sounded wonderful. Elias leaned back in the love seat and hung his arm over my shoulder. He propped his feet on the small coffee table and handed me the brown paper bag of food. I took one glance at it and shook my head. Nope, that was not happening today. Elias tried to hide his concern, but pushed the bag to the side and instead handed me a large Styrofoam cup.

"Hope you like bananas." I lifted the cup to my lips, took one sip, and sighed. It felt like heaven. I didn't realize how hungry I was until now. But man, was I thankful for this.

I picked up my phone and scrolled through Millie's response from the night before, feeling content that my update hadn't prompted further questions. That was a huge relief. Now all we had to do was work out our story.

"Come up with anything creative while you were out?" I whispered. Elias ignored me and pointed to the notepad, but I pushed it away. I'd have to talk to Millie and Eamon tonight, like it or not so might as well start now.

"You're not supposed to be talking." He insisted for the second time in twelve hours. I wanted to smack him, but considering he was trying to be helpful, I refrained.

"She said I should reserve it just in case. Not that anything was damaged," I insisted louder. Elias looked away, aggravated with me. He was used to getting things his way, and I never fell into step with that, but somehow over the course of our time together, I realized he was getting used to dealing with that part of me too.

Elias brushed me off and eventually answered. "Possibly. Ever rent bikes to ride around the park here?"

"You mean Schenley Park?"

"Yeah, I saw a flyer for bike rentals in the front lobby when we came in last night. I figured we could tell them that after we got breakfast, we rented two bikes to do some sightseeing—"

"It's not sightseeing for me," I reminded him, but he waved me off.

"It's sightseeing for me. Anyway, we'll tell them we went bike riding through the park when another rider collided with you and we had to get you medical care."

While he spoke, I cautiously lifted my hand to run my fingers along my jaw. The pain was not as severe as I expected, which was a relief, but it still made me tear up. Elias pulled my hand away from my face with a frown. "The second day is always the worst. Leave it be."

On instinct, I wanted to ignore him and see how bad it really was, but Elias held my hand tightly on his lap, so I didn't argue.

Elias glanced at his watch.

"If you message Millie in about fifteen minutes, we can manage this. We'll obviously have had to postpone our meeting with the museum until the afternoon, so we won't get back to your house until the evening. By then, your bruises should look the way they do without raising suspicion. As long as you keep them informed, I believe it should work," Elias trailed off as he observed my expression. "Or, if you prefer, we could always tell them the truth?"

I sighed, knowing that's what I thought I should do, but it was too great a risk. Eamon would surely blame me; Elias and Millie would call the police to file a report. They would probably throw another fit about me returning to Ireland soon after, and I didn't want to have that argument all over again after everything I had gone through to get here. No, telling them the truth was not an option. At least not now. I shook my head.

"I don't want to be cleaning more blood off the floor for a second day in a row," I said with the best smile I could muster. Elias smirked at my humor but visibly relaxed. "That reminds me, Dr. Balor wants a chat this afternoon. I told Lottie we could call, but it would be via FaceTime. She scheduled the meeting for two in the afternoon," he grumbled, frowning as he scooped another bite into his mouth.

I watched him closely now, my curiosity overcoming me. "What is your deal with him?" I asked. Elias froze.

"What?"

"Balor? What is your problem with him? You always seem to get irritated anytime he is brought up in conversation."

I thought back to that time in Glendalough and the strange comments Elias had made the day we uncovered the first clue. Elias was furious when I spoke over him at our very first meeting with Balor. He later mentioned, near the graveyard, about my being chosen by someone specific to join the team here. Could that person have been Dr. Balor himself?

Beside me, Elias shook off the question and returned his focus to our joined hands. He twisted and curled my fingers with his as he tried to avoid answering. "I just don't like the guy. He seems sketchy to me. You shouldn't trust him."

I folded my arms. "That's it? He's suspicious?" Something didn't quite add up. Elias licked his lips and turned his head now to face me.

"Balor has a rough past," he admitted. "He's been known to cheat to get the things he wants, including things like job titles. I have a hard time trusting anyone who doesn't earn their right to work here, the same way we have."

Okay, now that story I could understand. "And you have earned your right then?" I pressed, knowing full well it would annoy him.

Elias looked genuinely offended. "I'm sorry, you think I haven't?"

I shook my head and placed my hands on the table. "That's not what I said, I just don't know why a man of your age is still working as an expeditions advisor in a museum instead of taking on a regular job and exploring their field."

Elias looked flustered by this.

"And how old do you think I am?" he asked, trying to contain his smile. He knew he was putting me on the spot and I knew he was using it as a distraction.

"Forty-seven," I stated confidently. Elias shook his head, grinning now as he knew he had been played.

"Twenty-eight, actually." He looked away and took a moment to compose himself before replying. "Believe it or not, Miss Know-it-all, I actually enjoy the work I do here at the museum and have had the pleasure of being part of some very unique finds over the past few years."

"But you could do the same thing in a much more advanced setting, so while settling at the NMI, working with interns?" I questioned. Elias shrugged and sat back in his seat.

"Perhaps I knew something better was coming along," he mused. His lips curled into a sly smirk now, and I wondered what exactly he meant by that. Was it me he was referring to? Or this opportunity we were both currently chasing after—stolen jewels and precious secrets of groups long forgotten?

Elias pulled away and climbed to his feet to grab the remote for the TV. "You ask too many questions," he mused, but I ignored him.

The plan went smoothly as Elias had hoped. Millie took the bait, calling only once when I told her I was going to urgent care, and otherwise she patiently waited for my texts to update her. We managed connect to the hotel Wi-Fi so we could hold our team meeting without interruption. Elias looked relieved that Balor hadn't turned up as expected, which made the whole situation quite informal.

I allowed Elias to tell Calista all the details of our find in Carnegie and only interjected a couple of times once the facts became more focused on the writing. "The Ogham was on a slip of paper hidden inside the painting itself," I explained. "It's an old language we can decipher once we return, I have no doubt."

"I'm sure Elias can as well," Calista confirmed.

I watched Connor take notes throughout the whole interaction, but I could see the concern in his eyes the moment he had a good look at my face. I felt guilty. Amid all the chaos of the last twenty-four hours, I had forgotten to fill him in on what had happened.

"Dr. Balor is going to want the two of you home in the next few weeks for the fundraiser. But otherwise we're going to be taking a short break as he has business to attend to out of the country." Elias looked confused by this.

"Why does that matter to us?" he asked. I could tell he was trying to be professional, but you could hear the irritation in his voice. Calista sighed.

"It doesn't. You two are more than welcome to return in the next few days and start translating the Ogham if you wish. I'm sure Connor and I could assist you if you want, but honestly, I would love some extra time off. It's been so long since I've had a vacation, and I thought we could all use that time wisely if you catch my drift."

Connor's face did not hide his surprise at Calista's obvious hit on Elias, like I suspect he thought it did. Elias, however, was devoid of any emotion.

"I think we'll probably head back sooner rather than later. I agree with you, though, Lot. I have a few ideas of how to spend that time. Do you think you can get Ava and I on a flight by Friday?" he asked.

Calista grinned and started immediately typing something into her computer.

"Shouldn't be a problem, I'll send you all your information tonight. This will be great, Elias. I need your help picking out shoes to go with my dress for the fundraiser."

Elias ignored her comment and bashfully looked at his hands.

"Speaking of the party, would you be able to do me a favor, Lot?"

"What's up, buttercup?" Her voice sounded lighthearted. I tried my best not to scowl at the obvious perk up to Elias returning home.

"Ava's obviously going to be out of commission and in need of rest for the next few days. If I can get you her dress size, do you think you could pick out a dress for her? I'll cover the cost. She's going to be banged up as it is; I don't really want her to waste the time that she needs to heal, trying on dresses."

My eyes widened at this new piece of information, and I looked over at him stunned.

"Wha—?"

Calista's eyes slid over to me. "And . . . what's in it for me?"

He looked relieved at her playful tone, and for the first time since yesterday afternoon, gave us both a full grin. I found myself feeling even more confused. "Tell you what, you get Ava's dress and some shoes to match, and I'll let you use my money to pick out a necklace from Gear Jewelers."

Gear Jewelers was no joke. That place crafted stunning pieces and was extremely expensive. Again, I found myself wondering where we stood. Calista beamed directly through the phone, thrilled by this offer. I was surprised too. That was a lot of money Elias was risking, and all for two girls and a fundraiser. I briefly wondered how he could afford it, but decided to keep that question to myself. It wasn't kind to ask when he was going out of his way to make sure I was looked after.

"Aw, darling, you shouldn't have!" Calista cooed.

Elias chuckled at her. "Just let me know the cost, and I'll forward you the money."

"Whatever you say, hun. I have to go, though. Balor has been blowing up my phone since we got on, and I need to inform him of the situation. I'll send you the receipt and your flight details soon!"

We ended the call.

The next few hours were quite tense. When we returned to the house, I underwent an inspection by Millie herself, while Elias answered every single one of Eamon's questions. I was right not to tell them the truth. Considering how Eamon was interrogating Elias now, it reassured me he would have been ten times worse if he had known the true cause of my bruises.

Thankfully, I continued to improve quite quickly as the days blended into weeks leading up to the fundraiser. The bruising on my neck turned out not to be as severe as we initially thought, and by the first week, I was able to hide it with chunkier necklaces or infinity scarves. The rest of the bruises became smaller and less vivid in color. The cuts and scrapes healed day by day, and by the time we landed back in Dublin, I felt comfortable removing the glue strips from my jaw.

Things between Elias and me remained caught between flirting and friendship. He often kept me close, holding my hand almost everywhere we went. Aside from that, nothing much had changed. We still argued over silly things. But he never took things any further, and I decided that if he wanted me, he'd have to show it. Otherwise, I wasn't going to put myself out there.

Returning to Ireland had brought additional responsibilities for Elias, which ended up delaying our studies further, much to Calista's dismay. Hattie's barn was still a mess, so Elias decided to head to Glendalough once we arrived and spend a week or so with her, helping to fix up the place as best he could.

He had offered to see me safely back to my dorm at the NMI first, but I declined his offer. I had to respect his family's morals, and I knew he respected mine. Instead, I chose to have Connor pick me up, which caused a visible irritation to Elias's features as Connor's small yellowish car pulled into the lot. Elias looked down at me with a frown, and it was clear to me now that he didn't want me to go. This was the most emotion he had shown me since I woke up the day after the attack.

"Are you going to be okay on your own?"

What a silly question to ask.

"I was fine before you, I'll be fine now."

Elias grappled with his decision to leave for a second before leaning down and planting a quick kiss on my forehead. Butterflies lit up in my chest as he pulled away.

"Call me the second you need anything."

Chapter Thirty—Nine

Elias

Elias could not contain his resentment toward Connor as he watched Ava get into his car and pull away from the curb of the airport, leaving him behind. He hated having to part ways with her, but he had family obligations to attend to, and that couldn't be denied.

Elias turned and made his way toward the taxi station where he'd arranged for one to pick him up. He was Hattie's only family living in Ireland, so her care was essentially his responsibility. Not that Hattie would ever agree to being tended to. She was much too stubborn for that. But being older and single made her vulnerable, which was one of the reasons Elias had always stayed in Ireland, so she was never truly alone.

Elias walked up to a dark black car with a man leaning against the door of it and a sign that read *E. Lynch*. He tipped his hat to Elias to greet him as he approached. The man grabbed his bag and tossed it in the trunk, then jumped into the driver's side. Elias took his seat in the back and stared out the window as they drove.

Shortly after the barn fire, his phone had been ablaze with messages and calls of concern from his siblings. Even his father had crawled his way out of the woodwork and left him a voicemail while he was in Pittsburgh.

Elias barely even responded to that one. He knew Hattie would talk to his father eventually, and he'd be off the hook once again from any type of awkward conversation with the man. His sister and brothers, however, could not be so easily ignored.

Alana had practically had a meltdown when he had not answered his phone on the drive back to Dublin the following night, and Nathan had yelled at him for being careless and running into fire to save a horse. Tanner was the only one who acted like it was no big deal. This was no surprise as the kid was always on the move these days and barely had time to breathe, let alone text. He simply sent a *You good?*, and Elias responded with a thumbs up emoji and that was it. No drama, no issues, just chill, that was Tanner in a nutshell.

A half hour later the car pulled up to the inn where Hattie was waiting outside for him. She smiled wide, making the redness in her cheeks spread across her face, which pulled a reluctant smile from him as he got out of the car and tipped the driver. After retrieving his bag, the driver pulled away, and Elias walked freely into Hattie's open arms.

"My boy," she cooed. Her arms encircled his shoulders, and he hugged her back wholeheartedly for the first time in a long while. "It's good to see you, Auntie."

Hattie pulled him back at arm's length and peered at him with concern etched in her face. Elias couldn't handle her questions right now though and stepped away from her with a shake of his head. Hattie knew him well enough not to push him on this and followed him into the kitchen of the inn. "It's been a while since you've called me that," she noted with a chuckle.

Elias smiled and set his bags down by the table. He set his jacket on the back of a chair and proceeded toward the coffee pot she kept on hand for him. "That's because I've always got company with me."

"That ya do lad. Always workin' are ye." Elias spared a glance at her from over his shoulder. He could tell she was holding back, but he doubted that would last. Hattie never kept anything to herself for too long. He grabbed his coffee and came to sit at the table across from her.

"How are you doing, Auntie?" he asked, bringing everything back to the reason he was here in the first place. Hattie sighed and took the seat opposite him. She leaned her elbows on the table and folded her hands solemnly. "Doin' as best as I can, I suppose. It's hard lookin' out der and seeing it all in shambles," she frowned. Elias reached forward as a tear slipped down her cheek and rested his palm on her forearm.

"Don't worry, we're going to fix it up, you and me, it'll be just like new, I promise. You'll see." Hattie frowned and she adverted her eyes from him. "It's just hard because it was hers ya know? Ya know who built it don'cha?" Elias sat back and shook his head before taking a sip of his coffee.

"Yer mother did! Most of it anyway, with help from yer grandfather a'course. He started it and she finished it. They worked well the two of them did, ya."

Elias set his mug on the table and stood up to turn around and look out the window at the damage the fire had truly caused. The barn that once stood there was now a heap of burnt wood and hay. Ropes, saddles, barrels, and a miscellany of other farm tools were covered in ash or burnt to a crisp and scattered among the rubble. The grass around the barn was charred and would need attending to as well. Elias had a lot of work to do if he wanted to get back to Ava within a couple of weeks.

"How'd Nigel fare when the vet checked him out?" he asked, turning his attention back to his aunt. She looked worn out and emotionally exhausted, but she stood up and made to get rid of Elias's coffee.

He protested, but she gave him a stern look and he stopped.

"It's caffeinated. Are ya sure ye want that now? Ya got work that needs to be done early in the mornin', ya know," she explained and continued on. "He did alright, luckily you got him out quick or we might not have him here with us either. He's stayin' down at Pete O'Rourke's place along with the flock till we get this mess sorted out."

Elias sighed and came around to pull Hattie back into another hug. "We'll fix it up right and it'll be like nothing ever happened, Auntie. We'll put this behind us for good."

The plump and usually cheerful woman paused with her hands in the sink and lifted them to where his forearms met around her. She sniffled. "I'm glad yer here, Elias. I don't know what I'd do without ya."

Elias got to work the following day, cleaning the area and setting aside the things they could salvage. He managed to get in touch with Kayleigh and was able to get some help from friends sent up to Glendalough to assist him in rebuilding Hattie's barn. For two weeks, the men worked on rebuilding stalls and landscaping the grounds to restore them to health. Both Alana and Nathan sent money to help repair the damage, which gave them the funds to get Hattie all new equipment for Nigel and the flock.

Hattie enjoyed having members of her group stay with her; it seemed to be just the right dose of medicine for her. Hosting had always come naturally to her, and in no time Elias began to see her familiar bubbly smile reappear more often.

Elias kept in touch with Ava consistently over the time he was away. He hated not being close while she was recovering. Not that it had really done her much good after all. After that night in the hotel room, he had essentially pretended like nothing ever happened. Things had gotten a bit tense between them since they left the airport in Dublin. Her texts were cryptic and it felt like she was purposely shoving her time with Connor in his face. Every time he'd check in to see how she was doing, she was always at his apartment or out for coffee. Elias was beginning to lose his mind over the situation.

When the barn was nearly finished, with just a few minor things left to be done, they welcomed Nigel and the flock back with pride. Elias and Hattie thanked the men for their hard work and saw them off as they headed back to Killarney. With not a lot left to do, Elias finally took a breather and made his way toward the sitting room, prepared to sit back and put his feet up.

Hattie was perched reading a book in the love seat. He handed her a hot cup of tea before taking his seat in the lounge chair across the floor. She beamed up at him gratefully and laid her book and glasses down to enjoy the last evening she'd get with her nephew before he set back out to Dublin.

"Thank ya much!" she smiled and took a sip. "Boy what a ride, ya guys made good time!"

Elias agreed. At the beginning, he hadn't been confident they could finish it within his time constraints, but the boys had pulled through for him, and they managed to get it done quickly. Elias raised his mug in the air. "Ey! Here's to the Order," he toasted.

"I'll drink to that. *Sláinte!*"

Hattie climbed to her feet as a thought suddenly struck her. "Oh what are we doin' drinkin' tea? We should be crackin' open the good stuff!" she said and shuffled her way back into the kitchen to pull out a tall gold bottle with black labelling. She grabbed two glasses from the cupboard and brought them back to the couch.

"Hattie—" Elias warned.

"Aw hush."

Elias let a laugh escape his lips from behind his coffee cup. Hattie never was the subtle type. "We don't drink together for a reason ya know?"

Hattie smiled over her shoulder and popped the top off the bottle and began to pour the drinks. "Oh really, and why is that?"

She filled the first glass over half full and held her hand out to pass it to him. Elias looked wide-eyed at the large glass of whiskey and took it from her. He had to juggle a bit to keep from spilling the contents of both his coffee and his drink onto the floor.

"Because you're a bad influence! *Tiarna Maith*, Auntie, are you trying to get us drunk?" he exclaimed. Hattie just grinned and found her seat with her glass now safely in her hands. She swirled the liquid around a second then brought it to her lips and sipped it. She closed her eyes and smiled.

Elias set his coffee aside and shook his head at the old woman.

"Perhaps I am, What'er you goin' to do about it eh?" she challenged. Elias sat back and brought his own glass to his mouth.

He followed Hattie and swirled the drink around, then took a sip. "Nothing."

Elias knew better than to challenge his aunt. Hattie sat back in her chair. She finally looked back to her usual self. The sight warmed Elias's heart. It was tough to see her so upset about something completely out of her control. He knew the barn had sentimental value. He understood better than most would, but there was nothing they could do but move on and rebuild.

"Ready to go back to Dublin tomorrow and see our girl?" Hattie quipped.

Elias took another gulp of his drink. It warmed the back of his throat, which helped to chase the chill in the air. "Our girl?"

Hattie pointed a finger at him and sipped her drink. "Ya know exactly who I mean," she accused. Elias chuckled.

"She's not my girl Auntie. She never was."

"*Raiméis*! You two were made for each other," Hattie huffed. "Drink, lad. Or ya whiskey will get cold."

Elias eyed her but did as she said and threw another gulp back. He had noticed by the third sip that his insides were beginning to feel a little warm and his thoughts less guarded. He knew what she was doing but didn't care enough to fight her on it. So finally, he caved.

"She's trouble, Auntie," he said with a smile. Hattie gave him her all-knowing grin, bobbed her head, proud of herself for getting him to spill the tea.

"Ah, but the best kind, yeah?"

Elias weighed this thought.

"I suppose."

Hattie swirled her glass around thoughtfully and resumed her prodding. "The kind that'll make ya second-guess your life choices I suspect."

Elias threw back another gulp. Clearly, Hattie knew more about relationships than he did. Elias wanted to pretend as if he had all of life figured out, and until recently, he thought he had. But now, he wasn't so sure.

"Have ya spoken te yer sister about any of this by chance?" Elias's eyes shot up to meet Hattie's gaze. He'd been caught, and she knew it. Elias tried to regain his composure by taking another drink, but it somehow managed to slip down the wrong pipe. He coughed and cleared his throat, then ran a hand through his hair.

Hattie laughed at him and shook her head. "Oh boy, yer really smitten."

"Alana knows nothing of Ava," he countered, but Hattie knew better.

"But ya asked her about the ring, didn't ya?"

Lord, have mercy, why did this woman always have to know everything? She could never keep her nose out of it. Always forced herself right in the middle of everything. She was like a teenager that way, living off of gossip and whiskey.

"I only asked her where it was. I didn't ask her for it."

Hattie threw her hands up so fast she nearly spilt her drink. "And why the bloody hell not? It's just a claddagh ring, Elias, not an engagement ring."

Could have fooled him. The thought of it felt like a noose.

"Yer mother would have wanted her to have it," said Hattie. This softened Elias's attitude, and he looked away from his aunt, knowing she was right. "Tell me what happened that changed, because ya weren't this unhappy before you left last."

Elias didn't know what to say. Things over the last few days hadn't been going very well with them being a part. He had no idea what he was walking back into as he headed to Dublin tomorrow. But Hattie didn't know any of that. She had only seen what she wanted to see during their brief time together in Glendalough a couple of weeks ago. But beneath the surface, it was much more confusing. "I don't know, Auntie. I think I may have screwed this up."

"How?"

Elias rolled his shoulders back and shifted, feeling uncomfortable with the spotlight on him. "We had a moment . . . or two in Pittsburgh and then—" Elias shrugged to himself. "And then I never made a move. I don't know how I'm supposed to navigate all this with her in the picture. I can't give her the things she needs; I can only take them away. She's better off without me."

Hattie looked at him now with a serious expression. Her heart felt heavy because of the burden her nephew was clearly carrying. All of her sister's children had taken the oath, but none had lived up to its expectations as Elias had. Everything he did was for the Order. Perhaps it was time he learned to sacrifice something other than his desires for once.

"Elias, ya can't go on living your life in the shadows the way your great uncle did. That was no life, I can assure you. The Order will always be around, but ya won't find another girl like her out there again," she cautioned, and Elias knew she was right. However, that still didn't resolve the issue at hand. Ava needed money, and he was about to steal it right from under her nose. He shook his head sadly this time and threw back the last of the whiskey.

"Doesn't matter, soon enough she will hate me and there will be no coming back from that when she does."

"But why?"

"Because I'm about to be the reason her sister can't get her cancer treatments," he bit out through clenched teeth. By the look she was giving him it was clear she had missed a few details.

"It's a good thing I grabbed somethin' stronger. Yer gonna have ta explain that one to me deary."

Elias sighed and scratched the back of his neck. Then he proceeded to tell Hattie every single detail of his time with Ava. He dove all into the mess he had created and walked her through every minor issue they had along the way. Hattie listened intently, and when he was done, she remained still, watching him for a moment with her hands on her lap.

"So it's not a perfect relationship, I'll admit," Hattie said. She was trying to make him feel better about his chances, but Elias didn't think there was much to save. Once Ava found out, it'd be the end for them. Tired and a little groggy from the drink, Elias wiped his hand down his face in defeat. Hattie leaned forward and tapped her hand on his knee to comfort him.

"It'll be grand, Elias, you'll see. Everything will work itself out. Ava is a strong woman; she won't budge so easily if her heart's truly set on you. Just tell her the truth. The Order be damned. We will pick up the pieces when and if the time comes."

"She's going to be angry with me, Auntie."

"So what? Are ya sayin' you can't handle a little heat, Elias? Buck up! The money now is another matter. I can understand yer problem with that, however . . . I suspect we might be able to come to some sort of arrangement with the council if you and Ava are successful in your endeavors."

This caught Elias's attention. He removed his hand from his face and sat up straighter in his chair. He hadn't thought about going to the council about all of this. After all, that was their purpose: to help people. Perhaps he could present the case to them, and they might be willing to offer her some kind of a trade?

"You think that could work?" he asked her seriously.

With a pensive tilt of her head, she considered the pros and cons, then concluded. "Yes, I do. They stepped in to help yer mother after all, and she was never a member. They agreed solely on the grounds of all the good works your father had done up until then. We take care of our own. And if Ava is yours, they should respect that request as long as it's understood the severity of keeping our secret."

Elias took a breath of relief and rested his elbows on his knees. He couldn't believe he hadn't thought of this loophole earlier. Yes, the Order was eager to remain hidden, but they recruited new members regularly, and Hattie was right. They offered help to their people, who in turn supported them, and Ava and he succeeded—they would both have something to gain from the council. The Jewels had been missing for just over a century now, and they belonged to them. Returning them to the Order's hands was no small feat. It would be an honor. Perhaps there was hope for him and Ava after all.

Elias fished his phone out of his pocket and pulled up Ava's number. He didn't care how late it was; he knew she would get it anyway. He stood up and kissed Hattie on the cheek; she smiled at him in return as he walked away.

The message Ava woke up to was sweet and simple, bringing that fluttery feeling in her stomach once again. Lying back in her bed, she turned off her phone and savored the day ahead.

Heading back to Dublin tomorrow, beautiful. I'm excited to see you. I'll pick you up at seven. —E

1914

E,

It's odd not having you so close these days. After spending the last couple of years with you by my side, I realize how much I miss your company. Nevertheless, I must admit I am grateful for the time I have shared with Bridget. What a blessing it has been to reconnect with her after all these years. She hasn't changed, brother. Still as beautiful and as funny as ever. I cannot deny that she captivates me. What an opportunity I would have missed if I had stayed in Glendalough. It's as if we have been given the chance to live life here the way we always dreamed. With her performing nightly at the Abbey Theatre and coming home to meet me after a long day's work in the office.

Alas, I fear it is only temporary.

In more serious news, I regret to inform you that I will not be able to return anytime soon. With winter upon us and work piling up, the only free time I have has been spent on the Rising. Tensions are escalating here in Dublin, and I worry they might progress sooner than we anticipated. Collin is becoming somewhat more radical than I am comfortable with. Last week, there was an incident where he and his men assaulted an officer simply because no one was nearby. They left the man for dead. That's not the kind of behavior I can support. His increasing aggression concerns me.

I conveyed this in a letter to Abram, of course, but I am doing my best to de-escalate their anger and redirect their actions until a time when we can fully support them. However, I know the council is not prepared for that.

I worry that if something were to happen, I would have to step back and disappear from the city, at least for a few days, to protect both Bridget and me. While I can praise their bravery, they need to be patient until the time is right, and my loyalty will always stay with our council. If they order me to fight, I will, but until then, I will remain their dutiful informant.

May the road rise to meet you.

Until we meet again,
A. Lynch

P.S. Bridget says she'll be near Glendalough next month. She hopes "Andrew" can see her perform. Tickets will be at the box office under her name.

Chapter Forty

Connor

The look of absolute horror that crossed Connor's face when he first laid eyes on Ava after her accident was hard to hide. They had spun a story about a bicycle accident in the city, but Connor found that hard to believe. Ava's injuries were intense and not in places you would expect if she just collided with another rider. No—something about this whole story wasn't right, and it bothered Connor that the two of them were keeping secrets.

It bothered Connor even more that he had to find out about it over a FaceTime call for work. Why didn't Ava text him when she first got in the accident? If there was nothing to hide, why didn't she reach out to let him know what had happened? They spoke nearly every day at this point. So as long as they both had cell service, they were communicating. What had changed? Connor felt a little hurt and slightly offended. He thought they were close, but apparently not.

Furthermore, Connor also noticed the weird shift between Elias and Ava. It was pretty obvious they were growing closer to one another—enough to lie to his face. Even Calista had made a snarky comment afterwards about her distaste for their growing friendship. This concerned Connor only slightly, as he was still unsure if he trusted Calista.

When in a professional setting, she was normal, well-spoken and refined. But when she wasn't in a work state of mind, she was a little capricious and unhinged. Always very stressed and hostile toward anyone who wasn't above her pay grade. She only ever talked to Connor about work, and if they spoke personally, the conversation usually revolved around Elias. This was surprising because, according to Ava, Elias denied any current involvement with her.

Connor wasn't sure Calista was aware of that.

A week or so after the accident, Ava asked Connor to pick her up from the airport. With Balor out of the country on business, they essentially had the next couple of weeks free to do as they pleased until he returned. This gave Elias permission to head back up to Glendalough to help restore the barn that caught fire while Ava and Elias were staying at the Inn. Again, another odd circumstance, but what Connor found even more strange was Elias's insistence on going up to help rebuild it for her.

Calista had waved this off, explaining that it was normal since the NMI had been using Hattie as a place to shelter their interns on expeditions for years and that she had a particular fondness for Elias. However, Connor still found this out of place. Many things surrounding Elias didn't make sense. Nor did a lot of the things around Calista, for that matter. But when Connor pulled up to the side of the airport and saw Ava there waiting for him with Elias at her side, he couldn't help but smile.

He waited while Ava said her goodbyes to Elias. It was hard to watch as they leaned in close to one another and spoke in hushed tones. It was clear to him they were sharing a private moment, and while he didn't want to be rude, he also didn't enjoy seeing the two of them so close in person. It had been difficult enough to watch over the video conference. When Elias reached forward and kissed her forehead, though, Connor knew his gut had been right. There was something going on between them, and he had missed his chance.

Connor turned on his bright smile as Ava approached him and opened his arms to pull her in tightly. She squeezed his torso and didn't let go for a second. Connor watched Elias begrudgingly leave over her shoulder before he pulled back.

"You okay?"

His eyes traced down her length, taking everything in. Her face looked like it had endured the worst of it. Along her jawline, a long, purple and yellowish bruise embellished her face, with a vertical scar, about an inch long, healing in the middle. Two tiny bruises graced her neck on either side, in the same shade, though they were not nearly as visible.

Even her clothing was different; instead of sneakers and jeans, she wore sweatpants and Uggs—shoes that were practically slippers and not weather-resistant in the rain that was common in this country. Her smile was barely half its usual length when she saw him. She was exhausted and worn out.

No, Ava didn't look like her bubbly self, but she tried to put on a brave face for him anyway.

"Yeah, I'm okay. How about you? We've got so much to catch up on!" she said excitedly. Her smile lit up her face once more, but her eyes didn't show nearly the same enthusiasm. She was putting in a lousy effort to distract him from what he saw. He wasn't sure if it was embarrassment that kept her from being honest or simply the fact that they were out in public still but one way or another Connor intended to find out, and he knew just how to make that happen.

He grabbed her bags from her and tossed them in the back as Ava climbed inside the passenger seat. Once in the car, he started the ignition and pulled out onto the main drag.

"Do you have any plans today?"

Ava shook her head impassively and stared out the window.

"Good, because I've got just the thing you need."

Two hours later, they sat across from each other on Connor's bed in his dorm with coffee from their favorite local shop in hand. Snacks from Connor's storage lay atop the blankets. The Avengers played in the background on his TV.

Ava snuggled into his covers to keep warm, while Connor sat content on top of the blankets. The cold Irish air appeared to be bothering her more this time around, and Connor suspected it was because her body was still struggling as it was to heal itself. He turned down the volume on the TV and turned to her now, unwilling to wait any longer.

"So are you going to tell me what really happened? Or are you just going to keep lying to me?"

Ava pursed her lips. When she looked up and saw the emotion in his eyes that he could not hide, guilt washed over her. She knew he was upset about having to find out via the video conference. She thought maybe she could avoid the conversation and somehow make it easier for him, so they could move on. But he wasn't going to let this go.

Ava put down her snack and brushed the crumbs from her hands.

"Connor—"

"Please don't patronize me with an excuse," he whispered. He shook his head at the ground, disappointed. "I thought we were friends."

That felt like a stab in the chest to Ava. She never meant to hurt his feelings. Everything had been so chaotic, and Elias had taken control of almost everything at that time. So when he gave Calista and Connor the same story they gave the McKennas, she just went along with it. She wasn't sure why he didn't tell them the truth; she only figured at the time that Elias was trying to spare her more emotional damage by refraining from having to describe what happened.

"We are, Connor! And I'm sorry that it felt like I hid things from you; that wasn't my intent. Everything happened so fast, and it was still so fresh by the time Elias and I got on the conference with you that I just let him speak. I don't know why he lied to you guys, I swear, but please know that I never meant to."

Her words sounded sincere, but some things still didn't add up.

"Then why didn't you text me first? Why didn't you tell me?"

His voice still held onto its reproachful tone.

"When we FaceTimed you two, it wasn't even twenty-four hours after the attack. Forgive me, but I didn't have my bearings at the time."

Connor's eyes widened and Ava registered her mistake. Connor cocked his head back like he wasn't sure he heard her right. Surely she had used the wrong word, right? Annoyance was too little of a word to describe what he was feeling right now. Anger was more appropriate.

"I'm sorry, come again?"

Ava swallowed knowing that if she didn't explain now, he probably wouldn't forgive her. She took a second to collect herself. Forming the words at first was hard. Elias had been kind enough not to dwell on everything because he knew she wasn't ready to discuss it. But Connor needed to know.

"We were coming back from the Carnegie," she started. Her voice was shaky. Connor forced himself to wait and hear her out. "When we got to the parking garage, it was dark and my feet were shot from being in those heels so Elias offered to bring the car around."

"He left you alone, in the city at night?" Connor fumed but Ava held up her hand before he could make any assumptions.

"I told him to go and I stayed under the light near the elevator. It's not like I was standing in the dark."

Connor leaned forward and thrust his head into his hands.

"The guy came out of nowhere. He grabbed me from behind and tried to take me but I head butted him and he let me go. I think I broke his nose. I thought someone was coming to help when I saw car light flash over us, but turns out it was just the man's accomplice. So I ran."

Tears rolled down Ava's cheeks as she recounted the attack in Pittsburgh with clarity she wished she didn't have. Connor sighed in his hands and lifted his head feeling helpless as she struggled to force the words out.

"I honestly have no idea where we ended up but eventually they caught up to me and tackled me. I landed face first into the concrete. He tried to strangle me but someone shot at him—"

"Elias?" Connor questioned, confused.

Ava shook her head and returned her eyes to meet his. "No, we still have no idea where those came from."

Connor repositioned himself calmly now. He was trying to be strong for her even when the better part of him wanted to kill Elias for allowing this to happen on his watch. "The police couldn't track anyone down?"

Ava shook her head.

"We never went to the police."

That son of a bitch. "Why the hell not?"

"Because it was an isolated attack, the police would have wanted to speak to the McKennas, and I couldn't let that happen. If they knew what really happened, they'd never let me go back to Dublin with Elias."

"And for good reason!" Connor stood him now and began to pace the room. Ava tried to console him as best as possible, but he was pissed.

"Elias got there and intervened. He saved my life and got me the help I needed afterwards. Please don't blame this on him," she begged. Connor wasn't falling for it. If it wasn't his fault, then whose fault was it? He was the expedition's leader; he was the one in charge. It was his job to make sure she was safe, and he failed. In his mind, he didn't see how she could go through all of that and still think so highly of the guy. And not only did she think highly of him but they were actually together! Or so he thought.

"So let me get this straight, Elias leaves you to fend for yourself. You get physically assaulted, he steps in and saves you only after getting battered first, and then you see a doctor and ride off into the sunset together? Come on, Ava, I'm not buying this."

Ava crossed her arms over her chest and leaned back against the wall. Her irritation with Connor was now fully on display. "You're making him out to be the bad guy, and you know he's not."

"Then tell me how it is, Ava, because I don't see how you could go through all of that and still have feelings for that guy!"

Connor stopped when he realized his voice had risen to a shout and stepped back to give her space. He ran his hand anxiously over the back of his neck. Ava was silent for a moment; she wanted to give Connor a chance to cool down before they continued. She knew this was going to be a difficult conversation to have. But the problem wasn't what she anticipated. Connor's true faults lay with Ava, not with Elias; but right now, given her state, she didn't think he would admit to being upset with her, so he was choosing to take it out on the only other person involved.

"Is it that obvious?" she finally asked. Connor sighed and sat back down on the bed across from her.

"Yes. It was apparent you two were a thing when you separated at the airport."

Ava let out a huff of a laugh as if something about this was funny. If only.

"That's ironic because, apart from that and some hand-holding, he's barely touched me since the night of the attack. Nothing has changed." She finished in a whisper. Connor nibbled on his lip as he tossed the idea of saying something back and forth in his head.

"Everything has changed since you left for Pittsburgh. Don't you see? That's why I'm so frustrated with him, knowing all of this. You deserve to have someone at your side who will always show up at the end of the day. You're either all in it or you're not."

Ava thought over everything they experienced over the last couple of weeks. All the training and research, all the deep discussions about family and their history. The flirting, the clues, the attack, the kiss. It didn't matter that Elias was a little unconventional when it came to her, he showed up every time she needed him to. They worked things out and made a great team.

She was attracted to the man, and she knew he was attracted to her. Whatever secrets he kept that held her in the dark would soon reveal themselves, she had no doubt. And they would work through it together. They had been through worse. But Connor was right. If they were going to be together, they needed to make up their minds and take action.

She could only hope that Elias was ready to do the same.

Chapter Forty-One

Elias

Elias stood at the base of the grand staircase of McCarthy Lodge. The lobby was all but full because students and faculty alike had already made their way to Trinity College for the fundraiser. He leaned his elbow on the wooden railing and fiddled with his watch. He had chosen an untraditional navy blue suit with a dark gray vest, blue tie, and brown suede dress shoes. His hair was styled back, and he had shortened his beard to a scruff.

Elias shook out his wrist, trying to set his watch right. He was close to just taking the damn thing off and being done with it. Initially, he had hoped to have found his great grandfather Nathanial's watch by now so he could wear that one instead, but it hadn't resurfaced since Glendalough. He had decided to go with the one Lottie had picked out for him a couple of years ago. However, this thing was far too bulky, making him uncomfortable.

A lot had changed within the last couple weeks. After meeting Ava's family and getting the chance to spend some more personal time together, he was starting to see a whole new side of her—a side he liked. That enticed him, drew him in like a bee to honey. There wasn't really a way to hide it anymore.

After Ava's attack, he was struck by how she carried herself with dignity throughout everything. He had been so anxious; he could no longer deny the truth—he had feelings for her. He was enchanted by her, and in the best way. He only hoped that, now some weeks apart, returning to her would find her feeling the same.

Of course, this also made things complicated for him. It was going to be much harder for him to pull off the last part of his plan now that he knew exactly how high the stakes were for Ava.

Going back on his orders now would be a grave mistake. The jewels were so close he could almost taste them, and they absolutely could not fall into the wrong hands—Dr. Balor's. He had to keep focused, though he had to admit that with Ava now in the picture, it was going to be difficult. He was bound to be distracted by her. He wondered how she would react once she found out.

Elias shook his head to himself. *Stay positive!* he thought.

They would find a way to get the money Ava needed for her sister's treatment. He just had to be creative about it. She would understand once he explained it all to her. She had to. The very thought of her reaction made his stomach tense. That's when he heard Ava clear her throat from the top of the staircase.

He sucked in a breath and looked up as Ava began to descend the staircase. Patience had never been one of his greatest attributes, but just then, time stood still.

Ava was dressed in a simple yet elegant emerald silk gown with a swooping neckline and a slit up the side. Her minor bruising, still visible, was tactfully concealed beneath makeup. Her dress revealed a bit more leg than he really wanted her to, but it fit her perfectly in all the right places. That alone made Elias appreciate Lottie's taste in clothing.

Ava's brown hair was lightly curled, creating a waterfall-like effect flowing over her bare shoulders. She wore no jewelry except long diamond earrings. A scar still marked her jawline, though it had healed well since he last saw her, and even then, it was concealed with makeup to improve its appearance. Looking at her now, she was more than he had prepared himself for.

She tried to hide it, but she blushed when she smiled at him. And by the time she finally reached him at the bottom of the staircase, he felt like he couldn't breathe. Elias offered his arm, and she took it with grace.

"You look—" he stammered.

She winced. "Too over the top?"

He let out a chuckle and shook his head. "No, absolutely stunning." He took a moment to tuck back a stray curl, and she beamed up at him.

"I guess I have Calista to thank for that," she said sheepishly, as if her beauty couldn't measure up to the dress Lottie had picked for her.

Elias snorted. "You could have worn sweatpants, and you still would have been the most attractive one in the room."

Ava playfully looked Elias up and down. "I don't know. Currently, I have some pretty big competition," she said.

Elias rolled his eyes. "Hardly, but I will say Lottie has good taste. You look great." He stepped forward and held open the door for her. "Shall we?" She nodded.

The great hall at Trinity College was decorated like an American wedding. Small high tables had been strategically placed throughout the main area near the bar, leaving plenty of space for people to dance toward the back of the room. Glass candelabras sat on each dinner table along sides of the room, and mini candles decorated the high tables. The dance floor, which already had multiple interns on it, was stationed right in front of a giant glass window that looked out onto the gardens.

Elias glanced around, his arms curled casually around Ava's waist. *They have really outdone themselves this year,* he thought. He looked over at Ava. She seemed to be loving the grandeur of it all. So he hugged her closer as they entered through the glass doors into the ballroom.

It didn't take a server long to hand them champagne flutes. Ava made a face after she sipped it. She didn't seem to be interested in the stuff swirling in her glass, and that made two of them.

Elias noted that before long, they would have to make their way to the bar to get some real drinks. After all, they had earned the right to celebrate, and tonight, that's precisely what he expected to do—relax and enjoy the night with the woman in front of him that he couldn't seem to take his eyes off of.

Dr. Jensin, an older woman with graying hair and a love for preserving ancient text, stepped up to greet the two. Ava seemed to be in her element. She schmoozed and flirted shamelessly with people she had never met, with class.

Elias spent the next hour making little progress toward the bar as benefactor after benefactor approached them, asking details on their current expedition and wanting to know more about the girl Elias was parading about.

"What a gem. If you know what's good for you, you'll seal the deal with that girl before she gets away," Professor Grimes had whispered to him in a moment when Ava was deep in conversation with his wife. Elias couldn't agree more.

As soon as they had a moment alone, he whisked her away to the bar and ordered her a proper drink—Jameson with ginger ale, just the way she liked it. They stood side by side at one of the small high tables, lit only by the dim bar lights. Finally, alone, Elias bumped her gently with the side of his elbow.

"Are you enjoying yourself?" he asked her over the music in the background.

Ava turned, giving him her full attention for the first time in a while, and her smile widened. "Yes, I hadn't realized so many students were studying at the museum, though; I'm shocked!"

Elias shook his head. "Some of these interns are from Trinity College, so they stay in the dorms there; that's why it seems bigger to you." Ava nodded as if she had just realized something and turned away to look out at the dance floor again. He was distracted by her sudden head bobbing to the music. He hadn't noticed Connor and Lottie slither their way through the crowd toward their table.

Never to be outdone, Lottie was dressed in a dark red velvet off-the-shoulder gown with long sleeves. Her hair was pulled off to the side in a messy fit of curls. Elias couldn't help but notice the new diamond-encrusted necklace she had draped across her collarbone. He was sure that had cost him a pretty penny.

Connor was sporting the typical penguin attire. Elias perked an eyebrow at him as the two approached. Connor gave Elias a curt nod.

"Ava!" Lottie reached out and gave her a swift kiss on either cheek in her normal greeting. Ava's smile was guarded, but she accepted it and returned the greeting.

"I can't thank you enough for getting me this dress. It is absolutely gorgeous!"

"Yes, well, I do have a flair for fashion, though I must admit it was hard to find something that would shine you up appropriately enough for this event. But alas, it seems to have done its job!" Lottie said.

Ava didn't seem to notice Lottie's bitter tone, but Elias had. Elias eyed Lottie, making it clear he caught her bitterness.

"I told her before we got here, she could have worn sweatpants and still would have been the most beautiful person here."

"Oh, stop, Elias," Ava said.

Lottie tilted her head as if trying to hide her annoyance and ran her tongue over her teeth then beamed a fake smile. "Belle of the ball, it seems you are."

Ava shrugged, completely unaware of Lottie's intention. "He's just joking. He enjoys seeing me embarrassed. Ignore him," she said, waving him off.

Elias wrapped his arm around Ava and pulled her back to him by the waist. Ava smiled at him, and he returned the favor by allowing the corners of his mouth to creep upward into a discreet smile. "Is it working?" he asked.

Ava snorted and returned her eyes to the people on the dance floor. Connor followed her line of sight while Elias looked at Lottie. His smile faded. He knew this wasn't going to go over well, but he knew it was necessary.

Connor shifted his feet and looked away as if he hadn't noticed. "What do you say, Ava? Wanna grab a dance with a friend? I mean as long as Elias is okay with it," Connor added with a slight snip of his own.

Elias tore his eyes away from Lottie to give him a daring glare. But he eventually realized he had no real claim to Ava yet, and let her go. Though he had picked up on Connor's bitter tone toward him, he could also see what Connor was trying to do, and for that, he felt a little grateful.

Lottie wasn't going to leave him alone until he explained a little further, so he nodded and let the two go off and join the crowd on the dance floor.

Lottie waved over a waitress with a quick snap of her fingers. "God, I need a drink. Get me a glass of the Riesling now!"

Elias raised his eyebrows to himself and took a sip of his beer. "A *please* would have been nice," he said as the waitress disappeared.

Lottie sighed aggressively and settled her arms against the table in front of him. Elias flicked his eyes to the dance floor to check on Ava. However, when Lottie realized she wasn't getting the attention she thought she deserved, she rested her perfectly manicured hand on Elias's forearm.

"Well? Are you going to explain yourself?" she asked him. Elias chuckled and looked down at Lottie, who was sporting a very mischievously dark smile.

"You seem . . . smitten," she said with a grimace.

Elias shrugged and turned back to steal a glance in Ava's direction. If he was being honest with himself, he didn't know how to describe what he was feeling.

"I'm very tempted," he decided. He was tempted to make this work with Ava. *And maybe a little possessive, too*, he thought as he watched Connor dip Ava backward.

"Tempted?" Lottie scoffed. She squeezed herself closer to Elias, ran a nail up his arm, and rested her hand on his shoulder. "Remember when I used to be the one who tempted you?"

Lord help me, he thought. *What on earth is she doing?*

"Sure? But that was—" Elias faced her and gently grabbed her hand from his shoulder and brought it down to the table. Lottie looked like a snake had bitten her.

"A long time ago," Elias concluded softly. "Things have changed. I'm sorry, but I think you and I both know we're better as friends."

Lottie curled her lip and looked toward the dance floor, where Connor and Ava seemed to be enjoying themselves. Elias stole yet another glance their way but shook his head and decided to deal with Lottie head-on. He turned back to her and gave her an apologetic smile.

Lottie looked back at him with an ugly frown that she clearly wasn't trying to hide. For far too long they had danced around each other, flirting shamelessly and hooking up multiple times long after they had split.

They had led each other on for so long without actually being together that he realized that this thing they had between them—however unimportant it had been—was going to be hard for her to lose. Because as he could plainly read in her facial expression, it had meant something to her. And for that, he felt awful.

"You really are falling for her." It wasn't a question. It was an accusation.

He didn't know if he was in love just yet, but yes, he was, for all intents and purposes, off the market, entranced with her spirit. Love was a strong word, but hooked? Definitely.

"I'm sorry, Lottie. I know this is hard for you, and I am sincerely sorry if I have made it worse by leading you on for all these years, but I see something in Ava I definitely want the chance to explore. I hope you can understand that."

Lottie snatched her hand away from his, pure disgust spreading across her face. "Don't patronize me, Elias. You owe me the grace of treating me like an adult, for God's sake. I thought you simply took a side piece; I didn't realize you were stupid enough to fall in love with a child" Lottie said, her words dripping with venom meant to kill, not just sting.

Elias frowned and straightened himself to look down at her, slightly irritated now. It was one thing to be upset with him and call him names, but there was no reason to speak poorly of Ava. She had done nothing wrong. "Poor choice of words, don't you think, considering I am also a Yankee?" he asked and readjusted his cuffs.

Lottie crossed her arms and curled her lip up in a snarl. "Yes, but until now, I believed you to be much more intelligent than most. And here you are proving me wrong."

Elias shook his head. "It was nothing personal, Lottie. I love you, and I will always love you, but you and I both know we would never work. Come on, we're best friends; can't you be happy for me?"

Lottie, who had been looking down at her drink on the table in front of her, suddenly snapped her piercing eyes up to him, and Elias didn't like the look she gave him.

"Apparently not enough since you chose that pathetic tramp."

Elias scowled at her and narrowed his eyes. "That's enough, Lottie. There's no need for that."

Lottie threw her hands up. "Isn't there? We have been together for nearly five years, Elias! Five! I know you better than your own sister does! Better than yourself. I have been there for you through every high and every low. And the sex . . ." Lottie let out a small, irritated grunt. "You seduced me time after time; you made me feel wanted, made me feel desired, and I believed you. And yet, despite all that, you just walked away for some random piece of ass you found off the street!"

Elias closed his eyes and sighed. "Calista—"

"No! No, you don't get to end this after all that. After all we've been through together." Lottie came up, grabbed his hand, and held it. Her eyes pleading with him. "We are endgame. You know that."

He opened his eyes and looked down at his friend. His heart swirled with sorrow for having caused her so much pain. But it had to be done.

"No, Lottie, we're not," he whispered. "I'm sorry."

She stared up at him for a second before slowly pulling away. Elias let her go. Her lip curled back up into an ugly, angry snarl. "You will regret this, Elias."

He couldn't tell if it was meant to be a real threat from her or if it was merely just words spoken out of pain. "I don't think I will," he said gently.

Keeping in mind that the two had known each other for many years, he decided that he owed her enough and let her get in her nasty jabs at him. But the jabs didn't last long, for Lottie shook her head at him and muttered something about him being a lost cause and then started to step away from him and their conversation. He agreed it was probably for the better.

"I could have saved you."

With one last sigh, Elias whispered, "I was never yours to save."

Lottie let out a screech before she turned, stomping like a child, and disappeared into the crowd.

Elias stood there, guilty for letting all this get away from him the way it had. He should have cut things off with her a long time ago. He should have made his intentions clear from the beginning after they broke up, but he hadn't, and it looked like it may have cost him his friendship with her.

The music around him began to slow down, and people started to vacate the dancefloor while other couples flocked to it. Elias decided Connor had had enough time with Ava, and it was about time he stole her back. But first, he was going to need another drink.

19-14

Andrew,

It's good to hear from you. I am delighted to know you are doing so well and are happy with Bridget. You deserve to enjoy life. Take my advice, don't let your fear of what might happen ruin what you two share now. You can't possibly know how much time you'll have together until it's time to part ways, and by then, you'll have wished you hadn't spent so much of it living in fear of the what ifs. Just enjoy it together as best as you can. We will deal with the fallout of this conflict when it all boils over.

Speaking of the talented musician, you'll have to thank her for the tickets for me. It was wonderful to see Bridget perform. I genuinely enjoyed the chance to engage in public life once again. Just being among people who were happy and appreciating life for what it is, rather than constantly stressing over our declining country, was truly refreshing. The audience loved Bridget, and rightly so! She is an exceptional pianist and incredibly charismatic.

I am sure you are aware of this, but Abram has been considering appointing me to the council. Gidion is preparing to step down soon and when he does, Abram would like me to fill his place. I am not sure I am prepared for it, but I am willing to serve wherever they need me.

That being said, I am aware of the issues, and you should know, the tensions you are noticing no longer remain strictly in Dublin. We are receiving reports from all over the country about issues concerning the English. Nearly ten times the number of letters we attended to when you were still in Glendalough. We are trying to recruit new members, but unfortunately, we are losing the fight against time. There are simply not enough of us to go after their armies and still live to make a difference. I concur with your fear of the fallout should the Rising move too soon.

Please keep us updated as best as you can and try to get home soon. I hope to speak with you in person in the future.

The road rises to meet me, brother.

Until we meet again,
E. Lynch

Chapter Forty-Two

Ava

The music slowed down, but Connor and I couldn't stop laughing. He had been cracking jokes since the first song, and I just wasn't able to hold it in anymore. Of course, then he laughed at me, which left us looking like two crazy preteens caught in a fit of giggles.

If I were being honest with myself, I had missed how simple life could be. Things had been so confusing lately; I needed this—just one night to let everything go and enjoy my time on the dance floor with good food and a wonderful friend. And that's what he had become, my best friend. Very quickly. So quickly, I hadn't even noticed it at first, but he had, and it struck me as quite amusing.

Nearly two months ago, we had started this journey together, barely knowing each other. Now, here we were, drinking, dancing, and having a ball of fun together. I would be forever blessed for as long as we stayed friends.

After our minor fight in his apartment, my first night back, I convinced Connor to hear me out and come to terms with the possibility that Elias might be more than just a work partner. He, of course, had his concerns and was far from thrilled with the idea, but in the end, I was able to win him over by showing him pictures I had taken of Elias with my family. I don't think Connor ever thought of Elias as friendly or intimate, but seeing the way he played with Jules and Ryker at the zoo seemed to alter his thoughts on the guy enough to give him some slack.

It was hard to explain the connection between Elias and me. Of course, there was that undeniable attraction between us, but it was more than that; Elias felt like a safe space, a dangerous chemistry experiment, but most importantly, Elias felt like home. It had been a long time since I had felt anything close to that.

Thinking about Elias standing at the bottom of the staircase made my cheeks blush involuntarily. I stopped giggling for a second to scan the room for him. I had seen him with Calista at our table initially, but now they had both vanished from that spot near the bar, and I was having trouble pinpointing them.

"May I cut in?" Elias's deep voice sounded from behind me, raising the hairs on the back of my neck. I twirled my dress to face his broad chest. I looked up at him. I didn't wait for Connor's approval; I accepted Elias's immediately, and we moved to the back of the dance floor.

Elias's smile was subtle as if tainted with a tad too much to drink. He pulled me to a more secluded corner of the dance floor with dim lighting between the back of the staircase and a big open window giving us a full view of the stars. He twirled me once and tucked me in close.

He nuzzled against my ear as we swayed. I melted, leaned my head against his, and closed my eyes as I surrendered to the music and to him.

I didn't think you could feel this way about someone in such little time. Still, the feelings I had for him had been growing uncontrollably since Glendalough, against my better judgment. But as Millie had pointed out, I was happy, and that couldn't be denied.

"I guess you really can dance," I said quietly. I felt his smile brush my forehead.

"With the right person," he said sincerely, and that's when I got a whiff of his breath.

"You smell like Guinness," I giggled.

He didn't open his eyes, but I noticed his smile fade. "Things got a little tense between Lottie and me. I needed to cool down a bit before I found you."

This broke my spell of happiness, and I pulled back to get a good look at him. His dark brown eyes were a little heavy but not actually as bad as I had expected them to be, which was good because it meant he wasn't drunk, just a little tipsy, maybe. I frowned. "What do you mean things got tense with Lottie? What happened?"

Elias shook his head slowly, not in a drunken sort of way but more like a *please, do we have to do this now* sort of way. I softened. I knew how much Calista meant to him, and though I was definitely jealous of her at times and not thrilled with how incredibly close they were, that didn't mean I wanted her out of the picture. If she was that important to him, I could handle being her friend . . . hopefully.

"Nothing I couldn't handle." He tried to pull me back to him, but I didn't want that. I narrowed my eyes playfully at him but gave him a look to know I was serious.

"Elias, be honest with me. Tell me what happened."

Elias took a breath and a spare moment to look past me before looking down at the floor and answering. He never took his hands off my hips, but we had stopped swaying moments ago.

"Lottie is upset with how . . . obviously attracted to you I am. She could read me like a book when she walked in, and now I think she is hurt because she realizes there will never again be an *us* factor for her and I."

Elias looked back to meet my stare. He seemed anxious, as if concerned about how I would react. I had no idea why, though; he had just told me everything I had wanted to hear from him for the past several days ever since that kiss.

"Ava I—"

I studied his face, the way we study historical papers, with gentleness and precision. I wanted to know every inch, every detail of him that I could possibly soak in. I ran my hand up his shoulder, grasped his neck, and then slowly brought his mouth to mine.

The kiss was tender and slow, yet passionate as we reacquainted ourselves with each other's lips. The world around me seemed to fade into nothingness while fireworks burst behind my closed eyelids. Elias's arm snaked around my waist and pulled me as close to him as possible, crushing my body to his. He leaned me back slightly to deepen the kiss, and I let him.

When my shoe slipped on the linoleum flooring, Elias took the brunt of my weight, careful not to allow me to fall. My heart was racing, my breath being taken right from my very lungs and going into his. I finally pulled away to look at him. He opened his eyes and stared into the very depths of my soul.

"I am absolutely captivated by you," he said breathlessly. I let a slow smile creep onto my face, my blush returning. I brushed his scruff with my thumb as he spoke.

"I never wanted to hurt you or Lottie, but if I had to choose—"

"You chose me," I mainly whispered to myself. I bit my lip and let my hand wander back to his hair.

"Every time. If you'd have me."

I grinned and pressed my forehead to his. I had clearly been pining over this guy for the past several days. All this week while I had been recuperating in Dublin, I had missed him—longed for his touch, missed the moments we had shared in Pittsburgh.

Even then, I had already lost the battle of my heart to him. I sought out his attention, never pulled away from his touch, if anything I leaned into it. How could he not see all that? How could he not see what he did to me? I thought my feelings were pretty obvious, but I'm glad they weren't. This moment was so perfect, it was a feeling I wasn't likely to forget. It would be a memory I would come to cherish for many years. "Every day, Elias Cassedy, every day."

Elias briefly knitted his eyebrows together before giving me one last kiss on the lips, then he stood us upright and pulled away from me to grab something around his neck. I took the time to try and contain the blush that was no doubt spreading by now when Elias produced a beautiful silver pendant between us in his open hands.

The necklace was of two circular silver spheres, a little one on top of a slightly bigger one. On top of the little sphere was a silver rectangle encrusted with a few emeralds on the sides. The piece was obviously very old but stunningly beautiful.

Elias unclasped it and gently guided my shoulders, turning me around so my back was to him. Knowing where this was going but still loving the feeling of his hands on me, I just stood there and tilted my head to the side as he swept my hair off to the opposite shoulder. Using both hands, he clasped the necklace around my neck and then stepped forward and wrapped his long arms around my waist to hug me to him as we stared out the window at the stars.

"This necklace has been in my family for three generations. It's very important to me. I want you to watch over it. I trust you. And—" He once again brushed his nose into my hair, this time to nibble on my ear playfully. I couldn't hide my pleasure in the feeling. "It looks incredible on you. Will you keep it safe for me?"

I felt honored to be trusted with something so special to him. I slowly pulled away just enough so I could turn around and look at him, cupping his face between my hands.

Aside from being practically lit on fire from the way his hands were roaming, I was genuinely touched by his faith in me.

"Of course! It is beautiful." Elias grinned so big I didn't think I'd ever seen him this way and pulled me back for another unbreakable kiss. I was lost in a daze of sugar-coated kisses. Time seemed to stand still; I couldn't even remember why we were here in the first place.

"Ya know," Elias said between kisses, "Trinity College has one of the best libraries in all of Ireland." And his lips went back to leaving precious butterfly kisses down my bare shoulder, causing chills to run up my spine. "Better than the one we have on campus," he continued.

"Mhm, really?" But I wasn't really listening.

"We could go check out the library and see if we can translate this Ogham. Plus, the library at this time of night will be pretty secluded."

I pulled back and smiled wickedly at him. "Oh, talk dirty to me, why don't you?"

Chapter Forty-Three

Elias

It was easier to sneak out of the fundraiser than Elias had expected. For whatever reason, they really didn't have anything blocked from to the public, nor did they have any type of security for the event.

He had been to Trinity a couple times before, on other assignments, and he knew the layout pretty well—enough to sneak into the library, anyway. Ava had tried to hold in her childish delight as he led her through the hallways, holding her hand. Once in the library, he knew just where to look. The place was dark but not pitch-black. There were small security lights in multiple locations, casting a slight glow across an open array of tables.

Elias wasted no time guiding Ava through the library to a table in the middle of the room. He abruptly turned to her, hoisted her up by her waist, and sat her on the top. He planted a quick kiss on her lips and he felt too intoxicated by her scent to pull away. But he did so begrudgingly. They had work to do.

"Stay here, I'll be right back." He pulled away from her so swiftly that he could hear her suck in a breath as he left. Quickly, he made his way through the back section down an aisle to a section of books he had inspected many times before. His eyes landed on a deep purple book with gold lettering. He snatched it from the shelf and made his way back to Ava.

She was wiping her lip with her thumb, trying to preserve whatever was left of her lip stain. The slit in her green dress had fallen open and was hanging over the other side of the table, leaving her entire leg bare.

It was a vision that was more tempting than he thought he could bear at the moment.

He shook his head and plopped the book down on the table beside her. That was something he would have to attend to *after* they decoded the Ogham. Oblivious to the effect she was having on him, Ava turned her whole body around to look at the book. The change in position had given him a better view of her leg.

Elias took a breath. *Focus*, he reminded himself. This girl either really knew what she was doing or had absolutely no idea exactly how badly he wanted her. He blinked and began to flip through the book, looking for the chapter in Irish Ogham. When he found what he was looking for, he paused to look up at her impatiently. The sooner they decoded this, the sooner he could attend to her . . . well-being as long as she would still have him.

"Did you bring the paper you copied from Ogham? I'd look at my phone, but I left it in the car."

Ava reached into her dress and pulled out a folded piece of paper hidden from her cleavage. Elias sat frozen.

"What? This dress doesn't have pockets!" she said, but Elias had not heard; he did his best not to stare, but I caught him trying to regain his composure anyway.

"*Go dtuga Dia neart dom* . . . Woman, what are you trying to do to me?"

Ava just stared at him wide-eyed. An innocent smile played across her face. Until now, he had never spoken Gaelic directly to her, and she seemed pleasantly surprised. She handed him the page and bit her lip playfully. Apparently, she was a fan.

"What does that mean?" she asked. Elias lifted his eyes off of her bodice and brought them up to meet hers.

"May God give me strength," he hissed from between his teeth. He accepted the paper. Her smile widened with pride that she had such an effect on him.

Elias, beside her, got to work. He pulled out a pen from his jacket pocket.

The Ogham was created with a long vertical line in the middle, known as the stem and a series of strokes and lines going across it called twigs that make up the wording.

Elias took his time matching up the twigs and stems until he could arrange the letters, and finally, we had the next riddle. Ava watched over his shoulder the whole time; he had no doubt she was already working on the clue at hand.

He was keenly aware of how terribly close she was, but once he began to assemble his words, his demeanor shifted, as did hers. He felt the air in the room settle into a calmer state. And for that, he was grateful for the moment.

"The next clue says 'Surrender to a fire lit by many men. Atop of a cave from nineteen ten.'"

Elias sat back in his chair and ran his hand over his jaw. In truth, he had already suspected where they were going next, based on what Elijah had written in his brown leather journal, but he had to find the last clue to be sure. The part that didn't make sense to him was the end of the riddle. He hoped Ava would have an answer to that conundrum.

"It's Kilmainham Gaol," he said, not taking his eyes off the book. Elias reread the pages to make sure he had transcribed the entire riddle correctly. Ava, behind him, shook her head in confusion.

"How can you be so sure?"

"Andrew Lynch was executed at Kilmainham Gaol in 1917 along with other rebels by means of the firing squad," he explained.

Ava repeated the clue out loud thoughtfully. Her breath caressed his neck, sending goosebumps down his arms. Elias took a moment to himself, closing his eyes and once again regaining his composure before opening them and getting back to the topic at hand. "That doesn't explain the second half of the riddle, though. Atop a cave from nineteen ten," he stated.

Ava seemed frustrated she wasn't instantly getting this and tilted her head away from him as if that would somehow improve her train of thought. "Atop a cave . . . a cell?" she questioned. "From nineteen ten . . . Kilmainham Gaol closed in nineteen twenty-four," Ava concluded and shook her head again, trying to narrow down the list of possibilities.

"And it opened in seventeen ninety-six, so it's not that," Elias added.

"The Easter Rising happened in nineteen sixteen." Ava spun backward to lean back on the top of the table. He turned to watch her as her eyes flitted back and forth as if she was counting something out in her head. He raised an eyebrow, wondering what she could be thinking. "Can I see the pen and paper for a second?"

Elias handed her both, and she curled herself back around to scribble on the paper beside him. She wrote the numbers out together, 1-9-1-0, then down horizontally. "What if it's not a date, but a location?"

Elias looked from her to the paper with a puzzled expression, unable to piece it together as she had.

"First floor, ninth row, cell ten?" she asked.

Elias sat there staring at the paper, jaw agape and he tried to picture the inside of Kilmainham Gaol in his head. He mentally repeated what Ava had just said. And just like that, the light went on. He shook his head in disbelief. They had figured it out. The final piece of the puzzle was at the rebel cells in Kilmainham Gaol.

That is what Elijah had been trying to tell him when he described getting to see his brother one last time. He had been allowed to visit him before his execution in Kilmainham Gaol, which is where they traded places and hid in different locations! It was like everything he had been working on for the last four years came into place. Glendalough, the missing writing, Elijah's part in everything. It all made sense!

Elias looked over at Ava, who sat there thoughtfully, still reading over her numbers on the sheet, unaware of the importance of her discovery. He stood up, took her face into his hands gently, and kissed her.

"You are an absolute genius!" he said, and he pulled his lips away from her only to plant kisses over her cheek and down her neck. Elias shifted his position to steady Ava on the table, who had lost her balance in sudden advance. She laughed but pushed him away to see his face.

"Hold on for a second. I don't understand what just happened."

"Kilmainham, the numbers, you're right. They're not dates; it's his cell number. Andrew's cell!"

Ava seemed to know this already but narrowed her eyes in mock suspicion, only allowing her smirk to give her knowledge away. Elias continued. "Elijah must have left the final piece of the puzzle with him for safekeeping. You did it, Ava; we found them! We found the Jewels!"

Genuine confusion clouded her face. Elias realized his mistake before she even said anything but chose not to acknowledge it. Instead he redirected her attention elsewhere and distracted her with something she clearly was having trouble resisting right now.

Elias leaned forward and placed his hands on either side of her hips. He kissed her lips once, then moved his lips to the side, planting butterfly kisses along the opposite side of her face from where she was injured, before continuing south towards her neck. Ava's eyelids helplessly fluttered closed briefly, but she took a deep breath to focus and spoke again pushing him backward away from her.

"But there are two pieces to the puzzle. You and I both know that. We need the satchel and the key. One without the other is no good. How do you know they are both there?"

Elias came to a standing position, unable to hide his grin. He waited till he regained her eye contact to ensure she still trusted him, then tucked a loose curl behind her ear. "I'm betting they are both there. It's where Andrew took his last breath. Elijah would have insisted they stay with him."

It was a terrible lie, but for now, he had to lead her on until he could get her to a safe place where he felt comfortable telling her the truth.

Ava shook her head. He could tell she was still unsure about this, but it was apparent she didn't have any reason to oppose. A strong jab of guilt hit him when he realized she was caving in because she trusted him that much. And yet here he was lying to her blatantly.

"But the guards?"

"The rebel cells were darker and much more confined. Andrew could have hidden them without the guards noticing."

Ava was still questioning this. "I still don't understand what reason you have to believe they are both there."

"That's the thing. This whole time, we have been focusing on finding two different places: one that holds a key and one that holds the satchel and the jewels. But I think, given this new information, Andrew most likely hid them together . . . sort of. There is a place in the back of the Gaol where the rebel possessions were placed before execution. I bet any money that the key is in the cell, and that Elijah hid the jewels among the possessions before he left. The Brits had already sorted through and taken everything of value by that point. As long as they were locked in the case, they wouldn't have any reason to look through or even have access to open it, even if they wanted to. Those items are still there. Behind the glass, they haven't been touched." Another lie.

Elias was starting to feel a bit queasy about how easily Ava bought it. But when Ava's smile broadened into a dazzling grin, he knew there was no turning back now.

Soon, she would know the truth; she would be a part of fighting for the cause, and he couldn't wait until he was able to tell her everything. He would figure out the money for her sister later. The Order would come up with a way to save her as payment for Ava's part in returning the jewels to their rightful place. He was sure of it.

Without hesitation, Ava pulled him to her by the collar of his dress shirt, and their lips met once again.

Elias leaned into the kiss, wrapping his left arm around her waist while his right hand found the under part of her knee and lifted, sliding Ava closer to him.

Ava sucked in a breath at his sudden boldness, then shifted and used that same leg to wrap herself around his waist. Elias stopped himself and broke the kiss briefly. He gritted his teeth, putting his forehead to hers. This time, it was Ava who pulled him closer, leaning herself back against the table and pulling him down with her. Unable to stop himself, he obliged.

"*A Mhaighdean beannaithe.*"

Sweet Mother of Jesus. He breathed, the words spilling like a prayer into her hair. A tremor rippled through Ava, her body answering before she could register what he had said. Elias knew from that moment on, he would drench her world in Gaelic for as long as she would let him—every day, every hour—if only to draw that shiver from her again.

He shifted his position and rested his hand on the lower part of her bare thigh then slowly trailed its way up to the tip of where her dress split at the hip bone. Ava let a moan slip from her lips as her hair sprawled on the desk behind her.

Elias was thankful she was close enough to the edge that he only needed to lean down to kiss her thoroughly. Otherwise, he might have had to move them to a different location. As it was, part of him was cursing them for having a make-out session in the same place that held the Book of Kells. It felt somehow sacrilegious.

The better part of him chose to overlook that by focusing on the distraction of this stunningly gorgeous woman that lay before him.

Still, Elias knew he had to be careful. They were still fresh into this, and despite his actions, he wanted to take it slow. He wanted the opportunity to give this a fighting chance with Ava.

The last thing he wanted was for them to move too quickly and have it turn into the very same thing he had had with Lottie. But as Ava brought him back to her once more and her hands began to wander, it became increasingly hard for him to pull away.

Ava wrapped a hand around his neck initially to ensure his lips stayed precisely where she wanted them, then gingerly trailed her nails down his shoulder to the front of his suit. She took a brief moment to run her hands over the fabric there before grasping a hold of the buttons on his suit vest.

She spared no time unbuttoning them one by one. She pushed the vest off to the sides and explored his still-covered abdomen. Elias pulled his head back abruptly, afraid if he didn't, he wouldn't be able to later, but Ava grasped his neck once more before he could say anything and brought him back to her.

"*Cúramach!*" *Careful* . . . He growled a warning to her in desperation. But it fell on deaf ears.

Ava, ever the instigator, chuckled under her breath. She seemed to know exactly what he was saying and yet didn't seem to care. She replaced her hands on his chest and let them creep back up to his collar, where he pulled his hand away from her leg momentarily to help her yank his tie loose. Her nails brushed his throat as she undid the first button.

Elias replaced his hand on her upper thigh and pushed the boundaries of the dress as he squeezed the naked skin on her hip then slid backward.

The second button came undone under her fingers and yet again, he tried to shake his head free from her. He knew he was losing the battle, though; Ava wouldn't have it.

Then the third button popped, and Elias was prepared to give into her every desire when, all at once, the doors to the library opened. Elias's head shot up just as three dark figures entered the room.

Chapter forty-four

April of 1916, Glendalough

As the world entered World War One, tensions between the British and the Irish increased. People were being displaced from their homes, a war on religion had begun, and the Irish people were growing weary of foreign rule.

Andrew had moved to Dublin to serve as a spy for the Order within the ranks of the group known as the Rising. Although they were considerably smaller in number than the Order, their leader, Collin Leary, had gained prominence over the past few years by advocating that now was the time to unite and defend Ireland.

As the usual council members of the Order returned to Glendalough one by one, they began to discuss the situation. For the most part, they didn't disagree. The British were invading and taking things that didn't belong to them. The Irish people were clearly not safe, and helping individual families affected by their terrorism was no longer enough. The council had gone back and forth on what to do about the situation, but a decision had yet to be made.

Though the brothers mostly kept in contact through letters, Andrew had returned to Glendalough on many occasions to report concerning behavior to the council regarding the Rising's plans to move forward and start a war. In all honesty, these weren't ideas the Order hadn't already discussed, but they were not where they wanted to be. They were still not prepared to fight the British, even with the help of the Rising on their side. They needed more time.

The last time Elijah had seen his brother, he had reported Collin's plans to move forward with an attack the following week. Elijah had begged his brother to get out while he could, but Andrew had insisted on going back to Dublin to tie up some loose ends. He had left him with only his thoughts to keep him company.

Five days later, the Rising struck on Easter Monday. The group had revolted against the Brits in Dublin, taking claim of a local post office as their new headquarters and launching attacks on the small number of British soldiers that were there. They had to call in soldiers from other counties nearby to tend to the chaos as fighting and blood filled the streets.

In the end, the British had overcome the rebels. The rebels lost nearly sixty men, including many who Elijah had met in the first meeting with the Rising in Glendalough. One hundred twenty British soldiers had died in battle, and about 175 civilians had lost their lives in the crossfire.

Abram had read out the reports from newspapers to a solemn group of men who had gathered in the meeting hall. Elijah was among them.

Thankfully, Andrew had not been caught in battle. He had hunkered down, knowing his true loyalty had been to the Order and had not participated in the rebellion. His life had been spared. Elijah had been counting his blessings since receiving a letter from him two days ago.

Back in Dublin, Andrew had come out of hiding once the battle had finished. He had walked around the city surveying the damage they had left behind with sorrow. So many innocent lives were lost—so much devastation. Andrew had told Elijah that the British army was rounding up the captives—all the remaining leaders of the Rising—and transporting them to Kilmainham Gaol. They were to be shot by firing squad the following week after trials were held.

A bitter surprise throughout the entire ordeal was discovering that Seamus McDowell, who had been the reason Elijah sought refuge among the Order in the first place, was also caught up in all this chaos. He had also lived through the battle from behind hidden bunkers and had seen Andrew the day after the destruction, out walking the streets.

Andrew had not known it at the time, but Seamus had been hidden deep within the ranks of the Rising all this time and had seen Andrew join, knowing he was part of the Order. Seamus had never liked the brothers, and even after Elijah had passed, he had still watched Andrew from afar. Seamas was careful never to show his face at meetings for the Rising. So, Andrew had never known of his involvement.

Watching Andrew now, though, Seamus slithered through the crowd in the morning and approached a British soldier. He donned a face of despair and ran up to him urgently.

"Sir, I need to report someone! Please! I know for a fact he assisted in the battle with the British and may have even been a part of planning the entire attack!"

The soldier stood at attention and turned with a scowl to Seamus. He looked at him with the most profound form of distaste and eyed him up and down. Another soldier walked over, hearing the fuss. "What's all this about?" he asked.

The other soldier shook his head. "Says he knows one of the leaders of the rebellion."

The second soldier sized him up and then nodded in his direction. "Oh, yeh? And who is that?"

Seamus shook his head pretending to be so overcome by emotion that he couldn't breathe. "His name is . . . His name is . . ."

"Out with it, boy!"

Seamus looked up. "Andrew Lynch."

Chapter forty-five

Modern-day Dublin, Ireland

Elias

Elias reacted quickly to the intrusion and stood abruptly, moving in front of Ava so she could compose herself. She sat up and snagged the edge of her skirt, flinging it over her leg before attempting to tame her hair. Elias was surprised when the three came into view. Dr. Balor led the charge, with Lottie and Connor flanking him.

When his gaze fell on Lottie's dark locks, his blood ran cold. His eyes searched her face desperately, hoping to find some sign of reasoning within her expression, but she appeared indifferent to him. The conversation they had earlier had not gone over well, but to his knowledge, they were still friends. So there must be an explanation. Elias racked his brain for excuses on her behalf but in the back of his mind, he knew where they were heading.

Ava placed a hand on Elias's arm, and he glanced back briefly to ensure she was covered, before stepping aside.

Dr. Balor came a few feet in front of them. He smiled at the pair, glanced over at Ava approvingly, and clapped his hands. Ava narrowed her eyes, confused.

"Well done, Ava, well done! You played your part exactly like I hoped you would."

Elias clenched his jaw, but he didn't look at Ava. He had expected Lottie to betray him after the way she had entered the library but Ava was a far more haunting betrayal that cut deep. She glanced at him briefly before returning her gaze to the professor.

"I'm sorry?" she asked.

Elias kept composed and took another step away from her. Ava watched him for a moment before shaking her head and returning her attention to Dr. Balor.

"What are you talking about?" she asked.

Elias noticed Lottie's smile practically dripping with disdain as she watched Ava squirm. Dr. Balor pointed at Elias.

"Your assignment. Job well done. I must say I had doubts about your loyalty, but Calista reassured me you could do it. Elias had no idea you were stealing his family relics."

Elias took a deep breath and another step away from the woman he had come to know over the past few weeks.

Ava gasped at the accusation as if to object. She looked back and forth between Dr. Balor and Elias. When her eyes finally settled on Elias, she shook her head at him helplessly. "What? No! I didn't! I wouldn't! Elias, I would never!"

Elias straightened, his back going rigid, his cheeks flushed as Dr. Balor shook his head and produced his great-grandfather Nathanial's watch from his pocket—the very same watch he had misplaced in Glendalough. Determined not to show any signs of weakness, he buttoned his shirt and suit vest back up, refusing to look at Ava as she watched in horror.

Elias couldn't believe this. What a fool he had been to allow her to glimpse into his private life. He felt betrayed. He had given her his trust, and she had squandered it. What was worse is he had known better than to get involved with someone while on a mission for the Order. Elias glanced over to Ava, but he couldn't bring himself to look her in the eye. Instead, his gaze settled on the silver pendant that hung foolishly around her neck.

Good Lord. How could he have been so reckless? Now, what would he do? On top of everything, he had quite literally delivered the key right into the hands of the enemy. He would be stripped from his rank among the Order for sure. But that might not matter anyway, Elias realized, because now it looked like it might cost him more than just the mission. If he wasn't careful, it could cost him his life.

"You never said that was his; you told me that it was an artifact that needed to be returned to the museum!" she exclaimed, pointing the finger now at Calista, who grinned at Ava's expense.

"They did!" Lottie said innocently and stepped forward into the light. "Don't act like you weren't part of this plan, Ava. You begged us for more assignments so you could make more money. Correct me if I am wrong, but did you make a total of what, fifteen hundred dollars?"

Dr. Balor glanced over at Calista and nodded. "Yes, and she would have made more, but unfortunately, we have run out of time, and now I need to take things into my own hands. Calista, the journal, if you please?"

Elias's eyes widened, and he instinctively took a step back. How did they know about that? He spared a look in Ava's direction but was cut off when Calista stepped forward following Balor's orders. Elias took a second step back from her, away from his closest friend.

"With pleasure."

Ava had betrayed him, and now Lottie? No, he couldn't fathom it. There had to be an explanation. Ava was one thing, but after all this time being friends, Lottie couldn't have betrayed him. But as she stepped forward, he came face to face with the truth. His heart was breaking. Never in a million years would he have suspected her of such a betrayal. And all he wanted to know was why.

"Lottie—" he pleaded. They had been so loyal to each other for so long. What had changed? Calista walked toward Elias, who angrily pulled away from her and shook his head. Friends or not, he couldn't just hand over the journal.

"Oh, come now, Elias, don't be difficult," Calista said as she came to a stop, obviously annoyed.

"What in your right mind makes you think I'd give it to you willingly?" he snarled.

It was clear to Elias that she had chosen her side, and regardless of their friendship, Elias knew he had to stand his ground. For all intents and purposes, she was now the enemy. The stakes were too high.

Calista glowered at him, then turned back to look at Balor. The professor sighed and rolled his eyes. He then dug his hand into his suit pocket and produced a gun. He held it out, inspecting it nonchalantly. The barrel was pointed directly at Ava.

Elias's breath caught in his throat. Ava's eyes grew wide with fear, and she stepped back to the table. She was determined to put as much distance between herself and Balor as possible. Elias gritted his teeth and took a deep breath to settle himself fearing that if he didn't, he would wrap his hands around Calista's throat.

"Just a suspicion," Dr. Balor said.

Elias held his hands up and allowed Calista to step forward. She looked up at him with mischievous eyes as she made a show of exploring his chest before retrieving the brown leather journal from his left jacket pocket. He rolled his eyes, still refusing to look at Ava. He hated that he was still protective of her, given everything, but he wasn't about to see her get shot over a book. That wasn't a price he was willing to pay.

"Let her go. She has nothing to do with this," he said.

Dr. Balor shrugged as Calista brought the book to him. "Oh, I don't know. She seems to know just a little too much, don't you think?" he said, and he tilted his head suggestively in Ava's direction. Ava just stood there, frozen.

"She doesn't know anything. I swear. I haven't told her a thing."

Ava's eyes darted toward Elias, but he ignored her. It was for her own good. He couldn't allow them to see any more of a connection other than lust if there was any hope to spare her life.

Elias stood straight, letting his hands fall to his sides, and he leaned his head back, his jaw tense and eyes angry. His gaze bounced swiftly between Lottie and Balor in mutual disgust. Calista walked over and handed the book to the professor, who took it, gun still in hand, and began to page through it.

"You won't be able to read it without me," he threatened. But he knew it was an empty threat.

Dr. Balor glanced up at him from behind the book's old yellowing pages and chuckled.

"Please, Elias, we're in Ireland. Come now, you don't actually believe we can't find another translator, do you?" He shook his head as if remembering an old joke. Then he returned his eyes to the book and continued.

"No, but don't worry, I don't plan to kill you, at least not yet. I still have use for you. After all, you still have something I need, don't you?" he asked.

And for the second time since the group had appeared, Elias made the mistake of sneaking a look at Ava and that necklace. Balor was busy flipping pages, and Elias couldn't be sure if he had noticed or not.

"What is wrong with you?" Ava snapped. She was baiting him.

Balor chuckled. "Many things, my dear; take your pick."

"I thought this was a place devoted to history."

Dr. Balor looked up at her and snapped the book shut, then glanced around and held out his hands laughing. "Why, it is, child. But alas, I am not as dedicated as my colleagues may be."

"You're despicable. How could you do this? You'll completely destroy Elias's career!" Ava hissed, and Balor's eyes grew cold as he stared at her.

Elias sighed. *Stop sticking up for me. You're only making this worse for yourself,* he thought. He looked over at her, feeling guilty for having dragged her into this mess. He should have insisted on handling this particular mission on his own. He should have just done his research and not relied on an intern to do his dirty work. But it was too late.

Dr. Balor placed his gun back into his jacket, and Elias let out a breath. He handed the journal to Calista, then folded his hands in front of him and tilted his head at Ava menacingly. His patience was running thin by this point.

"You seem very defensive of him," Balor chuckled and shook his head again. "I mean, it's pathetic, isn't it?" Calista's nodded her approval. "Pining after someone who never truly thought twice about you!"

Elias stiffened. His eyes darted to Ava, who stared at Balor dumbfounded.

"What?" she whispered, then looked at Elias. He didn't know how to respond. This was not how he wanted her to find out, not like this. Ava looked at the doctor to continue.

Balor pointed at him accusingly. Elias closed his eyes, biting his bottom lip. He took in a deep breath, knowing what was coming next. Ava glanced at him, but Elias shook his head at her apologetically. "This has nothing to do with her," he said, exasperated.

Balor ignored his remarks and smiled. "He's been lying to you this whole time, Ava. He has more at stake in this expedition than even you do. All this time, you were hoping to make some money to send home to help your sister, and here Elias has been keeping a *huge* secret from you."

Ava shifted uncomfortably, watching Elias.

"You see, while he was promising to help you get the money to save your precious sister, he was actually making plans to steal the jewels before you could get them back to the museum—to take them for himself."

Ava slowly shook her head, unwilling to admit it. But she knew deep within herself it was true. Elias watched in dread as it all snapped together for her way too fast.

 Everything made sense. The little brown book, the way he seemed to know certain things before she did, even though she was supposed to be the brains of the operation. The way he took her to a friend's place instead of the hospital after the mugging because he said he didn't want to involve the police. His knowledge about the case, his strange demeanor toward Balor, and his desire to keep his life private all pointed to something.

Then her breath caught, and her heart seemed to drop from her chest. That's why he didn't want to pursue the relationship further. That's why it took him so long to commit. He never planned on sticking around. Deep down, she knew he had been hiding something, but she had just refused to believe it. But why would he do this? *How* could he do this to her? Even tonight, she could see clearly now, it was only ever about lust, not love. How could she be so stupid?

Ava looked at him. "Elias, tell me this isn't true."

He sighed and just stared back at her. That was the only answer she needed to confirm the bitter truth.

"Come now, Ava, stop groveling. You must have put the pieces together by now. The man couldn't even tell you his real name!"

Ava shook her head and swallowed hard. "No."

"His name isn't Elias Andrew Cassedy," Balor started, but Elias cut him off and stepped toward her, wanting to be the one to tell her himself. No matter what minor faults she had, she deserved this much.

"It's Elias Lynch," he told her. "I am Nathanial Lynch's great-grandson. I work for the Order of St. Patrick."

Ava's jaw dropped. In any other circumstance, she would have been excited and impressed. To find out that the secret society she had been researching and dreaming about her entire adult life was real—and not just that, but that she had been unknowingly working for them—was amazing!

But this was all at the expense of her sister. And everything this man had done and said to her up until this point had been a lie. A single tear rolled down her cheek as she slowly realized that everything she had done and everything she had worked for was a waste.

She would never secure the money she needed for Juliana's treatment. She not only aided in a set-up to steal the jewels, but possibly committed a crime. She had been made a fool of. And all of this, on top of discovering that the man she had grown to care for, the one she had actually developed feelings for, had used her to access the jewels for his own ends. No, this wasn't a dream; this was a nightmare.

Elias frowned as Ava's emotions played out in front of him. In the end, they had each betrayed the other. She unknowingly, and he intentionally, but the damage was done. They had both been played.

Ava glanced down at his forearm, which was showing from when he had adjusted his cufflinks earlier. There it was, in the exact place she had expected to find it—a tattoo of a triskele hidden under makeup that had mostly rubbed off during their escapades earlier tonight.

She bowed her head into her hands and turned away from him. She didn't know what was real and what was fake anymore. Did he actually mean anything he had said to her just moments ago? Did he genuinely feel for her the same way she did for him? Or had it all just been about sex to him? A way to get the jewels and catch her at her most vulnerable?

Elias watched as she unraveled. He wanted nothing more than to comfort her, but he couldn't. He had known what was at stake for her. And yet he chose to risk it in order to do what the Order expected of him. There was no reason he could see why she shouldn't blame him for everything she had to lose.

Balor shook his head and sighed loudly. "I'm tired of this drama. Come now, it's time to go. Bring them along please, Michael, and make it swift," he instructed, and he made his way out of the room as two more prominent men stepped in.

Ava closed the space between them, still unsure of herself, of him. She was breathing heavily, in a far different way than she had just fifteen minutes earlier.

Elias instinctively put his hands on her arms but kept his eyes on the men as they entered. He was trying to weigh his options when Ava forced him to look at her finally.

"I didn't know, Elias, I swear. You have to believe me," she whispered, her eyes had already filled with tears. They pleaded with him to understand the position she had been put in.

Elias sighed, looking down at her. He hated that he didn't trust her. Still, he realized how well they had used her like a pawn to do their bidding. She was not standing on the other end of the room with Calista, which spoke volumes, and Connor, whose involvement he didn't quite understand just yet.

Elias looked back at him. "Some friend of hers you turned out to be, Connor. I knew you were a coward." He snapped. Connor didn't respond. He hadn't moved from his place in the back of the room since they had entered, even with Elias's taunting. He had just stood there and watched it all play out with cold eyes. Now, though, he turned, giving Elias one last look, and followed Calista and Dr. Balor out of the room without a word.

The two men, Michael, who snarled as he approached, and another brute walked up slowly. Michael produced a second gun, and the other grabbed Ava by her hair and yanked her out of Elias's grasp. He glared at the man but knew better than to try and pull her back to him. Ava screamed and thrashed, and the man pulled her farther from him. Michael shoved the gun toward Elias and motioned for him to move to the door.

"Let's go, and quietly, or she gets it," he said, indicating the place where Ava had fought with all her might against the man who was twice Elias's size. Despite the fact that he was much bigger than her, though, the man was having trouble keeping his grasp. She was making such a ruckus that Elias feared what lengths they would go to get her out of here if he didn't intervene.

Elias knew they couldn't leave the room until the two of them were calm. One of two things had to happen: either Elias and Ava had to cooperate with the men, or the men would make her cooperate by force. Considering their weapons in hand, he assumed it was by any means necessary.

Elias abruptly turned toward the man pointing the gun at him. His hands were up. The man raised the gun a little higher.

"Let me walk with her. She will cooperate if she feels safe. And we can all walk out of here without anyone getting hurt or her making a scene."

The man glanced over to his companion just as he got fed up and raised his hand, slapping Ava across the cheek hard enough to send her to the ground. Elias's breath caught in his throat. *Get up, Ava, please, for the love of God, get up.* She slowly moved, bringing a hand to her cheek. Elias let out a steadied breath and closed his eyes, thanking God that she was still conscious after a hit like that.

Michael frowned at his partner. "Oi! Stop making a ruckus!"

The other man raised his shoulder. "What would ya have me do? She's fighting me tooth and nail. You want me to hit her again?"

Elias stepped between them and pleaded with the man with the gun once more. "No! That will cause people to stare if you carry her out unconscious. Let her walk with me. We will stay right in front of you, and people will just think we're a young couple leaving early for the night."

The man pursed his lips but eventually shook his head and waved Elias on. "Whatever, just get the bitch moving. We have a car waiting."

Elias thanked him and went to pick up Ava from the ground. He grasped her chin gently between his fingers, moving her face to the side so he could inspect the damage. She would no doubt have a bruise the next day, but ultimately, she would be okay.

"We have to move now, Ava. You can't stay here; we have to go."

Ava didn't respond but allowed him to help her to her feet. He wrapped his arm around her as she rubbed her cheek and leaned into him. Then Elias led her through the crowd of benefactors, out the front door and into the lion's den, back to the limo Dr. Balor had waiting for them.

Chapter Forty-Six

Dr. Balor and Calista were seated on one side of the limo, while Elias, Ava, and Michael, Balor's henchmen were beside her, the gun now tucked away. Connor sat in the front with the second bloke unfazed. Calista was sporting a dark-gray fur coat over her velvet gown. She stared out the window as they drove the short distance to Kilmainham Gaol. Ava was curled up next to Elias staring at the floor.

Elias didn't know how he was going to get the two of them out of this mess unscathed. His mind was racing with all the possible problems that awaited him once they got there while also trying to come up with ways to escape each one. It felt impossible.

He cursed himself for not keeping Kayleigh better informed. If he had just kept his tracker on his phone as she initially advised, he could have called for backup and the Order would have intervened. He could only hope they would encounter the night security guard once they arrived at Kilmainham, but luck was not on their side.

The limo rolled up to the entrance of the Gaol, where another man stood in the dark with a set of keys. And just when Elias gained a little bit of hope, it was dashed by the man offering Calista a hand and nodding to Balor as they exited the limo. Beside Ava, Michael pulled his gun from his pants and motioned for them to get out. Neither argued.

By now, the sky was pitch black, leaving only the moon to shine any light upon them. The cold Irish air was crisp as it whipped in all different directions. Rain was clearly on its way. Ava shivered as they stepped outside, and Elias scowled at Calista, who was enjoying the sight of Ava's suffering.

Elias removed his suit jacket and placed it over Ava's bare shoulders. Calista's smile faded. Ava pulled the top of the suit over her shoulders but didn't slip the sleeves through.

"The least you could have done was allow her the decency of grabbing her coat."

Calista rolled her eyes and walked away from them. Elias now understood why she had so "kindly" chosen such a sexy dress for the woman she didn't particularly like. She had known where this would lead. It made Elias's stomach churn.

"Stay with the car, Connor, if you don't mind, lad. You three, come with us." Balor motioned for the rest of them to follow as he and Calista entered Kilmainham. Elias followed with Ava by his side; one of the guards walked before them, and the other two brought up the rear.

Ava hadn't said a word since she had been struck. First the attack in Pittsburgh and now this. He knew he needed to reassure her in any way he could. He would get them out of this; he had to. He reached down and subtly (so as not to upset the men behind them) grabbed her hand and squeezed it.

Ava didn't look at him this time, but he noticed her take a deep breath in response. As they walked, Elias made sure to keep his eyes out for possible escape routes.

Balor led them to the location Ava had mapped out earlier: first floor, row nine, cell ten. The cell was kept farther back in a much darker part of the Gaol. The concrete walls and iron doors gave a very haunting vibe, and they came to cell ten. It was tucked away at the very end of the hallway. The door was partially opened as the others had been. Balor stopped and waved his hand in front of him as if to say ladies first. Calista stepped aside with Balor.

One of the men behind them propelled Elias forward, forcing him to break his contact with Ava. Ava moved quickly, trying not to be too far behind him. Elias tried to adjust to the darkness of the damp crevice, but without the lights on and no windows in the cell, it was no use. He felt Ava's tiny figure plow into him from behind as she tripped and clung to his arm.

One of the guards had the sense to produce a flashlight. He turned it on and shined it at another guard who held up an old torch. A dim, fiery glow lit the inside of the room as two of the men entered, followed by Balor and Calista. Elias scoffed. And all this time, he had assumed those torches were fake, just for the benefit of Kilmainham's tourists.

Calista scrunched up her nose at the damp mothball scent of the haunted cell and pointed her flashlight around it, no doubt looking for creepy things that crawl in the night. "I thought you said the key would be here," she complained.

Elias looked at Ava, who untangled her arms from around his elbow. Elias would have been proud of the way, given the circumstances, she turned to face Calista fearlessly before answering. "Elias believes it might be."

Calista abruptly shined her light directly on Ava's face causing her to recoil from the bright light. Knowing they wouldn't be leaving until they did as they had been asked, Elias scanned the top of the cell and walked in a circle, looking for a dent in the concrete, a loose brick, a hole, something.

"What do you mean 'might be'?" she asked in irritation.

"I mean, it's not going to be right out in the open. If his theory is correct, it will be hidden away. Otherwise, tourists would have seen it by now, or the people who run Kilmainham would have moved it," Ava retorted.

Calista moved to strike her, but Balor intervened, stepping between the two and following Elias's gaze thoughtfully around the top of the room.

"For our sake, we shall hope she's right. Otherwise, there is a good chance the jewels are long gone," Dr. Balor said. He brought his hand up to scratch his chin. Calista turned to him, then followed his gaze to Elias. He had stopped and was staring at a darker patch of concrete off to the side corner of the door.

"Atop a cave," Ava whispered.

Elias looked back at Balor and waited for further instructions. Balor glanced from him to the top of the door and back again with a smirk. He seemed to be enjoying this. He cocked his head toward it with his eyes locked on Elias as if to permit him to explore. "Go on."

Realizing the door was far too tall for him, and the bench beside him was now in crumbles, Elias looked back at Ava and Calista. Calista instantly shook her head and gave him a look as if Elias was insane for even thinking she would stick her hand anywhere near the walls.

His eyes then landed on Ava, and she stepped forward without hesitation.

Catching sight of the top of her dress as she approached, Elias took off his tie and vest. "I'd rather not be choked to death while she's up there looking," he told the men who had moved in closer, prepared to attack if needed.

Elias turned back to Ava and smiled wickedly. If it was a show they wanted, he was prepared to give it to them . . . even if it was regrettably at Ava's expense. If everything played out right, he may have just found a way to provide Ava with a bit of protection. He could only pray that she remembered *all* the moves he had taught her all those weeks ago in training.

After removing his vest, he balled up his tie. He shoved it down Ava's dress between her cleavage, the same place she had hidden the Ogham paper. He felt sparks in his veins as his hand briefly caressed her skin, but he shook it off.

Ava let out a gasp and took a step back from him, bringing her hand to her chest. Elias was now all in with his plan, so he gave her a grin that was sure to convince the others that his actions were merely that of sexual attraction and not for any other reason.

"Sorry, love, but that's my grandfather's tie, and I'd hate to ruin it. Plus, I'd be lying if I said I didn't enjoy every minute of that. Come on now, up ya go!"

Ava, still stunned, looked between Elias and Dr. Balor. She mindlessly patted down the tie in her bra and stepped forward, grabbing Elias's shoulders so he could hoist her up, wrapping her legs around his neck. Elias smacked her bare thigh once she was on top of his shoulder to proceed with the charade and looked up at her with a naughty grin from between her legs.

Ava snarled at him. "Touch me again, and I will knock you out," Ava said through gritted teeth.

"Enough," Balor cautioned. Elias noticed he seemed to be getting bored and close to losing his patience with their shenanigans, so he laid off, figuring he had done enough to be convincing.

Ava began to rub her hands over the concrete. She knitted her eyebrows together as she concentrated and knocked a few times at different spots on the wall. One in particular made a different sound. Ava turned to Balor and shook her head.

"I'm going to need something to make a dent in the mud, either a knife or a blunt object. Something."

Dr. Balor wasn't a fool, though, and motioned for one of the men to hand her a solid rock from the pile of crumbled benches. Ava took it and began to whack the wall. Elias shifted his weight with each hit. Finally, on the fifth try, the mud caved, and a hole the size of his fist fell into the wall.

He tried not to watch with such interest, but he couldn't help it. This was history in the making, one way or the other. Ava peeled back more and more of the wall until it looked like there was nothing much left for the wall to give. She glanced down at Elias, who was watching her from below, and stuck her hand in.

Dr. Balor let out a gleeful laugh as she pulled out a dark, significantly faded satchel covered in concrete dust from the wall. Elias smiled despite the circumstances and lowered Ava to the ground, where she kneeled and placed the bag on the floor for everyone to see.

Elias ran a nervous yet giddy hand through his hair as he watched in shock. A part of him couldn't believe it. They had actually found them. He shook his head, caught up in the moment. Dr. Balor pointed his flashlight to the satchel as Ava inspected it, but after running her hands over the top, she came to the same conclusion Elias already had. The zipper on the satchel had been ruined intentionally and was impossible to open.

"Cut it open."

Chapter Forty-Seven

1916, GLENDALOUGH, IRELAND

Word had spread within the Order fast. Andrew's trial had been set for two days from now, and it had everyone on edge, especially Elijah. The day before the trial, Abram asked to meet with him privately at his small cottage. Elijah had agreed.

When he arrived, however, he was surprised to find Terrance waiting in the shadows. Abram paid no attention to the boy, who had grown into a fine young man and vital member of the Order. Instead, he ushered them both into the cottage quickly and quietly. He made sure to check both sides of the house before pulling the door shut behind him. Abram led the two men by lanterns over to a table in the middle of the kitchen.

The old monk motioned for them to take a seat. His wrinkled hands were shaky as he pulled out Andrew's satchel, the same one he'd used to steal the Crown Jewels of Ireland the night this all started. Elijah looked up at him with uncertainty.

"I'm leaving for Dublin tomorrow. I'm going to testify on Andrew's behalf."

"Abram—"Elijah tried to protest, knowing it would only get him killed, too, but Abram held up his hand to silence him.

"I am old, Elijah, far too old to be of much use to the Order now. I will do what I can to try to free your brother. It is my fault he is under attack as it is." Both Abram and Elijah knew this wasn't the trust, but Elijah could see he wasn't in any state to see reason.

"You'll get yourself killed," Elijah said.

Abram nodded, looking exhausted. "If I am to perish, then at least it will be standing up for someone I have grown to have much more than respect for."

Elijah breathed in deeply and looked away. He understood what Abram was saying, and he couldn't be more thankful for his commitment to his family. He had always defended the brothers even when they had messed up, and here he was, willing to risk his life for one of them. Abram turned out to be the father they had both needed.

Abram smiled down at Elijah, who still refused to return his gaze, and Abram understood why. Elijah had grown into a fine young defender of the Order. He was proud of all he had seen the boys accomplish these past few years.

"That being said, I now leave you two with one last mission. It is to remain among the three of us. Is that understood?"

Elijah nodded at the floor, still not willing to look the man in the eye. Terrance glanced at Elijah before looking back to Abram and nodding himself.

"Good. I fear trying times are ahead of us. The Order may have to stand up in a war sooner than we were originally prepared for. That being said, the Crown Jewels cannot fall back into the Brits' hands. They must be protected at all costs."

At this, Elijah lifted his gaze to spy the satchel again.

"Elijah, from here on out, I name you the protector of the jewels." Abram reached forward and placed the satchel onto Elijah's lap. Elijah sat back, staring at the heavy leather satchel. "You must protect what rightfully belongs to Ireland for as long as you may live."

Abram reached up and removed a necklace that dangled from around his neck and placed it into Elijah's palm.

It was a beautiful piece made with two silver spheres. The bottom one was bigger than the top. On top of the smaller sphere was a silver rectangle encrusted with emeralds. It was the key. Andrew had hand-designed it for the satchel. He had planned to give it to a girl he had hoped to marry long ago, but she had up and left him for another man before he could do so.

"I will do my best," Elijah whispered into the darkness.

Abram turned to Terrance. "Terrance, you have become a strong and wise member of the Order. The best we have to offer. But now I ask for you to seal your loyalty to only one family."

Terrance peeked an eyebrow. Abram motioned to Elijah. "I ask you to seal your loyalty to the Lynch brothers, all *three* of them."

Elijah snapped his head up to Abram. Three?

"They will come before blood, before family, before the Order even. There is a good chance neither Andrew nor I will make it out of this alive. I'm seeking for your pledge of loyalty to Elijah and his brother Nathanial to ensure they remain safe and to assist them in any mission they should direct you on. From now on, you are family, as I was. I wouldn't trust this to anyone else. Do you accept?"

Elijah shook his head, but Terrance didn't have to think about it; he looked over at Elijah and nodded.

"That isn't necessary—"

"Of course, sir," Terrance said. "To the ends of the earth, I pledge my allegiance and seal my loyalty to the Lynches."

Abram smiled. Elijah looked over at Terrance, speechless.

Terrance had not forgotten the kindness both brothers had shown throughout the years. Starting with Andrew during the first heist and going all the way up to most recently when Elijah had nominated Terrance for a jump in rank. If he was able to return the favor to the brothers, he was happy to do so, no matter what was asked of him.

Because of Andrew, all those years ago, he had been able to feed his family. Because of his position here, he was able to relieve them from poverty. He would be forever grateful.

"Good, now Terrance, a new member, is being called into action. Elijah and I will be going up to Dublin for the trials. I need you to head toward the County Cork and retrieve his younger brother Nathanial. It is time he stepped into his brother's legacy." Elijah shifted his gaze back over to Abram, who winked at him. "Show him the ropes, Terrance; you will be the one to train him until a time when Elijah feels he can step in. You are to explain everything to him: Elijah being alive, Andrew's wrongful arrest. All of it. And hopefully, when we return, we will take over from there."

Terrance came to his feet, nodding seriously now. "Yes, sir."

"Good. You are dismissed, Terrance."

Terrance stood and held his hand out to shake Elijah's. Elijah accepted it graciously. Thankful for the commitment he had just pledged. Then Elijah watched him leave without another word. Abram turned to Elijah. He folded his hands behind his back and smiled down at the man.

"You've done well for yourself, Elijah. You should be proud."

Elijah shook his head. He didn't want to hear it; he didn't want to have this discussion. Not right now. Not with everything else going on. "There is always room for improvement," he said. "You sound like you're saying goodbye, Abram. I thought that those were beneath you," he said bitterly.

Abram wiggled his head back and forth the way only an old man could when he disagreed. "Certainly not. I'm merely saying until we meet again."

He took a step forward and sat down on the bench next to Elijah with his hand on his shoulder. Elijah dropped his head into his hands. This was all too much. He was already at risk of losing his twin, and now he was about to gain his other brother, only to lose Abram as well. He couldn't handle all of this on his own. Despite having Terrance, he felt like everyone was leaving him.

And Andrew, oh Andrew. His fate was practically sealed. Being on trial for unspeakable things meant he would most likely be put to death. How would he be able to move forward without him? Without his counterpart? Without his twin? They had always shared everything. Andrew had been not only his brother but his best friend and protector as well.

Abram sighed. "It's a long road ahead, Elijah, but as I have said before, you have a fighter's spirit within you. I know you will persevere no matter what the outcome is. And I will do everything in my power to save Andrew. You have my word."

Elijah sat up a bit and looked straight out the door that Terrance had left cracked open. The night sky coated the earth like a blanket. A soft fog hovered over the earth's floor. Elijah blinked. He would see this through for Andrew. He would hide the jewels and keep them from the hands of the British. He would not let Andrew's work go in vain.

Chapter Forty-Eight

Modern-day Kilmainham Gaol, Dublin, Ireland

Ava

One of Balor's henchmen stepped forward and pulled out a knife. I held my breath as he wasted no time and sliced through the old leather with ease. The man put his knife away and shoved his hand into the bag; he pulled out a small metal lockbox.

I glanced up and exchanged a look with Elias, who smirked before returning his attention to the box. Even with his deception, this victory was not lost on me. Regardless of whether we made it out of this alive, we still solved it. Together. It was a bittersweet moment.

I sat on my heels on the cold stone flooring, watching as the man held it out for Balor to inspect. I was afraid to move. Given the small space we were in, there was a chance that either I would get in someone's way and piss them off, or spook them into pulling out their guns again. Neither of those situations sounded like something I wanted to return to, so I stayed where I was.

As Dr. Balor looked at the box closely, I kept my eye on Calista. Out of everyone, she seemed to be the one who was the most unhinged. I expected that it had something more to do with Elias's conversation with her earlier, though, and less actually to do with me; nevertheless, she had, for some reason, chosen to take it out on me.

"It's locked," the henchman said. Dr. Balor let out a sigh of frustration and rolled his eyes.

"Yes, I see that you are a blithering idiot."

"Want me to break it open?"

Balor's eyes grew wide with mad concern. "Lord, no! You fool! You could damage the Jewels inside! They are priceless artifacts that will sell for millions! You damage a single diamond on them, and I will shoot you myself!"

Dr. Balor pulled out his gun and aimed it at Elias. Elias stepped back against the wall behind him and held up his hands. His expression never wavered. He never gave them the satisfaction of showing fear as he looked down the nose of the gun barrel and then back up to Balor.

"I know you have the key," Balor said calmly, but there was a new edge to his voice that hadn't been there before, and I realized they were running out of chances to escape. I shifted my eyes away from the two and flitted my eyes around the entryway of the cell in a desperate plea to find a way out from where we were.

"I don't have it. I swear," Elias replied.

"I'm not a fool, Elias Lynch. Give me the key, and I will promise to make your death as quick and painless as possible," Dr. Balor spat.

I snapped my eyes back to the pair and then turned toward Calista. Maybe I could play on her heartstrings and convince her to save Elias at least. "For someone who claimed to love him, you sure have a funny way of showing it," I whispered to her.

Calista's eyes flicked to me with disgust. She chose to watch the scene between Elias and Balor unfold without intervening. I was slightly more surprised when she slowly produced a gun of her own from underneath her dress. I sucked in a breath as she held it readily at her hip. I wasn't sure if she was preparing to defend Elias or Balor, but I decided, for now, to shut up as that gun was awfully close to my head.

"I told you *I don't have it!*" Elias hissed through his teeth at Balor from around the gun.

Balor considered this for a moment then acted as if none of this mattered to him and holstered his gun inside his jacket. "Fine, if you insist. Calista, dispose of the girl if you please, as she is no longer needed here tonight. If Elias doesn't want to give me what I'm looking for, maybe a glimpse at reality will change his mind."

What?

Everything happened so fast and I could barely keep up. Calista grabbed a handful of my hair, pulling it back so that I was forced to bend my head backward to look up at her. Elias lunged forward in an effort to aid me but was met with two guns pointed at him, this time from Balor's men, as they stepped in between us. Balor exited the cell.

"Gladly," she snarled wickedly.

I looked up at her with seething anger. I was beyond done with all of this. With the attacks, with the constant games, with the deception, the secrets, the lies, all of it. As I returned her venomous glare, I decided I wasn't about to give in to her antics again. If she wanted to kill me, she would have to work for it. "Good luck."

I used all my lower body strength, whipped my legs out, and swung them around so that I hooked Calista's legs and pulled them out from underneath her. Just as Elias had taught me on our first day of training. She dropped my hair, and I fell to the side as she hit the floor. She let out an enraged howl that echoed through the cell walls.

I tried to use my time wisely to scramble to my feet but came face to face with one of the guns. I was not nearly as brave when it came to firearms as Elias seemed to be, and I froze.

"Enough already! Calista, take Forton and get rid of her quickly! You two bring Lynch down to the center yard and tie him to the pole. I'm done playing games," Balor yelled.

I looked over at Calista, who had reached her boiling point with me. Her hair was now sticking up at the top from her fall, dirt and dust covered the bottom of her dress and coated the fur around her shoulders.

"You bitch," she fumed.

"Move," said the man pointing the gun. Balor had called him Forton.

I looked back at Elias. I didn't want to be separated from him. I threw my arm out to grasp him, but I came up short as Forton clotheslined me with his arm and began to drag me away from him.

Elias chased after me as Forton ushered me out of the cell, but the remaining two men seized him. One of them used Elias's distraction to their advantage and slugged him good in the abdomen. The last time I saw Elias, he was doubled over.

Once we made it past the cells and onto the center space, we exited the primary entryway into the backyard. Forton threw me onto the ground and my hands and knees met the loose gravel that surrounded us.

I slowly picked my head up and looked around. In the middle of the night, with nothing but the moon's glow to aid our vision, I realized I recognized precisely where we were. This was the same yard where the remaining leaders of the Rising had perished. This was where Andrew had died. This was the Firing Yard.

A fire lit by many men, the firing squad. They were going to execute me.

Still on the ground, I threw myself backward to see Calista towering over me with her gun in my face. Forton had taken a back seat, allowing Calista to play out her own dramatic scene, though his gun still hung from his hands. "Calista, please."

"Get up."

I held up my hands and scrambled backward on my heels as she slithered toward me step by step. "Calista, think about this. He will kill him. Balor? He won't let him live, you know that!"

"I said move! On your feet!" she screamed in outrage.

I didn't want to upset her more, so I obliged. Fear was setting in now; before, I had been running on adrenaline, feeding off of the excess courage that Elias had been giving off, but now that we were separated. I was alone. And that meant I had no one else's courage to fall back on.

Calista took a step forward. I took a step back.

"Calista, I'm begging you to hear me, please! After he kills us, he's going to kill you! He won't keep you around. Why would he?"

One more step.

"Tie her hands in front of her, Forton."

Forton took a step forward, and I shrank back.

"You have to know how much Elias still cares for you! You can still walk away from this; you can still save us. You can save him!"

Another step. I was getting increasingly desperate and tears began to roll down my face.

"Oh, I will save him. Don't you worry. And when I do, he will come crawling back to me, just you wait. But you? You were never really part of the equation. No, you will be better use to me dead."

Forton sealed the distance between us and snatched my hands, tying them together with a small rope. He dropped my hands and stepped away to stand behind Calista, who stood nearly ten feet away from me. Her gun was still at her side and she watched all my darkest fears come to light.

In reality, my fear of being alone was never my biggest weakness. Though I was not too fond of the idea, once my parents were gone, a new fear took root within me. I didn't want Juliana to ever feel the way I had when my dad left. I didn't want her to suffer as I did when Mom passed away. At that point, I realized that leaving Jules with the same fears I had was my greatest fear. I couldn't do that to her.

"Calista, please. I have a sister—"

"Shut up!" she screamed. "Do you think I care? Do you think I want to hear about your pathetic little family?"

"You can stop this. You don't have to do this. You don't have to be a monster," I said through tears.

"I'm not a monster! You are the monster! You're the one who took everything I loved away from me! You are the one who destroyed everything I had!"

"Elias will never forgive you," I told her. "How can you look at me, someone who considered you a friend? And kill me without a care in the world? Will you even be able to forgive yourself after this?"

Calista shook her head and paced around the spot in the gravel. It seemed as if she had finally lost her will to fight; her patience, too, had run through. She took a deep breath and faced me.

"I will have Elias one way or the other, Ava. And while I am sorry it had to come to this, my conscience remains clear."

Calista turned and raised the gun in front of her without another word, and I closed my eyes. If I was going to leave this earth, I did not want to see it happen. I began to count in my head in hopes of making it easier on myself. As I counted, the faces of my family showed up behind my closed eyes.

One . . . Juliana and Ryker running through the zoo. At least I knew Jules would always have him in her corner.

Two . . . Millie and Eamon out celebrating their anniversary together, holding hands.

Three . . . Mom's smile . . . Elias's embrace . . .

The gun went off three times, and despite myself, I let out a scream. I don't know where I had gotten the energy to scream, considering I had been shot at, but I did. I waited for the pain to set in, but it never came. Had I died instantly?

I opened my eyes and looked down at myself. Clean. Clear of any blood or bullet holes. What the? Where was it? Where was the pain? And the blood and comfort of death I was promised?

I glanced at Calista, but she was no longer standing. Instead, both she and Forton were lying on the gravel from where they had stood just moments before. Bullet holes were visible in both of their foreheads. I blinked in shock as blood pooled under Calista's head, her arm still raised. My eyes grazed the yard around me frantically. There was another shooter. Or possibly two?

It didn't take long for my eyes to narrow on the two men standing off to the side. My knees gave out. I fell to my knees, too stunned to stand.

This was a dream. It had to be. More like a nightmare. There was no way that man was walking toward me right now. There was no way this was possible. My body had simply gone into shock and I had lost it. That was the only feasible explanation.

Frozen in place, I kept my gaze on the first man as the second hurried over to me. He brushed his hands over my face, checking on me to make sure I was okay. My mind registered him before I actually laid eyes on him.

"Connor . . ."

"You're okay. You did great, Ava, but we have to go. Can you move?"

I don't think I responded, I just allowed him to help me up to a standing position. Connor pulled out a knife and cut the rope around my hands.

My eyes never left the tall, dark-haired man with gray sprinkling his goatee. His blue eyes pierced right through mine as he stood there sadly and watched Connor try to get me to respond.

Finally, Connor brought his two hands to my face and redirected my attention, so I was looking directly at him. "Ava, focus. We have to go. Elias needs our help. Are you ready? This isn't over yet. Can you stay with me?"

At the sound of Elias's name, my brain snapped back into the present. I blinked a few times and nodded. Connor dropped his hands and then started moving away.

"Good, then, follow us; he's in the center court."

The man in front of us started to walk away, urgently leading us toward the central courtyard. Connor followed him. As we passed Calista's body, I stopped and leaned down, finally coming face to face with the woman who had hated me enough to want me dead. Her eyes were still open, staring blankly, her perfect dark hair now soaked with dark blood. Even in death, she was still stunning. I frowned and slipped the gun from her hand before running to catch up with Connor.

As we followed behind the first man, I noticed he was watching me as much as I was him. I guess it was to be expected after all this time. Though I had honestly never thought I'd see him again, I was kind of glad I was now.

He wasn't the comfort I was searching for after these last two weeks of chaos; in fact, if anything, he added more stress to that, but he had shown up. For once in his life, he had shown up. And that was saying something.

My dad had proven years ago how little he had cared about me, and yet here he was saving my ass and leading the cavalry right back into a battle—one that wasn't his to fight.

Chapter Forty-Nine

ELIAS

Ava's scream pierced through the walls of the Gaol as the first shot rang out. Two more shots followed, stilling the space before Elias. The silence that remained destroyed him from the inside out. His heart dropped into the pit of his stomach. He stood praying for other sounds to follow, to prove that she was still alive, but all he heard was his own heavy breathing. She was gone.

He couldn't process it. The girl he had just spun around the dancefloor, the beauty who had wrapped her legs around his waist and seduced him just hours ago; the woman he had been willing to give his all to, was gone.

His mouth fell open in anguish. Despite the physical pain he was feeling from the blows, which Balor had been so graciously delivering himself, he hadn't reacted to any of it until now. Not until he heard her scream. Not until he heard that final gunshot.

Balor chuckled under his breath and looked down on Elias with pity. Elias's hands were tied behind his back around an old wooden pole that stood in the middle of the courtyard. Balor's henchmen were on either side of him with their hands folded at the waist, awaiting instructions.

How could he have let this happen? He knew better than to get involved. He knew anyone he loved could be manipulated and used against him. That was why he had remained so closed off to people before Ava had come along. He knew the price. And yet he had let her in. He had slipped up and allowed her to wriggle her way into his heart, and look where it had gotten her.

He had promised to protect her. She had trusted him, and he had instead led her to an early death. For this, he deserved anything Balor was going to do to him. He deserved the torture, the punishment, and he deserved to die. He would never be able to live with himself after this.

By now, the doctor had taken off his suit jacket and set it aside. The lockbox lay underneath it. Dr. Balor pulled out a white rag from his pants pocket and wiped away Elias's blood from his hands.

Blood from his split lip dripped from Elias's chin.

"All of this can just be over if you give me the key, Elias. I can end your pain if you let me."

He tried to take a deep breath in, but with broken ribs, the pain broke up his breathing. "You just destroyed it," he whispered.

Balor squinted at him as he waited for an explanation. *"What was that?"*

Elias didn't answer.

Another punch came, suddenly flying into his gut. The air that remained in Elias's lungs left him, and he doubled over, grimacing.

"What did you say?" Balor shouted.

Again, another blow. Elias spat blood onto the gravel and shook his head miserably. "I said you destroyed it when you killed her." All this time, he had been hoping that keeping that information from Balor would spare her life. But he had been wrong. It was a mistake that cost him the world.

"She had it?" Balor yelled, now irate. He stepped up, drew back his hand, and punched Elias in the face.

Elias stayed silent.

Kill me. Kill me now, he begged the saints above. He was utterly defeated in the worst sense; there was no fight left in him. Without her, the light that had been re-lit in his life was gone. He could not bear to walk around in the darkness again. Despite the fact that she had helped Balor steal his family heirlooms from him, she was still the one he wanted. He had known it even as Balor had revealed her deception; he had known he could never walk away from her.

"I will not end your miserable life until you tell me where that key is!" Balor yelled into Elias's face. Spit flung as he did so.

Just then, a clicking sound came from the dark corner behind Balor. Balor turned slowly to see a figure lurking among the shadows. Someone new had entered the courtyard. Elias looked up to see a man in his early fifties with dark brown hair streaked with gray. He stepped out from the shadows. Elias recognized him.

The man's name was Aiden. He was an older member of the Order. Elias had seen him around the grounds at headquarters, but they had never talked. Aiden, for the most part, kept to himself, only really confiding in the Order's president from time to time. Other than that, Elias only knew the rumors about the man, but who could say if they were real?

Aiden stepped into the courtyard's light, gun raised and aimed at Balor. Balor, having walked away from Elias, grinned as his sights were now set on Aiden.

"Never did learn to control that temper of yours, did you, Thaddeus?" Aiden asked him.

Balor shook his head wildly; the man was beginning to lose his grip on reality. "Oh, Aiden, I should have known you'd show up."

Elias looked between the two. Did they know each other? Elias had known Balor had been on the Order's radar for a while, but he didn't see any reason why Balor should also know Aiden.

"Wouldn't be anywhere else, old friend. Let the kid go."

Balor turned his head to smile at Elias then looked back at Aiden. "And why would I do that?" he asked, putting a hand on his hip.

"Because you're outnumbered."

From out of the shadows, Connor followed close behind Aiden with his own gun raised to Aiden's head.

Balor laughed. "Am I? Because it doesn't seem like it."

Connor suddenly spun on his heel and turned his gun on the guard closest to Elias. Michael returned his threat, pointing his gun back at Connor with sudden uncertainty. Connor flipped off his safety.

Balor sighed. "Are we really going to do this, boys? Now really? Aren't you tired yet, Aiden?"

Aiden took a step closer. "Tired of what?" he asked.

"Of all this drama? The running, the fighting? You've been hiding for how long? Almost eight years, and for what? You have already lost both your girls in this fight; just give up, old friend. Accept defeat. You have lost," Balor replied.

Both girls?

Elias had known of Aiden's story. Rumor was that he had lost his wife due to an accident, but he had always been told that his daughter had gone to live with her stepfather. Elias had expected that Aiden and his wife had divorced long before the accident and that she had remarried. But now, the way the two spoke made Elias think otherwise—something about what he had been told about Aiden and what was playing out between these two rivals wasn't adding up. Who was the second girl Balor spoke of?

Aiden smirked. "Oh, have I?"

Elias had just started to question everything he had known about Aiden and Connor when he heard a rustle of gravel from behind him. Connor shifted his feet at that moment to mask the sound from the guards. Elias subtly peeked back over his shoulder.

There, hidden in the back corner, covered by darkness, was a bright, yet filthy, emerald dress. Ava! She blinked at him twice, acknowledging his stare, then turned toward Connor, who returned the look with a subtle nod.

Ava kicked her heels to the side and quietly pulled out the black tie Elias had shoved down her cleavage earlier. He turned back to face front, aiding as best he could in the distraction.

"First your wife and now your daughter. Such a shame, isn't it?" Balor taunted him.

Aiden didn't hide the raw anger that seethed from behind his eyes as he took another step toward Balor. "You may have taken my wife from me, Thaddeus, and that is something you will pay for. But you have reached the wrong conclusion about my daughter."

Balor's smile dropped when he spotted Ava. She snuck up behind the man to Elias's left and wrapped the tie around his hands holding the gun, then threw all her effort into whacking his hands off the pole that held Elias. The man's big wrists made contact with the wooden pole, and the gun fell to the ground.

The man threw up his hands, which sent Ava flying backward, landing on the gravel. Michael turned, but Connor moved first and fired a warning shot through the guy's arm. He fell back, surprised and in pain. Ava, beside Elias, scrambled away from the man.

"Pant leg, pant leg!" said Elias. Ava grabbed Elias's left pant leg, pulled it up, and snatched the knife he had tucked into his boot. She scurried backward on her hands and knees and ducked, narrowly missing a swing from the man. She swiped the knife downward on the back of the pole.

The moment Elias felt the rope loosen, he intervened. He wasted no time pulling his arm back and returning the favor he had been graciously given just moments earlier. He struck the man twice in the face.

The guard stumbled and fell back.

Elias reached down and helped Ava to her feet before fleetingly grasping her face and kissing her with everything he had.

Gunshots erupted, and Elias was forced to break the kiss. Aiden, with the momentary distraction, had taken three shots at Balor and missed. Aiden was playing with psychological warfare. He advanced on the doctor now, and Balor stepped back.

The guard near Elias scrambled toward his gun lying on the ground nearby. But Ava saw it first and kicked it to the other end of the courtyard.

The man growled and reached out for Ava's ankle, but he came face to face with Elias's foot instead. Ava ran back to get the gun as Elias advanced on the man, fuming.

Michael watched Ava run past him to retrieve the gun. He pulled himself into a sitting position and faced the end of Connor's barrel. Abruptly, he grabbed his gun and aimed it at Ava, but Connor was quicker. He hit his target on the second try and sent the gun flying out of his hands.

As Aiden closed in on Balor, he holstered his gun. "Let's finish this, Thaddeus."

Balor grinned sinisterly. "Gladly." He lunged at Aiden.

Ava reached the discarded weapon and ejected the magazine, then checked to ensure no other bullets remained in the chamber. She threw it well out of reach and replaced the empty magazine that had been in Calista's gun with the new one she acquired.

She turned back to see all three men busy in battles of their own.

Her father and Dr. Balor were exchanging blows at the front of the courtyard. Their feud was evidently a long-standing one, and Ava knew it wouldn't end until one of them was dead. Elias had tackled the man from whom Ava had stolen the gun and was now engaged in a fight to the death of his own.

Connor had Michael cornered with his gun aimed.

Ava scanned the room anxiously. Then finally, she saw it. Over to the right side, under Balor's jacket, was the satchel with the jewels.

Ava weaved between the men. She crouched and lifted the jacket to search for the lockbox.

Connor wasn't paying enough attention and allowed himself to get too close.

Michael used his good hand to throw dirt and gravel at him, forcing Connor to pull one of his hands away from the gun to shield his face. He lifted his foot and kicked the gun from Connor's hands. The gun went flying, and he attacked.

Michael produced a knife from his back pocket and drove it into Connor's side. Connor took a brief step back before falling to his knees, letting out a hiss of pain. The man rushed past him.

Elias held his next punch as he heard Connor cry out. He turned to see the second guard running from where Connor sat on his heels with his hands on his side.

Connor was down, and the second man was heading for Ava.

Elias abandoned his fight to chase after Michael, but he reached Ava first. Micheal reached Ava just as she picked up the lockbox and swung it around her head, smacking him dead in the face with the jewel box.

Elias tried not to grimace. Her safety was more important than any jewels, he had to remind himself.

"Ava, run!" She sprinted past Michael, then Elias, who stepped between them and kicked him while he was down. She managed to get out through the main entrance, while everyone else was subdued then vanished into the darkness.

Elias took a brief sigh of relief, but it was short-lived. The first man from before had returned and grabbed him by the throat, pulling him into a headlock. Elias leaned backward and tried kicking with all his might. Michael came to a standing position and threw two punches into Elias's gut. The grip around his neck tightened, forcing the air from his lungs.

Aiden, in the midst of his fight, stopped briefly to look up. He assessed the situation quickly and knew this couldn't continue. He pulled away from Thaddeus, pulled out his gun one last time, and aimed. Balor breathed deeply from their struggle and bent down at the waist with his hand held up.

"Come now, brother. You're not really going to shoot me," Balor said between heaved breaths.

"We are not brothers," Aiden spat.

Balor laughed. "We were inducted together. We will always be brothers."

"Your title was renounced! And we are finished here, Thaddeus. I'm through." A single shot pierced the air once again. The shot landed right in the middle of Dr. Balor's stomach.

The sound made the guard who had Elias by the throat hesitate just long enough to throw him off balance. Elias pulled himself away from the two. He sucked in air desperately and doubled over as two more shots were heard finishing off Balor's men.

Elias looked up at Aiden, still gasping for breath. Aiden turned away from Balor's body. He was still alive but bleeding through the stomach, face down in the gravel. Both of Balor's men, however, were dead, and Elias knew he had made the shot to make Balor suffer for taking his wife.

It was over. They had won.

Elias looked back with his hands on his knees; his body was beginning to give out. He remembered Connor, but just barely.

Dr. Balor lay face down on the gravel, bleeding out more than just blood. Venom and anger poured from him like a waterfall. He couldn't allow this. He couldn't let the Lynch boy get away with his jewels! He had worked too hard and sacrificed too much.

Balor lifted his head slowly and pulled his gun from his pants pocket with a shaky hand. He looked up and raised the gun just barely off the ground pointing it at Elias. But just as he pulled the trigger, Aiden's daughter returned.

Ava felt like the world came to a stop as she watched Balor aim at Elias. Rain pelted her cheeks like tiny needles. Her breath was stolen away in a gasp. She had a mere second to make the choice. She raised her own hand without a second thought. Two shots sounded through the courtyard and both hit their targets.

# Chapter Fifty

1917, Glendalough, Ireland

Elijah sat on his heels in front of a gravestone etched with his brother's name. Behind him, a few feet back to give him space, Terrance stood paying his respects to his brother, who had once roped him into this grand adventure. Beside him, a curly, familiar redhead watched with tears in her eyes as Elijah bid farewell to his other half. Elijah was grateful for both of them. They had become great friends over the past few years.

Elijah sighed as he looked over his shoulder. The second row down had a second new stone with Abram's name on it. It had been a massive loss to the Order to lose them both within the same week. Elijah, though, had not been surprised.

The trial had not gone as well as Abram had hoped. He had shown up and testified on Andrew's behalf, but it had not been enough. Andrew had been sentenced to death with the rest of the leaders from the Rising. Elijah had never felt so heartbroken in his life. If he could take it all back, he would have. He would have suffered every blow, every beating till death if it meant his not joining The Order would spare his brother's life. He knew it was illogical, but he blamed himself all the same.

After the trials, Andrew was held at Kilmainham Gaol for a final week before his execution. Elijah was permitted one last visit. That final moment together was harrowing. Yet, amidst the pain, they plotted. As he clasped his brother's hand through the bars, they devised their plan to hide the jewels. They would need Nathanial's help, of course, but perhaps that was for the best.

Elijah wasn't quite sure how he was handling the news. It was one thing to find out Elijah was alive, but then to be told that he was instead losing his other brother on the same day. It was a lot for them both to handle. But Nathanial proved to be keeping up at the least and refused to show any tension. Elijah was impressed with his younger brother. Andrew would have been proud.

Shortly after the hearing, Abram collapsed in Dublin from cardiovascular disease. Elijah had been told he had died from stress, but he knew better. The final sentencing had destroyed him as much as it had Elijah, and it finished Abram off. Throughout all of this mess, Elijah considered himself lucky. Along with the Order, they had been allowed to take the bodies of Andrew and Abram home to Glendalough and bury them privately. This had permitted Nathanial the chance to mourn appropriately along with the rest of the Order, who held a quiet service for the two here on the grounds.

Now sitting in front of the newly chiseled gravestone, after all the plans, all the fuss, and the funeral services were done, Elijah found himself feeling empty as he stared at Andrew's name. He had long ago stopped shedding tears and now had come to terms with the significant loss.

Still, he bowed his head. "I'm sorry," he whispered. "I'm sorry I couldn't save you the way you had me."

Rustling behind him caused Elijah to turn his head. His eye caught the attention of Nathaniel, who had joined him, Bridget, and Terrence in the graveyard. Nathaniel stepped forward and stood behind Elijah, observing silently. Elijah looked back down and blessed his brother's stone before standing upright. Next to his younger brother, now in his mid-twenties, he towered over him. There was no doubt that Nathaniel still had some growing to do, but he would mature in time. If Elijah could do it, so could he.

Elijah patted his younger brother's shoulder. He then touched the chain dangling around his neck and lifted it from his chest. He held it out for Nathanial to inspect. His younger brother's eyes danced over the silver and emerald pendant with wonder.

"This belongs to you now."

Nathanial held out his hand, and Elijah dropped the pendant into his open palm.

"Protect this with your life."

Nathanial tilted his head. "What is it?"

"You will learn in time. But for now, all you need to know is that it holds Andrew's legacy. The legacy that you will pass on to your children someday."

Nathanial returned his eyes to stare at the necklace, then swiftly flipped it over his head so it hung around his neck.

"Good lad," said Elijah. And he pulled out his leather journal to jot a few of his thoughts down for the next generation.

# Epilogue

Two days before the fundraiser

Aiden stepped into the semi-lit office. A large cherry-oak desk that looked like it cost a fortune sat in the back center of the room, illuminated by floor-to-ceiling windows behind it. Large bookcases surrounded the desk, and an oval rug in the center gave the room a very regal look. A woman stood with her back turned to him. She was dressed in a sharp black suit and heels. Her presence screamed authority, but to him, she whispered temptation.

Aiden folded his hands behind his back; his eyes remained on the floor as he waited for her to turn around and address him. She took her time looking out the window, which gave light to the brilliance of her fiery red hair, and then, finally, she turned around. Aiden raised his eyes to meet hers. She merely raised her eyebrows at him, her mouth held in a firm line.

"You've been deliberately ignoring my orders," she growled.

Aiden wasn't as nervous as he should have been.

"Do you deny it?" the woman asked.

Aiden let out a sigh, breaking the formal tension between the two. "No."

The woman released a sound of frustration and threw her arms into the air as she came around the desk to speak to him face-to-face.

"Aiden! I gave you those specific orders for a reason. You are not to intervene with Elias's mission any further. Do not make me explain this to you again!"

Aiden held up his hand between the two to silence her. The action angered her even more, and she cocked her head back, prepared to give him another lashing of the tongue if he didn't start treating her as the superior that she was.

"Ava is *my daughter*—"

"I am well aware, Aiden, but she is in good, capable hands. Elias has proven himself committed to her safety many times, without even knowing who she was!"

"Yes, but I believe I have information that he doesn't."

The woman crossed her arms and scowled. It was doubtful that this was the truth and much more likely that Aiden was using it as an excuse to keep tabs on his daughter. The woman sat back and leaned against her desk, disapproving of him lying to her. "Oh really?"

Aiden frowned at her and stepped closer, knowing exactly what she was thinking.

"Yes. Really. And Ava is my daughter. I will protect her at all costs."

Aiden closed the gap between them and took hold of the woman's hand, pulling it out from under her other arm. Her anger seemed to fade with his touch. Her scowl softened into a less fierce frown. She looked over towards the bookshelf to avoid his gaze.

She was the president, the leader of the Order. Although she would never mention this to him, it sometimes bothered her how much he had influenced her decision-making.

"I have reason to believe that the men attacking them in Glendalough and Pittsburgh are not Balor's men. I believe them to be a different threat entirely."

Sabane's eyes grew wide and she shifted her gaze uneasily confused towards Aiden still holding her hand. "Another threat? What makes you say that?"

Aiden's eyes flickered over to the top of Sabane's desk, where a stack of papers was laid out to look like a flush of cards. "Have you received a report yet from Elias this evening?"

Sabane blinked, then stood up, forcing Aiden to release her hand. She walked around to stand behind her desk and began to shuffle through her papers briefly before shaking her head.

"No," she said. Her eyes continued to scan the various documents with Elias Lynch's name on them.

Aiden nodded and walked around the desk to stand beside her. "I've been watching Balor and his people. They need the items and information Ava and Elias are collecting for them. They want them to do their dirty work, as we suspected. But that being said, it makes no sense for Balor to have his men stepping in before they have what they want."

Sabane thought this through, nodding her head in agreement and then looking over to Aiden. "Did you get a good look at these men who attacked Ava in Pittsburgh the other night?"

she asked.

Aiden took a deep breath angrily and averted his gaze. The memory still had him fuming, but he shook his head and walked away.

"Not a good look. I had Kayleigh reach out to Elias to see if he had, but all he was able to describe to us was a big build, maybe late forties, with dark hair. But we lost contact with him after that . . . Elias did say, though, that Ava broke the guy's nose," he explained with a smirk. "My girl."

Sabane snorted and rolled her eyes. Aiden had always been the *strike now, ask questions later* type. It had been really hard for him to be considered an inactive member of The Order these last seven or so years. Initially, he had fought her on it. But when his wife was tragically murdered, he stepped back and listened. He was unwilling to put Ava and Juliana in the same danger he had no doubt put Triona. To this day, he still blames himself for her passing.

"Sabane," Aiden started again, stepping back toward her.

She looked at him with serious eyes. She already knew what he wanted but wasn't sure if now was the right time. Still, she didn't speak; this time, she let him finish.

"If what I think is true and there are *two* threats out there, then Elias and Ava could be walking into a death trap without proper support, and if we aren't able to reach him, this could end very badly."

He was right. Of course, he was right. She hated that he was right, but she also knew better than to question him at this point. Sabane thought for a minute. "Okay, so we send August and Bellamy. That keeps Ava and Elias out of immediate danger while still protecting your secret! Problem solved!"

Aiden's shoulders sagged. This roundabout he had going with her was getting old, and he was tired of playing games. Aiden took another step towards her, and she turned away from him, shaking her head and leaning forward with her palms on her desk. She hung her head in near defeat.

"You know I won't sit by this time and watch another member of my family get picked off Sabane. I have to be the one who goes."

Sabane took a deep breath in and shook her head once more. "If you do this, you will risk everything," she whispered.

"If I do this, I will finish what I started. Balor will not get the upper hand this time. I will end this once and for all."

Sabane turned her head to look over her shoulder at him but averted her eyes. She didn't want him to know how concerned she was at the thought of sending him back out into the field. "And the other threat?"

"I will assess that once I have located it."

Sabane finally nodded and pushed off the desk to come to a standing position. She turned to look at him directly. Her blue eyes danced across the features of his face. She sighed once more and crossed her arms over her chest. "And I assume you will want to enlist the help of Eamon for this task then, is that right?"

Aiden smiled mischievously at her and shook his head. "No, I don't believe he is ready to step out of the shadows quite yet."

Sabane narrowed her eyes in confusion as he took a few steps back from her, slowly making his way towards the door, pushing her response. "Then who?"

"Don't worry, my dear, I don't intend to work this case alone. I picked up a new recruit, you see, one whom I believe will be of great use to us. You might actually know him, come to think of it. His name is Connor Cook." Aiden had nearly reached the door when Sabane threw her arms down with her eyes wide in protest.

"You can't be serious!"

"Trust me! I wouldn't have chosen this if I didn't think it would work."

Aiden put his hand on the doorknob of Sabane's office and waited for the final order from her. Despite the fact that he typically had trouble following them, this was an order he needed to hear her give.

"You will stop at nothing, will you," she finally said, her voice as soft as a whisper. Aiden simply smiled in return. Sabane threw up her hands in utter defeat and let out a growl of frustration. "Fine! Ugh fine! Wake you, sleeping giant! Wake up and begin your first rescue mission. I, President Sabane Connelley of the Order of St. Patrick, reinstate Aiden O'Donnell into service. Go, you old fool! May your journey be blessed."

Acknowledgments

First and foremost, thank you to Jessica, Issac, and the team at Emerald Books for helping me turn this dream into reality and refine it to perfection. You have made me a better writer, and I have gained so much respect for you and the fantastic work you do. Thank you for believing in this book. I have been truly blessed to have had the opportunity to work with you.

To Allison, for daring to be the first to read all the rough drafts and picking apart every little detail. Your patience in waiting to see where the next chapter would lead you is what I lived for at one point. Thank you for your excitement and enthusiasm. Your interest in this story is what motivated me to push past the difficult chapters in my life and continue writing. PS: There's a cameo in this book specifically for you. See if you can find it!

To my parents, for inspiring my passion for writing and encouraging me to persevere. I am very grateful for everything you have done and thankful for the life lessons you've shared. I hope I can live up to your example as a mother and raise my children with compassion, love, and inspiration, just as you did for me. You've always supported me from the start, cheering me on. I hope this book makes you proud.

To Katelynn, Krysta, and Kait, for all of your support, love and excitement for this project throughout the years. I don't know what I'd do without you three. You truly are my favorite people in the world, and I wouldn't be half the person I am today if not for you. Special Thanks to Krysta for helping me bring this vision to life!

To Shawna, Heather, Abby, Rich, and Amanda for your help rearranging chapters, selecting titles, and literally red-penning everything! You all are incredible; thank you for willingly listening to me drone on for endless hours about plot development and history.

Lastly, to my husband Ric—As the very best parts of me belong to you, so too does this book. For every late night and every stressful moment, for the wild conspiracy theories and plot twist planning, for the unwavering love and confidence you gave me, I am endlessly grateful. Thank you for all the nights spent acting out fight scenes with me, for encouraging every spark of my imagination and for believing in me even when I struggled to believe in myself. This achievement is ours—We did it. Thank you for following me on this journey to a world where imagination meets reality.

About the Author

S.J. See is a second-generation American Scots-Irish author who lives in northern Illinois with her husband, two kids, and three lively dogs. She grew up just northwest of Pittsburgh, Pennsylvania, where the city's classic charm and rich history deeply shaped her sense of story and claimed her heritage-something she proudly carried into her writing.

Before becoming an author, S.J. worked with children of all ages, an experience that inspired her passion for writing young adult fiction. She loves to travel, explore new places, and challenge herself with new skills. Through her stories, she hopes to inspire and uplift readers, the way writing once gave her freedom at a young age.

www.ingramcontent.com/pod-product-compliance
Lightning Source LLC
LaVergne TN
LVHW012034070526
838202LV00056B/5489